WIDOW OF THE AMPUTATION
& OTHER WEIRD CRIMES

ERASERHEAD PRESS
833 Main Street #342
PORTLAND, OR 97214

www.eraserheadpress.com
facebook/eraserheadpress

ISBN: 978-1-62105-288-3
Copyright © 2021 by Robert Guffey
Cover art copyright © 2021 Matthew Revert

Printed in the USA.

WIDOW OF THE AMPUTATION
& OTHER WEIRD CRIMES

ROBERT GUFFEY

ERASERHEAD PRESS
PORTLAND, OREGON

To
RAY ZEPEDA,
Master
of
the
White
Buffalo
Robe
Lodge

CONTENTS

You Might as Well Die

1

Fade in:

The Pitch.

She pulled up outside the Hotel Roosevelt at 7000 W. Hollywood Blvd. The building looked as if it had been built as far back as the 1920s, complete with iron fire escapes zigzagging up the walls, a romantic alcove where illicit lovers meet and dirty deals are perpetrated between corrupt politicians, like the scene of a murder in a Chandler novel. It was across the street from Grauman's Chinese Theatre and a massive, gaudy-looking Virgin Megastore, the perfect visual metaphor for the clash of the old and the new in post-postmodern Tinsel Town.

Adrienne slid the car into a parking space behind the hotel. "You know, just recently," she said in a casual, offhand manner, "a guy with an AK-47 took the elevator to the top floor of the hotel down the street and blew away a room full of producers for no particular reason. The guy had no connection to them at all. It was totally random."

I didn't know what to say to that. So I said, "What does a single sperm cell and a Hollywood producer have in common?" Adrienne glanced at her watch again, then shrugged. "Each of them has a one in a million chance at becoming a human being."

She didn't laugh. I figured it was time I get out of the car. "I'll be back in a few hours to pick you up for the meeting," she said. "We have to be there on the dot. Fred keeps a tight schedule. This is your first trip to L.A., isn't it?"

I slipped my bag onto my shoulder. "'Fraid so."

"Enjoying it so far?"

Every cliché I'd ever heard about L.A. was true. My eyes were burning from the smog, and I felt like coughing up toxic waste. "So far."

She pulled away from the curb slowly. "Don't worry. It gets a lot less boring from here." And she was gone.

I staggered into the hotel lobby, a little stunned. I was still trying to get over the ride on the freeway. There were so many damn cars, all of them packed against each other bumper to bumper. That combined with the humidity is deadly. You never hear of cases of "road rage" in Wisconsin. There's a reason for this.

I went up to my room (it was far larger than I needed), put away what few clothes I had, and plopped down on the bed. I think I might've dozed off for awhile. The next thing I knew the phone was ringing next to my ear. It was Adrienne telling me to meet her in the lobby. I groaned something incomprehensible and hung up. I would've preferred to go back to sleep, but I knew I couldn't afford to piss off the Great Mr. Simms.

Great? Actually, I'd never heard of him before that first phone call of his. Of course, I'm not up on "who's who" in Hollywood. It's not a subject you concern yourself with when you're teaching esoteric subjects like the significance of the semi-colon in Tennyson to freshmen college students. Simms had run down a list of his credits during one of our phone conversations; I recognized some of them, which was a surprise. I don't get out to the movies very much, and I barely watch television. Some of the films were Academy Award winners. While coming over on the plane I'd wondered five million times why a big-wig of Simms's stature wanted to hire a novice like me; I'd only had a handful of stories published in a few mystery magazines here and there over the past few years. The man was used to dealing with literary icons ten times more successful. I felt as if I were being invited into a clubhouse that was far too good for lil' ol' Richard Angstrom.

I changed my shirt (which was wrinkled from having slept in it) and went downstairs to meet Adrienne, who was just as beautiful as before. Standard jazz, circa '30s or '40s, played in the hotel lobby. The music was as striking as her. Graceful. Intense. This time her clothes were formal but stylish: a beige top with three-cornered sleeves, a chestnut-brown, form-fitting skirt that hung down just past her knees, and classy high heels, all courtesy of Prada. Her long blonde hair was pulled back in a ponytail, her deep blue eyes distant and alluring. She hardly wore any make-up, but then again she didn't need any. Only a powerful producer like Simms could have a "personal assistant" like her. I wondered how close their relationship really was.

Adrienne asked how I liked my room as she turned toward the hotel entrance. As before, I found myself just one step behind her; her long legs outpaced mine with ease. I told her the room was a little larger than I was used to.

"Oh, all of Fred's writers get the very best treatment," she said.

"I'm not one of *his* writers yet."

She smiled. "I think you'll find his offer hard to refuse."

I bristled at the remark. That much confidence rubbed me the wrong way. I didn't like people who assumed my actions were foregone conclusions. Who did these people think they were? Were they so rich they thought they could buy anyone with an exaggerated dollar amount? During the drive over there I began to get more and more annoyed. I considered refusing his offer the second I entered the office just to show him his fancy trappings didn't impress me in any way.

Perhaps Adrienne sensed my thoughts. When she parked outside the ten-story office building on Sunset Boulevard, just off Alta Loma Road, she turned to me and said, "You know, any writer in Hollywood would kill to get a one-on-one meeting like this with Fred."

I spread my hands and shrugged. "I live in Wisconsin."

2

Close-up. Music swells.

I leaned against a pillar in the hotel lobby, wondering when Adrienne would arrive. Did she ask all the potential hired help out to dinner? I stared at the people swarming about me, listening to that jumpy Mingus bass in the background. I studied their clothes, their demeanor, their faces, wondered where they had come from and where they were going. I made up little stories about each of them, some of them quite elaborate. Sometimes I hit upon an idea that would be good for a Lincoln story. I would make a mental note to remember it, then shove it away onto the dusty shelves inside my head. I rarely took notes. I figured if you weren't capable of remembering an idea, it probably wasn't good enough to write about anyway.

I must've zoned out for quite awhile. What seemed like only a few minutes later, I heard a lilting, soft voice behind me say, "Mr. Angstrom?"

I turned. She seemed different from before. Same gorgeous face, of course… drastically different clothes. She was wearing what I could only describe as a psychedelic tunic, a beige mini-skirt, white stockings, and knee-high brown leather boots. The outfit was retro all the way, but on her it seemed as elegant as a Victorian gown. She'd released her hair from its restrictive pony tail, allowing it to flow halfway down her back. Her posture was less tense; her body wasn't rigid any longer. She no longer seemed as if she were standing at attention; she was smiling. Earlier in the day she'd had an invisible bubble encased around her that announced in no uncertain terms, "I'm on duty, keep your distance." That bubble had dissipated somewhat. She was more approachable. Or perhaps the change was only in my perception.

3

First Night in Hollywood.

For a brief moment there was silence as I watched the lighted signs and multi-colored stucco apartment buildings and garish fast food stands whiz past in the artificially bright night just outside the window of Adrienne's black Jaguar. The cool wind slammed into my face and knocked the jet lag out of me. Cigarettes, beer, movies, cars, newspapers, make-up, hair straighteners, cures for baldness, cures for impotence, cures for insomnia, cures for adverse reactions to defective cures; every conceivable product glared at you enticingly from huge billboards spotlighted by pure white light worthy of an angel. So this was my first night in Hollywood. Everything was so plastic, so two-dimensional and flat, a city-sized monument to artificiality: a Euclidean paradise shut off from higher dimensions by its own myopia. I hated almost everything about it. Yes, I said *almost*. As my father used to say, "It only takes one white crow to prove that all crows aren't black." There was nothing artificial about the woman sitting beside me.

She was my one white crow.

4

Character Development.

"It's all about writing, isn't it?" she said suddenly, pulling away from the restaurant: La Poubelle, this quaint little French place over on Franklin and Bronson. Up to that moment it had been a pleasant evening.

"What?" My turn to be confused again.

"That's what I've noticed most about writers, and I've dealt with a lot of them." As we sped past rows of street lamps, half of her face was cast starkly in darkness, the other in light; it was a haunting effect, granting an eerie glow to her smooth skin like the reflection of pale moonlight on clear waters. I focused on her pouty lips, unmarred by lipstick, glossed only in the strange Hollywood light. I imagined her as a spectral shadow trapped in an old black and white film, cloaked in film noir lighting.

"Every overheard conversation, every joke, every smallest detail is just grist for your mill," she said. "Even people's names. It gets to the point where you can't have a conversation with you people without snatches of it taken out of context." The tension had returned; her body was rigid once again.

"Sounds like you've been burned more than once."

"You can say that. My ex-husband was a writer." She paused, lost in thought for a moment. "Well, he still is a writer, actually. I don't know why I'm talking about him in the past tense."

"Wishful thinking?"

She laughed, some of the tension easing for a second. "Perhaps. I don't know, I just got tired of having our personal lives thrown up onto a screen for the whole world to see. Oh, he'd change the names, of course, but that didn't matter. All our friends knew what the story was really about, who the characters were. It was obvious, in-your-face, not subtle at all. Hector knew how much it bothered me, but he didn't care. He was a pisser, all right."

"Hector's a screenwriter, then?"

"You've never heard of the great and powerful, *genius* comedian, Hector Morales? Good. It's about time I met someone who didn't know who the fuck he was. He could pound out a full-length screenplay in a couple of days if he had enough speed inside him. He wrote *Blue Honeymoon* in four days."

"I've heard of it. I'm afraid I don't get out to the movies much."

"It was a dark comedy about marriage. It ends with the husband running his wife through a meat grinder. He gave me a copy of the screenplay on Valentine's Day."

"Charming."

"He thought so. He could never talk to me openly, so he'd plant these little jabs in his screenplays. His therapist said he was passive-aggressive."

"He was going to a therapist?"

She laughed again; it didn't sound entirely cheerful. "Of course."

I couldn't understand it. Why would a woman like this put up with such nonsense? "Did the therapist help him any?"

"I guess so, she married him. They were screwing around for a long time. I always wondered why his therapy sessions took so long. That was the basis for *Head Case*, his second film." I'd heard of that too. Hadn't it been nominated for an Academy Award or something? "It was about a successful screenwriter who's cheating on his wife with his therapist. That's when I found out about it, when I was sitting beside him at the premiere, watching the film for the first time. All my friends had already known months, maybe a year before. I was the last to know."

"That's horrible."

"He enjoyed it."

She grew quiet after that. It suddenly became uncomfortable in the warm, closed-in space of her heated car. I wondered why the hell she was telling me all this. Did she often unload her problems on people she just met? Or was she blaming me for Hector's hang-ups? Did she think all writers were the same? I worked up the courage to ask her point blank: "Not that I mind, but... why're you telling me all this? I mean, if it were me, I'd have a hard time sharing something so... personal."

She shrugged. "Everyone else already knows, so why shouldn't you? You'll hear the story eventually anyway if you decide to work for Fred. You might as well hear the story from me instead of through the grapevine. This city feeds off gossip." The lights from a passing billboard flashed across her eyes. "It wouldn't be able to live at night without rumors." She sighed. "Also, my therapist told me to try being as upfront as possible with people when I first meet them. I guess it's supposed to help me relate better."

5

Voiceover (with Montage).

Adrienne: Look at that homeless guy sitting on the sidewalk there. His name's Chuck and he's watching a television plugged into a street lamp; he gets better reception than I do. Every once in awhile I give him enough money for a new bottle. And look at those stairs over there, Laurel and Hardy once carried a grand piano up those things. And over here, here's where Hector set that famous scene in *Head Case* where the husband slams his fist into his wife's face for no reason. That's where Hector and I first kissed. I guess he thought that was funny. But I don't want to talk about that. Forget I mentioned it. See that cemetery over there? That's where Bela Lugosi was buried. His ghost was seen here once. There're ghosts all over this town. I saw one on a movie set a couple of years ago. The sound stage was empty and I was the only one around. I saw it standing in a doorway of a mock drugstore. It had a vague, misty outline, but I couldn't tell if it was a man or a woman. I know this sounds crazy, but it was smoking a cigarette. All I could really see was that orange cigarette butt moving up and down in the darkness, and clouds of smoke being exhaled from invisible lips. After a few minutes it vanished. Poof, like that. Finally I worked up the courage to walk over there, but there were no ashes at all. Some say the ghost of a dead extra haunts that sound stage, some unknown starving actor who committed suicide before he ever got a chance to be a star. I'm sorry, am I scaring you? No? Say, Fred lives right around here. Over there is where Nicole Simpson was murdered. A lot of people have seen her ghost too. Did you know the first cop on the scene of the Simpson murder was the same cop who first showed up at Roman Polanski's house the morning after Sharon Tate and her unborn child were slaughtered by the Manson Family? Isn't that something, the two most famous Hollywood murders being connected in such a weird way? If you like synchronicities this is the place to live. Oh, I feel so relaxed, like I could drive all night without getting tired. You want to head on up to the house where Sharon Tate was killed? Did you know Walt Disney owned that place before Polanski? Not only that, the Haunted House ride at Disneyland opened on the same day Tate was killed. If you—what? Oh, I thought I wasn't scaring you? Okay, I won't mention Manson again. Anyway, somewhere around here is where Bill Cosby's son was shot dead. In fact, now that I think about it, it was around this time of night too—

6

Mulholland Drive.

With Adrienne's ominous little stories as a soundtrack, we eventually wound our way up the darkened curves of Mulholland Drive, up into the Hollywood hills, where there were far more trees and far less lights and houses and grating mechanical sounds. As the road grew narrower, the lights below grew more and more distant. It was peaceful up here. Eventually we pulled off to the side of the road, stopped at the edge of a cliff overlooking the city lights below. I was amazed that something so artificial could seem so pretty from far away. I mentioned this to Adrienne, then said that this might make a great scene in the movie. "There you go again," she said, laughing. "Always living inside your head, like Hector."

"I'm not like Hector," I said. I reached out and ran my hand through her long hair. She closed her eyes. I brushed her hair for a few moments, then caressed her cheek. So soft. I leaned forward to kiss her, but at the last second she nestled her head in the crook of my neck and wrapped her arms around me.

"Just… hold me," she whispered. I said nothing. I didn't know what to say. She pulled back and looked at me with pleading eyes. "Is that all right?" No longer was she the hardened businesswoman with something to prove; she was like a nervous little girl.

"Yes," I said.

She smiled and returned her head to its cozy niche between my neck and shoulder. I held her for a long time, breathing in the sweet lingering scent of marijuana, petting her lustrous golden hair. My uncertainty as to what was supposed to happen next, or what she wanted me to do, made me anxious as hell. Sometimes I make up crazy stories in my head when I'm anxious. I did that even as a kid, before I ever thought of becoming a writer. I apologize if I sound like the unromantic type, but I wanted to do far more than just hold her. I tried to be patient. And in my patience I stared through the windshield and up at the stars. I saw a lone white bird fly up from the trees and into the dark sky, alighting upon a branch within a taller tree not far away. That shock of bright white against black would've inspired a beautiful haiku in someone more sensitive. Me, I thought of a Rorschach test, and all the possible neuroses its deep analysis might conceal.

7

The First Kiss.

...then the floodgates opened. We talked about little things, silly things, unexplainable things—childhood memories, parents, brothers, high school, movies, pets. I learned that she liked to eat toasted peanut butter sandwiches, which I never would've guessed in a million years. I learned that her favorite movie was *Santa Sangre*, a crazy foreign film about a boy named Fenix who's forced to slaughter women for his armless mother, a real lighthearted, happy-go-lucky flick; I should've been somewhat disturbed by this, but instead I was enchanted. Her favorite band was Sonic Youth, her favorite song "Brave Men Run." Her only pet was a stuffed toy, a black cat named Clover. (As a child she'd had a black kitten named Clover as well; it had contracted cancer, grown skinny and weak; her father had taken Clover from her ten-year-old arms in order to put it to sleep. Knowing the toy could never die, she could give it her full love without worrying about its inevitable death.) She loved coffee ice cream and night time soap operas, even though she knew both were bad for her. When she was growing up, every Sunday morning she and her father used to watch old Sherlock Holmes films starring Basil Rathbone. Her father was a psychology professor, her mother a professional psychic who had been one of his students, which I found hard to believe. Adrienne liked to read the horoscope every morning at breakfast because it reminded her of her dead mother. Today's horoscope had told her she would win the lottery. "Instead," she said, sighing, "I met you." I apologized for disappointing her. She smiled and said, "I'm not disappointed, not at all."

We passed the time in this way for over two hours, until at last she let go of my hand and said, "We should be heading home. It's getting pretty late."

"Or pretty early." I gestured toward the digital clock embedded in the dashboard. 4:16, it read. It had been a hell of a long day. I should've been exhausted, but instead I was charged-up. So much had happened, too much to process all at once. My mind was reeling.

We rode most of the way home in silence.

At 4:50 we pulled up outside the hotel. She turned off the engine. The silence deepened. "Well," she said.

"Well," I said.

"You're going home on Monday, right?"

"Yes."

"Fred's got me working out of town for the rest of the weekend. I probably won't get a chance to see you again before you leave. I'm sorry about that. Really... I am."

I spread out my hands, not really knowing what to say. After all, she had no obligation to me. I certainly didn't expect her to quit her job to help see me off. She was so altered from the woman I had met that morning: still graceful, still beautiful, but much less self-assured. This Hector had done an excellent job of destroying her inside. I couldn't imagine any man in the world abusing a woman like this, tiring of her and tossing her aside like used tissue paper.

In the end all I could think of to say was, "I hope I can talk to you again, even if it's just over the phone."

She smiled that innocent, little-girl-smile. She reached into the glove compartment, pulled out a notepad and pen, then scribbled down a phone number. She ripped the page off the pad and slipped it into my hand, leaned over and kissed me softly on the lips.

8

Blue Honeymoon.

The ride on the freeway was as mind-numbing as before, made all the worse by the driver's endless monologue explaining why the publishing world is in such a sad state of affairs. I couldn't help but wonder if Hector had been treated to similar lectures. Somehow I doubted it. At last he pulled up to an apartment building called Casa De Artista located on Bronson Avenue, just off Sunset Boulevard. It wasn't far from Simms's office. There were four buildings on the property, all of them designed with Spanish-style architecture. The buildings were at least eighty years old, quiet and charming; lots of trees decorated the narrow walkways between the buildings. Suddenly, the driver switched from extolling the many virtues of his unpublished masterpieces to the virtues of the building.

"Hey, this sure is a nice place," he said. "I'd love to be able to live here. Not many brats runnin' around. You'll probably get a lot of writing done, not like where I live. Oh, there's so much god damn noise at my pad I can hardly squeeze out a few sentences a day, you know what I mean?"

I told him I knew. He grabbed my bags and tried to bring them up to the apartment. I gave him twenty bucks to forget the idea.

"Oh, hey, I understand," he said. "Sometimes you need to be alone with yourself to let the creative juices flow. I'm down with that."

After he gave me the keys to the apartment, I grabbed my bags and started up the stairs toward 1531 ¾ on the second floor. When I was halfway up the driver called out, "So I'll just mail those stories to you, okay?"

I said nothing. I simply continued toward the apartment, feeling as if I were locked in a dull haze. Part of it was just jet lag, but most of it… most of it was the pull of gravity. I was still in freefall. I knew I hadn't yet hit the bottom. Can you imagine my trepidation as I anticipated the final impact? When would it come, what form would it take? While half of me wanted to prolong the fall, to delay impact as long as possible, the other half just wanted to get it over with.

Perhaps it was this half that directed me to set my bags down the second I entered the living room and urged me to pick up the phone. I was barely aware of my new surroundings. I was focused in on a single goal: dialing the number that had been burned indelibly in my brain so long before.

It rang eight and a half times before I heard her voice: "Hello?"

I breathed a sigh of relief. "Adrienne?"

"Oh, hello!" So casual, so innocent, so sweet. So happy to hear from me. "Fred told me you were coming in today. Are you in L.A. now?"

"I just arrived. I've been trying to get a hold of you for weeks." I attempted to filter the bitterness out of my voice, but it was difficult.

"Oh, I'm sorry. I've been out of town. Fred's been working me like a race horse lately."

I wanted to say, "You were never near a phone?" but I knew it would sound silly. What was I to her? She had nothing invested in me. I was the hired help. Always had been.

"I wanted to call you, but I never seemed to find the time," she said after a moment of tense silence. "You're not angry with me, are you?"

I realized how stupid I was being. If I started becoming possessive I'd never get anywhere with her. "No, of course not," I said. "I was just disappointed. I was hoping you'd pick me up from the airport. I've… I've missed talking to you."

"Really?" I could hear her smile the word. "I've missed talking to you too. For awhile there we were on the phone almost every night, remember?"

"How could I forget?"

"It was hard going to sleep without hearing your voice. Sometimes

I thought about calling you, but I was in San Francisco working. At midnight I'd get the bug to speak to you, but I didn't think I should wake you at three o'clock in the morning."

"I wouldn't have minded." God, I would've killed for that.

"I didn't want to be a bother."

"That's impossible."

"Not according to some people."

"Hector?" I interpreted her silence as a yes. "Have you spoken to him lately?"

"No, I wouldn't want to. I was referring to before, when he moved out. I'd call him at all hours just to hear his voice, to ask him for the hundredth time why he was leaving me. He'd say cruel things to me, hang up while I was in mid-sentence. I... I guess I just didn't want that to happen again. Y'know, sometimes I wonder if he didn't marry me just to have something to write about.

"In my most paranoid moments I think he already had the plot to *Blue Honeymoon* in his head, and he needed someone to belittle and destroy in order to work his little jokes out on. He had this talent to bounce one-liners off my forehead one after another like basketballs. One 'innocent' insult at a party in front of everybody could destroy me for the entire evening, but he'd just laugh and say it was all in fun. 'You're just making a big deal out of nothing,' he'd say. 'Maybe you *like* to be in pain. You can't have a thin skin if you're going to stick with me. If I can't try my material out on my wife, who can I try it out on?' Most of his material was made up of little clever jabs directed toward me. The sad thing is, I think that's the only way he knew how to communicate."

Her voice trailed away, as if she were now lost in thought. As she grew more silent, I grew angrier. If Hector had strolled into the room at that moment I definitely would've communicated with him, and I would've bounced more than one-liners off his forehead.

"I'm sorry," she said after a time. "I don't mean to talk about Hector so much. It's... it's become second nature for me by this point. Why on earth do I have to dwell on him this much?"

"Maybe you like to be in pain." I meant this sarcastically; I was making fun of Hector's idiotic comments. Adrienne didn't take it this way.

"Maybe so," she said. The fatality in her voice was depressing.

ROBERT GUFFEY

"But maybe… maybe you can help me with that?"

"Of course."

"Maybe you can write me into your screenplay and make sure I live happily ever after."

I smiled. "No one ever lives happily ever after in film noir, except maybe the villain."

She laughed then. Such a sweet laugh. I'd missed it so much.

9

Act One.

I had a ten A.M. meeting with Simms the next morning, but I was barely paying attention during it. At one point, while Simms was reading through the twenty pages of script I had brought with me, I said, "You know, maybe I'm not up to this."

Simms set the stack of papers on his desk and took off his glasses. He was in his early fifties, but wore his age well. He had distinguished silver hair, a tanned face creased with hard work and experience, mesmerizing bright green eyes. He was the type of person who exuded both authority and friendliness at the same time, a feat that would be an impossible paradox for lesser human beings. His dark business suit appeared to lack even the faintest of wrinkles, which made me feel like a real schlub in my wrinkled dress shirt and blue jeans. I was sitting in a swivel chair, facing him; his chair was just slightly higher than mine. He leaned forward with a concerned look on his face. "Why do you say that?"

"I don't know." I shot my head back and forth while lowering my gaze. "This whole thing isn't going as well as I thought."

Simms spread his hands. "But you just got here."

"I know, but I've been working on this screenplay for months and all I could come up with is twenty god damn pages."

"What I've read so far is fine," Simms said, flipping through the fifteen pages that he'd completed. "You may want to get more into the motivation of this bomber character. I mean, the basic idea works; it's really good, and rife with untapped potential. I can buy that this nut would kill two dozen people just to get at one person. But try to get inside his head more. I don't feel as if I know him as a real *person*. Oh, and you may have to cut down on some of the voice-over a bit, but other than that—"

"You see? I knew it sucked. I can't even write it directly into screenplay format. I've got to write it in prose, then *adapt* it into the proper format. It's the only way my mind works. That's why it's taken so long."

"Look, I don't care how you do it, just as long as you get the thing done. These pages seem fine, and the treatment you gave me is brilliant. Since you know exactly where you're going with the story, it should be no problem." Simms folded his hands on top of the desk and just stared at them for a moment. Then he glanced up at me and said, "What's the real problem here, Richard?"

I lowered my face into my hand and stared blankly at the tan carpet. I didn't know what to say. For a second I considered telling him the truth. When I'd come into the office this morning I'd hoped to run into Adrienne, but had had no luck. I'd casually asked Simms's secretary if she knew where Adrienne was.

"Oh, Adrienne hasn't come in yet," she replied, then added that it was the first time she'd been late in years. I asked if she'd called in sick, but the secretary said, "No, I haven't heard from her at all. I hope nothing serious has happened to her."

My first reaction was to try to phone her, but Simms had called me in for the meeting at that exact moment. Throughout the meeting I'd been thinking of nothing but Adrienne, but I wasn't yet comfortable enough with Simms to admit that. She was so sad so often... so often on the verge of what seemed to be a complete breakdown....

I glanced up from the carpet and said, "I don't know, I guess I'm just stressing out. I've never had this much pressure on me to write something before. I feel as if everyone's watching me, waiting for me to fall flat on my face. I'm just freezing up, that's all. You know, one time I saw an interview with Salman Rushdie. He talked about a conversation he'd had with Kurt Vonnegut. Rushdie was telling Vonnegut that he was just glad to be writing and getting paid for it.

Vonnegut turned to him and said, 'Just wait until you *have* to write a book.' That comment really horrified me, you know? I began this as nothing more than a hobby only a few years ago, and it's grown out of hand so quickly."

Simms sighed. "Well, if you really think you can't handle this I need to know now before I invest any more time or money into this thing. If you really want I can let you out of your contract now, you can take the money I've already given you and fly back to Wisconsin to work on your short stories. There're plenty of other writers I could've chosen with hundreds of professional credits to their name, but I decided to take a chance and hire *you*. Please don't make me look like an idiot. I can tell you now, I'm dedicated to making the best god damn crime noir film in the history of the universe. What're *you* dedicated to?"

Adrienne, I thought. Even after last night it's Adrienne. But I couldn't say that. I couldn't say anything. I remained silent and still.

10

Sex Scene.

After dinner that night she asked to see my new apartment. We sat on the couch for awhile amidst the clothes I hadn't put away and talked about how great our movie was going to be. That's how we'd begun to refer to it: "our" movie. I'm not sure when that began exactly, but it seemed quite natural at the time. For some reason I felt compelled to tell her about the fleeting thought I'd had the night we met, the metaphor of the one white crow. She had never heard the phrase before. Perhaps it was just a mid-west thing, I don't know. She seemed to like it, though. She seemed to like it a lot. At some point or another, in the middle of another sob story about that god damn Hector, I leaned over and kissed her. She responded at once. We kissed passionately for a time. I broke away from her eventually, but only to take her hand and lead her into my new bedroom. We sank into the rumpled sheets of my unmade bed, peeling off each other's clothes. I whispered in her ear, told her to lay on her stomach. First I ground my teeth lightly on the tiny white hairs on the back of her neck, then kissed her flesh. Beginning at the mid-point between her shoulders, I planted kisses all the way down her spine to her tailbone, from her tailbone down to her ankles. I told her to turn over, then covered her with kisses from her toes up to her throat. My palms brushed over the curves of her smooth thigh, across her ribcage, then upwards. I drew my mouth down to her left breast, sinking my teeth into the aureole while flicking my tongue over the tip of her erect nipple. My hand slid across her flat stomach, down between her legs. I massaged her clitoris while I moved my mouth from one breast to the other. Her moans grew louder, her hips gyrating faster and faster. For a moment I eased off, then covered every inch of her torso in the most gentle of kisses: her ribs, her stomach, her belly button, then down. Her wetness covered my lips as I flicked my tongue back and forth rapidly. Her hips spasmed against my face. She ran her fingers through my hair and pressed my head deep into her thighs. I couldn't have moved if I'd wanted to. I went down on her until she came, and her moans tapered off to a quiet whisper. She lifted her hands from my head, releasing me. I rose up onto my knees and just watched her lying there for a moment. At that moment my need to be inside her was greater than anything else in the world. I reached for one of my bags on the floor and scrounged around frantically in the mess for a condom. At last I found one, ripped it out of its package, and rolled it over my penis.

"What're you doing?" Adrienne said, closing her legs and scooting up to a sitting position.

I just stared at her for a moment. "What do you mean?"

She drew her knees up to her chest and began rocking back and forth. "I don't know if I'm ready for this."

"What do you—?"

"I-I think it'd be better if I just left now," she said, moving onto the edge of the bed and slipping into her panties.

I couldn't believe it. It was like that first night in her car, but a hundred times worse. I remained kneeling on the mattress, watching her put on her clothes. She was so close, and yet so god damn distant…. "Adrienne," I said, searching for something to say, "after what we just did—"

"I *know*," she said, her face distorted with worry, "I shouldn't have let it get this far. I'm not trying to be a tease—"

"Listen, I—"

"Don't say anything. *Please*." Fully clothed now, with her belt still unbuckled and her torn sweat shirt on backwards, Adrienne snatched up her purse and ran toward the door in tears. "I'm sorry," she called over her shoulder and darted out of the room. I heard the front door open and slam shut, followed by the sound of her Jaguar peeling away from the curb down below. Just like that, Adrienne was gone.

11

Soliloquy.

Can you stop with the sarcasm for one second? No one's ever made me feel the way you did last night. You were so sweet, and you paid attention to every… every part of me. Hector never made me feel that way. He was always so selfish. *I* always had to initiate everything, everything had to be done *to* him. I actually think he hated pleasure on a very deep, deep level. He resented sex. He only knew how to use it as a tool to manipulate people. Idiots like me. One time… one time, after Hector had moved out, I went over to his house and begged him to take me back. I was so low and so depressed I would've done anything to hear him say he loved me. So I told him… I was crying and I told him, What can I do to get you to take me back? and he said… he told me I could suck his dick. I was so messed up and confused, I did it. I got down on my knees right then and there and… and gave him a blowjob and afterwards he laughed and said, Now get the hell out of here, I'd never take you back… you're *nothing* to me. That was the last time I'd been with anybody… until I met you. I was scared of having that done to me again, of being ripped apart and humiliated so totally that you feel like tearing into your chest with your bare hands and clawing your heart out so you don't have to feel a damn thing any more. I was so scared of opening myself up again that I… I don't know, I was so overwhelmed last night it scared the hell out of me. I don't know what came over me, it was like, like having a panic attack or something. This wave of intense fear just swept over me all of a sudden and I-I had to get out of there. I'm sorry. You know… you know how some people are supposed to have a genetic disposition toward drug addiction? You think it's possible that I've got a "fuck-up" gene somewhere in my body that makes me screw up anything good in my life? Deep down I think I'm just like Hector. I hate pleasure, which is probably why I hooked up with him in the first place. Maybe I deserve him.

12

The Perfect Murder.

    I wrote down extensive notes, the perfect plan to execute the perfect murder. I reached into a suitcase and pulled out my copy of the script. I re-read the last few pages, then ran over to my computer and continued writing right where I'd left off. The path was clear. My fingers tapping on the keyboard blazed a clear trail through the rubble in my head and all the doubts and fears from the past few weeks fell to the wayside. I knew exactly where I was going for the first time in months. Oh, I might've had a detailed outline before, but every writer knows that outlines are written for the publisher's (or the producer's) benefit, not the writer's. Outlines always change, sometimes so radically that the final product bears no resemblance to what inspired it in the first place. No outline, no matter how detailed, can make up for a lack of inspiration. The inspiration is the key. The inspiration is what I'd been lacking up until now.

    No longer did I need the clumsy safety net of writing the story in prose, then adapting it into screenplay format. Now that I had fallen into the proper groove, I could just *go* and never look back. Ideas rained out of the sky. I added a major new character: Hector Morales the toy maker had an associate, a wife named Shannon Chatwood, a nutty therapist who shared with her husband a strange fascination for explosives. They were a mad bomber husband and wife team, the first in history. Once I thought of this everything else fell into place. I came up with the perfect death scene for Hector. When Shannon discovers that her husband is cheating on her with his ex-wife Adrienne she drugs him, locks him in a cheap motel room, ties him to the bed, stuffs a gag in his mouth, then connects a series of wires to his penis. The wires are connected to a specially made time bomb concealed beneath the bed. Upon first awakening Hector thinks his wife is playing a kinky little game with him until she whispers in his ear that she *knows*. Yes, she knows all about the sordid little affair between him and Adrienne. At this point he begins to worry. He grows a hell of a lot more worried when she informs him about the bomb. It will be activated only by a heightened pulse rate; if his penis hardens, the timer will begin. She then sends in a prostitute named Indrid, a real skanky whore, just the kind Hector likes, with all the right features and dimensions, the best one Shannon could recruit from the drug rehab clinic she works at on the weekends. She failed to inform Indrid of the bomb, of course. She simply flashed a wad of cash in her face and told her she had a patient with a little problem and to do everything she could to give him a hard-on. "Ignore the wires," she said, "he's into weird stuff." Indrid assured her that she hadn't failed yet and didn't intend to start now. She even promised to go that extra mile for the guy just to show Shannon how much she appreciated everything she'd done to help her kick her heroin addiction. Shannon tells her to wait about fifteen minutes before she begins her work; that should give Shannon enough time to drive well out of harm's way. We then see the terror in Hector's eyes as Indrid begins to dance for him. He wriggles around and tries to scream through the gag, but Indrid ignores him just like Shannon told her to do. This isn't all that unusual for her. Hell, she's had kinkier jobs in the past. Hector closes his eyes, tries to think clean thoughts, but it's not possible, not when Indrid begins the full body massage. We see his penis harden beneath the sheets. The time bomb begins to tick. Indrid wraps her lips around his penis, flicks her tongue back and forth across his foreskin. Close-up on Hector's face as he tries his hardest not to climax. Close-up on the timer ticking down to zero. Finally, inevitably, Hector orgasms, screaming with both pleasure and horror at once. The bomb detonates. Cut back to Shannon cruising down the road in her car, the exploding motel far behind her, a slight grin affixed to her face. And that's just the end of the second act. The moral of the story is, of course: Never fuck over a psychiatrist who's also a demolitions expert.

Before I knew it I'd finished fifty-six pages, the most I'd ever written in a single night. At one point I glanced up and saw the first rays of dawn shining through the window. I couldn't quite believe it at first. I grabbed my watch and lifted it up to my bleary eyes: 5:30 A.M. I suddenly realized that Adrienne never called. I suppose I should've been happy; it meant that she didn't have a lonely, sleepless night. But then again I guess another part of me *wanted* her to be lonely and sleepless, dependent on me and me alone.

13

The Fist Fight.

Simms's wife glided over to us through a room crowded with revelers, exuding absolute grace and contentment. I don't think I've ever seen a happier person. Her contentment had shown through even in the framed photo that stood upon Simms's desk, but the photo hadn't done her justice. Though she might've been very attractive in the past, she was now overweight and plain-looking. If anything, she had a matronly air about her; and yet despite all this she was actually quite radiant. She was one of those rare people who could seem attractive without really being so. I could see why Simms had remained married to her for so long. I, on the other hand, wouldn't be able to stand a permanent relationship with someone who was always that happy. For some reason I gravitate to the manic-depressive types, like Adrienne.

Valerie Simms took one of my hands in both of hers, patting the back of it like my grandmother used to do. "Ah, you must be Richard," she said through a wide grin. "Adrienne told me she was dragging you here tonight. She says you don't like people very much, which is understandable considering the statistics and all."

"What statistics?"

"Statistically human beings kill each other far more often than any other species on the planet, but that doesn't come as much of a shock to you, does it?"

"Well, no...."

"Good, then we won't mention it again. It just depresses everybody something awful, and that wouldn't be at all appropriate at a celebration, now would it?" Still holding my arm, she led me into the thick of the party. Adrienne followed close behind.

"What exactly are we celebrating?"

"Nothing in particular. Just being alive is enough, don't you think?"

"No, not really."

She laughed. "Oh, that's right, you're a cynic aren't you? That's how you're able to write all those perfectly horrible stories filled with crime and dead bodies and things, right?"

"It's easy. I just have to read the headlines."

"Tt. Headlines." She waved her hand in the air as if to say, "Who needs them?"

The crowd seemed to create a path for Valerie without having to be asked; instead of weaving in and out of the guests, she walked right through them in a straight line. Scattered throughout the crowd were a few people I'd met at previous parties, but prominent among them was Simms's affable grinning face. He was engaged in an intense conversation with five middle-aged men who were bulging out of their oh-so-expensive tuxedos second by second as they scarfed down a platter of *hors d'oeuvres*. It appeared as if Simms was attempting to convince the men of something or other, who knows what. I suspected that Simms saw these little get-togethers as more of an opportunity to work his verbal magic on potential business partners while they were either a bit tipsy or drunk out of their minds, rather than as a quaint "celebration of life" like his wife did. I wondered if Valerie was such a Pollyanna that she wasn't even aware of her husband's ulterior motives; it was hard to tell, really. I hadn't yet figured out if she was happy because she was A) smarter than everyone else or B) far dimmer than everyone else.

"I've heard so much about you," Valerie said, "from Fred and Adrienne. They both speak highly of you, you know. They say your stories are wonderful. Oh, but I wouldn't know anything about that. I don't read that kind of thing. I'll just have to take their word for it."

"Better their word than mine."

"Don't say that. I'm sure you wouldn't lie to me. Adrienne says you're the most honest man she's ever met. Isn't that right?" She turned to Adrienne, who hung her head slightly in embarrassment.

"You know, I didn't realize there was so much discussion going on about me behind my back."

"Where better to discuss you? Surely you can't expect us to have candid conversations about you in *front* of you, now can you, my dear? Of course, we could if you'd like, but that might be awfully embarrassing for you—"

"No, no, that's okay. But I would like to be a fly on the wall while you're all gathered together late one evening, long after midnight, hosting one of your many Richard Angstrom discussion panels in the smoke-filled stalls of the women's bathroom."

"Oh, no you wouldn't. You might learn things about yourself that even you never suspected." I glanced over at Adrienne, but she just smiled. I decided Valerie probably was very intelligent, otherwise how could she be so quick with a comeback?

Valerie led Adrienne and me to her husband, whose grin widened as he greeted us. "Richard!" he said. "I was wondering if you'd show up." He introduced us to the five overweight guys, whose names I forgot instantly. "Adrienne told us she was dragging you here tonight," he said.

"So I've heard."

Valerie pulled Adrienne aside and said to us, "Please excuse us while we retire to the bathroom to form one of our little covens." Adrienne waved goodbye as she was dragged into the crowd, leaving me alone with Simms. Well, alone except for the five fat guys, but they were pretty much talking among themselves by now. They could care less about what I had to say.

"So how're the rewrites coming along?" Simms asked.

"Well, *I* think they're great, but then again I always do… until you tear them up and tell me to start all over again, that is."

"Just trying to hone it to perfection, that's all. Believe me, I've been doing this for a lot of years. I'll know when it's perfect." Simms proceeded to lecture me for the hundredth time about the various elements that constitute the ideal script. I listened with only one ear, nodding at the appropriate moments, while also studying the faces in the crowd. So many drunken fools. Where did they think they were going, what did they think they were doing after the party was done? Sleeping it off until the working world reclaimed them on Monday morning? It all seemed so pointless. They were just staving off the inevitable.

As I continued to study the crowd, I saw the front door open and in walked two latecomers: a man and a woman. The man was short and olive-skinned, possibly Latino, and the woman was tall and skinny to an anorexic extreme. Her shiny black hair was so long it almost covered her butt. I thought her pale skin and black evening gown made her look a little like Morticia from *The Addams Family*. I was about to make a joke about this when Simms whispered, "Oh, Christ. I didn't invite them here. But I shouldn't be surprised. Leave it to him to crash a party."

"Who is he?" I said.

Simms seemed reluctant to tell me. "Hector Morales."

My head snapped back toward the man. A crowd had formed around him, and his little jokes were already making them howl with laughter. I couldn't believe it. After all I'd heard I was expecting some kind of tall, Don-Juan-type. Zorro without the mask and cape. Instead I'm confronted with this little troglodyte. He was no more than 5'5; I knew I could take him down within two seconds if I had to. Adrienne had described him as a handsome, debonair fellow: lustrous black hair, high cheekbones, dark flashing eyes, enticing lips, baby smooth skin. Now these features were marred by sunglasses, a goatee and a thin moustache, and a slightly receding hairline in the front. He even seemed a bit chubby. I realized that his companion, newly risen from the grave, must've been the therapist Adrienne was always mentioning—Dr. Julie Cavanaugh. It was hard to imagine talking over your problems with someone who looked like Vampira from *Plan 9 from Outer Space*; it was even harder to imagine paying for it.

From somewhere far away Simms said, "It's probably better just to ignore him," but I was barely listening. My eyes scanned the crowd for Adrienne. At that moment I saw her and Valerie emerge from a hallway on the right side of the room. (Hey, had they really been in the bathroom discussing me?) She stopped short upon seeing the crowd. Upon recognizing the man around whom the crowd had formed, she tried to retreat back into the hallway, but Valerie stopped her. She placed a comforting hand on Adrienne's shoulder and led her into the living room; she was obviously whispering encouraging words into her ear. Adrienne seemed frustrated and upset, but went along with her nevertheless. Valerie attempted to guide her past the throng, back toward the spot where Simms and I still stood. Halfway through some long-winded story, Hector's gaze alighted upon her. He called her name and pushed past the wall of sycophants hanging on his every word. They met in the center of the room. Morticia hung back, studying both of them with an amused expression. I couldn't hear what he was saying to her, but the superior grin on his face was enough to set me off.

"Uh, don't you think that's true?" Simms said, tugging at my sleeve. He'd asked me a question. I hadn't heard him. I'm sure it wasn't important. I pulled away from him and approached Adrienne and Hector at a slow, calm pace. She had her eyes locked on the ground and didn't see me coming. Valerie had moved to the side and was staring at Adrienne with concern. She spotted me before Hector or Adrienne did.

"Hello, Richard," Valerie said, I guess to alert Adrienne to the fact that I was there more than any other reason. It was clear that Valerie disliked Hector; I got the feeling she would prefer he vanish into thin air. "We were just on our way back to see you."

"Richard," Adrienne said, grabbing my hand tightly, "this is Hector Morales. Hector, this is Richard Angstrom."

Hector smiled and held out his hand. "Angstrom," he said. "I was just reading about you the other day—in a little article somewhere or other. So Simms was able to rope you into his empire, eh?"

I nodded my head once without giving him the benefit of even the slightest of smiles. While Adrienne still held onto my left arm as if for support, I shook his hand with my right. For a second all three of us were physically intertwined. *For a second.* It was over before it had begun, but for some reason that moment sticks in my mind to this day as a kind of turning point, the moment right before my path branched off toward a downhill slope right into Hell.

"I understand you're a mystery writer," he said, glancing down at Adrienne's hand on mine. The glance lasted for only a second, but it was long enough to betray his displeasure.

"Not strictly," I replied. "I'm interested in the more bizarre crime noir writers like—"

He waved his hand in the air, cutting me off in mid-sentence.

"So how long have you and Adrienne been together?" Adrienne's fingernails dug so deeply into the back of my hand that I thought she might rip my flesh off. Hector slipped a cigarette into his mouth and lit it over Valerie's objection.

"Long enough," I said.

"Yeah?" He blew clouds of gray smoke into the air, the only one in the entire room to do so. "Something tells me you haven't been with her long enough to fuck her. I can see it in your rigid posture, the way you're standing next to her. You're not as comfortable as you should be. She's keeping you at a distance, isn't she?" He waved the cigarette around like a magician's wand, in tune to the rhythm of his words. Out of the corner of my eye I could see some of his groupies closing like jackals in order to eavesdrop on his impromptu monologue. "It's not surprising," he continued, "your little girlfriend is frigid enough to give goosebumps to a cryogenically frozen head." The groupies roared with laughter. "In fact, you couldn't pry her legs open with a hydraulic excavator." More laughter. "Sex with her is about as happening as an all-expenses paid vacation to Garden Grove. Trust me, there's nothing going on down there. Foreplay for her is like holding an election in Iraq; it's just too much work for no results. Even *atom bombs* can't excite her. She could start out with the gun barrel of a Panzer tank just to get in the mood, then taper off with a Patriot missile and yet *still* her poontang would be as dry as the Gobi fuckin' desert." I heard Adrienne whimpering beside me. I heard Valerie telling Hector to stop. But most of all I heard the laugher of jackals. I imagined they sounded a lot like Hector after Adrienne had lowered herself onto her knees and sucked his dick. *Now get the hell out of here. I'd never take you back. You're nothing to me.* Months and months of pent-up frustration fired up within my brain. The sound of Adrienne's fingernail snapping off against my hand was the final cue. Tongues of flame lapped at the roof of my skull, and *snap*. Hector said, "Believe it or not, ladies and germs, but on our wedding night Adrienne was such a cold fish that my—"

I hauled off and socked the fucker in the jaw. He flew back into the crowd, his body flopping about like the Raggedy Ann doll that he really was, landing flat on his back with a dull thud. I didn't give him a chance to get up again. The surprised faces that surrounded him were a blur as I leaped onto his body, pummeling him with blow after blow directly to the face. Blood poured down the sides of his mouth. I hardly felt the horde of arms that attempted to pry me loose. I'm told it took them a good long while until they managed to do it. By that time Hector Morales's physical appearance bore a close resemblance to an anatomy chart on the wall of my old college Biology class, as if someone had taken his face and turned it inside out.

Three of the guests held me in place and yet still I struggled against them. If they'd only let me go I would've killed him right then and there, I know it. Everyone in that room knew it. They were staring at me with disgust as if I were some kind of distasteful animal, and yet *Hector* was the real animal. Why weren't they staring at him that way, why weren't they restraining *him*?

I didn't cease struggling until I heard Adrienne's voice beside me and felt her hand on my chest. She stroked my cheek and whispered, "It's okay, calm down… calm down, Richard, it's okay. Richard? *Please*, Richard."

Once I'd cooled off, the three monkeys in tuxedoes released me. For a brief second I contemplated jumping on top of him again, but I'd probably only get in a couple of punches before they yanked me away once more, so I figured it wasn't worth it. By this time the fog of hate that clouded my eyes had dissipated somewhat. I felt as if I'd been pushed out of my body for a time, and was just now settling back in.

Valerie ran up to me on the verge of tears and said, "I'm so sorry. He wasn't even supposed to be here. We specifically didn't invite him to *avoid* something like this."

Simms appeared at his wife's side. "We'll have him thrown out," he said. Then he glanced down at Hector, who was still lying flat on his back. "Uh, once he regains consciousness, that is."

"Forget it," I said, "I'm the one who's leaving. C'mon." I grabbed Adrienne by the hand and headed for the door.

We passed Morticia on the way out. She stuck a business card in Adrienne's face. "We recently moved our offices to another building. If you feel the need to discuss this incident, do give me a call, won't you?"

After Adrienne had accepted the card I dragged her out the door and down the driveway toward her car. We began the ride in total silence. I felt as if Hector had mentally raped me, as if he'd sucked the energy right out of my body like a vampire. My psyche was as deflated as a blown-out tire. All of a sudden Adrienne began to giggle, first softly, then hysterically. Her giggles intensified into choking guffaws. I thought I might have to take the wheel from her she was gasping so hard.

"You're not going nuts on me, are you?"

Tears were streaming down her cheeks. She said, "Remember those old Popeye cartoons, the ones with the Max Fleischer animation?"

"Excuse me?" She really had gone nuts.

"When Popeye would slam his fist into Bluto's jaw, Bluto's face would sink in as if it were made of rubber or silly putty and little stars would circle his head, remember that?" After every sentence she'd stop to catch her breath. "Well, that's exactly what Hector's face looked like when you knocked him to the floor. Did you see how fast he went down? *Bam*! Just like that. He toppled to the ground like King Kong. You never told me you could fight."

"Are you kidding? I've never won a fight in my life."

"Well, that wasn't a fight, it was a massacre." Half of her face was covered with a broad grin. She was obviously very proud. I guess at that moment I was her knight in shining armor, every little girl's dream. Perhaps I should have been flattered. Instead, as the scene played and replayed in my head, I began to grow angry.

"How on earth could you marry that guy?" I blurted out. "I wouldn't even buy a used car from him much less have *sex* with him."

She pursed her lips. "He was a lot different when I first met him."

"You mean he was human?"

"Physically. He was a lot different *physically*. He was much more handsome than he is now. Suave, debonair."

"Is that all that matters to you, what someone *looks* like?"

She laughed scornfully. "Oh, like that doesn't matter to you? Would you be here with me now if I was five hundred pounds?"

"If you were five hundred pounds I wouldn't be able to fit in your damn car with you."

She sighed. "I don't even know why I *try* talking to you."

"I don't know either. Couldn't you detect he was a scumbag right off the bat?"

"Maybe I'm attracted to scumbags."

"What's that supposed to mean?"

"Nothing."

"If that's some veiled insult directed toward me," I said, "I don't think it applies; I'm not a scumbag, and you're obviously not attracted to me."

"Why do you say that?"

Silence for a time. When she spoke at last she sounded as if she were going to cry. Yet again. "If Hector was so right about me, why did you even bother defending me?"

"I don't know." I think I did know, but I didn't want to admit it. Maybe I wasn't defending her. Maybe I was just angry because Hector was so right on-target.

Adrienne planted her left elbow on the door and lowered her head into her hand, operating the steering wheel with her right hand. I don't even think she was paying attention to what was on the road in front of her. She was on auto-pilot, even if the car wasn't. I don't think either of us cared what happened to us or the car at that moment.

Finally she whispered, "Don't you think I've ripped myself apart over and over and *over* again for falling for someone like that?" Fluorescent lights from the passing street lamps highlighted the tears that zigzagged crazily down her cheeks. They were no longer caused by laughter. "Don't you think I've stayed up all night asking myself how I could be so stupid? Don't you think I've wondered if there was something wrong with me? Don't you think I've tortured myself for over a year, exiled myself from all the friends I ever had just so I wouldn't have to hear Hector's name ever again? Don't you think I've suffered enough?" Her throat wouldn't allow her to speak all the words clearly. My imagination had to fill in the missing syllables and words. "The last thing I need is to be picked apart bit by bit by you. Fuck you. I love you."

At first I thought I imagined those last three words. "What?"

"I said I love you!" she screamed. "You're an *idiot*. I've been waiting and waiting for an opportunity to say it, but you've been playing hard to get all night. First you didn't want to go to the party, now this. You're a shithead. You give me the perfect opportunity by defending me, then you have to muck it all up by picking a fight with me. I hate you."

Ever feel like burrowing into the earth and pulling the ground over your head like a blanket? I'd waited months for this moment and this is how it turned out. What could I say? Well, I didn't say anything for a few seconds. Then:

"Look," I said, sighing, "I wasn't angry with you. I was just jealous. It's hard to imagine anyone else being with you, much less that guy. I've never met such a complete asshole in my life. It was a bit of a shock, you know."

"Try living with him."

"I'm sorry." I concentrated on my hands, which were folded in my lap. Those hands were the only things that existed in the world at that moment. "I love you, Adrienne. I really do. I've been waiting to tell you that for months, but I've been too scared. I was afraid, afraid of everything. Afraid of your reaction… afraid of a negative reaction, afraid of a positive reaction… afraid of *my* reaction to *your* reaction. You name it and I was probably afraid of it. I guess… I guess I wanted you to say it first, just because I didn't want to look like a fool."

"Oh, very brave. It's nice to know you're willing to risk so much to demonstrate your undying love."

"There's no need to be sarcastic! *I* know it wasn't brave."

"Sarcasm's about the only way you know how to communicate, a trait you share with someone else I know—a certain ex-husband of mine."

"There's a world of difference between him and me. He's doing it because he's evil. For me, maybe it's just a convenient way to hide my true feelings. You're not the only one who's ever been burned, you know."

She nodded. "I know," she said softly. I'd told her all about the girlfriends in my past. There were only a handful, but each represented another nail in my flesh. One in each wrist, one in each ankle, and a final one through the heart. The end of each relationship caused me to die a little more, my heart to shrink and harden and calcify like a fossil buried deep in the earth. I would never be able to hurt someone like that; a fist in the face is nothing compared to that kind of pain. As the song says, "Anyone who ever had a heart wouldn't turn around and break it." For some reason I had become a convenient port of call from which to launch into more "satisfying

ROBERT GUFFEY

relationships," a port of call that was sinking slowly from constant abuse and overuse. Adrienne was aware of all this, of course, and sympathized with my pain. I knew this merely from the way she said those two words: *I know*. She reached out and grabbed my folded hands, squeezed them both delicately.

"I love you," I said, wrapping her hand in both of mine. A smile broke out across her face; she turned to look at me as she echoed those three words: "I love you." The screenwriter in my head cued up the romantic music as we found ourselves lost in each other's eyes. Unfortunately, we held the beat a second too long. Neither of us saw the car until we slammed right into the passenger side.

14

The Car Crash.

It really wasn't our fault. This teenager in a brand new blue CRX ignored the stop light and sped into the intersection. Of course, if we'd been paying attention we probably would've been able to stop in time, but….

After I was certain Adrienne was all right, we got out and checked the other car. The entire passenger side had caved in. Thank God no one was sitting on that side. The driver, some blond surfer barely out of Drivers Ed., staggered out of the wreck and collapsed onto the cement. Both my life and Adrienne's passed before my eyes. I was sure we'd killed him. Adrienne just stood there in the street with her hands on her face. A small crowd of lookie-loos had begun to form. I dug Adrienne's cell phone out of her purse, but it wasn't charged. I didn't want to speak to a single person in that crowd, so I pushed through them and was relieved to see a payphone standing on the corner. I dialed 911 and after some useless babbling finally managed to explain the situation to the robotic-sounding lady on the other end. Then I rushed back to Adrienne, who was still standing in the middle of the street just staring at the kid and the remains of his car. The kid was now sitting up, his head resting against the crumpled metal of his CRX. Some overweight biker guy in a leather jacket was kneeling beside the kid, rapping to him casually. The kid didn't seem to be wounded or bloody, but that didn't mean anything of course. Internal damages are far more serious.

The ambulance arrived within five minutes. The paramedics examined the kid on the spot and told us he was strung out on something. He wasn't damaged by the crash, just stoned out of his mind. I can't tell you how relieved I was to hear this (I have to admit, the relief was more for me and Adrienne than for the kid). The lookie-loos were more disappointed, wandering away trailing bitter grumbles. No free bloodshed tonight. They'd have to get their kicks somewhere else.

The cops took us aside and interviewed us separately. All in all the whole process took about twenty minutes. By that time Adrienne was pretty much wiped out. She asked me to take the wheel. Despite the fact that the front of the car looked like an accordion, it still ran fine.

"You want to go to your apartment?" I asked, slipping into the driver's seat.

She eased into the passenger seat and strapped herself in. She wrapped her smooth pale arms around her chest and shook her head. "Can I stay at your place tonight?"

"Not a problem," I said.

My apartment wasn't far. Once we'd returned, Adrienne plopped down onto the sofa. She kicked off her high-heeled shoes, curled her feet under her. She stared at the blank television screen and said, "God, I thought that kid was dead."

I sat down beside her. "So did I. When he staggered out of that car and fell down on the cement... Christ, my heart just about stopped."

"Just think if we hadn't been wearing seat belts. What would've happened?"

"You really need to ask? We'd both be dead."

She glanced over at me, studying me for a moment, ran her fingertips down my cheeks, then leaned over and kissed me. She slipped her tongue into my mouth. We kissed passionately for a long time, until Adrienne broke away and whispered, "Richard, I'm still not ready. Please don't press me or ask me why. There's nothing wrong with you, trust me. It's entirely my problem and I have to get over it on my own. But I do love you, and I'll do everything else I can to please you. Okay?" As she spoke she ran her hand slowly down my chest, then grabbed my penis through my pants. She began massaging me with gentle, circling motions. "Okay?" she whispered again, this time directly into my ear. She nipped at my ear lobe, then my neck. After a few moments she removed her hand from my lap and said, "Can you go down to the car and grab the CD that's in the glove compartment?"

15

Sex Scene II.

CD in hand, I locked Adrienne's car and returned to the apartment. The living room was empty. Her black gown had been draped over the sofa. I laid her keys on the desk, then entered my bedroom. There she was on my bed, the sheets barely covering her naked breasts. "C'mon, give it here," she said, holding out her hands. I tossed the disc to her. She popped it into the CD player beside my bed. The opening, dissonant chords pulsed out of the speakers. Adrienne attacked me the second I entered the bed, covering my entire body with kisses. Her favorite song screamed at me as she tore at my body; bruises and cuts began to form before my eyes. I'd never experienced anything like it, nor had I ever fantasized about this. Until that night I didn't know how closely pain and pleasure were intertwined. At one point, after she visited her teeth upon them, blood dripped from my nipples, but I didn't care. I was only vaguely aware of Kim Gordon's sibilant whispers in the background. "Sudden days and sudden nights/Brave men run/In my family/Brave men run/Into the setting sun/Brave men run/Into captivity/Brave men run/In my family/Brave men run/Away from me." Adrienne went down on me for the first time to a relentless, maddening sample from the tail end of *Metal Machine Music*. Somehow she would know exactly when I was about to come and pull away just in time, allowing me to cool down while she focused on another part of my body. The *Metal Machine Music* sample segued into Thurston Moore's droning voice on "Society Is a Hole" and continued to be woven throughout the entirety of the second song. I remember those moments of ecstasy as if through a coma-like haze, slipping in and out of awareness, slipping in and out of Adrienne, pain then pleasure, pleasure then pain; sometimes it was hard to tell which was which, her teeth biting at my flesh, her nails raking across my thighs, the stentorian drone of two amps plugged into each other assaulting my ears. Finally the *Metal Machine Music* sample faded away to be replaced by a fragment of Iggy Pop singing "I'm Not Right," which then shifted back to Moore whining "I Love Her All The Time." I distinctly remember him intoning that phrase as Adrienne asked me to fuck her in the ass. She didn't bother to wait for my reply. She spit into her hands and rubbed the saliva all over my penis, then turned around and lowered herself onto all fours. She spread her ass cheeks wide and told me to shove myself inside her as roughly as possible. It was difficult at first; I didn't want to hurt her. I didn't yet understand that she wanted to be hurt. She told me to rub some more saliva on my penis. I slipped deep inside her, grabbed her by the hips and moved in and out slowly even as Adrienne yelled at me to go faster. I held back on purpose, frustrating her, learning to wound her the way she wanted to be wounded. As the opening feedback of "Ghost Bitch" howled out of the speakers like an urban banshee consisting of smoke and metal, she pulled away from me and ordered me to slap her. When I said I didn't want to she began to taunt me, relating in embarrassing detail everything Hector used to do to her in bed. "You know you hate me for letting him touch me at all," she snarled. "So show me. Show me how much you really *hate* me." She slapped me across the face three times fast. I grabbed her wrists and squeezed. She smiled innocently, like an angel, and spit in my face. That made me lose it. I shoved her back down onto the bed and slapped her across the face until both cheeks were bright red. I wiped her spittle off with my hand. "Spit on *me* now," she said. "Go ahead and do it. You know you want to. You've wanted to degrade me the second you saw me." No, I thought to myself. I never did. I just wanted to love you. But she wasn't having any of that. She bitched and screamed and nagged until I was convinced that she was right and I was wrong. I really did

ROBERT GUFFEY

hate her, I really did want to degrade her. So I did it. I spit in her face and trails of saliva dripped over the corners of her upper lip and into her mouth. She screamed in disgust and slashed me across the face. I pushed her again, holding her wrists down onto the bed. "You know what you want," she whispered. "Why don't you take it? I'm never giving it to you, you know. Never to a fool like you. Just take it then. Just *take* it, you asshole." Still clutching her wrists, I tried to mount her as she laughed at me. She attempted to hold her legs together but I pried them apart with my knee. At one point she kicked me near the groin, but I couldn't feel pain any more, not the way I used to. Her attempts to dissuade me just made me more insistent. I thrust my penis inside her despite her fake, teary-eyed protests. I rammed into her, my unusually sharp hip bones bruising her thighs, but I didn't care what I did to her any more. I just wanted what was mine, what I deserved after all these months of stupid cat and mouse games. Her protests grew less insistent with each of my violent thrusts. Soon they were replaced entirely by squeals of mounting ecstasy as I ejaculated inside her at last, at long last, oh God at long last. "Death Valley '69" reached a crescendo on the CD player. She jerked her wrists out of my hands and slid her fingers down my back, petting and stroking me gently, cooing like a tiny bird. I stroked her hair, her cheeks… gently. "I love you," she whispered in my ear, and I echoed those words between my fading gasps. The CD went quiet immediately after the end of the final song, somehow snapping me out of post-coitus limbo and back into the real world. I slipped out of her and plopped down on the bed, trying to catch my breath. Her hand reached out for mine and we lay there like teenage lovers, just staring at the ceiling, lost in our own alien thoughts. I had become someone new. My old self looked back at me down a very long dark corridor and didn't know if he liked what he saw. But my new self didn't care. For the first time in his life he knew the true meaning of love.

16

Synopsis.

Upon awaking the next morning at around six A.M. I suddenly realized how to finish the third act. All the plot threads converged at once in my mind in a brilliant white flash. (Maybe it wasn't as dramatic as that, but close enough.) I climbed out of bed, being careful not to awaken Adrienne, and rushed over to my computer. I banged out the remainder of the third act in a few hours. By the time Adrienne awoke at noon the only thing I had left to do was put the finishing touches on the rewrites of the second act that Simms had requested. I knew Adrienne had awakened when I heard her giggling behind me.

"Would you like to let me in on the joke?" I asked, not taking my eyes off the screen; I could barely see her reflection in it. Her head rose from the pillow, then she propped herself up on one elbow and just stared at my back.

"You look funny sitting there naked," she said. "I bet the seat is leaving little crisscross patterns on your butt."

"You think that's funny? What's even funnier is that I didn't know I was sitting here naked until you mentioned it."

"Damn, you're sure typing up a storm, aren't you?" I watched her reflection throw the sheets aside and pad across the floor toward me. Seconds later I felt her hands massaging my shoulders. "What's the hurry? Your deadline's not for awhile yet."

As my fingers whizzed across the keyboard I said, "What's the hurry? The hurry is I've finally finished this god damn screenplay. I'm St. George and I've just slain the dragon. It's dead and mangled and I've got my sword in its bloodless heart. The finish line is in sight and *nothing* can steer me from my course."

Adrienne took this as a challenge, of course. She reached down and began stroking my limp penis. I was concentrating so much on the screen I didn't even get a hard-on. Adrienne got pissed off. She lowered herself to her knees, wrapped her lips around the head of my penis and began flicking her tongue back and forth across the foreskin. My penis grew erect in her mouth within seconds. She was good, very good, but I never once stopped typing.

Synopsis: I come, she swallows, I'm done.

Fade to black and fade out.

17

Foreshadowing.

Fade in:

Ext. Cahuenga Blvd.—Day.

Richard Angstrom is driving through the sparse afternoon traffic in his girlfriend's beat-up Jaguar. Move in for a close-up of the passenger seat, where sits a fat manila envelope. His hand is resting on it protectively. He's got a shit-eating grin on his face and he's singing along with the radio, some up-tempo pop song he doesn't even know the words to. He's pretty damn happy, as if he's just completed a very long and arduous project.

Close-up on the clock radio embedded in the dashboard. As the blue digital numbers change from 1:59 to 2:00 the song segues into the regular news update at the top of the hour. We hear an emotionless, baritone announcer say the following: "We're receiving reports of an explosion in South Central Los Angeles that has caused a fire to rage out of control during church services at the St. Mark African Methodist Church located in the 12900 block of South Avalon Boulevard. Tenants from surrounding buildings have been evacuated while firemen attempt to contain the blaze. The cause of the explosion is so far unknown. We'll be updating you on this breaking story as it develops. In other news—"

The announcer's voice fades into the background as we close in on Richard's face, which bares a quizzical and maybe even frightened expression. He doesn't know what this story means, but somehow he knows it's significant. Though a cliché, the following description is most appropriate: He feels as if someone has just walked over his grave.

If I were writing this scene for a screenplay I would probably do it pretty much like that. Of course, much of this scene relies on having a good enough actor to pull off the job of expressing complex emotions for the audience to see on screen, but so what? I'm not the casting director. Let them find a professional actor and let me write the way I write.

It's a moot point. This scene will never be filmed in a movie, except for the one in my head. None of that's important anyway, not right now. I just want you to understand what really happened to me.

I'm innocent, and I always have been.

18

The Argument.

When I returned home I found Adrienne sitting in my chair reading something on the computer. All she was wearing was one of my old t-shirts and a pair of black panties. She sat staring at the screen, one leg propped up on the chair, her chin resting on her knee. She had a dour look on her face.

"Is something wrong?" I said from the bedroom doorway. The second the sentence left my mouth, I knew. Before leaving on my triumphant march to Simms's house I had asked her to read the screenplay from start to finish and then give me her opinion of it. Up to this point she had only been familiar with the initial outline. She knew of none of the characters I had introduced later, the ones so obviously based on Adrienne, Hector, and his screwy new wife. For some reason (and to this day I'm not even certain why), it had never occurred to me that Adrienne might be upset. All I can plead is the unconscious selfishness inherent in every living writer.

"What is this?" she said coldly, tapping her fingernail against the screen.

I leaned over her shoulder. She had just gotten out of the shower. Her hair was still damp and smelled water-fresh. My first instinct was to plant kisses on her neck, but instead I forced myself to focus on the screen. It was the scene where Adrienne's character is first introduced.

She's portrayed as a battered woman with a fragile self-esteem, unable to protect herself from her ex-husband's macho posturing.

"That's Adrienne," I said.

"And what's this?" She tapped her fingernail against Hector's name.

"That's Hector. Don't you love the way I kill him at the end?"

She spun around in the swivel chair to face me. "You *actually* used our names?"

"Not at all. I altered the last names." Thankfully I'd had the foresight to do that before showing Simms the first draft.

She glanced back at the screen. "From Hector Morales to Hector Moran?"

"Yeah, like 'moron.'" I released a weak little laugh.

"From Adrienne Coffee to Adrienne Folger?"

"Mm-hm. What's wrong with that?"

"Well, god damn, that disguises everything, doesn't it?"

"Of course it does… legally."

"I'm not talking about *legally*!" she screamed, rising up out of the chair. She got right into my face, jabbing her finger at me. "After everything I told you, I can't believe you went ahead and did this! After everything I went through with Hector's fucking screenplays, now you turn around and do the *same* fucking thing!"

"What're you talking about? It's not the same thing. Hector was actively trying to hurt you."

"And you're not?"

"Jesus, of course not." I placed my hands on her arms, just below her shoulders. She wriggled out of my grasp and walked away from me. She stared out the window down at the street below, her arms crossed over her chest. "I thought you would think it was funny."

She laughed scornfully. "Funny? What's so funny about reliving the worst part of your life all over again?" When she turned around to face me again, her eyes were glassy and bloodshot. "Why do you think I opened myself up to you? Why do you think I bothered to tell you over and over again what Hector did to me? I thought it might sink into your head. I thought… I thought you might sympathize with me just a tiny bit."

"I do. That's why I threw Hector into the screenplay in the first place. You think that shows Hector in a positive light? It's a complete *parody* of him. You can't see that?"

She got into my face again, enunciating each syllable as if I were a child. "I. Don't. Want. My. Life. On. Screen. Period. What don't you understand about that?"

"It's not your life, no one's going to connect it to you."

"No, only the people who know that Hector and I used to be married... namely everyone I've ever known in my entire god damn life. That's all. No big deal."

I sighed. "I'll change the names then. I'll make it more obscure."

"It's still my life."

"No one will know."

Her lips contorted into a crooked scowl, her face flushed red with anger. "It's a piece of *me* that you sucked out of *my* life like a vampire and squirreled away in your little story and now you want to display it on screens all across the country like some cute knick-knack on a mantel for everyone to look at and point at and *laugh* at? I... I can't even look at you." She stormed off toward the bathroom, still yelling. "I can't believe I fucked you. It's like making love to a bottom feeder, some fucking parasite."

I followed her toward the bathroom. She tried to slam the door in my face but I wouldn't let her. I pushed the door in and followed her inside.

"I don't believe you're even angry about this."

She backed up against the sink. "Fuck no, I just like raising my adrenalin for no particular reason."

"I think you do. What is this, some little sex game of yours again? Like last night?" I wrapped my arms around her waist, pressed my body against hers. "You want to rile me up, get me so angry I'll beat the hell out of you? Is that what excites you? Is that what gets you off?"

She tried to struggle out of my grasp. "Don't touch me!"

I grabbed her arms and pinned them to her sides. "Are you sure? Sure you don't want me to throw you to the floor and fuck you? How do I know what's real with you? One minute you're acting like a child, the next you're a character out of a god damn Marquis de Sade novel. You're so concerned with being betrayed and lied to, what about me? How am I supposed to know when you're telling the truth?"

"Let go of me, you're hurting me."

"Is that the truth or a lie?" I leaned down and tried to kiss her on the lips, but she jerked her head away.

ROBERT GUFFEY

"God damn, I swear I'll scream rape if you don't let go of me in two seconds."

"If the judge spent just three months with you he'd never convict me."

She just glared at me with eyes from hell. I released her arms. She scampered away toward the shower door. "Get out," she said.

"I live here."

"Get out!" She pointed toward the door. I backed out into the hallway. She slammed the door shut and locked it. What the hell was she doing now? I leaned against the wall and waited. A few minutes later she emerged from the bathroom wearing her black evening gown. "Where's my purse?" I followed her into the living room, where she began throwing all the cushions off the sofa and peeking under ash trays. "*Where's my purse?*"

Before she could begin ripping up the floor I said, "It's in your car."

She sighed in frustration and made a bee-line toward the door, slipping her shoes on at the same time, which seemed rather difficult. At one point I thought she might tip over, bang her head against the lamp, crack her skull open and die. But, alas, that didn't happen. Instead she walked right through the doorway.

"No parting shots?" I called out. "No clever *bon mots*?"

"Fuck you!" she said and slammed the door behind her.

19

We Interrupt This Broadcast.

I felt like zoning out, so I picked up the remote and switched on the television. I found myself staring at a freeway police chase live in-progress. This time the police were chasing a guy on a motorcycle, who was zipping in and out of cars like a mad stuntman on an obstacle course. Had he robbed a bank or was he just speeding out of control for no particular reason? Somehow I came to the conclusion that he'd had a fight with his girlfriend, but I was probably just projecting. The crazy cameraman, who must've been hanging out of the passenger side of the copter with the camera on his shoulder, had the motorcyclist locked in his sights. At the point that a flying mechanical object is tailing you, why the hell wouldn't you just give up?

The picture returned to the studio where the newswoman was explaining the situation as much as she could, which is difficult when you don't know a damn thing and there's nothing written on your teleprompter. Apparently the police didn't know why he was speeding. Just another senseless act of nuttiness in L.A.

Abruptly, they decided to switch from the chase to a sudden development in another breaking story. A middle-aged man in a suit and tie stood holding a microphone in front of a mass of blackened rubble, the charred remains of the burning church I'd heard about earlier. The firemen had succeeded in containing the blaze, but couldn't save the building itself. In the background a rescue team was in the process of pulling bodies out of the rubble. Some of it was pretty gruesome.

In the foreground the reporters stood interviewing a police officer who was sweating from the heat. The reporter, who possessed the most Aryan blond hair and blue eyes I'd ever seen and yet had a Latino surname, announced that the officer had new information on the arson.

"You do believe it was arson, don't you?" the reporter asked.

The officer replied in a stoic tone, "I can't deny that. Apparently the fire was the result of a bomb planted somewhere in the building."

"Do you think this could be the work of some kind of domestic terrorist group?"

"That would be jumping to conclusions."

"But wasn't this church the target of an arson a few years ago?"

"Yes, but no one was ever charged with the crime."

"But terrorists were suspected."

The police officer actually laughed. "You want to make this as dramatic as possible, don't you?"

"A bomb is fairly dramatic isn't it, officer? Listen, how do you know this isn't a part of a campaign of terror against black churches? There's been an inordinate amount of these church burnings in the past few years, hasn't there?"

"There's no evidence for any campaign of terror. As far as we know this is an isolated event. At this point it's useless to deny the fact that a bomb was involved… but any information on the purpose of the explosion would be pure speculation and very irresponsible." He looked like he wanted to get out of there as fast as possible. Somehow I knew how he felt.

"And the victims? How many are there?"

"About thirty. At least five of them are dead. Judging from the state of their bodies, they were probably at the center of the blast."

I pointed the remote at the TV and with the press of a button made the madness go away. The rest of the world remained the same. Too bad.

I went to bed early that night. I didn't dream.

20

Soliloquy II.

Richard? Are you awake? I'm sorry I'm calling so late. I don't know what to do. I think somebody broke into my apartment. All my stuff is moved around. No… no, I didn't touch *any* of it. Maybe he came in while I was at your place. I just got back from the office and… I think… I think it might've been Hector. I… don't know, I just have this fucked-up feeling. Why? Maybe to get back at me for what happened at the party? No… it'd be easier than you think. You see… well, Hector still has the key to my apartment. I know, I *know*… I just never wanted to ask for it back. I never wanted to see him again, so I just let it go…. Please, *please*, no, don't get angry with me. Don't let that son of a bitch come between us. That's what he *wants*. To set us against each other, to get us to do what we're doing right now! This is what he always loves to do. Somehow, within just a few seconds of meeting you for the first time, he can focus in on all your weaknesses. He has some… some fucking innate ability to divine exactly what it is you're most insecure about and build a whole house of cards on it, then he pulls the rug out from under you when you'll be most embarrassed by it. I got so *used* to being humiliated day after day I think I learned to enjoy it. He's actually got me *trained*. I can't even have sex now without… without….

Did you know the psychologist B. F. Skinner used to make his daughter Debbie live in a box? He even named it his "Skinner Box." He must've been so proud. He was curious to see how his daughter would turn out if she spent most of her childhood cut off from human contact. She grew up and killed herself in her twenties. Hurray for science. Sometimes… sometimes I feel like Debbie. Hector was a pretty damn good psychologist in a lot of ways. That's how he's able to satirize people so well in his screenplays. That's why I was so angry with you before. For a second, what with your writing and all, you just reminded me too much of Hector. But I… I overreacted. I know you're not doing it for the same reason he is. I love you, Richard, I really do.

He's a bitter, bitter man. I think he was unhappy the moment he was born. He really has no emotions, and he hates people who do. So he uses your emotions against you, works on you bit by bit, tears that house of cards down slowly, slowly. In our case that house of cards happened to be a marriage. In others it's a friendship or a business deal or a collaboration on some film script or just a… a simple transaction with a cashier at a supermarket. It never *ends* with him. He's always trying to one-up you, no matter who you are. You could be a kid down the street trying to sell Brownie cookies, it doesn't matter. He'd find some way to try to manipulate the situation so everyone would come out of it unhappy, as unhappy as him.

I know… sometimes I make him sound like evil incarnate. And maybe he *is*.

You don't understand. You don't know him. With most criminals, even murderers and rapists, at least I can understand their motivations. I don't sympathize with them, I don't agree with their actions, but at least there's some kind of definite *reason* you can put your hands on. A bank robber wants money, a rapist wants sex, a murderer kills for jealousy or power or fame, whatever. Those are concrete *goals* you can understand. Not with Hector. He has no goals. The shit he pulls, the crimes he commits, they're done for no reason at all. No reason at all. Just for the fun of it, to see if he can get away with it. To me, that's the ultimate evil. The Devil couldn't do any worse. Even *he* had to be pushed into Hell; he didn't leap into it with glee. Please… please, Richard, *please* come over here. I need you. I need to feel you next to me right now.

21

The Bridge.

It took me about twenty-five minutes to reach her apartment. She lived on the second floor of an attractive, well-kept building in Los Feliz on Franklin and St. George. In order to reach the apartment, I had to drive across an antiquated bridge constructed well over eighty years before, at some point in the 1920s. There was something eerie about that bridge. On four sides stood odd looking pillars that were hollowed out inside, as if they had once contained spaces for toll guards to stand in. Now there was nothing but emptiness: no guards, no trolls demanding recompense. Just the Hollywood night air, warmed by the Santa Ana winds. Every time I crossed over that bridge, between those pillars, I felt as if I was passing through some kind of threshold into another world, someplace far stranger than the world I was used to. Of course, that was just my imagination. Instead, the world on the other side always turned out to be the real one—this one—yet again. If, that is, you choose to call Los Angeles the real world.

I'm afraid I *have* to. I've got no choice.

Not anymore.

22

The Attack.

I didn't let Adrienne know what I was planning.

Dr. Julie Cavanaugh and her boy toy, Hector Morales, lived in a posh three-story house affixed to the side of a hill in Pacific Palisades. I followed a winding road up to a pair of locked black iron gates. From the top of each, a small security camera watched me. I punched a button on an intercom and asked to be let in. An old woman with a British accent told me to identify myself. I replied I was Richard Uphill from the IRS, after which I heard the old woman conferring with someone in the background for a few seconds. The gates soon opened all by themselves like a magical castle in a fairy tale. The IRS will do it for you all the time, at least that's what Lincoln always says. I'd had him use that trick a million times in my stories, but I never thought it'd work in real life.

I cruised up the driveway to an ornate front door. Obscure figures from Sumerian mythology had been hand-carved into the double doors. The only reason I recognized them was because of the shitload of research I'd done for a Lincoln story titled "Figures in Stone" about a serial killer obsessed with Sumerian culture. Dr. Cavanaugh was definitely an eccentric individual with unusual tastes.

I had become so paranoid, I wondered if this had been done as a reference to my story in particular—just to freak me out. But how could they know I would ever see it? And wouldn't that be a lot of trouble to go through just to put a scare into somebody?

Then again, breaking and entering was a lot of trouble to go through as well. And Adrienne's apartment had definitely been broken into, I knew that much for sure.

A few seconds after ringing the door bell, the door was opened by a kind old woman who said, "Yes? May I help you?"

She looked like my grandmother. All the pent-up hatred leaked out of me. I didn't know what to do. "Is… Mr. Morales here?"

"Yes. Would you like me to go get him? It might take a few minutes, but you're welcome to wait in the library. Would you like something to drink?"

I don't know what changed. I don't know what hit me.

I didn't even look back. I was having a hard time breathing. I ran. My flight took me across the front lawn, down the driveway, and back into Adrienne's car. I slammed the pedal to the metal and peeled out of there as fast as possible.

The fear.

My heart was pounding so fast I thought it was going to leap right through my chest. For the first time since my arrival I actually contemplated doing seventy all the way out of California and keeping my foot on the gas until I reached my beloved Wisconsin. I had enough money and credit cards on me to do it; it was within the realm of possibility. But then I thought of my screenplay and knew I couldn't abandon it. I'd gone this far, I had to see the entire project through to the end. And then of course there was Adrienne. The only way I could ever abandon her was if she told me to leave, and maybe not even then.

Within a few minutes my panic attack faded. I slowed the car down and turned on the radio to get my mind off the madness I'd just experienced, but I was only half-listening. I drove aimlessly along the coast, which was far out of my way. I stared at the vast pellucid expanse of deep blue waters stretching out toward the horizon, breathed in the clear salt-laced air, watched invisible people in dot-sized sailboats cruising about in the ocean a great distance away, and wondered how the hell so many royally fucked-up assholes could spring out of such beautiful surroundings. It was a fascinating paradox, one that my mind clung to and refused to release. Any writer loves a paradox, but mystery writers love them most of all. Where would we be without them? Unfortunately, this was one paradox that couldn't be resolved with a clue and a magnifying glass.

Dozens of news stories drifted up out of the radio, through one hole in my head and out the other. As I said before, I was only half-listening. It was just background noise. But then one news story in particular caught my attention. I turned up the volume and leaned forward in my seat.

"—Angeles has suffered the third devastating bombing in only two days. At exactly one o'clock this afternoon two bombings occurred simultaneously, one at a public radio station in West Hollywood and the other at a toy factory in downtown Los Angeles. While a massive explosion ripped through the studios of KPFK FM on Cahuenga Boulevard West an explosion of equal intensity devastated the Imperial Toy Corporation, which is based in a manufacturing district about two miles from City Hall. Due to the first explosion one person has been confirmed dead along with at least a dozen seriously injured, while the second explosion has left three dead and twenty-two injured. Fire officials will not yet confirm or deny rumors that these explosions are somehow connected to the bombing of the St. Mark African Methodist Church, which occurred early yesterday morning. Some experts speculate that this is the beginning of another Unabomber-type killing spree. Former FBI agent Ted Henderson…."

The broadcast then switched to the voice of Henderson himself: "I believe this is the dawning of a new age of terrorism in America. Before long Los Angeles will become the new Belfast. My investigations lead me to conclude that—"

I wasn't listening any more. I suddenly realized how cutting edge my screenplay really was. I know this might sound cruel, but I was actually excited by the tragedy to some extent. It meant that I was somehow tuned into the universe, that I was able to predict major events in my fiction before they even occurred in real life. When I had heard about the first explosion only a day before my reaction had been one of disgust, but now my first thoughts were centered in on myself: How did this affect me and my screenplay? When the movie came out would people think I was inspired by these bombings? Would the immediacy draw people to the theater or drive them away? Would this still be a major topic a year or so from now when the film would be ready for general release? Of course, I didn't want to see all of Los Angeles destroyed by terrorist bombings, but if it helped promote the movie maybe the universe would allow one or two to go off here and there just to keep the topic in the headlines....

Thoughts of leaving Los Angeles for good were now miles behind me.

But not my hatred of Hector Morales.

23

Assault on Precinct 13.

The police station was a whirlwind of chaotic activity: two scantily-clad prostitutes clawing at each other's faces, a teenager trying to burst out of his handcuffs as if he were a circus strong man, an elderly man who held his own wrist tightly as he complained about the invisible insects in his body carving through his veins with microscopic mandibles. Multiply these scenes over and over again, and this is what I saw as I tried to tell an overweight detective my story while he continued to go about his duties, which seemed to consist of filling out a variety of multicolored forms in between taking sips from a Styrofoam cup of perpetually steaming coffee.

I sighed, perhaps for the twelfth time during the conversation. "This man is stalking Adrienne. He's dangerous and I want to press charges against him."

"Whoa, wait a minute." The sergeant took his glasses off and began massaging the bridge of his nose. "At any point last night or today did you actually catch this guy in your girlfriend's apartment?"

"No, but I can tell you where his house is. Well, actually, it's his girlfriend's house. He lives up in Pacific Palisades. This guy's a real sick bastard. You need to go arrest him before something bad happens."

"If we arrested every sick bastard out there we'd have to drop bars around the entire city. Look, has this Hector guy ever actually assaulted you or your girlfriend?"

For a moment or two I said nothing. I just stared into his tired, baggy eyes. "You don't know what this guy's done to her," I whispered.

The detective slipped his glasses back on, folded his hirsute hands in front of him and said, "I'm afraid there's nothing we can do unless this person actually attempts to physically assault your girlfriend. Until then…." He spread his hands in the air and shrugged.

I felt myself growing angrier and angrier. "So what do you recommend for protection?"

The detective picked up his pen and continued filling out his endless forms. He said, "Buy a pit bull."

At that moment one of the screaming hookers slipped off her cherry-red shoe and began beating the other hooker in the forehead with the stiletto-sharp heel. Blood poured down her face. It took four cops to separate them.

Steam was still rising from the detective's cup.

24

Waiting Period.

I knew a baseball bat wouldn't be enough. A butcher knife wasn't much better. I needed something somewhat more… intimidating.

I went to a pawn shop in West Hollywood I'd passed by a number of times with Adrienne. Underneath a glass counter sat a .38 that would be perfect. They asked to see my ID and had me fill out an application. They couldn't sell me the gun until they ran the application through the NCIC to determine if I was a felon or if I had a past history of mental instability, which is ridiculous since your mental health profile is protected from such scrutiny by law. It's just a slight-of-hand game to keep all the "concerned citizens" and gun control lobbyists as happy as possible. Meanwhile, you can stroll into a Big 5 any time you want and buy a rifle over the counter to blow your head off or shoot up the White House or whatever random act of violence meets your particular fancy. The legal system is very strange, almost as if a giant white rabbit was sitting in a dark room somewhere pulling the laws out of a hat at random. Once I was at a Swap Meet in Janesville, Wisconsin where some fat Good Old Boy was selling .357 Magnums out of a rickety wooden booth that looked like a lemonade stand. Believe me, this guy wasn't concerned with IDs. I remember thinking about buying one just for the hell of it. After all, an opportunity like that doesn't pop up every day. Now I wished I had.

The fellow at the pawn shop told me I would have to wait seven days until he could sell me the gun. I hoped Adrienne would be safe in her hotel room at The Roosevelt during that time. I had convinced her to stay there for the time being. Once I had the gun I would ask her to move into my place. At that point, hell, Hector could do whatever he wanted. Slip in through the window at midnight, *please*. If I killed him in my apartment it would be legal.

I left the pawn shop around 4:30 in the afternoon and returned to the hotel around 5:00. When I entered the hotel room she wasn't there. I began to panic. I called the front desk to ask if Adrienne had left any messages for me, but they said no. I was just about to go looking for her when in strolled Adrienne with a small briefcase dangling from her hand.

"Hi," she said very cheerfully, as if all was right with the world.

"Where've you been?"

She set the briefcase down on the bed. "I forgot all the documents I needed for work. I was tired of waiting around for you so I decided to take the bus back to my place to pick them up."

"*You* took the bus?" The image of Adrienne on a bus was hard to visualize.

"Sure," she said, shrugging casually. She sat down on the bed and began riffling through the papers in her briefcase. "I used to take the bus all the time when I was in college. It's sure changed a lot, though. Do you know how expensive the bus is now? It's over a dollar! I can remember when it was *fifty* cents. How do these people afford it? Easier to buy a car."

I tried not to get angry. "Adrienne, the purpose of the hotel room was to keep you safe. How can you be safe if you're cruising all over town on buses?"

"It wasn't all over town, it was just back to my place. It didn't take more than an hour."

"Yeah, but—"

"What was I supposed to do, sit around here staring at my toenails? I've got work to do. Letting Hector put a scare into me like this is just as bad as being married to him, maybe even worse."

"So do you want to sleep in your apartment alone tonight?"

She put down the document she was studying and sighed. "No. But still, I can't hide underneath the covers either. Am I supposed to stay locked up in here forever?"

"Just for a week. Is that too much to ask?"

"Why, what's going to happen in a week?"

"You're going to move in with me."

"I am?"

"You said before you didn't mind. You said it would be fun."

"Temporarily, maybe. I just got out of one marriage, you know. I don't want to rush into another one."

"It won't be a marriage. It's the only way I can think of to keep an eye on you."

"I don't want anyone's eye on me."

"Unfortunately, you already have an eye on you and it belongs to Hector. Whose eye would you rather have on you, mine or his?"

She didn't even bother to answer the question. "So why don't I just move in now then?"

"Because I have to take care of something first. I went to the police and tried to press charges against Hector."

"What? Are you insane? They probably just laughed at you!"

I glanced at the carpet. "Well, yeah, pretty much."

"There's not even any evidence of a crime. How're they going to charge him with anything?"

"But the man's a stalker! Do you know what they had the nerve to tell me?"

"That they couldn't help me until I was physically assaulted. Welcome to patriarchy."

"It doesn't make any sense."

"Welcome to patriarchy."

I sat down beside her on the bed. "Listen, the next time you decide to take off, at least leave a message for me, okay?"

"You know, I wouldn't have to take the bus if you weren't using my car."

"Forget the bus. This isn't about that. Even if you're just joyriding in the car, I need to know where you are."

"Maybe you can inject one of those microchips in me like they do with pets these days. If the ASPCA accidentally catches me you can track me down."

I took Adrienne's hand. "I'm not joking. Hector's a twisted guy. We don't know what he's capable of. I need to know you're safe. I promise I'm not going to let him hurt you ever again." She stared at my hand on hers, then nodded. "Adrienne," I said, squeezing her hand, "I don't know what I would do if…." My voice cracked. I felt myself losing it. I drew her toward me and hugged her.

For some reason I couldn't exorcise from my mind those streams of blood spurting out of that prostitute's face as the ruby-red heel pierced her forehead.

An inappropriate image for such a tender moment.

25

Pronoia.

Later that night, after Adrienne assured me over and over that she'd take my concerns seriously, I returned to my place to pick up some clothes along with my laptop just in case Simms asked for some quick rewrites. We had decided I would stay with Adrienne at least overnight. If she wanted me to stay longer I would. Now that the screenplay was finished I had plenty of time on my hands, which meant my time was hers. To be honest, it was hard to believe the screenplay was even done. My life with Adrienne was inexplicably linked with it. How could one continue to exist without the other?

After I finished packing a small suitcase, I decided to call Simms and see if he'd read the script. I was dying to hear his opinion. In the past, every time I'd hand in a new exciting installment, he'd gobble it up within seconds. This time it was different.

"No, I haven't gotten to it," he said. "It's been a hell of a day. You know, every time Adrienne takes a day off the whole office goes to hell." He sounded a bit pissed. "Now what's this tall tale about a burglary?"

"It's not a tall tale, it's true. Adrienne's apartment was broken into." I wasn't sure how much I should say. The results of my conversation with the detective didn't inspire confidence. Nevertheless, I decided to march ahead. After all, Simms had seen firsthand how crazy Hector could be. As I grabbed the remote and flicked on the television across the room I said, "We think it might've been Hector."

"What, you mean because of what happened at the party?"

"That and a lot of other things. He's terrorizing us! The man's completely unhinged. I don't know how you can stand to work with him." The news was still covering the double explosions from earlier in the day. I found myself staring raptly at the charred bodies being pulled out of the rubble. Earlier, back at the hotel room, Adrienne had asked me to shut the TV off when they began showing such things. She had a weak stomach; she couldn't even handle fake violence in horror movies. I, on the other hand, had a fascination for death and destruction. Where would my career be without it?

"He used to be a lot different," Simms said. "Sometimes I think it's bad to have success too soon. The raves for *Blue Honeymoon* went right to his head. That's when things started changing between him and Adrienne, at least as far as I can tell. He's becoming something of a spoiled brat now; you never know what he's going to do. Sometimes I'd like to throw him over my knee and spank the hell out of him."

"Yeah, well, I'd like to throw him over my knee and plant a knife in his back." On the TV a mother was crying for her lost child. "Why couldn't someone blow up Hector Morales instead of innocent children?"

"Are you watching the news?"

"Yes. Isn't it crazy? It ties right into the screenplay. It's eerie. I almost feel like I caused it or something."

"Funny you should say that. Back in 1914 when World War I had just started Arthur Machen published a story called 'The Bowman' which had the angels of St. George fighting alongside the British Army. It was published in a newspaper a day after the retreat from Mons and hundreds of soldiers wrote in to say that such a thing had actually occurred."

"So what're you saying? You think Machen *caused* that?"

"In some sense. Maybe God read his story in the newspaper and decided it was a good idea."

"You think God reads the newspaper?"

"Sure. It has to get rather boring up there, don't you think?"

My eyes were still locked on the carnage playing out on the screen. "You believe in God?"

Simms sighed. "Sometimes, but not often enough to bother me."

"What the hell's that mean?"

ROBERT GUFFEY

"It means… most of the time I think you've got just one shot at life and you have to do anything you can to make a heaven for yourself here just in case there's nothing but blackness waiting on the other side. It'd be pretty disappointing to be a saint all your life and then die and there's nothing. No reward, no certificate from God congratulating you for being such a good boy."

I was thinking about that gun. I couldn't get it out of my mind. "So even if your happiness depended on hurting someone else you'd do it?"

Simms laughed. "That happens all the time in this town on a small scale. But if we're talking about something larger… well, I don't know, the payoff would have to be something pretty big. Something I absolutely couldn't live without." He paused. "Are we just being theoretical here?"

"Of course. Isn't that what writers are good at?"

"I don't know, I've never been one. Judging from you and Hector they seem to draw more from life experience than theory. 'Hector Moran,' for instance."

I smiled. "Have you gotten to his expanded death scene yet? I spent hours on it."

"It's pretty graphic, all right. You know we won't be able to show all of that on the screen."

"Misdirection and suggestion. The audience will imagine the worst of it on their own."

"Hell, that's what they're best at. The MPAA are even better at imagining things that aren't there. When Hitchcock filmed the shower scene in *Psycho* he actually made it far more graphic then he really wanted just so he could have something to take out after the censors got through with it."

Apparently the news was doing an entire half-hour segment on the bombings. They just wouldn't let it go. Now the reporters were camped out on a lawn belonging to the family of one of the victims, trying to catch a brief shot of their angered, tear-stricken faces through the drawn curtains.

"Too bad God doesn't have a censor board," I said.

"If it did all of us would cease to exist. Do the police have any suspects in this bombing? I've got the sound down on the TV."

"So do I. The last I heard they weren't releasing any information. Everybody always jumps to the conclusion that Middle Eastern terrorists are responsible. Hell, maybe it's some right-wing militia group. You know, like Timothy McVeigh? Those guys toss bombs around like Easter eggs. You could wallpaper the Taj Mahal with the amount of pamphlets they sell on explosives and sabotage and booby traps and derailing trains and I don't know… poisoning sheep. You name it, they've got a pamphlet on it. Where do you think I got all my information for the screenplay?"

"From militia groups?" Simms said. "You're kidding."

"Of course not. You can order a pamphlet from them for about a buck-fifty. God knows what they do with the money." I swiveled around in my chair and pulled some of the well-worn pamphlets out of my bookshelf. The cover of one of them was decorated with a garish illustration of the Founding Fathers locked in hand-to-hand combat with blue-helmeted UN troops, most of whom had dark skin. "They're probably using all of it to buy a used nuclear submarine from Russia or something. There's a lot of these guys out in Wisconsin."

"There's plenty out here too, I hear, just up north."

"Yeah, but there's a big difference between the two. The ones out in Janesville, Wisconsin are more likely to be Klan members, while the ones out here are like New Age hippies with guns. During the week they munch on their yogurt and granola bars, then on the weekends they go up into the hills and blow the heads off squirrels. Really weird."

"Aren't you afraid to be ordering their books? You're probably on some government list now."

"Jesus, I'm already on a list. We all are these days."

"That's kind of paranoid."

"Nah, just realistic. I've invented a new word. I'd love to figure out how to get into fulltime *pronoia* instead of paranoia."

"What the hell're you talking about?"

"Pronoia is where you think everyone in the world is working very hard to make you happy."

Simms laughed. "Now *that's* insanity."

Judging from the news, I couldn't help but agree. I had to get my mind out of this negative rut. Adrienne was a godsend, but life with her was like taking up residence on a roller coaster without seatbelts. One minute she was Pollyanna, the next she was on the verge of slitting her wrists. You could get whiplash from her mood swings. I figured I needed to hunt out some more positive and upbeat friends, just for a change of pace. Simms's wife would certainly fit the bill. Besides, I had some unfinished business with her.

"Listen," I said, "is Valerie home right now? I haven't gotten a chance to apologize for Saturday night."

"There's no need to apologize. She knows it's not your fault. Besides, she's not here right now. She's at her mother's house. The matriarch's been sick lately and needs constant care." He sounded annoyed.

"Hey… you two don't get along? You and Valerie's mother, I mean?"

"Let's just say you and Hector get along better."

"I don't think that's possible. I'm sure you and her never got into a fist fight."

Simms laughed so hard he began to cough. "Have it your way. Why don't you and Adrienne come over for dinner one night?"

"I don't know…."

"It'll just be the four of us."

"Well… then I accept. Adrienne would love it."

"I feel I need to make up for Hector's grandstanding. Maybe I should call up Hector and give him an earful. If he's really terrorizing you and Adrienne I should—"

"Please, don't bother. There's no need for you to get involved in this. I've got to handle it on my own."

"I understand. I promise to get back to your script as soon as possible. I'm up to my neck in other projects, though. It may take awhile."

"How long?"

"Let's say… seven days."

Seven days. The waiting period. I remembered something Adrienne had said to me months before: "If you like synchronicities, this is the place to live."

26

Dream Sequence.

Just as I once looked forward to leaving Wisconsin and being with Adrienne forever, I now longed to hold that gun in my hand. For some reason I felt it would end our problems for good. It was the key out of our self-imposed imprisonment within that hotel room. It had become a symbol for my obsessive love for Adrienne. Once I possessed it Adrienne could move into my apartment, safe from Hector's abuse, protected by me and enough firepower to blow Hector's twisted brains halfway across the state if necessary.

After living with me for even a little while, she would know this was meant to be. She would ask to move in permanently. Marriage wouldn't even be necessary. I didn't believe love needed to be bound by such things. For the first time in my life I began writing a love story.

Unfortunately, over the course of the next seven days reality seemed to drift further and further away from the fantasy in my head. Adrienne became more and more distant and aloof. She was hardly ever in the hotel room. Most of the day would be spent at the office—of course, that's natural. But long after six she'd still be working overtime, either at the office or somewhere else; in Hollywood, one's social life was simply another name for work. Most annoying, perhaps, were her dinners with potential new writers… but

I did my best to reign in my jealousy. If I began holding something like that over her head, my jealousy would never end.

On the second night I called her office a little after six. They told me she'd gone home. For now "home" was this hotel room, with me, but she didn't return until nine. She told me she'd been out having dinner with some potential financial backers for one of Simms's projects; she said her work kept her out late most of the time, and that if I wanted to live with her I better get used to it. The conversation got out of control. I yelled at her, she yelled back at me. At one point she said I was smothering her to death, then accused *me* of breaking into her apartment just to drive her further into my arms. I told her flat-out she was crazy. She threw a lamp at me and told me to get the hell out, so I did. The second I returned home the phone rang. It was Adrienne, sobbing like a little girl again. She wanted me to come back to her. A roller coaster without seatbelts.

The entire week went like this. It was as if someone had decided to compress the ups and downs and twists and turns of our entire relationship into seven short days. Concentrated madness. It was enough to drive anyone over the edge.

On the eighth day I bought the gun. A sleek black .38, the kind cops carry on their hips. It cost a hundred and sixty dollars.

"Always aim for the head," said the old man behind the counter, smiling as if we shared some kind of private joke.

I brought the gun back to my place and hid it in a drawer next to my bed. It was like slipping the final piece of a puzzle into its appropriate niche. The key was now in position. The lock could be turned, the doors flung open wide.

Adrienne moved into my apartment the next night. It was a Tuesday. Adrienne arrived at my door at seven. She dropped her overstuffed suitcase on the floor, then collapsed onto the sofa. Work hadn't gone well, she said. The backers she'd taken out to dinner a few nights before had run out of money. Simms wouldn't be pleased. She hoped this wouldn't affect our movie. I told her not to worry, it didn't matter; at best it was just light on a screen, at worst some words on a page. She lay on the couch with her legs resting on my lap. I slipped off her shoes and massaged her feet through her stockings. She pulled her pipe out of her purse and took a few hits off some marijuana, then fell dead asleep within seconds. I couldn't move for fear of waking her. I sat there with her feet in my lap staring at the seven o'clock news. Two more bombs had exploded, one at a park called Pershing Square in downtown Los Angeles near the Metro Red Line, another way out in Orange County. Fortunately no one was hurt in the first explosion, but in the second one a whole house had been destroyed. They reported that one woman was in critical condition, but had no information on her identity. All in all it was a most inauspicious start to what should've been a romantic evening.

After the news I slipped out from beneath Adrienne's legs. I draped a blanket over her, then retreated into the bedroom to fiddle around with my new story. I went to bed at midnight.

I had a strange dream. I was lying in my bed, but not the one here in Los Angeles... my old bed in Wisconsin. In the dream a fluffy white cat with green eyes was sitting on my chest. It was Sox, who had died when I was eleven. Sox was saying, "Only one of you will know." Somehow I knew he meant that only one of *me* would know; I was crying and turning my head away so Sox wouldn't see. Over and over again I sobbed, "Who else don't you want me to tell?" Then I looked straight up at the ceiling and saw a long yellowish centipede scurrying fast across its granulated white surface toward the area right above my head. I could hear my own voice whispering urgently, "It's just a dream... wake up."

My eyes snapped open. I knew I needed to urinate. I was sweating; I had left all the windows closed and the room had become stuffy. Adrienne was leaning over me in the early morning darkness. She was still wearing her work clothes. She was clearly upset. "Are you awake?" she asked.

I glanced over at the clock. It was 2:26 A.M. "What's wrong?"

"I woke up in the living room and you weren't there. For a second I didn't know where I was."

"You fell asleep," I said, still trying to regain my wits.

"I know, I'm sorry." She patted my chest. "Do you forgive me?"

"Of course." My mouth was dry. I needed a drink of water. I was just about to ask her to open a window when she leaned down and ran her tongue over my shoulder blade. She slid her hand into my boxers, the only piece of clothing I was wearing.

She whispered, "Make love to me, please. Right now." She pulled my boxers down low enough to reach my penis and stroked it until

ROBERT GUFFEY

it was totally erect. All thoughts of urinating vanished. She planted a few kisses on my neck and chest, then broke away to remove her nightgown, not even bothering with her usual striptease. She straddled my thighs, playing with her own nipples as she rode me. She closed her eyes and tilted her head back, sank her teeth into her lower lip. I turned my gaze straight toward the ceiling. It was cloaked in darkness. Anything could be hiding up there.

As I ejaculated inside her I thought of centipedes and green-eyed cats.

27

Morning Edition.

I awoke again at around 8:30 the next morning. Adrienne had already left for work. I staggered into the living room and found the morning paper, still unopened, lying on the arm of the sofa. Adrienne must have tossed it there on her way out the door. I picked it up and entered the kitchen. I popped some bread into the toaster, then sat down at the kitchen table and slipped the rubber band off the paper. I opened it up to the first page and was about to begin reading when I heard the front door open. I tensed, thinking about Hector. The gun was in the other room....

Adrienne came storming into the kitchen.

"What're you doing home?" I began to say, but then stopped. Her face was as white as a newly-painted wall.

"Have you read the newspaper?" she asked.

"No, I was just about to." The toast popped up in the toaster, but I ignored it. Adrienne ripped the paper out of my hands and laid it flat on the table. She pointed at the lead article, which was about the twin bombings from the previous day. The tip of her index finger landed on the name of the sole victim.

Valerie Simms.

28

Over the Edge.

She had died in the hospital earlier that morning. The home in Orange County that had exploded had belonged to Valerie's dying mother. Ironically, the mother had survived while Valerie had died what was no doubt a lingering, painful death. The article ended by saying that Mrs. Simms was survived by her husband, famous Hollywood producer Frederick Simms, who could not be reached for comment.

Adrienne and I sat at the kitchen table in total silence for a very long time. There were no words to say, none that really meant anything.

At last Adrienne whispered, "You should call Fred." I just stared at the ghostly, face-like patterns in the stained wooden table. "Richard?"

I took a deep breath. "Adrienne, if you were capable of breaking into someone's home, wouldn't you be capable of murder too?"

She looked confused. "What?"

I jabbed my finger at the paper. "Hector did this."

She laughed. "That's... insane."

"Is it?"

Adrienne lifted the paper into the air. "*This* was a random act of violence. Now Hector may be an asshole, but never in a million years would he—"

"Why're you protecting him all of a sudden?"

"I'm not protecting him. Why on earth would he do such a thing?"

"Because of what happened at the party. He's embarrassed and he blames Valerie for letting it happen."

"Oh, c'mon, that's crazy."

"Yes, that's what crazy people are good at—being crazy."

"So you think he's responsible for all the other bombings as well?"

"Maybe, I don't know. Maybe he came up with the same idea I had for the screenplay. Obscure one specific murder by surrounding it with random ones. It's easier to get away with twenty murders than just one. Ask any military strategist."

"If you're not going to call Fred, I am." Adrienne got up from the table and snatched her phone from her purse, which was sitting on the counter dividing the living room from the kitchen. She dialed Simms's number, but it went straight to voicemail. "Damn," she whispered while slipping the phone back into her purse. "He's not answering. Jesus, I don't blame him. He's probably getting calls from a whole bunch of different newspapers and TV stations. Maybe we should go over there." I said nothing. I continued staring at the faces in the wood. "Well, what do you think?"

"I think we're in danger."

She sighed. "No, I think *you're* in danger—of going over the deep-end. You're becoming more obsessed with Hector than me. You act as if *you're* the one married to him." At that moment the phone rang. She lifted it to her ear and said, "Hello?" Pause. "Yes, well, I'm staying here more and more now." Pause. "I just saw it in the paper, I couldn't believe it." Pause. "You are?" Pause. "Oh, sure. That'll probably be more convenient." Pause. "Okay, see you soon. Bye." She hung up.

I said, "Who was that, Dr. Cavanaugh? Offering you cut-rates on a therapy session? 'How to Deal with the Death of a Loved One?'"

"How can you fucking make sick jokes now?"

"How can I *not*? The whole situation's absurd."

"Now you sound like Hector." I shut up. "That was Marin," she said, "in case you're interested."

"Who?"

"Marin, Fred's secretary. You've met her hundreds of times before."

"Oh." I'm not good with names, unless I'm making them up for a character in a story.

"Fred called the office and told everyone to go home. Marin wants to go visit him, but she doesn't want to go alone. She wanted to know if I would drive over there with her. She doesn't live far from here. Do you want to go with us?

"I don't think it's a good idea. He wants to be alone."

"How do you know?"

I shrugged. "I just know. I would want to be alone if you died."

"Well, maybe not everyone's like you. People handle grief differently, you know."

I didn't look up from the table. I couldn't. Adrienne sighed again and stormed out into the living room. I heard her sit down on the sofa. Silence filled the apartment for the next ten minutes or so until a car horn honked twice from the curb below. I heard Adrienne rise from the couch.

"That's Marin," she yelled. "Do you want to go with us or not?" I said nothing. I heard the front door open, then slam shut behind her.

I waited five minutes, rose from my seat in the kitchen, walked softly into the bedroom like a sleepwalker. I pulled the gun out of the drawer and hefted it, testing its weight. It was far heavier with the bullets in them. I put on a simple white t-shirt and blue jeans with a heavy black jacket that had deep pockets. I slipped the gun into the inside pocket. It fit perfectly.

From the closet I removed a wire hanger, which I bent out of shape. Adrienne had taken her purse with her, and her car keys were always in her purse. I needed to improvise. One time Adrienne had locked her keys in the car and I opened it with a piece of wire lying in the road. It wouldn't be difficult at all. Even the resourceful Mr. Lincoln couldn't do any better.

Within ten minutes I was in Adrienne's car cruising down the 405 freeway toward Pacific Palisades. It was a clear fall day with few clouds in the sky. You could even see the mountains far off in the distance, which is a rare sight in Los Angeles. The sky was as clear as my mind. I knew exactly what I was doing. I knew exactly what I was *going* to do. I felt peaceful inside, the most peaceful I'd been in months. I was going to avenge the deaths of many people and save the lives of a whole hell of a lot more. Maybe it's true what all my colleagues said back home, that everyone in California is callous and shallow and care about nothing except themselves. Maybe. But it only takes one white crow to prove that all crows aren't black. I know *I* live here and I care a very great deal about what happens to other people. I care so much I'd even kill for them.

Here I come, Hector.

Your one white crow.

29

Horse Feathers.

Once again I followed the winding path up the hill to the pair of black iron gates, both of which stood wide open as if enticing me inside. Upon topping the rise of the hill the house came into clear view… or what was left of it. The entire three-story house had caved in, resembling photos of the Alfred P. Murrah Building in Oklahoma City. Fire engines and ambulances jammed the driveway while firemen and paramedics darted about the disaster site in a state of composed panic, if such an emotion even existed. Lookie-loos from the neighboring houses stood at the perimeter of the scene with expressions of frightened bemusement on their well-preserved faces, watching plumes of smoke rise from the hot rubble like dark ghosts. You could see it in their eyes: the violence of the wicked big city had bit them in the rear and it disturbed them as much as discovering a speck of dirt under their fingernails.

I parked the car at a crooked, haphazard angle then ran up to the nearest bystander, not even bothering to shut the car door behind me. I grabbed an old woman by the elbow and said, "What the hell happened?"

"I don't know. I live in the house down the road and we heard this massive explosion about an hour ago. We ran down as soon as we heard the fire engines." She pointed at a fat balding man, who was far closer to the carnage, trying to get a better view I suppose. Her husband, I assumed.

"Was anyone killed?"

"A paramedic told me they're bringing three bodies out. Oh, I hope it's not Dr. Cavanaugh. She's an excellent therapist. She cured me of my obsessive-compulsive disorder last year. It'd be such a waste if—" She gasped and clutched at my shoulder. She pointed an arthritic, claw-like finger at the front door. "They're bringing out the stretchers now."

The sparse crowd closed in on the bodies the second they appeared. I pushed past every single one of them. Most of them moved aside like straw men. I shouted, "Get the fuck out of my way!" at the ones who didn't. I caught up to the first stretcher just as they were sliding it into the back of the ambulance.

"Stop!" I said, grabbing one paramedic by the arm. "I need to see!" Another paramedic tried to pull me away, but I wrenched my arm out of his grasp and leaned over the stretcher. Half of him was gone, but he was still recognizably Hector Morales. Yes, the Great Academy Award winning screenwriter reduced to a head and a torso. I glanced up at the second stretcher a few feet away: the housekeeper. She was in better condition than Hector, but no less dead.

"Where's the third body?" I asked.

"She's still in the house," one of the paramedics said. "Why, you want to take a picture with her? Get out of the way!" They slid Hector into the back of one ambulance and the housekeeper into the other.

"Is she still alive?"

Most of them didn't say anything. One guy, the youngest, shook his head and said, "There's hardly anything left. I'm sorry, man. Did you know her?"

I nodded yes.

He patted me on the shoulder, then ran back into the house. The ambulances screeched away, their sirens howling for the dead. I just stood there for a moment, watching them pass through the gates.

The old woman hobbled up to me and said, "Is Dr. Cavanaugh dead?"

"There's hardly anything left," I whispered. I staggered toward Adrienne's car, eased myself behind the wheel, and drove down the hill at a slow, measured pace....

I had no thoughts. I cruised aimlessly for awhile at high speeds, losing myself in the serpentine twists and turns of the rolling hills.

ROBERT GUFFEY

I'm not sure how long this lasted, but by and by I found my body steering the car toward home. I drove back into Hollywood with a blank slate for a mind. For some reason I was reminded of that Groucho Marx line from *Horse Feathers*. After Groucho and Chico crawl through the door of a speakeasy, Groucho rises to his feet and says to Chico, "Get up! That's no way to go into a speakeasy, that's they way you come out." I thought of that about a block away from my apartment. For some reason it made me laugh for about five minutes straight. That's a long time when you're laughing, particularly when there's no one else around. I had to pull over to the curb. By the end of those five minutes tears were running down my cheeks and I couldn't breathe.

Finally I calmed down, wiped the tears from my face, and gathered my thoughts. I had almost committed murder. Little more than chance and crazy circumstance had prevented me from being one of those wild-eyed guys you see on the nightly news during dinner time, one of those lone nuts who make you turn to your wife or husband and say, "What the hell do you think happened to him to make him so fucked up?" I remembered saying the same thing to myself dozens of times throughout the past few years. To almost be on the opposite end of that question gave me a vertiginous, sinking sensation. At the same time I felt both fearful and relieved: fearful that I was capable of such violence, relieved that the choice had been taken from my hands.

I removed the gun from my jacket, just stared at it. What if Adrienne was already back from Simms's house? I didn't want her to find it. It might scare her away from me for good. Mr. Lincoln would probably say that the best hiding place is in plain sight. I smiled and almost laughed out loud again. Of course. I slipped the gun beneath the trash under the passenger seat. It blended quite well with the old grocery bags and banana peels. If she hadn't cleaned out her car in the past eight years, why should she start now?

I pulled away from the curb and drove the remaining distance to my building, thinking of Hector's bleeding face. I knew it would haunt me for some time to come. After all, *I* might've caused the same amount of damage. Dead is dead, whether by a bullet or a bomb. My hatred was too great to hold any sympathy for him, however. I was still certain he was guilty. This last bombing only proved it.

My instincts had been correct. Clearly Hector was storing his little bombs at Julie's house, but something had gone wrong. Perhaps it was stored improperly or they had detonated on accident. Plenty of similar incidents had occurred in the past. Leave a dozen mad bombers on a desert island and half of them would find some way to blow themselves to smithereens. In the final analysis I didn't care how it had happened. I was just glad the nightmare was over.

I parked the car beside the curb outside my building, locked it behind me, then lumbered up the stairs toward my apartment. Two men were standing outside my door. They were both fairly short, shorter than me, and yet they exuded a strange aura of intimidation. One was in his late twenties and looked like the kind of bland fellow who always died before the end of the first act in a cheesy horror movie. The other guy was middle-aged, bald with the last remnants of a Jewish afro wrapped around the back of his head. The middle-aged guy said, "You Richard Angstrom?"

I hesitated. "Yeah?"

He flashed a badge in my face. "Detective Merril, Trevino." He gestured at his partner with his thumb. I didn't know if he meant he was Merril Trevino, or if he was Merril and his partner was Trevino. "We'd like to ask you a few questions."

I think my first reaction was something along the lines of, "What the fuck?"

30

The Trial.

They brought me down to the police station in West Hollywood, stuck me in a little room with a two-way mirror that I guess I was supposed to ignore, and grilled me for about three hours straight. I couldn't believe it. I felt like Joseph K. at the beginning of *The Trial*. At first I had absolutely no idea why they were asking me my name, my profession, who I worked for, where I was born, why I was in L.A., who my next of kin was, did I have a lover, was she a man or a woman, what was her name, did I love her, can I chew gum and whistle at the same time, what's the capital of Nebraska, what's the capital of the Chase National Bank, how many Frenchmen can't be wrong, and suddenly I was back in a Marx Brothers routine again. Perhaps it didn't get as absurd as that, but almost.

Within the first hour I figured out that the middle-aged cop was Merril and the younger guy was Trevino. They did a pretty good rendition of good cop/bad cop, with Trevino being the good and Merril being the bad. But they performed their parts with such intense disinterest that you felt they might abandon their roles at any moment and begin assaulting you with batons and plungers just to relieve their terminal boredom. They were intimidating without being shrill, confrontational without once raising their voices. Perhaps most annoying was their patronizing attitude, as if you were a problem child who needed a good talking to.

It wasn't until the second hour that I understood they suspected me of an actual crime, that this wasn't some bureaucratic error or a vast practical joke. Some moments later it sank in that they not only suspected me of a crime, they suspected me of murder—quite a lot of them, in fact.

"You do a lot of writing, don't you?" Merril said.

"It's my job."

"I bet that takes a lot of research, doesn't it?"

"Sometimes."

"Ever order away for research material, like books and stuff?"

"What kind of books?"

"I don't know. Books on how to make bombs, maybe."

My God, I thought, Simms was right. They *do* have a file on me.

"Is that against the law now, reading books?"

"Depends."

"On what?"

"On what you do with the information."

Merril then proceeded to lead me down a meandering, disorientating labyrinth carefully constructed of words in an attempt to incriminate myself of something I hadn't done and never planned to do. Replaying in my head was the dialogue in the opening scene of Orson Welles's version of *The Trial* when two policemen barge into Joseph K.'s apartment in the middle of the night.

1st Policeman (lifting up the rug in the middle of the room): What's this?

Joseph K.: What's what?

1st Policeman (studying the floor): A circular line with four holes.

2nd Policeman (taking notes): Circular—

1st Policeman: No, it's not really circular. It's more ovular.

Joseph K.: Don't write that down, for Heaven's sake.

1st Policeman: Why not?

2nd Policeman: We can't not write it down just because you say we shouldn't.

Joseph K.: Ovular's not even a word.

1st Policeman: Do you deny there's an ovular shape concealed beneath this rug?

2nd Policemen: He denies everything.

Some of Merril's lines were just as memorable. Fortunately I'd done plenty of research into interrogation techniques. *Verbal Judo* is the book most cops read. Pick that up if you want to be prepared. Take it from me, you never know when you're going to be in this situation. I'd written plenty of surreal interrogation scenes just like this for my Lincoln stories, but I never thought I'd be in one. Cops generally run into two different types of people: hostile smart-asses and talkative kiss-asses. If you really want to annoy them remain silent. Totally silent. Pisses the hell out of them. Don't let them rope you in. I kept wanting to jab back at their straight lines with my scintillating, crystalline wit. Of course, that's exactly what they wanted.

And that's exactly what I gave them.

In the third hour they dropped a pile of papers in front of me. I tried not to show the surprise on my face, but I think I probably failed. Sitting in front of me was a photocopy of *You Might as Well Die.* A million questions swirled in my head at once. Where had they gotten a copy? Who had given it to them? Why did they have it? What the hell were they getting at?

"You write this?"

"That's my name on the first page, isn't it?"

"Interesting parallels between your little movie here and the bombings."

"Hey, I'm impressed. Is 'parallel' your new word for the day?"

"You know Hector Morales?"

"Not any more. He's dead."

"Do you know Hector Moran?"

"That would be difficult since he's a fictional character."

"I hear you're some kind of a professor."

"You've heard right."

"Would you care to do some literary analysis for us?"

"How much you payin' me?"

"Isn't it very interesting that Hector Moran died in an explosion in your screenplay, and Hector *Morales* died in an explosion in real life just this morning only a week after you threatened to kill him?"

I tensed up and almost walked out on both of them. By this point Trevino had fallen into silence while walking around and around the table, sucking on a cough drop, glaring straight through me. "I never threatened to kill anybody," I said.

At this point Trevino withdrew a small recorder from his pants pocket and hit play. I heard my own voice, muffled as if taped through a phone receiver: "Yeah, well, I'd like to throw him over my knee and plant a knife in his back. Why couldn't someone blow up Hector Morales instead of innocent children?" Trevino stopped the machine.

Merril leaned into my face. "What's your interpretation of that, professor?"

Simms....

"That's not my voice," I said. Another mistake. I should've just told them the truth or not said anything at all. That's why they're so good. They make you hang yourself. Slowly.

"It sure sounded like you," Merril said.

"A lot of people sound like me."

Trevino started the recorder again. I heard Simms's voice saying, "Are you watching the news?" His voice was remarkably clear, as if it had been taped from his end.

"Who would you say *that* is," Trevino said, "a celebrity impersonator?"

I shrugged. "You can manufacture anything these days. Blood stains, photographs, phone conversations. Look at the O.J. Simpson case."

"O.J. was guilty," Merril said.

"Is that what the jury said?"

"Are you actually saying this isn't your voice?"

I clapped my hands together. "Congratulations, your ears are in excellent condition. You want to do an eye exam next?"

"I have a feeling your phone records will say different."

"Then why don't you go check them instead of talking to me?"

Their interest in me seemed to dissipate like a block of ice on a summer sidewalk.

"What? Aren't you going to arrest me?"

"No, no." Trevino said. "It was probably all one big mistake anyway. You know how bureaucracies can be. Well, have a nice day."

I think I liked the good cop even less than the bad cop. I grabbed my jacket and pointed at *You Might as Well Die*. "Can I have my script back?"

"No," Trevino said, "I think I'd like to read it before bedtime. That's the only chance I get to read, you know, right before I go to sleep. Man, I sure wish I had your job. I bet you get to read all the time, don't you?"

ROBERT GUFFEY

I rolled my eyes and started out the door.

"Oh, try not to take any sudden vacations," Merril said, "it might look… well, peculiar, to say the least."

Trevino just smiled.

Apparently the price to leave the room was to let them have the last word. I did so and left. Outside the police station I tried to call my apartment, but Adrienne wasn't home. I had to take a bus back to my building. But my mind was focused on other matters, most of all Simms, and I got on the wrong bus. It took me awhile before I realized I was heading in the opposite direction. By the time I returned to my neighborhood the sun was just beginning to set. The sky was an orange-red color smattered by thin black clouds that looked quite like the smoke that had been rising from the remains of Julie Cavanaugh's house earlier in the day. It was as if the entire sky was on fire.

As I approached my building I noticed that Adrienne's car was still parked beside the curb. When I entered the darkened apartment I knew no one was home. I picked up the phone to call Simms, then hung up before I had even finished dialing. The questions I wanted to ask him needed to be asked in person. I wasn't feeling too kindly toward phones at that particular moment.

I decided to take Adrienne's car. I sped off towards Simms's house. I wasn't even certain what I would say to him. I just wanted to see him. And look him in the eyes.

The clock in the dashboard said it was 8:30 when I reached Simms's neighborhood. Simms lived in a lavish house on South Bundy Drive not far from where Merril's friend O.J. Simpson used to live. According to Adrienne, tourists still drive to the scene of his wife's murder and take pictures of themselves waving for the camera. "Say cheese!" "Hi, Mom!" Souvenirs to hang up on the refrigerator door. Walk down that street at night, even without any knowledge of what had once occurred there, one picks up the impression of death-like stillness, as at a festive celebration where all the champagne has gone flat, the bitter atmosphere created by reality's hot breath invading a gated paradise. At the moment it was quiet, very quiet, perhaps as quiet as the night Nicole got her throat slashed. The Hollywood aristocracy who dwelled in these posh surroundings paid a lot of money for that quiet. They didn't like it when it was disturbed.

I parked a block away from the estate, turned off the engine, and just sat there for awhile. I stared at myself in the rearview mirror. I had come so far from Madison, Wisconsin. Back in my home town I always felt so grounded, as if my feet were rooted to the earth, as if nothing in the whole world was out of place. Now I felt like I was floating in the endless black vacuum of space, totally cut off from any other habitable star in the solar system. Sometimes I wish I could go back to this precise moment and… but no. People can't go back in time, except in science fiction stories.

To this day I'm not sure why I did it, but I reached under the passenger seat and slipped the gun out from beneath the pile of soft brown banana peels and held it to my chest. I knew I needed to bring it with me. I felt as if I was in danger. I had to protect myself. From who or what I didn't know.

I had to protect myself. Whole countries had been destroyed for that same reason.

I stuck the gun in my jacket. I closed the door behind me, being careful not to lock it, then walked the rest of the way toward Simms's estate. It was a warm, pleasant evening. I passed an old lady walking her dog. "Nice night for a stroll," I said through a boyish grin. She smiled back at me. It was a pleasant moment.

I approached the estate from behind. Simms's house was surrounded by a big black gate. Why announce my presence if I didn't have to? I glanced from side to side, making sure no one was around, then scaled the gate within a few seconds. I climbed halfway down the other side and leaped the rest of the way. I tried to land on my feet, but instead ended up falling on my butt. For one terrible moment I thought I might've sprained my ankle. I sat on the wet grass, wondering what the hell I would do if I couldn't even walk. I forced myself to rise. I found myself limping a bit, but other than that everything was fine. I continued toward the house.

There didn't seem to be any lights on. Was anyone home? I crept through the back yard and around the side. The soft grass muffled my steps. As I neared the front of the house the peace and quiet vanished. Loud music could be heard drifting from one particular window. I froze upon recognizing the band and the song.

Sonic Youth.

"Brave Men Run."

31

The Gun.

I entered the house through the front door. It wasn't locked. All the lights were out. I waited for my eyes to adjust to the darkness, then followed the music into a large bedroom. Two naked bodies lay on the bed. The man lay on his back, mewling like an animal. The woman was on top of him, sucking at his nipples. Was that a thin stream of blood trickling down his chest? He had his hands in her long blonde hair. He was petting her as if she were a dog. Her hands clawed at his broad chest with great violence and passion. Was he moaning her name? Perhaps not, but I heard it. I heard it distinctly.

"Adrienne... Adrienne...."

I watched Simms open his eyes. His moans stopped when he saw me. I felt myself slipping the gun out of my jacket. Simms tried to pull Adrienne's head away from his chest, but that just made her even more excited. At last he managed to whisper my name.

Adrienne's head snapped upwards. Her eyes filled with fear. She moved away from her lover as if he were suddenly infected with a fatal, contagious disease.

"I'm sorry—," Simms began to say. At least I think he did. I'm not sure. I fired two bullets into Simms's chest, a third in the face. Blood splattered all over the elaborate wooden headboard behind him. Mad brush strokes of red sprayed across Adrienne's naked flesh along with pieces of brain and bone. She screamed and fell out of the bed. She crawled on her hands and knees into the corner of the room. I followed her.

"*Why?*" I said, aiming the gun at her head.

She was crying and screaming at the same time. I told her to shut up. I told her to shut the fuck up or I'd shoot her right then and there. She wouldn't stop screaming. I leaned over and grabbed her by her blood-caked hair. I snapped her head upwards and told her once more to quit screaming. At last she stopped. But the crying continued. That soft, girlish sobbing.

I pressed the barrel of the gun against her skull. "How long?"

"Since… since before I met you," she whimpered.

"*Why?*"

"Why do you think?"

"You loved him?"

"Of course."

I wanted to beat her. I wanted to beat her until there was nothing left to recognize. "Why? Why bring me into all this?"

"I told him not to, I swear I did. It was his little game. He didn't want to wait. He wanted to marry me as soon as possible. He knew Valerie would never let him leave her, and Hector would do anything to keep me from being happy. The only way was to kill them. He wanted the perfect murder… h-he said you were the perfect scapegoat because he could hire you to frame yourself with your own ideas. He always said writers were easy to manipulate. Just stroke their egos, he said—"

"And you went along with all this? Do you know what you've done? The police think *I* killed all those people!" I leaned into her face. "Damn you, tell me the rest of it. *Now*." She hesitated. I shook her violently until she began to speak again.

"He… he had me plant evidence in your apartment. They're probably finding it right now. He wanted to drive you mad, make you hate Hector more and more. I didn't want to, I never did, but he made me. He *made* me. How could I refuse? I wasn't supposed to fall in love with you either, but I did. I swear I did." She reached upwards and tried to stroke my cheek.

"Don't give me that shit!" I slapped her hand away with the gun. "If that was true you would've stopped this a long time ago."

"No, I couldn't, don't you see? Fred had me right where he wanted me. He was using me. He hired someone to plant those bombs. Once the first one went off I couldn't back out. I was an accomplice to murder."

"Why didn't you back out before then?"

"I was confused. I couldn't help it." She reached for me again. This time I allowed her to stroke my cheek. Her fingertips were moist with blood. I stared into her eyes. Those clear blue eyes. I kissed her on the lips. I could taste Simms's blood on both of our tongues.

I closed my eyes and said, "Get out."

"What? But… why? We can leave together, go somewhere far away, they'll never find us—"

"I said get out before I change my mind!"

Adrienne scrambled to her feet, snatched her clothes from the floor, then ran out of the room. I collapsed against the wall, dropped the gun on the carpet, lowered my face into my bloodstained hands. I sat there for a very long time. I don't know how long. It must've been awhile.

The CD had long since stopped playing by the time I crawled toward the phone.

32

The Letter.

It's been a lot of years since that night. About three, I think. I don't count the days any more. Why bother? I'm serving the first of two consecutive life sentences. I just barely avoided the gas chamber. The majority of Americans think that's rather unfortunate. I agree.

I'm probably one of the most famous mad bombers in history. My name will go down in infamy with the likes of Kaczynski and McVeigh. Sometimes I wonder what made *them* so crazy. Or are they crazy? Are they even guilty of their crimes? Is anyone? I wonder.

You Might as Well Die was never filmed. That's no surprise. I finished the romance story, though. Turned into a horror story. Perhaps that's no surprise either. It was published in an anthology called *Stories By and For Serial Killers*. It's something of an underground classic, I understand. Look for it next time you're in a used bookstore. Oh, and I hear someone's created a website about me. It's supposed to be pretty good. I wouldn't know, I've never seen it. I'm rarely in the mood for fiction these days.

Life is funny sometimes. Weird synchronicities pop up out of nowhere. I received a letter today. Well, I receive a lot, actually. From admirers. Mad bombers are very popular among teenagers for some reason. Anyway, this was a very special letter. Perhaps the universe decided to send it my way to coincide with the end of this memoir.

The letter was from Adrienne. It was the first I'd heard from her since the night I killed Simms.

Richard,

I wouldn't be surprised if you tore this note into tiny pieces before even reading it, but I have to try. I truly did love you, though I tried hard not to. It was already too late. Fred's little game had been set into motion and like a runaway car it couldn't be stopped, at least not by me. I'm too weak and always have been.

I have this terrible feeling inside me. It's very close to the feeling I had when Hector broke up with me, long before I started seeing Fred. Fred was so helpful in the beginning, so gentle. It always starts out that way, doesn't it? The manipulation comes later, at least it seems to in my life. Except with you.

My fingers ache to call you but I know I shouldn't. I shouldn't be feeling like this right now. Everything turned out so wrong in the end. All because of me. I'm so confused. I'm sorry the handwriting is so bad. I've only had three hours sleep. I can't sleep any more. It hurts to be awake because then I remember.

It could have been so perfect. I could be at your side right now in your little apartment there in Hollywood, living happily ever after. Why did I sabotage it? What did I hope to gain? Why didn't I just leave Fred?

I know I should pull away from you, but it's hard. Missing you increases exponentially to the pain I feel—and to your pain, which I can only imagine. I'm still not the person I've pretended to be. I thought if I pretended long enough it would be real. And some of it is, but some things got glossed over and forgotten. I've been too busy playing the victim and I had forgotten how much pain I could cause.

I can no longer feel innocent. After all the questionable things I've done I still felt innocent. I realize now how misplaced that feeling was.

I'm so afraid of the ugliness inside me. I'm afraid to look but I know I have to. If I don't I'll never become a better person. My dreams will never come true if I don't start thinking more clearly, if I don't stop airbrushing away my faults and pretending they aren't there waiting to pounce at the last critical moments.

I feel a heavy weight inside me, not just because of my mistakes or your rightful feelings of betrayal, but because you're not here to greet me when I come home like you used to during that strange, wonderful, final week we had together. You're far away and I feel very alone and sad.

I've had some very bad moments in my life. The moment I realized I was not the person I thought I'd become tops them all. I want to crawl into a hole and disappear but that would be too easy. I need to find the courage to look deeply into myself and find all the holes and rotten spots I've been covering with pretense and bullshit. And I'm scared, so scared.

A month ago I met a strange little girl at the park that's just down the street from my home. She said something that scared me very deeply, although I didn't realize why at the time. She had dark hair and pale skin. Her lips were a deep shade. But her eyes—they were violet, more violet than Liz Taylor's. They were framed by thick eyelashes. She was seven and looked like she was born wearing makeup. She asked me my name and then climbed into a lookout tower on the playground. She looked at me. She made direct eye contact, and as she probed deeply for something behind my eyes she looked as though she were standing much closer to me than she was. "Now I can see everything about you, Adrienne," she said.

Something snapped inside me and I thought "those eyes" and knew she was telling the truth. When she smiled after she said it, I knew she understood things about me that I didn't even know. My tower of make-believe makes me ignorant; the tower of make-believe she was seeing me from gave her a clarity of vision I can only aspire to.

I miss your energy filling my house. I miss your jokes. I look at the mess in my car every morning and know there will be no more hot nights with you up in the hills, watching the lights of Los Angeles far below. You are a brilliant light in this world, Richard. If that little girl could see you she would know it the second you told her your name.

There is a space in my life that will never be filled. I'm sorry if this sounds so clichéd but my sentiment is genuine. I love you so much more than I realized. I'm filled with regret that we aren't even. I'll make it right, I promise.

Please give me a second chance.

Love,

Adrienne

I sit here now in my little cell turning the letter over and over in my hand. She included a phone number as well as a return address. She lives somewhere in England now. Somewhere near a park. A park with a playground. Children. Laughter. Games.

I'm thinking of our first night together up in the hills, the long conversations over the phone, making love slowly in the shower. I'm thinking of so many things, intense moments that passed so quickly you couldn't even describe their importance to another human being. How much of it was real, and how much of it was part of the game?

I'm thinking... I'm thinking of that Groucho Marx line, believe it or not. I'm laughing.

Get up! That's no way to go into a speakeasy, that's the way you come out. Oh God, I think I... I think....

33

Fade out.
 I think I believe her.

Rocket City Murder

1

In Which We Meet Mr. L, (d/dx)c=0, (|x| >= 1), and Ms. N(n)

Mr. L paused outside the door. He was alone again. It seemed to him, sometimes, as if he'd always been alone. Except for a brief period of time, so long ago….

Mr. L took a deep breath, then pressed his left palm against the glass scanner embedded in the wall. A brief flash of green hit his palm. The light was neither warm nor cold. It felt like nothing.

The smooth steel doors slid open. Inside stood the control room which contained a console and video screens overlooking the Welcome Room. A bird's eye view. Whoever sat behind the console could observe everything that occurred in that little room.

(d/dx)c=0 spun around in his padded swivel chair. A steaming cup of coffee sat on the console. A bit of a pick-me-up, no doubt. Drugs weren't allowed on the premises, not recreational drugs. And it was going to be a long night… or so the guard believed.

"Oh, hello, sir," said (d/dx)c=0. He appeared startled, and he knew it. He tried to regain his composure. "You're up late, aren't you?"

"We have some business to tend to," said Mr. L. "Get on the phone. Have Ms. N(n) brought here. We need to talk to her. It can't wait any longer."

(d/dx)c=0 nodded. "Of course, sir." The guard picked up the phone on the console and repeated the demand as if it were his, with the same terseness and authority. A pyramid of orders. A pyramid of words.

"I'd like you to ready the Welcome Room for me while I make sure everything here is as it should be," said Mr. L.

"But… I'm not supposed to leave my post. You yourself—"

"It's important that not a single syllable uttered by Ms. N(n) during the next few hours goes unrecorded. I want to be personally assured that the equipment is in working order. If you recall, I used to do work like this myself."

(d/dx)c=0 smiled for a moment, as if the very thought of the great Mr. L actually performing a thankless task similar to his was far outside his comprehension. Perhaps it seemed funny to him. Nonetheless, (d/dx)c=0 rose from his seat and said, "I'll make sure everything is ready by the time she arrives. Oh, be careful of this seat, sir. I think the screws are a little loose."

"That's not my concern… for the rest of the evening I won't have time to be sitting down, *relaxing* on the job. I can't waste even a second with this one. I've wasted too much time already."

"Yes, sir. Some of 'em are stronger than they seem, sir, and others… well, I've seen three-hundred-pound men, real gorillas, just fold after a few minutes or so. One time—"

"My patience is wearing a tad thin."

(d/dx)c=0 nodded quickly. He knew he'd overstepped his bounds. It was acceptable to exchange a few friendly words, but going on and on like this like a chatty school girl… it was unbecoming.

(d/dx)c=0 left the room. Mr. L sat in the black leather chair and watched on the monitor as the guard entered the Welcome Room. He watched him remove the restraints from the chair as well as the various electrodes that trailed away from it into the featureless, padded walls. Mr. L glanced at his watch. It was after midnight. Everything had to be timed just right. He pulled a pair of gray gloves out of his inside jacket pocket and began to slip them on. He knew how long it would take to escort Ms. N(n) from her quarters to the Dome. Just enough time for the guard to complete all the necessary preparations.

Mr. L swiveled the chair toward the keyboard. The seat *is* a little loose, he thought. But no time to think about that. He had important business to tend to. His fingers danced across the buttons, calling up obscure programs embedded deep in the computer; he disabled all the monitoring equipment in the control room. The video screens blinked out at the same moment.

He smiled, the first time he'd done so in years.

He rose from the chair and headed toward the door. Just as he was about to wave his palm in front of the screen, the door swung open on its own. There in the doorway stood Ms. N(n), and looming behind her a new guard, ($|x| >= 1$). The guard had a mean-looking rifle in his gloved hands; he knew he had to take every precaution with this prisoner. She had given them a lot of trouble over the past few weeks.

And she was about to give them some more trouble, the most frustrating kind of all.

She looked up at Mr. L with those clear, blue eyes. Blue, bloodshot eyes that had seen so much.

"What're you *doing* here?" said Mr. L.

Even through the plexiglass visor that covered half his face, the guard looked confused. "Sir, I thought I was told to bring Ms. N(n) directly here, sir."

"To the *Welcome* Room!" Mr. L shouted and pointed down the long gray corridor. The corridor was built this way on purpose. It was supposed to look as bleak and sterile as possible, for the benefit of those being interviewed. That long walk toward the Welcome Room caused some of them to break down and talk before they even reached the door. "The Bridge-of-Sighs," those on the inside called it.

Mr. L pushed his way into the hall, waved his palm over the outside scanner, shutting the doors behind him with a metallic hiss. He did not look at the woman in the eyes. He couldn't. He maintained his wild-eyed stare on the guard, who said, "Yes, sir!" then spun widdershins, grabbed N(n) by her elbow, and pushed her toward the Welcome Room with abrupt little shoves. The woman did not complain. She hardly ever said anything to the guards.

Mr. L walked a few feet behind both of them. "Open the door," Mr. L ordered the guard.

The guard said nothing. He followed orders, as everyone here did. *Almost* everyone.

As ($|x| >= 1$) pressed his hand against the glass scanner, Mr. L pulled a .22 out of his jacket and pumped a single bullet into the back of the guard's neck, the only area not covered by armor and padding. Blood splattered all over the scanner and the bare walls that surrounded it. There was a brief, green flash. ACCESS APPROVED, said digital crimson words that materialized on the screen.

N(n) spun around and pressed herself up against the smooth gray wall. She watched as Mr. L switched the gun from one hand to the other. The door *sssshhhhhhed* open so quietly. And on the other side of the door stood $(d/dx)c=0$. Before he could say a single word, Mr. L lifted the .22 and fired a bullet into the guard's face. He looked so surprised. The body tumbled on the floor comically, like a scarecrow stripped of life.

Mr. L faced Ms. N(n) at last. "Inside the room," he said. "Hurry."

She obeyed.

He followed her inside, carefully placed the gun on the ground, right next to $(|x| >= 1)$'s vacant-eyed remains. "We don't have much time," he said.

"We never did," she said.

They just stared at each other for a moment. They were both covered in blood. He approached her. And they hugged for so long....

It was N(n) who broke away.

"Jennifer," Mr. L whispered, "I'm so sorry... I wish...." He reached out for her again. He felt like taking off his gloves, just for a second, to feel the warmth of her cheek....

"You said it yourself," she said. "We don't have much time. Let's just get this over with."

Jennifer wore dark slacks, a black turtleneck sweater, a black jacket, sneakers. Standard fare hereabouts. Such a dull uniform for such a striking woman. She was in her late thirties, just as beautiful as she had been when Mr. L had first met her almost twenty years ago. She had short, shoulder-length blonde hair parted down the middle, the chubby cheeks of a little girl, a svelte athletic figure, and long legs that could incapacitate several armed men with the right kick, at the proper angle. Such strength, such resolve in those haunting blue eyes. She had far surpassed the potential she'd demonstrated way back in college... two decades ago. Had it been that long? God, how much the world had changed since then. For both of them.

Mr. L was in his late fifties, slightly overweight, with a full head of silver hair. He was so out of shape. This place would do that to you, if you allowed yourself to get comfortable. That was his mistake. Believing their ridiculous promises. Everybody has a weakness, and his was wishing to think that his opinion mattered to the people above him....

His word meant nothing.

He was *nothing* here. He always would be.

What did Jennifer think of him?

"Jennifer…," he started to say.

She cut him off. "We've been over this," she said, "there's no other way."

"We could try to escape, both of us."

"You know we'd never get past the gates—maybe you would, but not both of us. There's no way. They can track me down wherever I go. They put something in my body." She massaged her arm with an expression of detachment, as if it were no longer a part of her.

"We don't know that."

"I know it. Just do it. You have a long night ahead of you."

Tears streamed from Mr. L's eyes.

Jennifer sank her teeth into her bottom lip. At her side, her hands clenched into tight fists. "Don't do this," she whispered. Then she threw her arms around him again. "I can't say goodbye again."

"Then don't. I *love* you."

"God, you know I love you. I always have. I'm so sorry it didn't… work out the way it was supposed to."

It was his fault. All his fault. Rivulets of tears streamed down his neck. "God, I can't do this."

"You know what'll happen to me if—"

"Don't."

She pulled away from him again. She sat down in the chair, the one they would use on her in twenty-four hours if something wasn't done about it.

"Maybe something will happen," he said. "They'll realize they're wrong."

"They never realize they're wrong, not until it's too late. You know that."

Yes, he knew… in more ways than one. "I brought the needle too, just in case. I thought you might—"

"No," she said. "This way is better. The other way leaves too many questions. I don't want you to get in trouble for helping me."

"I would gladly take your place if I could."

"I know." She opened her mouth, as if to say more, then said, "I *know.*"

Mr. L picked the gun up off the floor and pointed it at her face… his gloved hand wavered… then pointed it at her chest… her stomach….

"Everett… don't *think* about it," she said.

"You're not… you're not afraid at all, are you?"

"You trained me *not* to be afraid. Don't disappoint me."

He let the gun fall to the ground. "I can't do it." He dropped to his knees on the shiny, cold plexiglass floor and cried into his hands. So many people had died at his hands. Why did this have to be any different?

"I don't want you to feel any pain," he cried into the ground.

"How much pain will I be in if you don't do this?"

He said nothing. He just whimpered.

She stood and walked toward him. She lowered to her knees… hugged him. "You have the needle?"

"Yes, of course… but how will we explain…?"

"Give it to me, then leave me alone."

"No."

"You can't handle it. I understand. If the situation was reversed, I couldn't do it either."

He looked up at her. "Is that true?"

She nodded. She patted him on the cheek. "Yes. Of course."

He breathed deeply, grabbed the handle of the gun, rose to his feet. "This way it'll just be like going to sleep?" he asked.

She nodded. He reached into his jacket, the right side, and pulled out the needle.

They kissed one last time, gently, like father and daughter. Is that what they had always been? Really? She took the needle from him and sat down in the chair. She pulled back the sleeves of her sweater. She squirted out a bit of the liquid, then lowered the needle toward her vein.

"If I could do it all over again," she said, "I never would've left you. I need you to know that."

He smiled, and the tears came again. "If I could do it all over again… I guess I never would've kissed you. I would've left you alone. You deserved far better than me."

"I'm glad you didn't hold back. I love you, Everett."

"…*wait*. Don't. Let me do it."

He had to be strong. For her. He could not let her do it to herself.

He kneeled down at her feet, as if he were about to propose. He grabbed her elbow gently, took a deep breath, did not look her in the eye… *no, don't look at her eyes, just focus on her flesh… her arm…*

so many times he'd covered it in kisses... sank the needle into her vein, pressed the plunger down. The clear liquid drained into her pulsing blue veins... blue, like her eyes... he looked up... her eyes fluttered... she leaned back into the chair... the chair she once swore would never take her... and, like always, she was right. She was right.

The chair didn't take her.

He kneeled beside her and took her hand in his. He watched her eyes close. Held her until the final trembling of life had left her warm flesh. Still so beautiful. He took off one glove, stroked her chubby cheek with the back of his hand. "I love you," he said once more, then rose.

Work to do... so much work... so little time....

Don't think about it.

First he pulled off the other glove and wrapped the used needle inside it. He slipped them inside his jacket pocket. He needed to get back to the control room before the next patrol came along. He'd timed it a dozen times before. It couldn't fail.

Don't look back at her... just don't....

Mr. L fled the room. He stepped over the body of the dead guard and rushed back down the Bridge-of-Sighs. The stairs leading to the incinerator were to the left, next to the control room. It would only take him a few minutes to dart down the stairs and get rid of the gloves and the needle. Then he could—

Wait, voices. The sound of boots clomping down the corridors. Were they coming this way? He saw shadows cast on the far wall, just down the hall to his left. The shadows grew larger.

He muttered curses under his breath, waved his palm over the scanner outside the control room, then slipped inside. The doors slid shut silently behind him.

He sat down in front of the console and punched in codes only *he* knew to lock the doors from the outside. They would have no reason to suspect... as long as he put up a good front....

Mr. L banged on the closed doors with his fists. "Let me out! Help! Let me out! Somebody! Come quick! *Help!*"

That's when he remembered what lay inside his jacket: the gloves and needle. He glanced around the little room. He needed these damn things out of his possession, immediately. He could come back and get rid of them later. Didn't he have free reign of the premises morning, noon and night? It shouldn't be that much of a problem.

His gaze alighted upon the padded leather swivel chair in front of the console. *Oh, be careful of this seat, sir. I think the screws are a little loose.* A metal tube between the seat and the wheeled stand at the bottom of the chair allowed the height to be adjusted.

Perfect.

He grabbed the back of the chair and lifted up. The screws were indeed already loosened a little bit. He turned the chair over, loosened the screws even further, then separated the seat from the tube. The tube was hollow inside. He dropped the gloves and needle into the tube, then replaced the seat on top of it. He heard footsteps approaching. He tightened the screws as much as possible. He sat back down in the chair, tested its strength. It held. It wouldn't come apart, unless someone purposely tried to pull it apart. Why would they? It only needed to hold for a few hours, until things calmed down, then he could sneak back down here and….

A muffled voice penetrated the steel door: "Is there somebody in there?"

Mr. L rushed toward the door, began banging on it with his fists. "Let me out of here!"

"Who's there!"

"It's *me*, you idiot!"

The doors opened almost immediately. The guard was white with fear. "I'm sorry," he said, "I didn't know."

"At ease."

The man relaxed; he knew now he wouldn't be punished, not today at least. Oh, there was so much power in just two little words. Power that existed only because brainless idiots like this one *allowed* the words to have power.

Mr. L was sick of them. The words and the people.

"What's going on here?" Mr. L asked. "Why was I trapped inside that room?"

"I think there's something wrong, sir, down the hall—"

That's when they heard the alarm bells echo down the Bridge-of-Sighs.

"Follow me," Mr. L said to the frightened guard. "Let's see what all this is about."

"Yes, sir. Of course, sir."

Within seconds the halls would be aswarm with mindless drones like this one. Mr. L, for one, had had quite enough of all of them.

Quite enough.

2

In Which Bandini Arrives

It was always the same. Lt. Bandini woke with an overwhelming desire to remain in bed, a desire that could only be overcome by sheer force of will… a force of will he didn't have. Usually he hit the alarm and then went back to sleep for a few minutes. He'd do that three or four times until his wife got pissed off at him and told him to get the hell out of bed already—he was gonna be *late* again! He was always running late. This annoyed his superiors, or at least it seemed to, but he didn't think the Captain really minded. Nobody with as many closed cases under his belt as Bandini could be faulted for a few eccentricities here and there.

But this morning was different. His wife did not yell at him to get up. His wife was not there. He reached out for her, expecting to feel the familiar softness of her belly (she was always promising to go on a diet, not that he really cared one way or the other—he liked her just the way she was) and instead felt a rumpled blanket. An empty, rumpled blanket.

This was the first sign.

He shot up to a sitting position. The arc of sunlight filtering in through his clean white blinds was different than normal. The sunbeams were too low. It wasn't morning. This was afternoon sunlight.

The blinds. Clean. His blinds were never clean. No matter how much the missus tried to keep the dust off them, it was impossible.

Maybe it was the pollution in Los Angeles. All that dust made his son's asthma act up from time to time, but there was nothing he could do about that except leave Los Angeles, and he couldn't do that, not yet. Whatever it was, dust particles loved his bedroom blinds, that's all he knew.

But not this morning. Those blinds looked like they'd just come right off the assembly line.

He thought about his son's asthma attacks. And he thought about the air. He took a deep breath. The air was cool and clean. So damn clean....

It reminded him of the few times he and the wife and the kids had packed everything in the van and gone up into the mountains for a weekend camping trip. Some fishing, some hunting. The family didn't do it that often. He wasn't good at hunting. Hated guns. Even though he'd been a cop for years, he still hated them. He taught the kids how to hunt just because his father-in-law thought he should. Most of the time, though, he just taught them how to fish... on the placid lake, in the fresh mountain air....

Air like this.

Bandini dragged himself out of bed and called his wife's name. She didn't answer. Was she at work? Why wouldn't she wake him up? What day was this? Did he have to be at work?

Then he realized... of course... no, he didn't have to be at work. He'd resigned from the LAPD only a day before. For a moment it all felt like a dream. Why would he resign from a job he loved almost as much as his wife and his kids?

Then the memories flooded back... of course....

His heart started beating fast. Where was his wife? Where were the kids? The house sounded so quiet....

He shuffled over to the window, his bare feet dragging across the clean new carpet, and stuck his fingers between the blinds. He spread them apart just slightly, so he could peek outside. He expected to see the Greenfields' bright yellow house glaring at him from across the street (that yellow was just a little too bright for his tastes), and his beat-up old black convertible parked in the driveway. But that's not what he saw.

He expected to be on the second floor, but instead he was on the first. And outside were a series of featureless bungalows made of corrugated metal, the kind of shoddy affairs the local elementary schools had taken to throwing up on campuses in order to accommodate floods of new students. He'd seen several bungalows like them at the elementary school his oldest son had just started attending.

The bungalows were facing each other at an angle, forming a ragged "V." His bungalow lay at the very tip of this "V." Beyond the bungalow lay a series of small hills that grew progressively larger as they dwindled into the distance. At the top of the highest hill stood a large copper-colored dome. Weaving in and out of the bungalows, covering the hills, were lush green bushes and trees that loomed high overheard adorned with fresh, young leaves. He'd seen trees like these in the mountains surrounding Los Angeles. Overshadowing even the impressive copper dome stood even higher mountains, their peaks capped with pure white snow.

Bandini wasn't the kind of guy to become easily afraid. He'd grown up in the Bronx, had served on the NYPD as a beat cop for years before moving to Southern California. He knew how to handle fear and overcome it. But that was easy when you were dealing with known quantities. Whether it was a thug with a knife in his fist or some rich bastard with the power of a thousand attorneys behind him, Bandini knew how to handle intimidation. He'd had plenty of loaded guns pointed at his face, and he'd dealt with all of them by remaining calm.

Bandini was no longer calm. Where was he?

He raced over to his closet, pulled open the door. His clothes were gone. What were these? Dark slacks, a turtleneck sweater, a funny black jacket. Multiple copies of the same outfit. Seven of them. Plus sneakers. Sneakers? Where were *his* clothes? Where was his raincoat?

His. Raincoat. Was. Gone.

It looked like it was cold outside. The one time when it was actually cold outside, and he didn't have his damn coat.

His fear was now giving way to anger.

He threw off his boxers and got dressed, then hurried outside.

The air was cool and fresh and harsh on his lungs. Suddenly, he was glad for the turtleneck. So quiet. Was he totally alone?

All the other bungalows in the "V" were locked up. No lights inside. If they were occupied, their inhabitants must have been holed up in a closet somewhere, remaining very, very still.

ROBERT GUFFEY

He felt no eyes upon him. He did not feel watched at all. He felt as if he were totally alone. That's what disturbed him the most. Never, not for one second, did you feel isolated in L.A., even when you desperately wanted to be. This total isolation was not only unexpected, but deeply disturbing. A slight sense of panic began to coil up into his chest from deep inside his gut.

He began walking, fast. A dirt pathway led up the center of the V-shaped formation of silent bungalows. He kneeled down and inspected the dirt. On either side of the path: bright green grass—brighter than any grass he'd seen in the middle of L.A. The path had been made by the constant tread of feet, a lot of them, over the course of many years. Fresh tracks stained the path. Judging from the imprint of the shoes, they were sneakers very much like his own. All of them leading uphill. He was not alone.

The panic began to subside.

Bandini continued up the path. He could hear distant music. By the time he reached the top of the hill he was out of breath. He bent over and gripped his knees. Too many cigars. Too little exercise. Most of his life was spent behind a desk, filling out forms. His wife was always telling him he needed to get into shape. "What if you have to chase a suspect?" she'd say. And he'd just laugh. Jesus, he hadn't chased a suspect since he was working the beat in New York. The kind of chases he'd been on since making detective didn't require too much physical exertion, and he couldn't be happier about that. Still….

There was something to be said about being in shape.

He collapsed onto his butt and surveyed the scene below. The dirt path continued down the other side of the hill and into a little mockup of a city square, like the kind of thing you might see in an old black and white movie. It reminded him of this quaint little place he and his wife sometimes visited in the South Bay. It was called Alpine Village down in Torrance somewhere. It was a little outdoor mall where all the stores were made up like little wooden shops from the late 19th century. They served real good polish sausage there, and sauerkraut. His wife hated sauerkraut but he liked to have it from time to time. It depended on what kind of mood he was in. Alpine Village had swing dancing on Thursday nights. Bandini couldn't dance, but it was fun to watch the other couples dancing. It was a nice place to take the wife once in awhile, when she wanted to dine out. That's what the scene down below reminded him of. There were little wooden booths set up in the square and festive banners strung up everywhere and multi-colored balloons and a little brass band playing polka music. There were well over a hundred people down there having a nice time, dancing, drinking, singing, chatting. It was as if someone had plucked up Alpine Village and dumped it in the middle of nowhere.

Having finally regained his breath, Bandini rose to his feet and followed the path all the way down. The music grew louder as he neared the street that led to the fountain and the square. The dirt suddenly gave way to a cobblestoned path that took him through a wide street flanked on either side by vendors selling various items like steaming apple cider and blackberry pie and meat on a stick and buttered corn on the cob and yo-yos and poppers and wooden puppets and tiny kites shaped like fat men with astonished looks plastered on their painted faces and paper insects that flew. All of them seemed to pay no special attention to Bandini. He was just another face in the crowd, another potential customer. Many of the revelers were dressed in Alpine-style outfits, everything from fat little burgomasters to buxom beer maids, while many of the others were dressed in clothes very similar to the ones that Bandini had discovered in his closet. All of them seemed to merge together into one anonymous blur. Ignoring the vendors hawking their wares in sing-song voices, Bandini approached an old man sitting on the side of the marble fountain. The old man was reading a newspaper.

"Excuse me," Bandini said.

The old man looked up. "Eh?" the old man said, lowering the paper into his lap.

Bandini had to speak louder in order to be heard over the din of the brass band. "Excuse me!" he said. "May I borrow your paper for a second?"

"What?" the old man said.

"May I," Bandini said, speaking ever louder, "borrow your paper, please?"

"What?"

Bandini sat beside him on the side of the marble fountain. He pressed up close against the old man. He pointed at the paper for a second. "May I see the paper? Just for a second?"

The old man's mouth widened into an "Oh," but uttered no

noise, then he handed Bandini his paper. The old man pulled a big black cigar out of his jacket, crossed his long skinny legs, and lit up. It smelled good. Bandini tried to ignore it as he turned to the first page. Thank God, the paper was in English. At least that narrowed down the possibilities. Bold, cursive letters announced the title of the paper: THE SCOPE. The main headline on the first page screamed: TRIPLE HOMICIDE IN THE DOME. Bandini glanced at the first few sentences: "Emotions ran high in the Dome today where two guards and a New Arrival were found dead in the central chamber known to many as The Welcome Room. When asked for a comment, Mr. L said, 'The culprit will be brought to justice sooner than later.' The two guards, $(d/dx)c=0$ and $(|x| >= 1)$, ages 23 and 21 respectively, were on night watch when tragedy struck. Both were fatally shot with the same .22 revolver, according to authorities. No information has been released regarding the circumstances of the New Arrival's death, only that it was most likely perpetrated by the same suspect. Because this marks the second breach of security at the Dome in as many weeks, Mr. L assures us that security will be growing even tighter in—"

Bandini was confused. This was like no newspaper he'd ever seen. He glanced through every page, but could find no reference to any known city or state or even country. The first few pages of the paper seemed to be dedicated to "local news" (the triple homicide was the only dramatic news story mentioned) while the rest of the paper was filled with brief squibs about breakthroughs in science; all the bylines indicated they were excerpts from various science journals. Bandini had never heard of these journals, but then again he wasn't one to keep up on science news. It was hard enough keeping up with the real world.

There was one very long article about Pluto being restored to the status of a planet by a prominent astrological society in Switzerland. This made Bandini happy, at least for a moment. When Bandini was in elementary school, he and a bunch of other kids had to get into groups and create paper models of all the planets in the solar system. Bandini got stuck with Pluto, even though he wanted Jupiter. He spent weeks gluing yellow yarn on construction paper to get the look just right. Then to find out it wasn't even a planet.... All that effort, for nothing? It just didn't seem right.

Bandini sighed and gave the paper back to the old man. "Thank you very much!" he yelled. "May I ask you a question? What city am I in?"

The old man's brow creased in confusion. He cupped his hand behind his ear.

"Where. Am. I?" Bandini repeated, even louder than before.

The old man just spread his hands in the air. "Me? No…." He spread his hands in the air, then began reeling out a long series of staccato sentences in a language Bandini didn't recognize.

Bandini sighed and stood up. "Thank you anyway."

The old man opened the paper to the funnies and continued looking at the simple black and white drawings—the only feature of any apparent interest to the man. Bandini rose, thinking he might ask someone else. Then the old man tugged at his sleeve.

"You," the old man said. "New?" He pointed at the ground.

"New?" Bandini said. "Here?" He mimicked the gesture. "Yeah, you could say that."

The old man smiled, turned halfway around, and used his black cigar to point upwards at the far high hill, at the looming copper dome.

"You," the old man said. He sounded Hungarian. "Go. Sign." He made a motion in the air as if he were signing an invisible check with the tip of his burning cigar.

Bandini stared up at that dome apprehensively. It didn't look very inviting. He smiled back at the old man and placed his index finger against his own temple and pulled his thumb down, as if he were shooting himself in the head with his finger.

The old man waved his hand in the air and laughed. "No, no, no," he said. "Not you. Not yet."

"Not yet? Well, that's inviting." He glanced around, wondering if he should ask someone else for directions. The people around the fountain were mostly teenagers. They all seemed so happy, so wrapped up in their celebration, that he didn't want to intrude. So he turned back to the old man and nodded with a smile. "Thank you," he said. The old man nodded back. Then Bandini started on his long walk toward the Dome.

The cobblestone path that led away from the fountain wound off into the city (was it a city?) past little storefronts, improvised bungalows, drab featureless warehouses, apartment houses stacked on top of one another like Legos, industrial areas where heavy machinery could be heard hissing and grating and pumping, but most of all the city (what else to call it?) seemed to be dominated by sterile white office buildings identified by numbers that looked more like mathematical equations than addresses. No sound at all came from these buildings. These grew more and more numerous as Bandini neared the Dome.

Past him sped little golf cart style vehicles that made a metronomic, *clackety-clack* sound as they skittered across the cobblestones. Eventually, the cobblestoned path widened into a flat, concrete-paved street down which an occasional black bus would drive silently. Bandini was alarmed to see that all these buses were adorned with barred windows. On the side of one bus was the first identifying mark he'd seen: a green triangle with a purple lightning bolt passing through it. He'd never seen such a symbol before. The black buses all seemed to be headed for the Dome as well. He didn't feel like asking any of them for a ride.

He passed another area that seemed similar to the bungalows in which he'd awoken: one-story, compact living areas with an exact amount of distance between each one. Outside one of these bungalows a bit of a commotion appeared to be brewing. He'd seen this same type of commotion a thousand times before outside a thousand different crime scenes. One of the black buses that had passed him some time before was now parked outside the bungalow. This bungalow was marked with a large letter "D" and it seemed to be written in the same font as the title of the old man's newspaper.

A gang of black-garbed security guards were streaming out of the bungalow. The guards looked a lot like the Homeland Security forces he'd seen patrolling the ports of Long Beach when he and his wife had visited the Queen Mary only a few weeks before. They had thick bulletproof vests, padded gloves that made their fists look grotesquely huge, plexiglass visors, heavy leather boots, high-tech pistols strapped to their hips. A crowd of lookie-loos stood outside their bungalows staring at the guards, trying to catch a glimpse of something new and exciting, any yet they made sure to stand well back at the same time. They seemed intimidated by the guards, all of whom flanked a single man they were now leading toward the black bus. Two of the guards parted for a moment, revealing the prisoner.

He was handsome in a typical sort of way, tall, blond, blue-eyed, obviously in shape. The clothes he wore were similar to Bandini's. Except for the handcuffs on his wrists, there was nothing about the man that should have piqued Bandini's interest. You could see men who looked like this all around L.A. And yet... Bandini stopped and stared at the prisoner as intensely as the lookie-loos.

Bandini recognized this man.

He'd once worked with him on the force. He was a homicide detective who'd served on the LAPD for a brief period of time before disappearing abruptly. Bandini couldn't forget that face or that distinctive sneer. He was the cause of the worst year of Bandini's life. His name was Lt. Charles Duvall.

And now he was in handcuffs being led along by jackbooted stormtroopers towards a black bus with barred windows?

He never thought he'd see such a sight, not even in a dream.

For a moment, the very briefest of moments, that scowling face looked up from his bound wrists just long enough to lock eyes with Bandini. Those piercing blue eyes widened. One eyebrow arched with surprise... surprise and recognition.

Then it was over. The crowd of stormtroopers closed in again, cutting Duvall from view. That mass of bulletproof muscle disappeared into the bus. The doors slid closed; colorless, odorless exhaust escaped from the back. Nothing could be seen through those dark windows. The bus took off down the street, uphill yet again, toward the Dome.

Never once did Bandini think he'd be happy to see Lt. Duvall. And yet a familiar face, all the way out here, wherever he was, wasn't something to sneer at. After all, what were the chances? Perhaps this was a reason to hope... to hope that there was a rational explanation for all this, that he wasn't just going off his nut at long last... that a return to normalcy was still within reach.

Bandini followed in the wake of the bus.

3

In Which Bandini Is Introduced to Mr. L

About twenty minutes later Bandini reached the base of the hill. He saw the black bus, along with several others, parked at the base of the hill. He followed the winding path that led up to the Dome's green double doors; they were decorated with wooden reliefs depicting pagan gods and goddesses, like something out of a PBS documentary about ancient India or Egypt or some God forsaken place like that. (Bandini didn't like watching PBS, but sometimes his wife did, and he caught that stuff by accident.)

He couldn't bring himself to knock on the door. He was afraid of ruining the carefully carved images. Further carved images surrounded the massive door: images of wild animals like tigers, cheetahs, jackals, panthers, lions, hyenas, bears, creatures he couldn't recognize. After studying them for a few moments he finally discovered a button unobtrusively hidden within a wooden carving of a tiger's head. You had to stick your finger in the tiger's mouth in order to ring the bell.

Somewhere inside he heard the distant, muffled ringing of chimes. He leaned against the wall, trying to catch his breath. Walking so damn much first thing in the morning, with no coffee? It was almost too much to handle.

At last the doors opened. Inside stood a child wearing a tuxedo. The little boy stared up at him with a dour expression on his pudgy face. He was about ten years old. He looked Bandini up and down as if evaluating a piece of meat at a butcher shop, then nodded, as if having reached some sort of conclusion about him. The child waved his white-gloved hand over his shoulder, motioning for Bandini to follow.

What else was he going to do? So he followed… down a long, carpeted corridor decorated with original paintings that looked very old, very expensive. One painting caught his eye: black crows circling above a golden wheat field. A sense of desperation and loneliness emanated from the canvas. Animals everywhere.

At the end of the corridor stood another set of doors, just as impressive and intimidating as the last, though these bore no carvings whatsoever. They managed to exude a kind of ominous authority with their stark whiteness alone.

Just as they were about to reach the doors, another group of people emerged from a corridor to the right: black-garbed soldiers, armed with the same hi-tech weapons he'd seen earlier, surrounding a familiar looking prisoner: Lt. Charles Duvall. Duvall caught Bandini's eye again and glared at him with anger and suspicion. This was unusual. Never before had Bandini seen the man be anything but self-assured and arrogant.

They were clearly headed toward the same room as Bandini and the child. He wondered what they were planning on doing with Duvall.

Surprisingly, the child raised his hand in the air and all the guards stopped marching. Whoever this little boy was, these muscle-bound guards respected him… or at least feared him?

The guards remained in place. The child turned, motioned for Bandini to remain where he was, then continued into the room beyond the doors. The child shut the doors behind him.

Bandini didn't know what to do. He reached into his jacket pocket for a cigar, then realized for the seventeenth time that day that he didn't have his cigars.

The guards remained motionless, waiting for their next order. Duvall was simply meditating on his handcuffs, as if trying to burst through them with psychic energy alone.

Bandini rubbed the stubble on his face… a nervous tick… the first time he'd done so all morning. He realized his beard was much thicker than it should be. Bandini caught a glimpse of himself out of the corner of his eye. A large ornate mirror hung on the wall beside him. Looked like hell. His mop of dark brown hair hung to one side, as if he'd been lying on it for a very long time. Bags under his eyes. Streaks of red ruining the whites of his eyes. Yes, a three-day growth at the very least. He'd been out of the game for several days. A slight tinge of the old panic returned for a moment, but he suppressed it.

He glanced back at Duvall. Duvall was now staring at him. If eyes could bore holes in flesh, these very well could. He looked like he wanted to strangle Bandini. Why? Bandini was just as helpless as he was. Wasn't he?

That was the problem: Bandini didn't know what he was. Where he was. Never before had he felt so disorientated.

The doors swung open. The child-butler had returned. With a swift, graceful motion, the butler pointed at Bandini and crooked his finger ever so slightly, motioning for Bandini to follow once again. Bandini scratched his head in confusion, using the opportunity to flatten down the uncontrollable mass of hair on his head without being too obvious about it. In order to follow the butler into the room, he had to walk right past Duvall. Duvall stared at him with such tangible hate, Bandini almost got the feeling that Duvall blamed *him* for his arrest.

A steep ramp led down into an extremely large room that had no corners. It was the inside of an oblate spheroid. Wrapping around the top of the room was a panoramic screen filled with the kind of abstract images Bandini often saw on his wife's computer. What were they called? Screen savers? Wallpaper? Somethin' like that. Bandini had no use for computers. At home he still used a Smith-Corona electric typewriter. He just liked old stuff, always had. Sometimes he wondered if he'd been born in the wrong century.

Amorphous red blobs darted about on the giant screen. The lights cast weird shadows that swam across the curved walls of the room. Beneath the screen stood a circular bookshelf packed with hardcover books. They looked old. On the wall, in between some of the book shelves, stood gray metal file cabinets. And above one of these file cabinets, mounted on the wall, hung an ornate sign framed in glass. Inside the frame, bold black words read: "IF POWER ASKS WHY, THEN IS POWER WEAKNESS." You could just barely make out the words in this dim light.

The blobs were so distracting, it took Bandini a few moments to notice the large white spherical chair sitting in the middle of the room. And in the chair, a man.

Late '50s, overweight (fat, to be truthful), perfectly silver hair, dull gray eyes, the blotchy skin of a man who drank far too much. The man leaned forward, both oversized pale white hands gripping a stylish silver cane. "Greetings," he said. His teeth straight and white—too white for his age. Perhaps they weren't real. "I knew you were on the agenda for today. Didn't know when you'd arrive, of course. We might as well get this rigmarole out of the way, though. I have far more pressing business to tend to." He had a slight British accent, like someone who had been displaced from the nation of his birth for a very long time. The accent had been fading away for several years. Judging, however, from his desperate attempt to maintain his British airs, Bandini decided that this displacement had not been entirely voluntary.

"Yeah?" Bandini said, scratching the top of his head. He motioned toward the doorway behind him with his thumb. "I saw the entourage out there. They waitin' for you?"

The fat man smirked. "Do you see anybody else in here?" In front of the fat man stood a silver tray on wheels. He leaned forward even further in order to spread some jam on a biscuit. Two silver trays sat on either side of the platter.

"Uh, no… no, I can't say I do." Bandini turned and saw that the door had shut behind him.

"They're not locked," the man said. "You can leave whenever you wish. Consider yourself to be free while you're here."

"That's good to know." Bandini brushed his palms together nervously. "That's something I'd normally take for granted—being free, I mean."

"Oh, come, come. Dear me, my good man. You're a policeman. Certainly you know by now you shouldn't take *anything* for granted, eh?"

"Oh, I try not to, sir. I try not to. My wife always tells me I'm a bit of a… what d'ya call it? You know, when you're too hopeful about things?"

"An idealist."

Bandini snapped his fingers and pointed at the fat man. "That's right. An idealist. Thanks. That's what she says I am."

The fat man raised one eyebrow. "That's a dangerous thing to be these days, particularly in your line of work."

"Oh, I'm just behind the desk most of the time. Filling out

reports. Signing them. Filing them away. That sort of thing."

The fat man nodded while stuffing an entire biscuit into his mouth. He chewed vigorously, swallowed, then took a dainty sip from the porcelain cup sitting beside the platter. His pinky stuck straight out to one side.

"A functionary," said the fat man. "How charming. Please, have a seat. You're my guest. Would you like some tea, some biscuits, coffee?"

"Oh, coffee would be fantastic, sir. I haven't had breakfast this morning. My wife always tells me breakfast is the most important meal of the day, and yet I just always seem to skip over it somehow. I think I'd be much healthier if I ate better, but it's so hard to find the time."

He sank into a padded, spherical seat that faced the fat man's chair. He seemed to sink into it. Bandini noticed that the fat man's chair was bolted to a white platform roughly thirteen inches higher than Bandini's chair. He was certain that gave the fat man a sense of security.

"Well, yes, the time must just *slip* away from you when you're filling out all those forms," said the fat man. He didn't even crack a smile. "Let's get down to brass tacks, as your people like to say." He watched with disgust as Bandini dunked a biscuit into his black coffee. "I'm sure you're wondering why you're here."

"The thought had crossed my mind, sir. Where do you get these biscuits? I've never tasted anything like them."

The fat man just stared at him for a moment before replying, "They're imported. From England."

"All the way from there? We went there once, me and the wife. Lovely place. But I never had anything like these biscuits when I was there. My wife gets stuff *kinda* like this from Costco, in bulk."

"Not like these, I'm sure. You *are* interested to know why you've been brought here, aren't you?"

"Yeah, of course. Did I interrupt you? I'm sorry, sir. Go on."

The fat man gritted his teeth. "Do you recall the suicide of a Dr. Keri Davidson?"

"Hold that thought. Have we been introduced? I mean, like, properly?

"My name," the fat man said, "is Mr. L."

"That's it?"

"That's it."

"Well, okay. Who am I to say?" Bandini wiped his right palm on his pants leg, then held out the hand. "Mr. L, my name is Lieutenant—"

"Not anymore." Mr. L just stared at the hand until Bandini finally withdrew it.

"Not anymore?"

"No. Your new title is Mr. V(a). You've just been hired on."

The fat man held out a card decorated with a symbol: a series of interlocking molecules that almost looked like a series of artificial planets floating in deep space. Above this symbol were the words: MICROPOLIS, INC. Below the symbol were the words: Mr. V(a), File Clerk. Pollen Hill—Trace Sector V.

Bandini glanced up at the man and tried to smile. "I… didn't even know I had applied."

"More coffee?"

"Oh, sure. I'm not the kinda guy to refuse a second cup of coffee."

"You don't take cream or sugar or—?"

Bandini waved his palm. "Nah, black for me. The earlier in the morning, the blacker the coffee."

Mr. L laughed, genuinely this time. "Yes, I know what you mean. So how do you feel about your new position?"

"Well, to be absolutely truthful with you, I've never seen myself as a file clerk."

"But I thought that was your specialty."

"Sometimes. In some ways… oh, thank you very much," Bandini said as Mr. L finished pouring the cup.

"Clearly you didn't plan on remaining a homicide detective, otherwise why would you resign?"

"I planned on setting up in business for myself."

"Private detective."

Bandini shrugged. "Who knows? There's a world of possibilities out there. At least that's what my wife keeps sayin'. You know how wives are. Always pushin' you to advance and stuff. Advancement's very important."

"To some. Tell me, do you ever think for yourself or does your wife do all the thinking for you?"

"Oh, I get an original thought in this skull from time to time."

Mr. L waved his index finger in the air. "You never answered my question."

"What question was that, sir?"

Mr. L clenched his back teeth. "Do you remember the death of Dr. Keri Davidson?"

"Of course. That's the case I was working on." Bandini took another prolonged sip of coffee. "When I resigned."

"And what details about the case can you share with me?"

Bandini dunked another biscuit into his coffee. "These biscuits go real well with the coffee. You should try it."

"No, thank you."

"Uh… now what were we talkin' about? Oh. Dr. Davidson. You see, I believe that her suicide was not exactly a suicide."

"And why do you think that?"

"Well… it's very odd, but my memory's not the best. My wife's always telling me to tie strings around my fingers just to remember to pick up a carton of milk on the way home from work? So these little details about specific cases kinda get dropped along the wayside, if you know what I mean. If I had my report in front of me, I'm sure that would refresh my memory. But that's back at headquarters."

Mr. L spun around in his chair, pulled open a drawer in a file cabinet, and removed a thick manila folder from it. The folder was marked DR. KERI DAVIDSON. He dropped it on the silver tray in front of him, causing several biscuits to fall to the floor.

Bandini stared at it in surprise. "That's real clever of you. Is that a copy?"

"Your entire report, word for word."

"Have you read it?"

"Every phoneme."

"Huh. Well then, I've got an idea. Why don't *you* tell me what's in it? It'd probably be easier that way."

"If that's the way you want to play it. You believe Dr. Davidson was murdered due to her specialized knowledge of microbiology. You believe her position as chief microbiologist for the Ministry of Defense had given her access to dangerous tidbits of information… and these tidbits were so sensitive they required her immediate assassination by persons unknown. These conspirators had influence over the honorable organization for which you had toiled so dutifully for so many years. These… no doubt *shadowy* and *nefarious*… entities somehow convinced your superiors to not only take you off the case, but to officially designate Dr. Davidson's death a suicide, despite numerous aspects of the case which you believe do not coincide with that particular viewpoint. Is that a fair assessment?"

Bandini smiled. "I wish my memory was as good as yours."

L tapped the folder. "Well, I've been studying. And not just this report. A lot of documents. You have a brother?"

"I've got a lot of brothers. I'm the youngest."

"A brother who lives in Virginia?"

"That's Al! He's the oldest. Been meaning to call him lately."

"I'm sure you have. He lives in Virginia?"

"Yes."

"He works for the FBI."

"Oh, yes. Has for years. The whole family's proud of him. Do you know he's the main reason I wanted to go into law enforcement in the first place?" Bandini leaned back in the chair, more relaxed now. "You know, there was this one time back in high school when Al—"

"He also works for the CIA."

Bandini paused. He leaned forward again. "You kiddin' me?"

L pulled out a second folder and dumped it on top of the first. "There's your brother's entire record with the Agency. Now answer me a question and please refrain this time from the transparent distractions and stalling. Who are you working for?"

Bandini had a faraway gaze in his eyes. "That explains all them business trips. Son of a bitch. Al." He smiled and shook his head.

L slammed his fist into the silver tray, leaving a huge dent inside it. Steaming coffee spilled everywhere, all over L's bare flesh. He didn't seem to notice this. "Please answer the question!"

Bandini looked shocked. "What question?"

L shot to his feet. "*Who do you work for?*"

Bandini spread his hands in the air. "Nobody. Anymore."

"You *must* be working for someone else!" L began pacing the room. "Why stay on the case so damn long? You know how many times we tried to warn you off? To threaten you, your family, your co-workers? Why? Why hang on? Why the leaks to the press? Why resign? Why keep *at* it? You know full well you intended to keep on the case even after it was closed, under the guise of opening some two-bit private detective agency. You weren't going to drop it. *Ever.* We *know* this. Why? What's in it for you? Who's putting you up to all of it?"

Bandini's confusion was palpable. "I'm not sure what you mean. I'm just a guy doin' his job. You know, I pick up a paycheck at the end of the week, go home, watch some pro wrestling, play with the kids, eat sandwiches, hang out with the wife, you know. I'm just a normal guy. I think you've got some kind of inflated view of me. I don't know if I'm the right person for the job you're offering me. I may have to turn it down." He gently set the business card on the silver platter, in the middle of the deep impression L's fist had made.

"You'll *take* it all right!" L's jowls were jostling about like the neck of a turkey. His face had deepened to a purple bordering on crimson. "I'll tell you what you'll take and what you won't. I'll *tell* you what kind of a man you are. You cops are all the same. Brainless bloodhounds. All instinct. No real intelligence. Someone in authority gives you a job to do, you do it... without even *thinking* about the consequences. About the future. You should've listened to the first warning. But you were too god damn arrogant to imagine for even a second that there might be someone else out there in the world smarter than you are. You're stubborn, like all perfect idiots. Some human beings are like animals. They don't think—that's their blessing, you see. Other people are cursed. They're too smart for their own good." He slammed his cane down into the floor three times fast. "They have to be thinking all the time, all the time, *all* the time!"

He was gasping for breath now. He retreated into silence. He just stared at the white floor, trying to regain his breath.

"Are you all right?" Bandini asked.

"'Course I'm all right! And if I wasn't, I wouldn't need any help from you. I have plenty of people here to help me. In case you hadn't noticed, I'm in charge of this facility. This entire city."

"Well, I wasn't sure what your job was. I imagine it's difficult, whatever it is."

"You'll find out everything you need to know... in time."

"I have to admit, I'm not that smart. Not like you. I see you've got a lotta books here." He stood up and approached the massive bookcases. "I'm not much of a reader I'm afraid. My wife, she's the one who reads." Bandini reached out and pulled out a leather hardcover book at random. "She's always tryin' to get me to read stuff, y'know, but I just don't have the patience to see a book through all the way to the end. I get impatient. The last book I read was, uh, one of them Dirk Pitt novels. Y'know what I mean?"

"Dirk Pitt?"

"Oh, I doubt it's your kinda thing. Wow, this is thick. What's this one called?" Bandini read the title aloud. "*The Foundation of Impermanence.* Jeez. Sounds serious. It's gotta be over... what, a thousand pages?"

"Something like that. It's by Johann Strauss. He's one of my favorite authors—my *favorite* author, actually."

"Yeah? What's it about? Is it a western? I really like westerns, like the ones in paperback that Elmore Leonard used to write. Those're real good. Perfect to read right before you go to sleep."

Mr. L released a long, drawn-out sigh. "That's *not* fiction. Strauss was a philosopher."

"Oh, so he must've lived a long time ago then, right?"

"He died in 1961."

"Oh? I thought philosophers lived a long time ago." Bandini began flipping through the pages.

"There are great philosophers alive right now. Perhaps I'm one."

"Yeah? Really?"

"Yes. I've been meaning to write a book based on Strauss's theories. But I just don't have the time. I have to deal with people like you all day."

"Yeah, that *is* time consuming. So what was Strauss like? What're his theories?"

Bandini shoved the thick book back onto the shelf, then pulled out another volume. This one was called *The Misuse of Fiction.*

"It's rather complicated," said Mr. L. "I'm not sure you'd be interested. Strauss believed most of the human race was so ill equipped to handle the essential truths of the universe that they needed to be spoon-fed pretty lies in order to endure their inferior existences. Philosophers, on the other hand, are higher beings who can face these truths: that God does not exist, that the universe cares not one bit about the fate of mankind, that all of human history is nothing more than an insignificant blip on a giant screen... a blip that will vanish without a trace before too long. There is no morality, no good or evil. The duty of the philosopher is to feed the ignorant with the religious and moral beliefs they require in order to survive. This is the only route to take, Strauss believed, if truth is to survive on this planet for longer than a microsecond."

"Pretty heady stuff." Bandini pulled out a third volume: *The Lie Machine*. Then another one, the smallest of the bunch: *Is Power Weakness*. It was a slim red volume, only about seventy pages long. Bandini read the title aloud, then said, "Well, this one looks like it's more my speed. I think I could actually get through this one."

Mr. L seemed to grow nervous, then walked very quickly over to the bookshelf. He carefully removed the slim volume from Bandini's hands. "That's the book I wrote my Ph.D. thesis about. It's the most important of Strauss's books, though it's little known. This is a very rare volume. A first edition." Strauss put the book back on the shelf. Daintily.

"Yeah? What's that one about?"

"It's hard to sum up, really."

"But you wrote your thesis about it. You must understand the book well enough to give a kind of a synopsis of the entire thing, right? Don't ya gotta do that kinda thing when you write a thesis?"

"Of course. Basically, Strauss believed that true power lay *behind* the throne, not within it. Beyond that… well, you'd have to read the book."

"Oh, I doubt I'm readin' that copy, sir, judgin' by the way you handled it. Hey, what's that one there?"

Bandini crouched down and pulled out a large picture book from the bottom shelf. The fancy lettering on the front of the book resembled the sort of lettering Bandini often saw on the fairy tale books his wife read to the kids right before bedtime. Bandini read the title aloud: "*Micropolis Stories for Children*. Strauss didn't write this one, did he?"

Mr. L chuckled. "No, Strauss was long dead before that volume was completed. Our own personal staff wrote that book. It's an introduction to our facility. It's a limited edition, intended only for special guests." Mr. L reached down and pulled the book out of Bandini's hands.

"Children?"

"Some particularly gifted children are allowed to be visitors here, if they prove they can demonstrate they have something to offer us." Mr. L slipped the volume back into its proper niche.

"Like the butler?"

Mr. L snorted—a kind of a chuckle. "No, not like him. He's not a child at all. He just looks that way."

Bandini reached out and ran his fingertips over the golden lettering that made up the word "Micropolis" on the thick spine of the book. Briefly, an image of his own children flashed through his mind. He pushed it away, then stood up.

"I've never heard of Micropolis," Bandini said.

"Few have."

"It's a corporation?"

"It's your new home. Your new source of gainful employment." Mr. L walked away from the bookshelf. He sat back down in his swivel chair.

"Well, I'm always happy to be of service in any way I can. What's your main specialty here? Your product?"

"Officially? We write brochures."

"Really. All this, just to write brochures? I mean, it's a pretty big facility."

"You don't know how big. The subbasement levels are quite entertaining. Perhaps you'll see them sometime."

"I'd like my wife and kids to see all this stuff. I'm sure they'd be impressed."

"I'm sure they would too, but they won't get the chance."

"Why is that?" For the first time, Bandini's pleasant smile had vanished.

"My superiors decided we wouldn't need the whole family this time. Your presence here would suffice. Your wife and children are back at home, where they've always been. Safe. And they'll remain that way, as long as you do your job and cooperate."

Bandini settled back into his chair. "Is there any room for development in this new position of mine? Any chance of transferring out of here?"

"Of going back home you mean? Certainly. Just tell us the truth. Tell us who you're really working for. Why they're so interested in the suicide of Dr. Davidson."

"I can't tell you something I don't know."

"You don't know? You mean because it's a compartmentalized operation?"

"I don't know because there is no operation. If I'm part of some conspiracy, I'm not aware of it."

"Indeed. Perhaps you're not. Well, we'll find all that out. In time, in time. Now... I think I have some other business to tend to." He glanced toward the door.

Bandini held up his palm. "Excuse me, this is all kinda new to me. I mean, the last thing I remember is playin' mahjong with the kids; next I know I'm wakin' up out in the middle of nowhere in a room that looks exactly like my bedroom back home. That was real clever how you pulled that off. I want to give you credit on that. I mean, that's a lot of trouble to go through to accommodate the needs of a nobody like me, just to make me feel at home. And I just wanted to thank you for your kindness. As you know, there are other types in this business, real uncivilized types, who would've been a little more harsh with me. I think you know what I mean."

"What're you prattling on about now? *Kill* you, you mean?"

"Oh, I wouldn't want to be impolite... or uncouth or out of place...."

"*Kill* you? Why on earth would we do something like that? You have something we need. You're an anomaly. We prefer to keep you well-preserved, like a rare and beautiful insect stored inside a bottle. A statistical outlier, subject to our careful analysis. Not everybody is so honored, you understand. We need to understand chaps like you. Where your attitudes and quirks come from. How your mind works. Who you might be working for. Minor details like that."

"Well... I'm willing to do my patriotic duty, of course. I'd be happy to cooperate in any way possible. But not for too long. My wife and kids are gonna start wonderin' where I am. The wife gets worried real fast about things like that. She's the suspicious type."

"Look at it this way: The longer you're gone, the happier they'll be when you return."

"Yeah. It's good to always look on the bright side of a situation, that's what my grandmother always said." He sighed and rubbed his palms together. "So... anything you need me for, sir, I'll be right here for you."

"That's an excellent attitude to have, my good man. You're already off on the right foot. For now just report to your quarters until I decide we need to see you again. The butler will show you out. Oh, and your first duty is to tell that entourage out there that they may come in now."

"Thank you for your time, sir." Bandini turned and started walking toward the door. The doors swung open, all by themselves. "That's quite a magic trick," he said. He flashed Mr. L an "ok" sign with his thumb and forefinger.

On the other side of the door, Bandini walked right up to the guy who seemed to be the head guard and said, "Uh, Mr. L said he'd see you now." The head guard nodded once, like a wind-up mechanical doll. He motioned for the other guards to follow him through the doors.

Bandini stood and watched as the parade of guards pushed Duvall in front of them, herding the man into the room like a piece of prize cattle. The butler appeared beside Bandini and offered to show him to the exit. Bandini was just about to follow him when he heard a guard's muffled voice call out, "We've brought the suspect, sir, just as you asked!"

Bandini paused, turned, stared at the white doors as they closed slowly behind the entourage. He broke away from the butler and walked fast back toward the doors. He opened the door just as Mr. L said, "Did he offer any resistance?"

"No, sir," the guard replied.

Bandini felt something tugging at his sleeve. He looked down and saw that it was the butler furiously pulling on the sleeve of his new coat. The butler motioned with his thumb down the hall, clearly wanting him to follow. He seemed annoyed. Bandini opened his mouth, intending to explain that he just wanted to stay for a few more moments, when the front doorbell rang. The butler looked flushed and concerned. The doorbell could not be left unattended, could it? The butler sighed with frustration, then scurried off down the hall to answer the call of the bell.

Bandini remained standing in the doorway. He watched the scene unfolding at the base of the ramp below, as if it were a stage play being enacted for his benefit alone. Duvall stood in front of Mr. L's chair, his eyes fixed firmly on L's pudgy face. Duvall was tall, well over six feet, and towered above the fat man with a regal sort of presence. There was a certain amount of dignity about the man that could not be stripped away, no matter how many chains you threw around him. The guards surrounded Duvall and L, their weapons ready to be employed at the slightest provocation.

L stared at Duvall with contempt. "So," he said. "Your countless schemes have finally reduced you to *this*. But it was inevitable, wasn't it? An anarchist like you, with all your 'harmless' little protests and demonstrations, couldn't be satisfied for long with non-violent disobedience. Eventually it had to happen. Eventually you had to take the law into your own hands."

Duvall cocked one eyebrow, calmly. "And *you've* never taken the law into your own hands? There's not a single person in this room who hasn't violated the laws of *several* countries simply by following your orders." As before, Duvall spoke with a slight Irish brogue. It had been so many years, Bandini had almost forgotten what his voice sounded like.

Mr. L placed his cane down on the floor and leaned his full weight on it. "So... you admit to what you've done, eh?"

"You know full well I had nothing to do with whatever it is you're accusing me of."

"What *are* we accusing you of?"

"I wouldn't even hesitate to guess. I woke up this morning to your welcoming committee celebrating the Equinox on my forehead with several unnecessary swings of a baton."

"I'm sorry your holiday had to be interrupted, Mr. D, but I'm afraid we at Micropolis take murder very seriously here."

For the first time since entering the room, Duvall seemed taken aback. His bound hands clenched into fists. "Murder?"

"Triple homicide, as a matter of fact," said Mr. L. He pulled a fountain pen out of his inside jacket pocket. "You locked me in the control room downstairs, proceeded to kill two of my guards as well as a recent arrival to our facilities, then fled the premises and returned to your bungalow as if nothing had happened. Did you have a pleasant night's sleep afterwards? I wonder." Mr. L shook his head in disgust. "Would you like to sign the confession now or later?"

"I'm afraid the only way *my* hand is signing any document of your contrivance," said Duvall, "is if you sever it completely from my arm, place the fountain pen inside my bloody clenched fist, and manipulate the hand... in my absence."

Mr. L leaned in close. "That can be arranged, Mr. D, quite easily."

"Let's not be too hasty," said a voice right behind Bandini. It was such an authoritative, booming voice that Bandini nearly jumped when he heard it. Bandini had to step to one side of the doorway to allow this new entourage to pass through. An old man, in his eighties at least, came striding into the chamber. Despite his advanced years, he carried himself well. He was thin, but he didn't seem frail at all.

His body appeared to be muscular, toned, like someone who swam every morning. He had a full head of pure white hair, and eyes almost as blue as Duvall's. He took no notice of Bandini as he swept past him, the entourage of armed guards following in his wake.

Mr. L rose from his chair. He was visibly shaken. This was clearly an unforeseen development. Whoever this man was, he commanded a great deal of respect. Mr. L's guards saluted him as he entered.

"Oh, at ease, at ease," said the old man, almost as if he were annoyed by the pomp and circumstance of it all. The guards relaxed. The old man slipped a cigarette into his mouth and lit it. Bandini felt jealous.

"I'm so pleased to see you," Mr. L said through a strained smile. When Mr. L smiled, it looked like he was suffering from a hernia. "What brings you all the way out here?"

"As if you didn't know?" The man's mocking laugh turned into a cough. He had a distinct British accent. Bandini had an uncle who moved to London for business reasons, and after living there for awhile, he started to talk exactly like the locals. This accent sounded very similar. "They sent me as soon as they heard. I don't appreciate having to drop all my work in D.C. just to tend to something sordid like this. I left everything in your hands because I thought you were competent enough to handle it. Maybe I was wrong?"

"Sir, perhaps we should discuss these matters later…."

"We'll discuss them *now*!"

"Of course, sir, of course, but there was no need to send you all the way out here. I have the situation well in hand."

"Do you realize there hasn't been a murder in the Dome since the day the last cornerstone was laid down? This isn't a minor infraction, man! Three homicides in one night?"

"That's why I realized how important it was to wrap up the matter as quickly as possible—which, as you can see, is exactly what I've done." He gestured toward Duvall.

The old man looked Duvall up and down. "Oh, I see. You again. You know, we've gone out of our way to accommodate you while you've been here. You've received privileges other visitors have been denied. Is this how you reward us? By stirring up a lot of unrest? By butchering innocent people, guards who are just doing their job. Even a fellow visitor? Is that right?"

A look of surprise appeared on Duvall's face. "Fellow visitor?"

He almost whispered those two words. "Excuse me, but… when is all this supposed to have occurred?"

Mr. L slapped Duvall across his right cheek. "Wipe that smirk off your face," he said. "You know bloody well when it occurred. Last night. When you broke out of your chamber, snuck in here, and shot two guards to death. Isn't that what you did? *Isn't it?*"

"That's impossible. I was in my chambers all night. Check the closed-circuit cameras. They'll show you."

"We already tried that," Mr. L said, "but you disabled them. Neither the cameras in your chambers nor the cameras in the Dome were working last night."

Duvall snorted a frustrated little laugh. "How convenient. And where am I supposed to have gotten the gun? Through mail order, perhaps?"

"While in the Dome you retrieved your gun… the very same gun you had on your person the day you came here."

"I wouldn't even have known where the gun was stored except for the fact that you went out of your way to show it to me. Last week."

"That was a mistake on my part. I was merely showing you what could be yours again, if you cooperated."

"It wasn't a mistake. It was a purposeful action necessary to *frame* me for murder!"

"And why would I want to frame you, my good man? Why? Haven't I been kind to you? Haven't we played many a fine game of chess together in the square? Haven't we shared many a pleasant brunch? Haven't we been… well… something like friends?"

"If 'something like friends' means 'enemies,' yes."

"Wait a moment," said the old man. "Why on earth would Mr. L here want to frame you for murder?"

"There's no reason," said Mr. L. "I need you. We *all* need you. I think we've made that very clear by now. I would have nothing to gain from this. If anything, I seem to have a lot to lose." He glanced briefly at the old man. "There's simply no motive."

"It's absurd," said the old man.

"Nonetheless, it's happening," said Duvall. "I can't be expected to explain something I don't understand."

"It's hard to keep your story straight, isn't it?" said Mr. L.

"What about *my* motive?" said Duvall. "If you have no motive, then neither do I!"

"On the contrary," said Mr. L, "your motive has already been established. Shall I show you?"

Duvall nodded. Mr. L waved his hand in the air, no doubt activating motion sensors embedded in the ceiling. The amorphous blobs on the screen were replaced by a video of Duvall speaking to Mr. L in this very same chamber. Duvall was leaning over L's desk and shouting: "You think you've trapped us here forever? You think you're *safe* in this little room forever? As long as I've got an ounce of breath left inside me I'll do everything I can to cause as much chaos in this godforsaken concentration camp as I possibly can before you finally take me out in the center square and shoot me for the entertainment of the others. And that'll be a very happy day for me, because at least I won't have to stare at your pitiful, toad-like face ever again. Good day." Then Duvall spun around and marched up the ramp, through the white doors, and away. While Mr. L sat behind the desk, looking very amused by the outburst.

He still looked amused. L waved his hand again, shutting off the scene. "Is that enough?" said Mr. L. "Or do you want to hear more? There are plenty of other similar outbursts recorded for posterity. They make for illuminating viewing, when strung together in chronological order."

"I'm sure they do," Duvall said quietly, sounding very tired. Tired and defeated.

"You may get your wish now," the old man said. "Our penalty for murder here is very clear."

"Execution," L said.

"In the center square," Duvall said, smiling sadly. "For the entertainment of the others."

"For the *education* of the others," L said. "There is a difference."

"Um, excuse me, sirs," Bandini said, strolling down the ramp, "but may I offer my services?"

"What're you still doing here?" L said. "The butler should've shown you out long ago."

"Uh, he kinda got distracted, sir," Bandini said. "You know...." He turned toward the old man. "I've worked in homicide for, oh, a lotta years now, and I've been able to solve a lotta crimes kinda similar to this one. Of course, I don't have the resources of the LAPD science lab at my immediate disposal, which is kind of a handicap I suppose, but even so I'd be willing to take a shot at it if you'd let me try. Mr. L here already told me he wanted me to start helping out around here, and I'd really like to give it a go. I think you've got a good operation here. Very efficient. I admire them kinda qualities. If the LAPD was run this way, well… the LAPD would be different, I'll tell ya that."

The old man turned toward Mr. L with a confused look on his face. "Who is this little man?" he said.

Mr. L smiled pleasantly, put his arm around Bandini, and started leading him back toward the ramp. "He's our most recent visitor. He was just leaving. He has a lot of forms to begin filling out."

"Wait a minute," the old man said, "you're a homicide detective?"

Bandini smoothly moved away from L's arm and walked back toward the old man. "Yes, sir, I am, sorry to say. My parents wanted me to be an accountant. But it just wasn't in the blood. Y'know."

"We don't get many homicide detectives around here," the old man said. "Mostly scientist types. Oh, and they can be *such* a bore. Such pushovers."

"Oh, I understand what you mean, sir, believe me.

"What job has Mr. L given you to perform during your stay here?"

"I'm gonna be a file clerk it seems. Y'know, I don't know if that's gonna work out so well. I mean, my parents wanted me to be an accountant and I ended up running away from home. So I thought maybe I might be of more use to you fellas if I applied my expertise to solving your little problem here. Surely you want all remaining doubts addressed before going through with executing a possibly innocent man." Bandini glanced at Duvall and Duvall met the glance with a cold, unemotional gaze.

"Of course. By no means do we wish to be cruel. We simply do what needs to be done to maintain security. The safety of many nations rests on the activities of this facility, you understand."

"I don't doubt it, sir. From what I can tell so far, you have a very vital operation goin' full guns here and I'd hate to see it jeopardized in any way. After all, what happens if you publicly execute this man only to have another murder occur afterwards? It would certainly make you seem incompetent not only in the eyes of other visitors like myself, sir, but also in the eyes of your superiors. The efficacy of all subsequent public executions will have lost their impact. Do you understand what I mean?"

"I certainly do."

"So I would suggest ironing out all the bugs right away. Crimes such as these are most easily solved within the first twenty-four hours, at least in my experience. So if you'd give me permission to have full access to the crime scene, I'm sure I could get to bottom of this whole nonsense in no time at all. That way you'll have definite proof that this prisoner here is your man; if your superiors demand any proof as well you'll have it readily available; and all doubts will have been removed and filed safely away under the category 'Solved, Case Closed,' and you can wash your hands of the whole affair and go back to tying up all your loose ends in D.C. See what I mean?"

The old man remained silent for a moment, then said, "Remove the prisoner from the room. Put him under house arrest for now." The guards began leading Duvall away.

"But, sir," Mr. L said, "we should begin—"

The old man cut off his words with a wave of his hand. Duvall glanced back at Bandini with a look that suggested confusion, suspicion and perhaps a little bit of hope all at the same time. The second the doors had closed shut behind Duvall, the old man turned back toward Bandini and said, "I like the way your mind works. Have we been introduced?" The old man glanced at Mr. L.

L said, trying to suppress the rage in his voice, "This is Mr. V(a)."

"Mr. V(a)," the old man repeated. "A fine juxtaposition of letters. Are you Italian?"

"Yes, sir, I am. Have been my whole life."

"I could tell right away. I've always liked the Italians. They're very full of life."

"We try. My old man was from Sicily. I've always been very proud of my family name. Would you like to hear it?"

"Oh, dear me, no, we mustn't have any of that! *No proper names.* You understand why."

"Sure… of course. Uh, could I ask you for a favor?"

"Ask away."

"Do you have any more of them cigarettes? I've been dying for one since I woke up this morning."

"Certainly." The old man reached inside his jacket and pulled out a fancy metal cigarette holder.

ROBERT GUFFEY

"We don't really have time for *cigarettes*, sir," Mr. L said. "We should be—"

"Everybody has time for a little leisure in their lives, my dear man. Everything's going to be under control now. You don't object to letting Mr. V(a) try his hand at this thing, do you?" He handed Bandini the cigarette, then lit it for him.

"But he's a *visitor*... a recent one at that. I don't think it would be wise to—"

"Tosh. Who could he harm? It's always advantageous to introduce a new perspective into the mix. Wasn't that the whole point of this facility in the first place?"

"Yes, of course... not in this particular context, though, sir."

"Nonetheless, a similar principle applies." He turned back toward Bandini. "You have at it then, my boy. See what you can come up with. How's that cigarette?"

"Oh, it's wonderful, sir. Thank you very much. This was rolled by hand, wasn't it?"

"That tobacco's from my own garden. There's no pesticide in that cigarette, none at all. It's not the tobacco that's unhealthy, you see—it's those awful pesticides they spray on it."

"I've heard that, sir. By the way, I don't think we ever finished our introductions...."

"Ah, yes." The old man laughed, almost to himself. "You get so used to everybody around you knowing who you are, you just assume everybody on the whole planet knows. My name is Mr. L(Prime)."

"So... I'm guessin' you were the acting Mr. L before the current Mr. L? Is that right?"

"I left everything in his hands. I'm hoping—" The old man threw a hard glance at Mr. L, then turned back toward Bandini to finish the sentence. "—that your investigations will find any and all holes in the current security system. When I was Mr. L, the security here was nearly flawless."

"Well, sir," Bandini said, "every system, no matter how foolproof, is gonna have some holes in it."

"Our goal here is to eliminate *all* holes, in this system or any other. I hope you can help us with that."

"I can certainly try, sir."

"That's all I can ask for."

"Now, the first place I should start is the crime scene itself. Is there any sort of identification I need to grant me access?"

The old man turned to Mr. L and said, "Please make sure that a full access identification badge is made up for Mr. V(a) within the hour. In the meantime, I'll escort him to the crime scene myself. The Welcome Room, no?"

"Yes, sir," Mr. L said, though he didn't sound happy about it at all.

4

In Which Bandini Investigates the Scene of the Crime

"According to the report I received this morning," said the old man, "it all happened right around this corner. The times I spent in here…." The thought trailed off, no conclusion in sight.

They paused at the mouth of a long gray corridor blocked off by yellow tape. They began walking down the corridor, the sound of their footsteps echoing back at them. The corridor led toward open double doors. The bodies were still in place: one guard lay crumpled on the floor in front of the open doorway, facedown, while the other lay face up on the opposite side of the doorway, his arms spread out like Christ on the cross, legs splayed far apart.

Two guards stood in front of the tape. "This is Mr. V(a)," the old man said to them. "He's helping out with the investigation for now."

Those last two words were significant to Bandini. He interpreted them to mean that he had only a limited time to produce results, or he might be taken off the case. And everything else. Permanently.

It wasn't so different from working for the LAPD, except for the fact that your life was rarely in danger from your superiors when you were working for the LAPD.

Bandini crouched down and walked underneath the tape. The old man followed. They walked down the hall toward a second pair of guards who stood over the corpses.

"Have these bodies been touched?" Bandini said to the guards.

Both shook no.

Bandini kneeled down beside the first body and examined it closely. He kept going "Mm-hh, mm-hh," as if agreeing with a voice whispering in his ear.

The old man stood behind him and watched. "What do you see?"

"It was definitely a revolver. A .22. Did Mr. L say he had access to what he thought was the murder weapon?"

"Yes, he did."

"Was the murder weapon found at the scene?"

"That's what I was told."

"Any fingerprints on it?"

"I'm not certain."

"I'd like to take a look at that a little later."

"Of course."

Bandini stepped over the first body and entered the doorway. That's when he got a good look at the third corpse lying at the base of a chair in the center of the room. A woman. Pale and lifeless.

He ignored her for the moment and focused on the body in front of him. This one's throat was torn up. A nice, clean shot, though. Whoever had done this was an expert shooter. He recalled Duvall's shooting scores out on the range. He was one of the best the Department ever had—he remembered everybody saying so. Bandini, on the other hand, had always been one of the worst.

"The same weapon," Bandini said, rising to his feet, "I'm pretty sure of that." The old man had followed him into the room. They now stood next to each other. "Each victim got it one by one. The guards just happened to be in the way. A lone shooter. All to get to her."

Bandini walked over to the third corpse. The woman was different from the first two, he could tell that right off the bat. No blood. No bullet hole. She had died some other way.

"These other two guards," Bandini said as he examined her inch by inch. "What were they doing with this woman? Do you know?"

"I'd say they were getting her ready to be questioned," the old man said.

"About what?"

"About her knowledge."

"Yeah? Knowledge of what exactly, if you don't mind me askin'?"

"Microbiology, of course. She was an expert in her field. It's too bad, really. She could've made *such* a contribution." The old man sighed.

"Contribution to what?"

"Why, to the cause."

"What cause?"

The old man merely stared at Bandini as if he were mad. "*Our* cause."

"Okay. And how do you usually go about questioning people like her?"

"We use simple techniques. Techniques that *work*. Nothing illegal, if that's what you're implying."

Bandini held up his palm, as if to bat away the old man's sudden annoyance. "I'm not implying anything, sir. I'm just trying to get to the bottom of this thing. I need to have as complete a picture as possible, y'understand?"

The old man nodded.

Bandini stared closely at the woman's bare arm. The sleeve on her right arm was folded up above her elbow, but the other wasn't. Why would that be? He examined the flesh closely… and yes, there it was. A pinprick. The telltale mark of a hypodermic needle.

Bandini sat on his haunches, pulled the cigarette out of his mouth, rubbed the stubble on his face. Why? he thought. Why…?

"It doesn't make any sense," Bandini mumbled. "Why would he storm in here, shoot two guards with a revolver, then switch to a different murder weapon when he got to her?"

"Switch?" the old man said. "What're you talking about?"

"Do you *know* the suspect, sir?"

The old man laughed. "I certainly do. We all do. He's been here for some time now. He's been giving us quite a lot of trouble."

"Would you say he's an uncooperative man?" Bandini said, almost pressing his face up against the dead woman's arm in order to get a better look at the pinprick.

The old man laughed again. "To say the least."

"Is he subject to sudden fits of rage, would you say?"

"Oh, absolutely," the old man said. "We have numerous examples of such outbursts on video, if you'd like to see them."

"Nah… I don't think that'll be necessary. Would you say the suspect would have the capability of flying into a *murderous* rage?"

"He's tried to kill various guards in the past."

"In self-defense?"

The old man clasped his hands in front of his waist and squared his shoulders primly. Proudly. "Anybody who is brought here, Lieutenant, is brought here because we wish them to remain *alive*. This is a philanthropic organization. We're saving their lives by bringing them here."

"But it is against their will, isn't it?"

"It's a complicated world. Sometimes complicated solutions are required."

Bandini stood up and nodded. He rubbed his chin again, still deep in thought. "The ends justify the means," he mumbled.

The old man was growing impatient. "Are we still talking about the murders, Lieutenant, or are we talking about the facility?"

"Both." Bandini suddenly darted over to the doorway and pointed at the bodies of the two guards. "Look at how these bodies are laid out. We've already established that they haven't been touched, right?" He glanced at the guard standing by the door, waiting for confirmation. "Right?" he said once more.

The guard nodded.

Bandini stared at the old man. "The bodies haven't been touched. See the guard in the hall? He's lying *face*down. The bullet hole's in the *back* of the head. There's only a very small space for the bullet to hit, only a small space not covered by the helmet or the armor. See?" He kneeled down beside the body and pointed directly at the bloody hole in the man's skull. "I'd say the bullet was fired from a very short distance from the man's head. Maybe only a few inches. How could the guard not hear the suspect creep up behind him? Why would the guard be *facing* the door? You don't hire negligent guards, do you, sir?"

"I should say not," the old man said. "They're paid handsomely not to be. Many of them were handpicked personally by myself out of a very small pool of possible applicants. They undergo rigorous psychological exams before even being called in for the interview."

"Well, that's what I thought you'd say, sir," Bandini said. "You seem like a methodical man to me. If all that is true, and I have no reason to think it's not, then there's *no* reason why the guard would be facing a door he's been hired to guard. And even if he were, he certainly wouldn't have a problem hearing a man coming down this very long corridor. Did you notice the way our footsteps echoed as we approached the door? No, I think it's clear the only reason he would have his back to the suspect would be if he trusted the man. Trusted him with his life. Someone he would have no reason to fear. Someone he saw every day."

The old man stared at the body, his forehead creased with worry. Before the old man could open his mouth, Bandini continued: "Now look at the second body. He's lying face *up*. A bullet to the throat. Judging from the wound, I'd say the shot came from a little farther away than the last one. From a few feet. Maybe from *here*." He placed himself at the feet of the first dead guard. He held his arm out, pantomiming the fatal shot. "Bang. Right in the Adam's apple. This guy's a good shot, we know that much." Bandini walked over to the glass scanner embedded in the wall. He took a drag off his cigarette as he studied the scanner. "This, uh… one of them things that scans the palm? That's how the door opens, right?"

"The most sensitive areas in the Dome are protected in that way," the old man said. "That was my idea."

"Only a few palm prints are approved for admittance into the room?"

"Of course."

"Okay. I'd say the suspect asked the guard to open the door, and as he was doin' it… bang." He pantomimed the gunshot again. "The first guard goes down. The door slides open. The second guard's on the other side of the door, facing the suspect. Bang. He goes down." Bandini strode into the room. "Now this is where things get tricky. The woman may have been sitting in the chair, I guess? Why? Why would she be there that late at night?"

"As I say, the only reason would be if she were about to be interviewed."

"But by who? The guards?"

"No. Mr. L, perhaps, or one of his colleagues."

"So the interrogation is interrupted before it can even begin." Bandini kneeled down in front of the dead woman once more. He pressed his hands together in front of his face. It probably looked like he was praying over her. "The suspect puts the gun away, slips it into his pocket, pulls out a hypodermic syringe, and injects something poisonous directly into her veins. Look here at her arm. Can you see the pinprick?"

The old man leaned over his shoulder as he grabbed her arm and pulled it upward. He placed his thumb right below the pinprick. "Yes," the old man whispered, "I can see it. We can have an autopsy performed on her to find out what it was that killed her."

"All the comforts of home," Bandini mumbled as he lowered the woman's arm back to its resting place on her stomach. "Notice there's no sign of a struggle. She does not resist. Why? If a raging madman had come blazing into this room, I know I'd put up a hell of a fight before I let him come anywhere near me with a syringe. And why would a man in a rage use a syringe? Why would a man in a rage take the time to ask a guard to please turn around before he shot him? How could a man in a rage be so *precise* when shooting a fully armored man using a .22 revolver? If your suspect pulled this off, he certainly wasn't in a rage when he did it. I doubt it was him." Bandini stood and stared directly into the old man's bluish-gray eyes. "All the evidence points against it. The man or woman who shot these people knew all three of them. I'd say the murderer is one of your own employees."

"But why do you say that? The detail of the scanner points *away* from that possibility. Someone with access to the Welcome Room wouldn't need to shoot the guards in order to get inside. It looks to me as if the murderer, whoever it was, pulled a gun on the guard and threatened to shoot him if he didn't turn around and open the door with his palm print. Therefore, the murderer was someone who didn't work in the building."

"There are plenty of other explanations. The guards might have been asked to open the door simply to give the murderer a better shot. It's always easier to shoot a man in the back."

"I couldn't imagine any of my employees being capable of such a thing. I don't think you understand how rigorous the psychological exams are that the applicants are forced to undergo before they're even—"

"You take pride in your operation here, sir, and that's an admirable quality. However, I wouldn't allow it to affect your judgment. As I said, every system, no matter how foolproof, is gonna have some holes in it. And this proves it." Bandini gestured toward the bodies on the floor.

The old man had no response.

5

In Which Bandini Asks Messrs. $\sqrt{-1}$, x^3 and L Several Questions of Import

Mr. L sat in the control room, observing Bandini's activities through the array of screens laid out before him, nervously picking at a hangnail on his right thumb. Through the speakers he could hear everything he was saying to Mr. L(Prime). He could hear him say, "Now I'd like to talk to Mr. L if you don't mind."

He just wanted them to stay in the Welcome Room a little while longer. The tech boys were almost done fixing the control room. Mr. x^3 was sitting at the console behind him right now, putting the finishing touches on his repair job. The second the boys were done, Mr. L would have the time he needed—just a few minutes, that's all—to pull the chair apart again and retrieve the offensive items. This damn room and the halls outside had been swarming with guards and tech people all morning and all afternoon....

"By all means," said Mr. L(Prime). "You're my guest here. Feel free to go anywhere you wish."

"I just need to ask him a few minor questions," Bandini said. "Y'know, just to get the timeline straight in my mind. You understand."

"Certainly," said Mr. L(Prime), following Bandini out into the corridor.

They disappeared off the central screen, reappeared in a different screen at the end of the console, the one that covered the Bridge-of-Sighs. Mr. L stood up quickly, straightened his jacket, and called the remaining technician into the control room.

Mr. $\sqrt{-1}$ strolled into the room with a typical slacker attitude, his shirt hanging out of his pants, his iPod plugged into one ear, a stupid smile plastered on his acne-ridden face. The tech boys could always get away with that attitude. They didn't have a thousand eyes watching them every second of the day. They didn't have reports to fill out, people to answer to. All they had to do was wander into a room, hit a few buttons, then wander away again, off to who knows where. They could fly under the radar. Not so with Mr. L. Not ever since he lost his name.

"Are you quite finished yet?" Mr. L said.

"Looks like we got everything workin' again, doesn't it?" said Mr. $\sqrt{-1}$. Mr. $\sqrt{-1}$ was eighteen years old.

"Another epic series of obstacles surmounted by Mr. $\sqrt{-1}$ and Mr. x^3!" said Mr. x^3. Mr. x^3 was sixteen. Both of them had lived and worked at the facility since they were only thirteen years old. The consequences of hacking into the wrong computer could be unforeseen—a most hazardous hobby.

Both Mr. $\sqrt{-1}$ and Mr. x^3 high-fived each other while saying things like, "The dynamic duo strikes again, dude!" and "If they haven't broken the mold yet, they sure oughta!" and "Hey, has anybody gotten around to copyrighting the two of us yet?"

L could feel his fist tightening at his side. "Quiet!" Mr. L said. "Tuck in those shirts! Pull that damn plug out of the hole in your head! Do you absolutely need that throbbing noise pouring into your skull twenty-four hours a day? And wipe those smiles off your faces! Stand up straight! Mr. L(Prime) is visiting the premises. Do you want him to think I'm running a circus here? *Do* you?"

The second Mr. L opened his mouth the pair immediately followed his orders. Shirts got tucked in, the iPod got unplugged, the smiles vanished, and the pair attempted to straighten their postures with little success.

"Jeez," Mr. x^3 said, "even Mr. L(Prime) knows the circus hasn't been through these parts in ages."

Mr. L just stared at the pair for a few moments, a few moments that seemed to last forever, his frustration growing with each beat of his heart, then hauled off and slapped the boy in the face. The bristle on the boy's unshaven cheek chaffed the back of Mr. L's hand. "If you only knew what it was like to have some *responsibility* in your miserable little lives, you'd know what *I* have to—!"

Mr. L cut off the tirade in mid-sentence. Suddenly, out of the corner of his eye, he caught a glimpse of Mr. L(Prime) and Bandini standing in the doorway of the control room. Staring at him.

"That will be enough, Mr. L," the old man said calmly. "Who are these boys?"

"They're part of the technical crew," L said between heavy breaths. "They came here during your term. Remember the Mt. Weather case, sir?"

"Ah, yes, the hackers," said the old man. "How could I forget? My, you've grown considerably. At ease, boys, at ease." Mr. $\sqrt{}$-I and Mr. x^3 relaxed, reverting to their normal postures. Mr. x^3 massaged his chin, a wounded expression still distorting his face. "What're you both doing up here?" said the old man.

"We were asked to fix the security cameras," said Mr. x^3, "and we did. What's... what's so wrong with that?"

Mr. L(Prime) patted the boy on the shoulder. "Nothing. Nothing at all." The old man looked at all the screens, now in perfect working order. "What was wrong with the camera?"

"They'd been sabotaged," said Mr. $\sqrt{}$-I. "Somebody managed to dismantle them somehow."

"Just the cameras in here?" Bandini said.

"No," said Mr. x^3, "other cameras outside the Dome were dismantled too. Like these." Mr. x^3 walked over to the console, sheepishly inching around Mr. L's considerable girth as if afraid of being hit again, and slammed his skinny fist into a white button. One of the screens switched to an overhead shot of Duvall pacing back and forth in a quaint little living room, nervously sipping a cup of tea. "And this one." He hit another button, and a different screen switched to an exterior view of Duvall's bungalow.

"I assume these cameras can be dismantled from this room?" Bandini said.

"Of course," said Mr. x^3. "That's why it's called the control room I guess."

"Do you think that's what happened? The cameras were dismantled from here?"

Mr. L could feel his heart pounding faster and faster and faster.

"No," said the boy. "The only person who was in this room was Mr. L."

"Really?" Bandini took another long drag off his cigarette. One of the old man's cigarettes. "So based on that, you think the culprit probably figured out a way to dismantle the controls from somewhere else?"

"It's not impossible. I could do it, if I wanted to. Either of us could." The boy gestured toward his friend. The other boy looked uncomfortable when Mr. x^3 said this.

"Has anybody ever managed to do something like this before?"

"Yes," Mr. L interrupted. "In fact, the suspect has. At least once before. That's one of the reasons he *is* the suspect. He caused chaos here for an entire week. We had to upgrade the system because of his shenanigans."

"Yeah, I can attest to that," said Mr. $\sqrt{}$-I. "It took the two of us at least five days to figure out how he'd done it. So we built some new firewalls to prevent the same thing from happening again. Apparently they weren't strong enough, though. I can't figure out how he did it this time."

"You two should be at work trying to figure that out, not standing around here jabbering," said Mr. L. "I want a report on my desk by tomorrow morning. Hop to it."

Just as the two boys were about to leave the room, Bandini said, "Oh, just one more thing. Would either of you say it's… oh, *unusual* for Mr. L to be in this room so early in the morning?"

Before either of the boys could respond, Mr. L said, "It isn't when I'm going to perform an interview. I always need to make sure the recording equipment is in working order."

"Who normally oversees the control room?" Bandini said.

"His name's $(d/dx)c=0$."

"Can I talk to him?"

"No. I'm afraid not. You were just ogling his corpse a few minutes ago."

"I see." Bandini sighed and ran his hand through his messy hair.

Mr. L glanced over at the boys and said, "You may go now." They left the room, silent and sheepish.

"So why wasn't he here in the control room doing his job?" Bandini continued. "Why was he down the hall in the Welcome Room?"

"Because I asked him to make sure everything was ready for the interview. There's nothing unusual about that."

"How long were you alone in the room?"

"Until the guards managed to pry open the door."

"Pry it open? Why'd they have to do that?"

Mr. L glanced at the old man, expecting him to step in and terminate this line of questioning. This *interrogation*. But he didn't. He simply looked on, as if waiting for a response. Mr. L sighed and pointed at the screen. "(d/dx)c=0 called me in here at roughly two A.M. Some of the screens had gone dead. He told me he'd been trying to fix them for about twenty minutes straight with no success. He assumed it was a simple malfunction. So did I, in fact. Such things have happened before. We had an interrogation scheduled, so I told him to go prepare our visitor while I tried to fix the problem myself. I've done so in the past with little difficulty. I have evidence of that, if you wish to peruse it. And that's when Mr. D locked me in here. I wasn't released until later. The guards let me out after they found… the corpses." All he had to do was think of Jennifer's still body in order to conjure up a genuinely distraught expression. "You can talk to the guards as well, if that amuses you."

"That might be helpful, thank you, but not right now. Who's this Mr. D?"

"The suspect we arrested. The man you saw in handcuffs only a few minutes ago."

"Okay, I get it. And you *saw* him lock you in?"

"Not… not exactly *saw*. I heard something behind me, a noise." Here Mr. L sat down in the padded chair and began to reenact what happened. "I turned around, but by that time the door was already closed. I bolted up out of my seat and tried to open the door with the scanner, but it wasn't working. I banged on the door, yelled for help. That did no good. Then I tried to pry the door open. Then I heard gunfire. I didn't know what had happened, not until the guards released me. Well, when I saw the carnage, naturally I suspected Mr. D. When we checked his locker, where we keep all his personal belongings, I noticed that his .22 revolver was missing. According to the doctors I spoke to, the fatal bullets had been fired from a .22."

"That's right," Bandini said. "And that revolver's been found?"

"Yes. At the crime scene."

"There were prints on the gun?"

"We didn't find any."

"Mn, I was afraid you were gonna say that." Bandini sighed, shook his head.

Mr. L tried to ignore the little man's comments. "Coupled with the fact that the cameras monitoring Mr. D's residence had been disabled as well, I drew the logical conclusion. That was reason enough for me to order the arrest. Don't you agree?" He turned toward the old man, who nodded in silent agreement.

"But… why would you immediately assume that Mr. D was responsible when you first saw the bodies?" Bandini said.

Mr. L laughed. "Perhaps Mr. L(Prime) would like to answer that question." Mr. L returned to his seat, crossed one leg over the other, folded his hands on his knee, and watched as a broad smile broke out across the old man's face.

"Well, Mr. D has given us a great deal of trouble lately," said the old man. "Not a week goes by when we don't have to waste precious time preventing some kind of crazy scheme the man tries to cobble up in order to avoid our hospitality."

"How ungrateful of him," Bandini said.

The old man spread his hands in the air. "I don't understand it myself. If we hadn't taken him here, he probably would be dead by now."

"Why do you say that, sir?"

"The information contained within the heads of some people is of great value to other… well, entities, shall we say? Without the proper protection, they wouldn't last long in the outside world. As I said before, we bring them here for their own protection."

"That's kind of you. I'm sure everyone here appreciates your efforts. Even Mr. D."

"If so, he has a strange way of showing it."

Mr. L studied Bandini's expression. He tried to pierce through the man's harmless exterior. How stupid could he really be?

"I'd like to talk to Mr. D one on one," Bandini said. "I think he might be able to give me some useful information."

Mr. L shot up out of his seat. He addressed the old man: "I really don't think Mr. D should have contact with anyone right now. Who knows what he might do? We've seen what the man's capable of. He's a raving maniac."

"I don't think the lieutenant will be in any danger," said the old man. "After all, we can monitor their meeting from here and if—"

"But, sir, I don't want any more visitors coming to any harm after what happened last night. I refuse to have any more deaths on my watch."

"I'll take all responsibility for the lieutenant's safety. I'm curious to see where his investigations lead. He asks good questions. And he has excellent taste in cigarettes."

"Thank you, sir, I'd roll them myself if I wasn't so damn lazy."

The old man laughed. "See what I mean." He slapped Bandini on the back. "I'll have a guard take you to Mr. D's bungalow. You don't have to worry. You'll be perfectly safe."

"Well, you have to be willing to put yourself in dangerous situations when you're in my line of work."

"Of course, everyone here could say the same thing, eh?"

"Of course."

"Follow me, lieutenant."

Bandini began to follow the old man out of the room, then abruptly paused and turned around. He faced Mr. L. "Oh, just one more thing… is it unusual to have one of these, uh, interviews scheduled in the middle of the night?"

Mr. L crossed his arms over his chest. "No. We find our visitors seem to be more willing to be open and frank the *later* the conversation is scheduled. Perhaps you'll see what I mean one day."

Bandini nodded. "Okay, thanks a lot, you've been a lotta help, sir. See ya later."

Bandini left the room. Mr. L released a long, relieved sigh. He stared at the array of screens in front of him. He reached out on a whim and hit a button. Suddenly, he himself appeared on the screen. Slouched in that chair. Wearing an expression not unlike the one he'd seen on Mr. $\sqrt{}$-I and Mr. x^3. Sheepish and silent.

Mr. L grew enraged and slammed his fat fist into the screen. The glass did not break. There he was. As clear as before. He wanted to strangle that disgusting mass of flesh he saw on the screen. Strangle him till he was dead and motionless and relieved of all the tension and pain that came with being Mr. L.

He brought his fist down again, cutting off that mercilessly objective view of himself. The view that only a hidden camera could provide.

Now that he was alone, it was time to retrieve what he had hidden. He stood up to close the doors so he could have privacy at last.

"Oh, just one more thing." Suddenly, the lieutenant was there again, in the doorway. Would he ever be free of this annoying little man? Mr. L was beginning to regret approving Bandini's admittance into the facility. "Uh, I'm sorry, I'm real forgetful sometimes. Mr. L, the *other* one, he said you'd have some paperwork for me. Do you have that now or should I come back later an' get it?"

"Please, no. Do *not* come back later." Mr. L reached into his jacket and pulled out a small piece of paper with Bandini's photo on it. The facility had all sorts of information, photographic and otherwise, stored away in Bandini's file—the one labeled Y(a). "I had one of my assistants bring it to me while you and Mr. L(Prime) were down the hall. Thank you for reminding me." Mr. L pulled out a fountain pen and signed the bottom of the card, then slipped it between two sheets of clear plastic. The badge was attached to a metal clip.

"Huh, that's funny," Bandini said.

"What?" said Mr. L, looking up slowly. He wanted to be elsewhere, far away from this little room and the little cop inside it. "What is?"

"I've got a brother who's left-handed. Just like you."

"The same one who lives in Virginia?"

"That's him."

"Perhaps I'll meet him somebody."

Bandini smiled. "Anythin's possible, I suppose."

"Clip this to your collar," said Mr. L, handing Bandini the tag. "Keep it on at all times, except when you're asleep. It gives you unlimited access to the facility, per Mr. L(Prime)'s orders. Keep in mind that this privilege is only a temporary one… while Mr. L(Prime) remains on the premises."

"Oh, believe me, I don't want to overstep my bounds. It don't need to be anything more than temporary. Thank you very much."

Bandini waddled out of the room, still smoking the old man's cigarette, that perpetual little smile plastered on his ugly face.

Mr. L breathed another sigh of relief, sat in the chair, swiveled back toward the screens. Quickly, in a calm panic, he switched to another shot, one of the old man being led down the hall by the butler. He watched them until they had left the Dome completely. Wait a minute… where was…?

"Oh, sir?" Bandini stood in the doorway again. "I'm sorry to be such a pest again, but I guess your boss had to go do somethin' else so he asked me to ask you to assign a bodyguard for me, so's I can go visit with the suspect. Y'know, it's a routine kinda thing. D'ya mind?"

Mr. L shot to his feet and darted out of the claustrophobic room. "Get inside and watch the monitors," he snapped at the guard in the hall. "Make sure at least two guards are here at all times, do you understand? Nobody enters or leaves the control room unless I say so."

"Yes, sir," the guard said.

"Follow me," Mr. L said to Bandini without even turning around. "Your wish is my command."

"That's awfully kind of you to say so," Bandini said. "But you don't have to go that far."

6

In Which Bandini Visits the Abode of the Infamous Mr. D

Bandini paused at the entrance to Mr. D's bungalow. Behind him stood the guard Mr. L had assigned to him. Bandini suspected the guard's purpose was not only to lead him to Mr. D's residence, but to make sure Bandini himself didn't get any funny ideas. Meanwhile, Mr. L(Prime) was off somewhere else, tending to other pressing matters in the Dome. He said he would meet Bandini later in the day to check on his progress.

There was already an armed guard standing outside the door. Judging from the nasty looking rifle in his fists, nobody here was taking any chances with the infamous Mr. D. Bandini turned toward his chaperone and said, "Say, I really appreciate Mr. L sendin' you along to keep me company, but I think I can manage from here. In fact, I think things'll go a lot smoother in there if I just go in by myself, y'know what I mean?" The guard seemed hesitant. "Look, Mr. L wouldn't have given me this badge if he didn't trust me, right?" Bandini lifted the badge up higher, so the guard could get a better look at it.

The guard nodded.

"Okay… I won't be long. But if you hear any trouble in there, come runnin', y'know what I mean? Say, either of you want a cigarette? Mr. L(Prime) just gave me half a pack, and I don't want to hog all the riches, y'know? Aw, c'mon, don't be a spoil sport. You're not gonna turn down a present from Mr. L(Prime), are ya?"

ROBERT GUFFEY

Both guards now stood on either side of Mr. D's front door. They both held out their hands. Bandini lit both cigarettes with the one that was still burning in his mouth. It was only his second cigarette that morning. He felt like he was lagging or something. If only the old man was fond of cigars….

The two guards now stood happily smoking their cigarettes. "No need to thank me, boys," he said. "It'll all come back to me eventually. Now how do I get inside here?"

The guard raised his hand, as if to wave it in front of the scanner on the outside of the door. Bandini stopped him. "Wait, hold on a sec, I don't want to just barge in. We've got to go about this whole thing the right way. It's a delicate operation, talkin' to dangerous criminals. I'm gonna try this the old fashioned way, okay?" Bandini wrapped his knuckles on the wooden door.

Nothing. He listened carefully, but could hear nobody within.

He knocked again. Nothing.

He knocked again.

At last, the door swung open. And there stood Duvall, looking the same as he had in Mr. L's hi-tech, gaudy office—except for the lack of handcuffs binding his wrists.

"I was expecting a visit from you," Duvall said. He had that damn superior smirk on his face, the same one Bandini had seen a million times before when they used to work together on the force.

"You were?" Bandini said.

"I didn't think it'd take long for them to send in the cavalry, as you Americans like to say."

"Uh… well, ya mind if I come in?"

"Surely…." He stepped aside with a grand gesture, as if he were admitting a prince into a king's chamber. "After all, you're going to do so whether I like it or not. Are you not?" Duvall cast a glance at the two armed guards.

"I'm just here to ask a few routine questions," Bandini said as he stepped into Duvall's bungalow. "You know the drill." It was a quaint little place with a kitchen attached, a bear skin rug on the floor, pastoral landscapes hanging on the wall.

Duvall closed the door behind Bandini. "I certainly do. Would you like a drink?"

"Sure could use one. What d'ya got?"

"Coffee. Tea. Scotch?"

"Jesus, a Scotch would be great… are you havin' Scotch?"

"Tea. Earl Grey."

"Right. Better just give me the coffee. I never drink when I'm workin' anyway. They, uh, let you have Scotch in this place?"

"As long as you have enough credits."

"Huh. Guess it's just like the outside world then."

"It's *exactly* like the outside world." Now he lowered his voice to a whisper. "Only *more* so."

Jeez, did that smirk ever fade from his face?

Duvall reached out and turned on the radio full blast. Jimmy Buffett, "Cheeseburger in Paradise." "There's only one station here, I'm afraid," Duvall said. "But it seems to be effective in counteracting their listening devices, at least to some extent. You preferred black, if I recall."

Bandini pulled up a stool and sat down at the bar that divided the kitchen from the living room. He watched carefully as Duvall picked up a glass coffee pot and began pouring steaming black coffee into a large, handmade ceramic cup. The cup was Duvall's handiwork; a very small D could be seen in the inner rim of the broad handle. "I've gotta hand it to ya," Bandini said, "you've got a good memory."

"It's a quality that can get you into trouble sometimes. If I didn't have such a good memory, I might not be here."

"That's what landed you here, your memory?"

"Sometimes one remembers things that others do not wish you to remember. Or, conversely, one remembers things that others would desperately like to know as well."

Bandini raised the cup to his lips. It tasted good. Real good. Bandini lowered his voice as he said, "You're aware your place is under constant video surveillance?"

Duvall's smile wavered for a moment as he added some sugar to his tea. "Of course. You're the first to admit it, though. I'm surprised to see you here, quite frankly. You never struck me as the… corporate type?" Duvall took a sip of his tea.

"Corporate type?"

"Did they think that drudging someone up from my past would actually make me open up? Mm? Get me into a spot of trouble, then send in the trusted colleague from the Good Old Days to lend a shoulder for me to cry on? One never knows. I'm in such a vulnerable state, it might actually work this time. But why you? Have you always... *done them favors*... or did they just call you up out of the blue and offer you a job? I must say, if you were working for them during the Good Old Days, I'd be quite surprised. You struck me as a real 'Joe Amurrican' type, a 'meat 'n potatoes' man. To think you were living a double life the entire time... well, I guess you can't judge a book by its cover."

"Well, I've learned not to myself. For your information, I just arrived here today. I'm as confused as you are—probably more so."

"Of course, you *would* say something like that, if you were trying to get on my good side."

"Listen, Duvall, I don't have time to—"

Duvall held up his palm. "Ah, ahh, please, no proper names. Isn't that right?"

"I wouldn't know. What the hell's all that about anyway?"

"Shouldn't I be asking you that?"

"Look, think whatever you want, but I'd very much like to save both our hides and get us the hell out of here. Is that okay with you?"

Duvall took a very long sip from his cup of tea, then said, "I'll humor you. Why not? I have nothing to lose. I suspect I'll be dead soon. I'll play your game, but only as long as it's amusing to me."

"I'll try to keep you entertained. Now can I ask you some questions?"

Duvall's smiled broadened as he used his thumb and forefinger to pantomime the shooting of a gun.

"How'd you end up in this place? How long you been here?"

"Take a good guess."

"Jesus. Okay, let's start out by giving *you* some answers then. You don't even need to ask me the questions. I'll just give you the answers for free, okay? I woke up today in my own room. My bedroom. Then I look out the window and I'm in the middle of nowhere. My clothes are gone. My wife is gone. My kids are gone. And right about now I'd really like to have them back, and I don't know about you but I'm willin' to do whatever I can to *get* back to them. You have a family?"

Duvall's smile disappeared. "A fiancée."

"Yeah? How long's it been since you saw her last?"

"Well, the last time I saw her...." He sighed. "I wasn't myself. It was a long time ago."

"Let's hope she's still waitin' around. Do you have any idea where the heck we are?"

"Hard to say." Now the smile returned. "I've heard rumors from some of the older… visitors… that this place used to be a Nike missile base back during the Cold War. A multinational corporation bought the base, closed it off to the public, and set up a private research center here in the middle of… nowhere, as you say. Do *you* have any ideas?"

"A Nike missile base," Bandini mumbled. He rubbed his chin once more. "Yeah, I think I got an idea. I think we're in the Santa Monica Mountains, just outside Los Angeles."

Duvall raised one eyebrow. "That precise?" He took another sip of tea.

"Sure. I recognized this place immediately. Me and the family took a drive up into the mountains not long ago. 'Bout a year ago. I recognize the trees, the way the air smells, everything. You live in the city all your life, you don't forget things like that. And now that you mention the missile base, that clinches it. I remember some of the locals at this little market in Topanga Canyon mentionin' the missile base and how the whole area was closed off to the public for miles around. There were rumors about what the heck was goin' on there. Rumors about some secret government project. I thought it was just a buncha malarkey. Now I know what they were talkin' about. Boy, do I know."

"Just outside L.A." Duvall paused for a moment. "I have to admit, that possibility never really occurred to me. It certainly makes some kind of cockeyed sense, though. I always hated Los Angeles. Now I know why."

"If you hated it, why'd you move there? Why'd you ever accept that job with the LAPD?"

Duvall's smile broadened. "You haven't figured it out yet, a man with your laudable ratiocination skills? I'm afraid my name is not Duvall. Never was. Nor is it Schmidt nor Peter Smith nor Steinmetz nor anything else. I was sent to work for the LAPD on a *mission*."

"A mission? What kind of a mission?"

"Of an intelligence nature."

Bandini slowly brought his palm down on the formica topped surface of the bar, then pointed at Duvall with an elfish grin on his face. "You're a spy. You were a spy back then."

"I was a spy back then."

"Workin' for who?"

"Wouldn't you like to know?"

"What was the mission?"

"You can't guess?"

Bandini paused for a moment, then said in a whisper, "All that trouble you gave me on the Senator Channing case, the way you obstructed my investigation. You were *told* to do that?"

Duvall nodded.

"But why? Why didn't you want me to get to the bottom of Channing's death?"

"I don't think I need to tell you that some conspiracy theories are *true*."

"So who was responsible for Channing gettin' offed?"

"Obviously, the people I was working for at the time."

"Are you still working for them?"

"I wouldn't be here if I was."

"You know… I'm not the kinda guy to judge another man, really I'm not, but I don't think I could prevent justice from taking its natural course just 'cause some higher up told me to, or just 'cause somebody paid me a lot of blood money."

"*Blood* money? That's a harsh term for somebody who's not judgmental. That's not why I did it, not for the money. I did it because… well, I thought I was helping save the world, as ridiculous as that sounds. I was young and stupid. I believed everything I was told. I was told that you were the enemy, I was told Senator Channing was the enemy, I was told *everybody* was the enemy. Everybody but… well, the people I was working for. And when you allow yourself to fall into that kind of mindset, anything is justified." Duvall's eyes glazed over; it suddenly seemed as if he were a thousand miles away. "Until one day you wake up, catch a glimpse of yourself in the mirror, and realize you can't feel your hands anymore." He held up his hands and stared at them with increasing wonder. "And the doctors can't tell you what's wrong. And they suggest you're going crazy. Reality becomes too painful to ignore or explain away. What you've always known was true is finally made obvious, even to you. To someone who's not young anymore, but still just as stupid. And so you walk away. You run away. But the past catches up with you very quickly. And you end up here. In this very moment. Talking to Lt. Bandini of the LAPD. Whoever would've thought?" He paused for a moment, reflecting on the ripples in his cup. "You know, it's ironic. I concede that you were right in trying to solve the Senator's death. If I'd let you continue, you would've busted the case wide open. You were on the side of justice. You always were. I wasn't. I never was. And yet, in the end, both of us... we ended up here, didn't we? In hell. So what good was it all? What good was it?"

"So... that's why you're not workin' for them anymore? Your conscience got the better of you?

That far-off stare in Duvall's eyes vanished abruptly. He snapped back fully to the here and now. "You think you're very clever, don't you?"

"What're you talkin' about? I'm just tryin' to get to the bottom of this mess. Just like I tried to do with the Channing case. I'm just tryin' to help you out. You and me. At the same time."

"Yeah? Then tell me... why're you here?"

"I resigned. For the same reason you did. My conscience was killin' me. I was investigating the death of a famous microbiologist named Dr. Keri Davidson. She was the chief microbiologist at a secret facility run by the Ministry of Defense at Porton Down in England. She had been workin' for the Institute of Virology at Oxford and so she brought a lot of her fellow Oxford scientists to her new job. Within the last two years most of those scientists have ended up dead. All suicides or unexplained accidents. But Davidson was the first casualty. She was makin' headlines just before her death 'cause she had leaked information to the British press that proved the Ministry of Defense had exaggerated the threat posed by them terrorists to jumpstart the war in the Middle East."

Duvall's brow furrowed. "England's at *war* now?"

"Jesus... you have been here for a long time, haven't you? Listen, let's just boil it all down to this: Davidson posed a threat to both the British *and* American governments because of her opposition to the war. She had the information she needed to prove they were lying about weapons of mass destruction being stored in secret facilities beneath the Middle East. It was all a lie, and Davidson knew it. She was going to testify to that fact. In fact, she was in Los Angeles to give a speech at UCLA. They were gonna broadcast it live on CSPAN, to let the whole world know about what she knew—that's according to her husband, who I interviewed. Instead she ended up committing suicide at a rest stop just off the 405 the night before she was supposed to go on the show. I was *this* close to crackin' the case wide open when I was stopped. Shut down, just like you blocked me on the Channing case. I could see what was happenin' and why it was happenin'. I was warned off the case by my superiors. The higher ups wanted it closed down. I turned in my badge. I planned to start up a private detective agency and keep the case goin' in my spare time. Instead I ended up *here*. Now... I want you to make up for all the B.S. you pulled back when you were on the LAPD. I want you to help me out. You say a private corporation runs this place. What's it called? Is Micropolis its real name?"

"Supposedly. Their specialty is microbiology. I think you'll find that most of the microbiologists you think are dead or missing have actually ended up *here*. Bodies can be easily replaced, autopsies altered. These microbiologists are the most important scientists on the planet from a defense perspective. They're too valuable to be allowed to roam free. So they're kidnapped, forced to work in isolation where they can't share their information with the public, or with the enemy. A Brain Drain. The same thing was done in Germany during World War II. Rocket scientists were abducted and forced to work for the Führer in Rocket City. The analogy hasn't been missed by the scientists. That's why some of them have taken to calling this place 'Rocket City.' The fact that this place used to be a missile base just makes the moniker even more appropriate. More coffee?"

Bandini nodded as Duvall took the cup away from him and filled it to the brim. "Scientists, huh? You've spoken to 'em? Where are they?"

"Just down the street. They're having their annual Spring celebration today. I suppose one can't work all the time."

"All *those* people out there? They're all microbiologists?"

"Well, all *scientists*... for the most part." Duvall slid the filled cup back across the formica. "Microbiologists. Quantum physicists. Biologists. Mathematicians. Zoologists. Mostly virologists. Such knowledge is priceless. They're encouraged to *cooperate*, of course. And if they don't... well, there's always the Welcome Room. Few of them can withstand the pain for long. Eventually, they cooperate... or die resisting. Most of them choose the former, though." A bit shamefully, Duvall said softly, "I helped bring some of them here, back in my idealistic youth. I think that's called karma. You know, there used to be an unspoken rule in intelligence that the private sector will always be twenty to thirty years *behind* the military in terms of scientific research. Micropolis is trying to put the lie to that rule."

Bandini stared into the blackness of his coffee. "Incredible. It's so huge."

"Makes one want to give up and go back to sleep, doesn't it?" Duvall poured himself a second cup of tea.

Bandini raised his cup to his lip and took a long sip. "Good coffee, by the way."

"Thank you."

Bandini held up his index finger. "Nothing's impossible. I learned that a long time ago. No matter how impenetrable a case seems to be, you just gotta keep pushin' against it. Little by little. One little step at a time, like puttin' the hundredth chair in a pattern, or layin' down the next brick in the wall. Pretty soon, you got enough bricks, the building's done. The case is over and you didn't even notice while it was happenin'."

"Persistence. A very American trait. Where do you suggest we begin? By the way, I'm going to be executed for murder soon, so you better think fast. I've been thinking about giving up entirely for a change. A different strategy might be in order now."

"That's fine, let me handle this. I know where we're gonna start. With the present. With *you*."

Duvall sighed. "Please keep in mind that I've tried to escape about one hundred and thirty-six times now. Nothing has worked."

"I'm not talking about escape. I'm just talking about dealing with the immediate problem. Keeping you from getting killed."

"Why on earth would you want to bother with that? What's in it for you?"

Bandini spread his hands in the air, as if the answer should be obvious. "I don't want to see an innocent man go to his death?"

"But how do you know I'm innocent?"

"Who benefits from the murders? You? I don't think so. You only have two possible motives: to silence the woman or to bring about your own execution. You have no *reason* to silence the woman. What could she know that would endanger you? After all, you're already imprisoned here. Could her knowledge condemn you to death somehow? Well, by the very act of silencing her you condemn yourself to death anyway. The crime cancels out the motive, see?

"Now, there's another motive. That you're tired of being trapped here. You want someone to kill you, but you can't bring yourself to do it. So you want someone else to put you out of your misery. A 'Suicide By Cop' situation. But if that's the case, why deny having done it? Mr. L claims you did it in a blind rage. Temporary insanity? I don't think so. Whoever pulled it off was very methodical.

"Means. Opportunity. Motive. You didn't have the means, you didn't have the opportunity, you didn't have the motive."

"That brings us back to the main question," said Duvall. "Who benefits?

"Mr. L. It was made pretty clear to me by the old man that you've been a thorn in the side of this operation for a long time now."

Duvall laughed. "I can say with some modesty that *I* was the one who drove the first Mr. L out of here."

"Then getting you out of the way would be pretty convenient. And yet, if you die, there goes all the information in that precious little skull of yours... all those memories they want to keep around. So there's more to it than that. The two guards were simply obstructions, we know that. It's obvious from the crime scene. Whoever it was had to get them out of the way... to get to the woman. But who is she?"

"If she was in the interrogation room," said Duvall, "she was no doubt a scientist."

"Another microbiologist. But why her? Why would Mr. L choose *her* of all the microbiologists that come through this place?" In the distance, Bandini could just barely hear the sound of laughing and singing. The sound of a brass band. "The only reason you're brought here is if you know something unique, something irreplaceable. Why kill her? Why *her*? Mr. L had the means, the opportunity... but what's the motive? What could a man as powerful as that possibly want?"

"Who knows how a man like that thinks? All I know is that I've managed to have some fun bedeviling him for quite awhile now. Mr. L(Prime) left the facility in his very, very incapable, *oversized* hands. The Peter Principle in action. Throughout my years toiling away for my country in the intelligence world I can assure you that the people who rise to the top are, for the most part, clueless bureaucrats. They land in positions of power by accident. If they could have their way, they'd be much happier in a position with far less responsibility—but with the same amount of pay, of course. Only when I realized that I'd become as mindless as them did I turn my back on the whole lot of them. Or at least I thought I did."

The sound of singing was growing quite loud now. Bandini sighed. He smiled. "Y'know, it's nice to know that even under conditions like these, people like that can find a ray of sunshine in all the darkness here. They haven't given up hope. They still find a reason to sing and dance."

"Or you can look at it another way," Duvall said between his final sips of tea. "That all this jabberwocky is just symptomatic of a human being's never ending ability to deaden himself completely to the harsh reality staring him right in the face. The writing on the wall is there for everybody to see and yet we refuse to see it, even when the letters are ten feet high and staring us straight in the face. That singing out there could be seen as just another form of entertainment. Just another meaningless distraction."

"Yeah… the writing on the wall," Bandini said almost to himself, as if lost in another world. "*The writing on the wall.* Jesus, that's it. You hit on it."

"Excuse me?"

Bandini slapped Duvall on the shoulder. "Excellent job, Duvall!"

"May I remind you my name isn't Duvall?"

Bandini's widened impossibly. "It always will be to me."

7

In Which At Least One Autopsy Is Performed

Mr. L stood beside Mr. L(Prime), patiently listening to him as he waxed nostalgic about his days working in the Dome. About how perfect Micropolis was in those days. Everything ran so *smoothly*. No murders in the halls, no violence of any kind. Smooth.

If he loved it so damn much, why did he ever leave in the first place?

Mr. L had been stuck here for hours, trapped in the old man's memories.

They were standing in the huge chamber at the very top of the Dome. This was the observatory. It was the largest observatory on the continent, larger even than the one in Griffith Park or the one sitting atop Palomar. All the astronomers brought to Micropolis as guests were allowed to work in this observatory in order to continue their important research. Today, no research was being conducted here. The only two people in the observatory were Mr. L and Mr. L(Prime).

The old man peered into the giant telescope, as he used to do so often in the old days, staring at the surface of the moon. "I wonder when our boys will get back," the old man said.

"Not for awhile yet," said Mr. L. "They still have a lot of work to do."

"I wish it was me up there instead of them."

Mr. L had to refrain from saying, "I know what you mean."

"Did you ever have dreams when you were a little boy?" asked the old man.

"Of course… too many of them."

At that moment a loud knock came to the double doors behind them, and in came Lieutenant Bandini.

"Sorry to intrude," said Bandini, "but the guards downstairs said I could probably find you both up here."

"Ah, I was just thinking about you," the old man said. "Did you ever have any dreams when you were a kid? Anything you wanted to be when you grew up?"

"Oh, sir, I don't know. I think I just always wanted to be a cop. I remember tellin' my mom when I started elementary school, like when I was about five or so, that I wanted to catch crooks for a livin'. It was just in the blood I guess."

"You're a very fortunate man. Not everybody knows what they want to do at such a young age. I did… but I turned my back on it." He pressed his eye against the telescope again.

"That's a mighty big telescope you got there," Bandini said. "Did you wanna be an astronomer or something'?"

The old man did not look up from the eyepiece. "An astronaut."

"Well, who knows? You're never too young, that's what my grandma always used to say."

"Never too *young*?" The old man straightened up, smiled. "Yes… it'd be nice if we could start all over again. Reel the film back as it were, eh? Snip out a scene there, replace it with a new one, then let the film continue again."

"Sometimes we're just stuck with what we have, sir. We've got to make the best of it."

"I suppose so." The old man stared off into space for a moment, then said, "I always wanted to travel in space, ever since I can remember. I wanted to stand on the surface of the moon and look back down at the earth. A tiny blue dot in all that vastness. It'd be the closest you could ever get to being God. The closest you could ever get…." The old man turned toward Mr. L. "What about you? Did you want to be an astronaut when you were a kid?"

"No, sir, outer space never appealed to me for some reason."

"Well, what did you want? There had to be something. Some crazy dream."

"Yes. I think…." A faraway expression leaked into the eyes of Mr. L. "I think I wanted to be invisible." Mr. L smiled nervously then, and added, "But we all grow out of such nonsense sooner or later."

"Yeah, we do," Bandini said, "sooner or later."

The old man turned back toward Bandini. "I hope you've come with some good news. Have you made any progress?"

"I think I've got a pretty good picture of what happened now." Mr. L could feel his entire body tightening up. He doesn't know anything, he told himself, he *couldn't* know anything. "But I don't have any proof." Mr. L breathed a silent sigh of relief. "But I think that's gonna change soon." Then the tension returned. "I just ran into the medical doctor that you assigned to the case, sir. He's gonna perform the autopsy in a few minutes from now. I was wonderin' if either of you wanted to sit in on it. Y'know, to observe."

"Autopsy?" The word came out as a whisper. Mr. L could feel a bottomless chasm opening in his heart. "Autopsy on *who*?"

"Oh, I'm sorry." Bandini glanced at the old man. "I figured you would've been informed by now. We need to perform an autopsy on the woman, y'see. Uh, what'd you call her? N(n), I guess? Somethin' like that. Anyway, yeah, I'm gonna go sit in on it right now if you want to join me. Sometimes autopsies can be fun, y'know. It's not like you get the chance to do it every day."

"I most certainly will not sit in on any autopsy, and neither are *you*!" Mr. L could feel his face turning crimson as his hands wilted into fists. "I'll be *damned* if I'm going to let some outsider like you sit by and watch as—as a *visitor* to this facility is cut open like some common piece of beef! For *your* entertainment? I think not."

"Calm down," the old man said. "It's nothing to get upset about it."

Mr. L turned toward the old man. "You can't allow this to happen. It's a *travesty*. My authority has been trampled on every which way since this—this *man* arrived here. Now he's ordering autopsies on my visitors? I won't have it. I'm lodging a formal complaint. With you, sir, right now. I *demand* that this gentleman be kept under house arrest in his bungalow from this point forward. Until *I* say so."

"First of all," the old man said calmly, "he did not order the autopsy, *I* did. The responsibility for this lies on my shoulders, not his."

"I beg to differ, sir, but any visitor who arrived at the facility under my watch is *my* sole responsibility. I can't just have her body *desecrated* like this for no good reason. Not only is it unseemly, but it's—!"

"My good man, you couldn't even prevent the poor woman from

being murdered, and now you're concerned about the state of her remains? You're acting very strangely, Mr. L."

Mr. L calmed down suddenly. "I'm sorry." He glanced at Bandini. Bandini just kept staring at him with those beady little black eyes of his. He looked like an overgrown ferret. "It's just that I've been under a lot of stress today. I want to do a good job for you."

"You better," the old man said, "or I might have to demote you." The words hit him like a face full of ice cold water. All the tension in his body vanished, like magic. "Now pull yourself together. I think all three of us should attend the autopsy. What do you say?" He turned toward Bandini.

Bandini shrugged. "Sounds good to me, sir."

"I'll lead the way," the old man said, and started toward the door.

Mr. L found himself walking side by side with Bandini. He was staring at the old man's back. "May I at least ask why you think an autopsy is necessary?" Mr. L said.

"The lieutenant found a pinprick on the dead woman's arm," said the old man as they started down the metal spiral staircase. "He thinks the woman was injected with some kind of poison."

"And if so," Mr. L said, "what would that prove?"

"That Mr. D isn't the killer," Bandini said.

"How so?"

"His only real plausible motivation for committing the crime would be blind rage. You implied as much yourself. But a man overcome with rage doesn't kill two people with a gun, then switch to a hypodermic needle. Only a very *methodical* man would do that. A man with a purpose. A clear motive. Maybe several of them."

"What about the gun?" Mr. L said. "His .22…."

"Another piece of evidence in Mr. D's favor," Bandini said. "Does an enraged man, a man who's temporarily *insane*, remember to wipe off all his fingerprints from the murder weapon before conveniently leaving it behind at the crime scene?"

"So you're suggesting Mr. D is being framed? You're taking *his* side in this? Mr. D is clearly an anarchist. His record is clear for anyone to see."

"Listen, sir, I'm not taking any sides," Bandini said.

"We just want to cover all the bases," the old man said, "for the record. That's all."

For the record indeed! The old man had his own superiors to report back to. A hierarchy of threats and intimidation. Mr. L was sick of it. All of it.

They entered the autopsy room several minutes later. The small white cubicle was located in the first sub-basement. Mr. L rarely had reason to come down this far.

The dead woman lay spread out on a slab. She was naked, pale, devoid of life. A small man, even smaller than the lieutenant, stood behind the table with a scalpel in his hands. He was an ugly man with a nasty, bushy brown moustache and frizzy gray hair ringing a bald pate. He wore thick glasses with wide frames. He had a thick German accent.

"We've got a quite a crowd I see," said the German doctor. "Are you all here for the show?"

"The lieutenant is advising us on the investigation," the old man said.

The doctor shrugged. "Okay, fine by me. Here we go. You got here just in time. I'd offer you some popcorn, but I don't have any more left." He opened his mouth and flashed a gap toothed smile filled with brown, crooked teeth.

"We don't have time for jokes," said the old man. "Just do your job."

"Okay, okay… sorry. Just tryin' to lighten things up, y'know? Here is one for the gipper, as they say." The doctor bent over the corpse (Jennifer… her name was Jennifer… her name *is* Jennifer… Jenny… I), stabbed Jenny's throat with the tip of the blade (love you I), sliced downward slowly, ever so slowly, peeling back her beautiful flesh, the flesh he used to smother with gentle kisses (love you I love) revealing Jenny's insides for all to see… a grotesque striptease (you I love you I love)… spilling blood down the right side of her neck and onto the cold lifeless surface of the metal slab… both the same, Jenny and the slab… both the same….

Mr. L couldn't take it anymore. He'd had enough. Enough of everything. He bolted out of the room, slammed his body against the wall in the corridor, dug his fingers into the plaster, closed his eyes, wanted the hellish visions to go away… go away… go *away*… Jenny….

A gentle hand on his shoulder. "Sorry about that, sir. It can be awful tough if you've never seen it before."

Mr. L knocked the hand away. "Get *away* from me!" He pressed his cheek against the coolness of the wall. He just wanted to be left alone. Forever.

"Of course, sir, I'm sorry. I know how difficult it must be. You must've loved her a great deal."

Mr. L opened his eyes and turned toward Bandini slowly. "What?"

"You loved her. A great deal. Isn't that why you killed her?"

"What're you talking about? How do you—?"

"The needle, sir. You could've shot her... but you didn't. That's the act of someone who's in love. No signs of a struggle. She trusted you. You were in love with each other."

"You're just guessing. You don't know anything."

"I know enough, sir. I figure she was pretty strong willed, and wasn't going to cooperate no matter how much you begged her to do otherwise. You didn't want to see her tortured. Now *that's* a guess. How close is it?"

"You... you can't prove anything."

"I can prove enough. I can prove that Mr. D is not responsible."

Mr. L laughed. Suddenly, he was grateful for the cop's arrival. It gave him something else to think about, something other than Jenny's decaying body. The way her eyes would sparkle when she smiled. This stupid little man was a convenient distraction. A worthy adversary. Just another one of the sheeple to be fooled.

"How?" Mr. L said.

Bandini pointed at the autopsy room as he lit another cigarette. "When the doctor finds the poison in that poor woman's body, I suspect he'll determine that it's a type of poison Mr. D has no access to. But *you* do."

Mr. L smiled broadly. He straightened up. He fixed his jacket, smoothed out the wrinkles. "You think you're smart, don't you? You think you're really smart. But you know nothing. All right, Lieutenant, I'll accept your challenge. Do whatever you want. Investigate whatever you want. You'll find nothing. You'll prove nothing. As long as the old man is on the premises you're in an enviable position. The second he leaves, however... well, that's a different story, isn't it? You don't have your brainless boys in blue protecting you here. All you have is yourself, and that's just not enough. Shouldn't you be a little wary? To be confronting me with all this? After all, if I'm such a methodical assassin, what would stop me from killing *you*?"

Bandini nodded. He wasn't smiling anymore. "I don't have much time. I know that."

"You better hope the doctor in there pulls through for you. Tell the old man I have more pressing business to tend to. We have new visitors every day you know. There'll be more tomorrow, and more the next day." Mr. L walked away, knowing there was very little the idiot cop could accomplish.

The autopsy would turn up nothing.

8

In Which Bandini Is Stymied and Mr. L Demands a Punchline

Later that evening Mr. L sat in his study, rereading choice passages from Johann Strauss's first published book, when Bandini barged into the room.

The butler stood behind him, gesturing helplessly toward Mr. L.

"That's all right," Mr. L said to the butler. "It's not your fault. Leave us alone, please."

The butler walked out of the room, casting uneasy glances back at Bandini. Bandini remained standing on the ramp.

The second they were alone Mr. L said, "Just because you have a *temporary* unlimited pass doesn't mean that all decorum must be thrown out the window. A brief knock at least would be appreciated before you come marching in here like a Gestapo agent."

"I'm sorry, sir, it won't happen again. I just have some important news."

"Oh? Did the doctor find anything of grave import? Have you come to slap the cuffs on me? Surely the old man would be with you if that was the case."

"No, sir." The lieutenant looked quite distraught. "There was no evidence of any poison whatsoever in the woman's system."

"Oh, how unfortunate," Mr. L said. "How very, very unfortunate for *you*. For all of us, in fact. After all… I want to catch the man responsible just as much as anybody else." He went back to reading.

Bandini stepped off the ramp and started walking toward him.

"Some of the most brilliant microbiologists in the world are being held captive here. You're in charge of this entire facility. How difficult would it be for you to get hold of a fatal substance that kills instantly and leaves no trace in the victim's body afterwards?"

"I don't know, *how* difficult? Oh, wait… this *is* a joke, isn't it?" Mr. L slipped a bookmark into Strauss's book. "There is some sort of punchline coming, isn't there?"

"Depends on your definition of a punchline, sir." Bandini walked right up to Mr. L's desk. "I just came here to tell you what I know. I know you killed three people here last night and you're trying to pin the crimes on an innocent man. I can't let that happen. It's against all my training. I don't care if this place is outside my jurisdiction or not."

"It'd be hard for you to know if it's outside your jurisdiction, wouldn't it?"

"Yes it would, sir. Nonetheless, I won't rest until I've proved you're guilty."

"You'll rest when I *tell* you to rest. You can't prove I'm guilty. Now get out of here. I'm tired of wasting my time with this nonsense."

"I'll prove it when I finish analyzing the needle."

Mr. L quietly closed the book. "What're you talking about?"

"There's only two things you could've done with the needle after fleeing the scene. You either destroyed it immediately or you hid it. Since I'm guessing you were in a near state of panic, knowing you might be caught by your own guards at any moment, you probably didn't have time to destroy it. I'm bettin' you hid it somewhere, which means it's possible for me to find it again. I suspect you probably removed your gloves in order to share a final moment with the victim before she allowed you to euthanize her. I suspect that in the tenderness of that moment you forgot to put the gloves back on. I suspect that the syringe has your fingerprints on it. And there'll still be traces of blood on the needle that'll connect the syringe to the victim. And when we analyze the liquid inside, we'll be able to confirm that it's poison… through and through."

"You suspect a lot."

"I'm a suspicious person. An occupational hazard."

"Too bad you don't have the needle."

"Oh, I've been known to find much smaller knickknacks in even bigger haystacks. Just ask my wife. When she loses an earring she always comes to me fir—"

Mr. L slammed his fist into his desk and shot up out of his chair. "Get out! I've had enough of this!"

Bandini gently wrapped his knuckles against the wooden surface of the desk. "I'll have that syringe in my hands by morning." Then turned around and walked slowly up the ramp, back out into the halls of the Dome. The doors closed behind him.

Mr. L had the urge to hurl the Strauss book across the room, but stopped himself at the last moment. Instead he reached out calmly and ran his palm over the leathery surface. Over and over again. Stroked the book, as if it were a purring pet and he its one and only master.

9

In Which Mr. L Composes a Masterpiece

It was almost ten o'clock at night when Bandini left his office. Mr. L turned toward the monitor on his desk, hit a few buttons, and accessed the various cameras in the Dome. He watched Bandini return to the observatory where the cop talked to the old man for a little while about nothing significant, not even mentioning the case at all. The two of them took turns watching the moon.

He switched to a separate view: an exterior shot of the main control room. Two guards were standing outside, just as he had requested. Mr. L remained sitting behind the desk for several hours after that. He tried to read more of Strauss but couldn't. So instead he pulled out his notepad and continued working on that book he'd started so long ago. A work of fiction, inspired by Kafka, about a lone man beset by the mindlessness of the masses, a man trapped in a village from which there is no escape. The hero is the last honorable man on Earth and the antagonist... the rest of the world. He was thinking of calling it *The Last Man in Europe*, Orwell's discarded title for *1984*. Even Orwell's considerable achievement would be overshadowed by this new masterpiece. The trouble with most dystopian novels is that they were never written from a *sympathetic* point of view—a realistic one, one not marred by the intrusion of simplistic morality. Mr. L's novel would rectify that problem. Of course, he wouldn't be able to publish it under his real name, but no matter. Most artists in his position were forced to take the same measures. Orwell himself, for example.

He worked long into the night, completing an entire chapter in which the hero is regressed into his childhood by advanced mind control technology in order to break him down psychologically. But perhaps that chapter would be more appropriate for later in the story…. Well, he couldn't decide now. He was much too tired. He had to go to sleep. It had been such a long day.

He hoped he didn't dream.

Jenny….

Forget it. Don't think about it. Just don't.

He rose from the desk, glanced at the monitor one last time. The guards were still at their post. The observatory was empty now. The old man had always been pretty strict about the curfew. In fact, he was the one who had implemented it. He was probably in bed by now. And Bandini… what did it matter where he was? Once all this was over, he wouldn't be his problem anymore. None of this would be his problem.

Mr. L stretched and yawned. He returned the Strauss book to the shelf, then slipped the thick yellow notepad back into its place inside his desk. Someday, when it was finished, he would type it into the computer and send it on the rounds to the various publishers. Then the world would see.

Mr. L went upstairs to the master bedroom. He stripped off his jacket, his button-up shirt, his undershirt… collapsed onto the mattress. He fell asleep on top of the covers.

He saw Jennifer standing on a stage, naked, peeling off her flesh for a roomful of drunken men. Jimmy Buffett was playing over a loudspeaker somewhere. She was dancing to that Buffett beat. Pulling off an eyelid here, a breast there, a piece of her right cheek here….

Mr. L was in the audience. He'd paid for the best seat, but now he was trapped at the back of the crowd, trying to push through them all. "No!" he yelled at her. "Stop, Jenny! Please stop!"

She ignored him. Maybe she couldn't hear him? Smiling, she reached into her chest and ripped out her own heart and tossed it into the crowd. They went for it like animals. He was knocked down by the rush, got lost beneath their feet, trampled by the mad rush for her blood. His head hit the sticky floor and he couldn't breathe anymore… he couldn't *breathe….*

He woke up gasping, his body covered in sweat.

Mr. L jumped out of bed, trying to catch his breath. *Couldn't breathe.* He rushed into the bathroom, tore out of his pants, and crawled into the bathtub. He ran the water all over himself. The water felt good against his flesh, like a young woman's touch... like *Jenny's* touch....

He had to exterminate this feeling somehow, this feeling of perpetual doom. As if Jenny's shadow was lurking in his peripheral vision, accusing him of not loving her enough. If he had, if he had begged her to stay so long ago, none of this would've happened.

He had to cut himself off from the past. Stop thinking. Be like Strauss. A rationalist to the end. See through all the illusions society tries to build around you like a prison. The past doesn't matter. The past is as illusory as the future. As illusory as guilt. Didn't Strauss always say that the only way to be truthful to oneself was to be untruthful to others? That's the way it had to be, the way civilization had been set up. By kings and bureaucrats and little men. But people like L didn't have to go along with that game. Superior intellects like L had to survive by breaking the rules while forcing the rest of the world to follow them. Otherwise, there would be nothing but chaos.

Chaos and kings and little men. Little men like Bandini.

He had to get that man off his back once and for all. Then he could rest.

He could rest and have peace of mind and finally complete the novel.

But first he had to get rid of all these incessant questions that kept scraping against the inside of his mind. *Did* he take off the gloves to stroke Jenny's cheek? Yes... yes, he did. At least he thought so. Did he *keep* them off? He couldn't remember... he just couldn't. He didn't *want* to.

He put on his robe over his still wet body and opened the door to his room, ever so slowly. The entire Dome was silent, as it usually was this time of night. It had to be at least two in the morning. Around the time he and Jenny had last spoken to one another.

Forget it. Cut off the past. Cut it off.

Mr. L descended the staircase, put his hands in the pockets of his robe, and strolled down the corridor that branched off from the Bridge-of-Sighs. There, in the early morning darkness of the corridor, stood two guards. Hardened killers with postures as straight as steel. No man could get through them. Certainly not Bandini. Only Mr. L could call them off.

The second Mr. L appeared in front of them, the two guards saluted him. "At ease, men." They returned to their previous posture. "Has anybody been by here?"

"No, sir," the two guards said simultaneously.

"Anybody try to get into this room?"

"No, sir," both guards said.

"Excellent. I'm going in now. I don't wish to be disturbed in there, you understand? If anybody comes by here, send them away. Is that clear to both of you?"

"Yes, sir," they said.

Mr. L waved his palm in front of the scanner. The door slid open. He entered the control room. He made the same motion on the opposite side, shutting the door behind him. Now he was alone in here at last.

He didn't even bother to turn on the lights. Just as he had done last night, he quickly unscrewed the bolts at the bottom of the seat. He pulled the seat off its metal perch, then reached inside the tube. They were still there: the gloves and the needle. His last connection to Jenny. His last connection to the past. His last connection to guilt.

Behind him, the door slid open and light flooded the room.

Mr. L spun around and saw a silhouette standing in the doorway. The silhouette of a little man lazily smoking a cigarette. He watched the trail of smoke rise toward the ceiling.

Behind the silhouette stood another figure. The figure pointed at him.

"Grab whatever's in his hands." The voice of the old man.

The two guards descended on Mr. L and pulled the gloves and the needle out of his hands.

"Be careful with that stuff," Bandini said. He took it from the guards and showed it to the old man. "What'd I tell ya? It's all there, laid out for you in the form of three simple objects. Two gloves and a needle. Now there's a story you don't need a thousand pages to tell, right?"

"You were right all along," the old man whispered.

"You're going to believe him over *me*?" Mr. L screamed as the two guards dragged him to his feet. He struggled to break free of them, but it was no use. They were too strong. Micropolis only hired the best. The old man had seen to that long ago. "I've worked for you for *years*!"

"That's why I'm so distraught right now," the old man said. "So

ROBERT GUFFEY

disappointed." He waved his hand over a sensor in the wall, turning on the overhead lights.

The sudden glare made Mr. L squint. "Disappointed? I was trying to *help* you. Bandini told me about the missing needle, so I tried to find it. I've been wandering up and down the hallways all night, looking, *looking*. D must've planted it in here. Nobody thought to look in here, but I did. *I* did. And now you're punishing me for that?"

The old man said to the guards, "You can release him, but make sure he doesn't move."

"But I'm telling you the *truth*."

"I'm afraid that story's impossible, sir," said Bandini.

"What're you talking about?" Mr. L said.

"How could Mr. D have hidden the needle in here if, as you say, Mr. D was the one who locked you in the room in the first place? He could only have ditched the needle *after* committing all three murders. So when did he have access to this room? You were locked in here until the guard released you. Isn't that what you told us?"

"Yes, of course, but—"

"And D fled the premises sometime after the crime and *before* you were released, right? That's a very small window, sir. During that window, you were the only one who had access to this room."

"That's not true. Can't you see?" He laughed like a little girl. It was the first time he'd laughed in years. "There are other explanations—"

"There are *always* other explanations. And then there's the right one. The right one is this: You got hit in the face with your own past when the kind people you worked for abducted a woman you once loved. Maybe she was a sister to you. Maybe she was like a daughter. Maybe she was your girlfriend. I don't know, and I don't need to know. All I know is that you *loved* her. Loved her enough to kill her. Heck, I dunno, maybe she was the one who came up with the idea." Bandini shrugged. "Either way, she's dead. And that's probably a good thing, if what goes on in that room down the hall is anywhere near as bad as I think it is."

"I don't understand any of this," Mr. L said. "How could you possibly expect anybody to believe that I'd—"

"The thing that clinched it was the needle mark. You should've just shot her. I never would've known. Nobody would have. The needle mark was on her left arm, y'see. If I'm kneeling down in front of a woman who's sitting in a chair, I would take her right arm to inject her with a needle. But that's because I'm right-handed. And so is Mr. D. But you...." Bandini pointed at Mr. L with his lit cigarette. "You're left-handed."

"So are a lot of people. So what?"

"So... I suspected the woman was euthanized from the very beginning when I didn't see any signs of a struggle. I wasn't sure, though, until I saw your reaction at the autopsy. Even that wasn't enough. Even that didn't give me the final clue. Because you didn't just have *one* motive in this. Oh, no. You had two. Wait, scratch that. You had *three*.

"You wanted to save the woman from the pleasures of your little Welcome Room. And you wanted to frame Mr. D. Why? Anybody would do, but you chose D.

"Because that was the main task that had been dumped in your lap. Mr. L(Prime) retired because he couldn't break D, so he left it to you. And if you couldn't do it, you'd probably be punished very severely. Just as severely as all your other 'visitors.' Wouldn't that be ironic?

"And that's too much responsibility for someone like you. How to avoid it? You could murder D, but that wouldn't do. You were ordered *not* to. He's too precious. That's why he's still alive. No, if he was taken dead all of a sudden under your watch *you'd* be blamed. But... what if D killed somebody *else*? A scientist just as valuable to Micropolis as D is, maybe even more so. If you followed the twisted rules of this place to the letter, why... you could justify killing D in broad daylight. And it wouldn't even be at your own hands. The situation's resolved, and *almost* everybody comes out happy.

"But there's even an extra bonus. Your superiors wouldn't be happy about this at all. Two valuable visitors dead, under your watch? You'd be punished, that's for sure, but not nearly as harshly as you would be if you killed 'em both yourself. Your punishment? You'd be *demoted*. You'd be allowed to crawl back into the woodwork. You'd be able to go back to being invisible.

"This was the final clue." Bandini reached inside his jacket and pulled out a small red paperback decorated with the words *Is Power Weakness*. "Strauss's book. It's a good thing Mr. D is a literate man. He had a copy of this book in his bookshelf. Ironically, *you're* the one who gave it to him. As a birthday present, he said. How charming.... I read it. Tonight. Didn't take long at all. Seventy pages? That's nothin'. You should see the reports I have to fill out. When I read this, I saw the writing on the wall.

"Literally. I remembered the sign on your wall. That's what did it. When I first saw this book on your bookshelf, I thought the title was a question. Is Power Weakness? But no, it's a statement: If Power Asks Why, Then Is Power Weakness. That's Strauss's whole philosophy. You're more powerful if you're *behind* the scenes, but you got thrust to the top by accident. Because Mr. L(Prime) decided to leave. Because he knew he couldn't break D. And he knew it would look bad if the guy who succeeded him managed to do what he couldn't. So he promoted the most ill-suited person to the job, the person who was bound to fail. That person was you. You weren't invisible anymore, and it was tearin' you up inside. So much so that you were willing to sacrifice *four* lives to break out of the trap.

"You might think you did this for love, but that was just a small part of it. Y'know, it's funny, in a lot of mysteries the motive to kill is ambition. Look at *Macbeth*. I mean, I haven't read *Macbeth* or anything but my wife has an' she told me all about it. I can't tell ya how many times I've seen someone driven to murder 'cause they were so hell-bent on gettin' a promotion they didn't even deserve. But you're the only person I've ever met who killed to be *de*moted."

Bandini tossed the Strauss book toward Mr. L, who fumbled with it, but managed to hold on. He hugged it to his chest.

"You had access to Mr. D's gun," Bandini said, "access to the crime scene, access to the control room to cover it up. Means. Opportunity. Motive. All three applied to you. So... you want to sign the confession now or later?"

Mr. L hugged the book to his chest even tighter, his gaze focused on the ground, as he whispered, "Please preserve my manuscript. It's in the top drawer in my office. I think it's a masterpiece."

"Take him away," said the old man.

"Please promise me that," said Mr. L, "please."

The old man said nothing. Bandini could hear Mr. L's raving screams dwindle all the way down the corridor.

"Where're they gonna take him?" Bandini said.

"We'll leave him in the Welcome Room. For now." The old

man smiled and held out his hand. "Congratulations. You're a very observant man. Very intuitive."

Bandini ignored the hand.

The old man did not withdraw it. "I'm very impressed. I'm not impressed by a lot of people, you know. The visitors who come through here are all brilliant, no doubt about that, but they're almost all pushovers. Namby-pambies, my father would say. You're different. You and Mr. D both fascinate me. That can be both good and bad. In Mr. D's case it's bad. In yours… well, we could use a man like you in a position of power here. If you played your cards right, you could eventually end up in my shoes."

Bandini took the final drag off the last of the old man's cigarettes. He had a feeling it would be his last for awhile. Too bad. He liked that hand rolled kind. Aw, what the hell, the wife was always on him to quit anyway.

"Sounds like a piss poor deal to me," Bandini said and let the orange butt drop at the old man's feet. "I mean, think about it. How much did those shoes cost you?"

The old man had no reply. His hand withdrew slowly—a pale, emaciated snake crawling into its hole.

10

In Which Bandini Matches Wits with the Infamous Mr. D

Bandini and Duvall sat at a small table outside Duvall's bungalow. Duvall was drinking tea. Earl Grey. Bandini was drinking coffee. Black.

Bandini had dropped by to see how he was doing. And Duvall had responded by challenging him to a game of chess.

"You must be feelin' better now that that whole execution thing's been taken care of," Bandini said. He looked up at the blue sky. Not a single cloud up there. He wished his family could see it. The city was probably choked with smog. He tried not to think about how much he missed it.

"I have mixed feelings about the whole affair," said Duvall. "I was rather looking forward to that final second. Right before the bullet hit. I have a feeling such a heightened moment of tension might inspire great illumination. Tremendous creativity."

"Jesus, not for long. Sorry I saved you from that experience. I guess you'll never know now, huh?"

"I suppose not. Until *next* time then. Your move, by the way."

Bandini stared at the board, amazed. "Son of a bitch. Another rook? How'd you do that?"

"Don't feel bad. I've been playing this game longer than you have."

"Well… I hope I'm as good as you someday."

"Let's hope not. Let's hope you won't have to be here that long."

"I'll drink to that." He took another sip of his coffee. "Hey, I get the feeling you're actually startin' to trust me a little bit."

"That, my friend, would be a bit premature."

Bandini grunted, then went back to studying all the pieces on the board.

11

In Which Bandini Wakens from a Peaceful Repose (Again)

Always the same. Bandini woke expecting to find himself snuggling against his wife's warm body, waiting for that horrid alarm to sound.

The bell never rang.

He woke up, approached the window, and looked out. So many trees, so much green. Such fresh air.

Some visitors said he was lucky. But he didn't feel lucky.

It was going to be a perfect day in Rocket City. A long, perfect day. A day of fun and games.

Just like all the others.

"Why don't you just tell us what we want to know and get the whole thing over with?" somebody will no doubt ask him for the five hundredth time.

And Bandini will smile, remembering those eight words that used to hang on Mr. L's wall.

Widow of the Amputation
or
Charlie's Adventures Underground

Somewhere: the sound of ravens.

At twelve years old, in April of 1946, Charlie stood in a courtroom holding the hand of his mother. She usually didn't hold his hand. He wondered if she was doing it for the sake of the judge.

Charlie barely listened to his mother's words. He stared at all the other people in the courtroom, none of whom were paying any attention to him. They were too busy with their own lives to notice the fiery anger of the boy, who was unusually small for his age.

The anger was buried deep inside. He rarely showed it to others, except when the bigger kids attacked him at school. Then he allowed it to flow from the pit of his stomach outward to his fists, which became like steel balls when he was pounding his way out of a pile of kids.

Amidst the chaos of his school life the sole anchor had been his mother, the mother who had pleaded with one of Charlie's many "uncles" the night before, pleaded with him not to leave, please, please don't leave me.

"I'm telling you, I'm moving on. You and I could make it just fine, but I can't stand that sneaky kid of yours."

"Don't leave, be patient. I love you and we'll work something out. *Please.*"

Please. Charlie knew what that word meant. It meant "goodbye, Charlie." It meant pawning him off on another set of reluctant relatives.

But not quite. They had run out of such relatives long ago. Charlie was a burden not only to his mother, but to everyone in the world. Even to the state.

The judge looked bored as he listened to Charlie's mother tell her story.

"You see, I just can't provide for Charlie like I want to. Life's been such a struggle, moving from job to job, state to state. Oh, I don't mind. It's all been for my little Charlie here." She patted him on the head. He tried to jerk away from her, but she held him fast. "I realize now that I'm hurting my son by moving around so much. He needs a stable home, like a normal child. That's why I'm asking you, judge sir, please find a proper home for my Charlie until I land myself a steady income so's I can take care of my son the way he really deserves to be."

The judge almost yawned as he shuffled some papers in front of him and said, without even looking at Charlie and his mother, "Until there is capable earning power by the mother and a decent stable home for Charles to return to, I am making him a ward of the court and placing him in a boys' home." He hit his gavel against the wooden surface of the table so lightly there was barely a sound.

Charlie's mother squeezed his hand, squeezed it with pent-up giddiness and joy, as she thanked the judge for his time in a sad tone of voice. The judge waved his hand in the air as if dismissing a pair of flies.

At thirteen, in the Indiana School for boys in Plainfield, Indiana, Charlie learned about the hierarchy of pain. In fact, he referred to the school as "Painsville."

The school was a microcosm for the outside world: society being a pyramid of suffering, each level inhabited by fucked-up, twisted souls whose main joy in life was preying on the weakness of those below them and kissing the asses of those above them. More than anything else, Charlie wished he could leapfrog over the levels above and somehow elbow his way into the capstone of the pyramid where there would be no one looking down on him, only a universe of victims awaiting Charlie's final judgment.

In Painsville the victims were the inmates, the boys sent there to be reformed by the Old-Testament-style teaching methods of the school. The inflictors of pain were the "supervisors," men like Fields who had chosen Charlie as his personal stooge. Charlie discovered this on his very first week.

"You, the short one," Fields said, pointing at Charlie near the end of the work day in the dairy. Fields had ordered the twelve boys assigned to the dairy to line up for a headcount.

Charlie glanced around, searching for someone shorter than him.

"I'm talking to *you*," Fields said, grabbing Charlie by the collar and yanking him out of the line. "Pull your strides down, shorty, I want to see if you've been getting fucked."

Charlie stared into Fields' gray eyes, hoping he was just grandstanding for the benefit of the other boys. He couldn't be serious.

"Are you deaf?" Fields shouted. "Pull down your god damn pants!" Fields slapped him upside the head. When Charlie still refused to obey, Fields pushed him onto the ground and yanked his pants down to his ankles. The other boys began to titter. Fields turned to them and yelled, "The first punk who utters even a cough will get the same treatment as the faggot here!"

Everybody shut up.

Fields scooped up some raw silage from the ground, spit tobacco juice onto the green fodder, then shoved the whole mess up Charlie's ass. As Fields left the dairy he said to the other boys, "I got him lubed, so fuck him if you get the chance." He laughed and locked the door behind him.

None of the boys took him up on the offer.

It wasn't long before Charlie tried to escape. He got as far as the river that bordered Plainfield on one side. Halfway across, he noticed the men and dogs waiting for him on the opposite bank. For a moment he considered sinking to the river bed below and allowing the water to fill his lungs and take him away, away from this hell forever. He couldn't bring himself to do it, though. The fear, the fear that had defined his life, was far too great.

Instead he received thirty lashes from Fields' escape strap. By the time his punishment was over his ass was crisscrossed with crimson railroad tracks, thin scratches from the whistling whip. He wished, prayed he could overcome his fear and end it with a single leap from the rooftop of the institution.

That night, the night of the beating, Fields made Charlie do the work of two men. He hauled heavy sacks of horse feed from the feed bin to the stables. Fields appointed two guards to watch over him at all times. At around two o'clock in the morning, while he was picking up what seemed like his hundredth sack of grain, two of the older inmates cornered Charlie in the bin. They had been eyeing him for months. Krause and Miller were both sixteen at the very least; even boys his own age were much taller and stronger than Charlie.

He knew the only way they could have gotten in was if the guards had allowed them to do so.

He knew what was about to happen. Despite the pain, despite his exhaustion, he put up a fight. It wasn't good enough.

Miller pinned his arms behind his back. Krause ripped off Charlie's pants, purposefully laughing like Fields himself. Charlie screamed and struggled to be free. They stuffed a gag in his mouth and beat on him until he could fight no longer.

Krause and Miller took their turns with him, reopening the fresh wounds on his ass, then left him bleeding on the floor. After a few minutes the guards appeared and ordered Charlie back to bed. He wondered why they didn't force him to continue working. Maybe this was their own way of giving him a "break." And maybe they just didn't give a shit one way or the other.

About an hour later Charlie lay in bed, wanting desperately to see his mother for two paradoxical reasons: to apologize for being such a burden on her,—plead for her forgiveness until she accepted him back—to scream at her and let her know just how much he really hated her.

Amidst all this tension and pain and hate he wasn't sure how he managed to go to sleep. Perhaps he never did. All he knew was this: at around a quarter to five he opened his eyes to see a large figure standing beside his bed. At first he thought it was one of his rapists coming back for another go-around. He tensed, ready to scream.

The figure didn't attack. He merely stood there, not uttering a word. Charlie glanced from side to side, staring at all the other boys sleeping in the large room. As far as he could tell, they were all sound asleep.

"Who—who are you?" Charlie whispered.

"Some call me the One-Who-Blinds-With-Death, others Father-of-the-Slain. I have many names. You may call me Bringer-of-Ecstasy." The stranger's voice was both quiet and powerful. He knelt beside Charlie's bed. The figure was thin and tall with a long gray beard that almost touched the middle of his chest. A hood was drawn low over his face, a dark robe covered his entire body. He reached out and touched Charlie on the forehead. For some reason Charlie didn't pull away. "Listen: You needn't overcome fear. Fear is just another form of awareness. When you're afraid, you're truly living in the 'Now.' Simply become one with fear, and fear will do the rest."

The stranger seemed to become translucent, for Charlie could see the rest of the room through his body. He transformed into a being of luminous colors, then Charlie felt his eyelids growing heavy....

His next memory was the sound of Fields banging a baton against a trash can, something he did every morning at exactly 6:30 A.M.

"All right, assholes, wakey wakey! You can count on this being another shitty day!"

Even though he couldn't have gotten more than ninety minutes of sleep, Charlie felt as refreshed as if he'd been snoozing in his old bed at his grandparents' house. Everything was clear. He knew what he had to do. He leaped up out of bed and stood at attention, awaiting Fields' inevitable scrutiny.

Sure enough, Fields strolled over to Charlie's bunk and poked him in the shoulder with the baton. "Have a nice workout last night, boy?"

"Yes, sir," Charlie replied.

Fields tapped him against the side of the head. "I didn't hear you!"

"Yes, sir!"

Fields leaned into Charlie's ear and whispered, "If you don't want another workout like last night, I suggest you behave from here on out, you got that, boy?"

"Yes, sir!"

Fields nodded, then strode toward another victim.

During the entire inspection Charlie remained as rigid as a soldier on parade, while deep inside him something quivered and seethed.

As he filed out of the housing unit with the other boys, he saw Krause and Miller emerging from the unit next door. Miller winked at him while Krause just smiled—that damn superior, mocking grin. Charlie faced forward and ignored them as best he could.

Charlie didn't talk to anybody the rest of that day and focused on the tasks assigned to him. With his newfound enthusiasm he did the work of two men, just like the night before. Fields was so impressed he complimented him in front of the other boys.

That night, an hour after lights-out, Charlie slipped out of bed and crept over to the window nearest the door. In order to close the window, one had to turn an iron handle that was almost twelve inches long and weighed three pounds. With as little noise as possible Charlie turned the handle until the window was shut, then kept turning it, and kept turning it, eventually unscrewing the handle from the window sill. He hefted it into the air, slapped it into the palm of his hand. It wasn't a baseball bat, or Fields' escape strap, but it would do. There were so many windows and doors in the housing units that were in need of repair, no one would even miss one pitiful little crank.

Charlie knew security came through the housing units twice a night for a head count, so he'd have to do this quickly. He slipped out of his unit, padded across the dirt and gravel in his bare feet, then crept through the front entrance of the housing unit next door.

Charlie tip-toed from bed to bed, searching the faces of the sleeping inmates. He spotted Miller near the front door, but he wasn't the one Charlie wanted the most. It was that damn mocking smile that caused the seething creature in his breast to twist and turn.

He found him on the opposite end of the large room, sleeping peacefully like an innocent child. Charlie sneered at the thought. Whether a child or not, no human being was innocent.

With great care Charlie lifted the blanket over Krause's head, then brought the handle down against his skull. The fire in his stomach seemed to erupt outward into his arm, down into the iron bar itself as he clubbed Krause over the head again and again and again. At last he stopped and stared at the motionless lump of flesh lying before him. Charlie felt light-headed; ecstasy filled his brain. He stared at the iron bar and marveled at how much damage such a tiny weapon could cause. He'd never felt better in his life.

He didn't even wait to see if he'd killed the boy. He walked silently toward the front door, streams of sweat trickling from his armpits to his ribs. On his way out the door, he paused long enough to slip the iron bar beneath Miller's blanket.

The door closed quietly behind him. In the warm night air, Charlie stood on the porch of the housing unit and glanced from side to side. To his right he couldn't see a soul. To his left, however, he spotted the door to the guard house creaking open.

Fuck, Charlie thought, fuck! He ducked under the railing that bordered the porch and hid behind a large bush. He watched the overweight guard waddle toward the housing unit with a Styrofoam cup of coffee in his hands, thinking, C'mon, *c'mon*, I don't have all night, you fat pig! The second the guard entered the building and closed the door behind him, Charlie emerged from behind the bush and retraced his steps back to his own unit.

He slipped into the building as silently as he'd left it. He wondered if the Fat Pig In Uniform would do a thorough enough head count to notice the bleeding boy. He hoped not. He hoped the boy wasn't discovered by morning. Perhaps that would give him enough time to bleed to death, if he hadn't died already.

The alarm sounded a few minutes after Charlie's head had hit his pillow. All the inmates were rounded up out of bed and searched. An ambulance came to the school and drove Krause's unconscious body away. An hour or so later the weapon was found in Miller's bed. He became the prime suspect.

Every inmate in Painsville knew who had committed the crime. For the first time since his arrival at the Indian School for Boys, Charlie felt genuine fear and respect radiating from the other boys. It felt good. From that point on, Charlie's ass was "off-limits."

Charlie fed off the fear and became more powerful day by day. The fear invigorated him. He got off on it, just as Krause had gotten off on him.

Someday, somehow, he knew the rest of the word would radiate the same fear at the mere mention of his name.

Somewhere: the sound of ravens.

On February 2nd, 1969, Aldrin could think only of a cool beer as the old Indian shaman poked bird feathers into his arms. It was a long, tedious process. Every few seconds or so the Indian would jab the end of a feather into his skin, reminding Aldrin of the dreaded vaccination shots he had received as a child. The shaman would ease the feather into his arm as deep as it could go. His entire left arm had almost been covered by the multicolored feathers; the right one had been covered long ago. He felt as if he were actually changing form, from man to bird, rather than just allowing himself to be poked by dead feathers. These shamans called genuine shapeshifters "skinwalkers." It was one of the few facts Aldrin had been able to squeeze out of the reticent old men. Every time he tried to initiate a conversation they just ignored him. Pretty soon he got the hint. He closed his eyes and tried to forget that he was standing naked in the middle of the Nevada desert beneath a scorching sun, surrounded by a trio of peyote-popping Hopi Indians with hocus-pocus on the brain.

Ten feet to the right of Aldrin, Armstrong was being tended to by yet another Indian. Every time the old men jabbed him with a feather, Armstrong let out a brief cry. A third shaman stood between both of them, singing a bunch of mumbo-jumbo at the sky. Aldrin had no idea what any of it meant, but it was sure annoying. Mumbo-jumbo or not, he knew it was intended to help them get to the moon. That's all he'd ever wanted.

When Dr. Farouk El-Baz, a geologist who worked at NASA, had informed the astronauts of his plan, Aldrin's immediate assumption was that his leg was being pulled. Perhaps this was yet one more psychological exam the astronauts were forced to undergo. After only a few seconds, however, when Aldrin saw the utter seriousness in El-Baz's eyes, he realized the secrets of NASA were far more esoteric than even he had ever dreamed.

Aldrin opened his eyes for a moment and stared at the green fruit bulbs of the plentiful saguaro cacti that could be seen dotting the sandy soil of the arid desert. He studied the white flowers growing from the giant, spiked cactus and wished they were aluminum cans filled with All-American Budweiser. Pretty soon he thought he saw a six-pack dangling from the arms of the cactus, at which point he closed his eyes once more, convinced he'd been standing in the sun for far too long. He wanted to ask the shamans when he and Armstrong would be allowed to leave, but he knew it would be useless. They would just ignore him as always.

Aldrin ignored the sweat beads dripping off his forehead and onto his eyelids and thought of El-Baz. The inner circle of the Apollo Program called El-Baz "the King." This had always mystified Aldrin until that first secret meeting in his office, the one during which he was told about the harsh ordeal that would follow. Since January of 1964 Aldrin had undergone rigorous examinations and torture tests at Wright-Patterson Air Force Base, among other high-security locations, in order to prove his worth to the program. He and two others, Armstrong and Collins, had somehow risen above the twenty-five other semifinalists to land the cream of the NASA assignments: the first flight to the moon. After such an ordeal it was somewhat disconcerting to learn that he would have to begin the process all over again; that what he had believed to be the top of the pyramid was, in fact, the base.

Such an analogy was appropriate, since El-Baz was rather fond of comparing the Apollo Program to the Great Pyramids in Egypt. In fact, El-Baz himself had grown up in Cairo; not only was his father a prominent Egyptologist, but he himself had an advanced degree in Egyptology as well. How El-Baz had gotten from Cairo to Cape Canaveral was mysterious to Aldrin, but he'd learned not to ask questions. Instead he just sat back and allowed the King to command his court. El-Baz seemed to believe the American space program was fulfilling some kind of ancient Egyptian prophecy involving Isis and Osiris.

One time Aldrin had wondered aloud in El-Baz's presence why the mission to the moon was named after the God of the Sun and not Diana, the Goddess of the Moon. For a moment he thought El-Baz might strike him as he softly advised Aldrin with a quivering voice to follow more orders and ask less questions.

It was Collins who later made the connection between Apollo and Osiris: both were gods of the sun. But why this was so important to the space program was utterly mystifying. Nevertheless, Aldrin did as the King suggested and stopped asking questions. He did as he was told and hoped to God he could reach the "proper degree of illumination" (as El-Baz often said) to enable him to reach the moon.

Aldrin turned his attention on the cloudless blue sky and wished Collins could be here with them. He had been the first and only casualty in El-Baz's "crash course in illumination." Collins had freaked out in the last week, just before reaching the 32nd degree, claiming his soul was being sucked away from him. He locked himself inside the test module and screamed for hours on end about demons ripping through his skin. Apparently these were flashbacks from the LSD tests in the isolation tanks. It was too bad, but perhaps for the best. After all, they couldn't risk taking a potentially unstable personality all the way to the moon.

Aldrin used his free arm to shield his eyes from the sun. The sun: Apollo in his flaming chariot, streaking across the sky; Osiris and his consort staring down upon their faithful subjects, awaiting recognition. The Aeon of Osiris was the Aeon of Death.

And Death always demanded a sacrifice.

Armstrong squeaked in pain once more. Aldrin turned toward his friend just in time to see the final feather sliding into place. Blood soaked his arms and dripped toward his ribs in meandering streaks. Standing there erect, clad in nothing but the panorama of the sky behind him, blue-white-black-brown-red feathers lodged into his sunburned skin, he looked like some kind of lost demigod, the forgotten progeny of a midnight tryst between a Greek god and an innocent Indian maiden: The Winged White Warrior clothed in blood.

Aldrin felt a strange yearning in his gut, an alien passion building within his groin. His penis became erect as he imagined yielding to the majestic man before him, melding with mythology in one extended second of pure ecstasy: Osiris and Apollo locked in a passionate embrace. *Ah, yes....*

For the first time in many hours the shaman revealed an actual emotion; he glanced down at Aldrin's erection, cleared his throat, and laughed slightly. Aldrin felt his cheeks flushing. Luckily, his back was to Armstrong. His erection remained hidden. He focused on the vultures circling far overhead, hoping to keep his mind off such embarrassing matters.

The third shaman's chant reached a heightened pitch, as if he were echoing the racing heartbeats of both Aldrin and Armstrong. The final feather was at last shoved into Aldrin's shoulder. Though the experience had been painful indeed, he felt like thanking the Indian. After all, this ritual would enable him to conquer the sky.

Aldrin opened his mouth to say something to the old man. "Hey, look, I know I don't know your name or anything, but I just want to th—" The words were cut short when the old man shoved his fingers into Aldrin's mouth. Something circular was placed on his tongue, something hard and rough like old leather with about as much taste. The old man removed his fingers, then told him to chew. Aldrin was reluctant at first, but then turned and saw that Armstrong was undergoing the same treatment. This was clearly part of the ritual.

He bit into the object and winced at the bitter taste. After awhile chewing became an enormous chore, for his whole mouth had grown numb; he felt as if a dentist had just injected him with Novocain. Nevertheless he forced himself to keep moving his jaw up and down, until at last the object had been shredded to numerous flaccid strips. The old man gave him a cup of water and told him to spit out the remains. Aldrin tried to swirl the water in his mouth, but was afraid he might swallow. He'd lost almost all control over his mouth. Instead of spitting out the remains, he crouched down and let the water dribble onto the desert floor. He felt like sitting, but the Indian grabbed him by the shoulders and urged him to rise.

Rise....

Aldrin felt the world slipping away from him. Time seemed to slow down. He was already sixty feet in the air before he realized he could no longer feel his arms flapping.

Early on July 16th, 1969, the morning after the girls cut off their hair and buried it in the desert to prove the death of their egos, Charlie ordered his family out of the Spahn Ranch to avoid the Black Panther raids that would no doubt descend upon them any day now. Charlie didn't want to be caught unawares. If he'd learned anything during his life spent behind bars it was that the niggers were bloodthirsty and unforgiving, more dangerous in packs than alone.

Unlike in prison, however, Charlie now had an intricate network of friends here in Southern California, friends who possessed secret knowledge—knowledge they didn't mind sharing with Charlie as long as he did them a few favors in return. He'd received a rather disturbing message this morning. Apparently the final black/white war was set to begin August 1st. This was bad news, for it gave him less than three weeks to uncover the Hole in the desert that would lead his family to the vast underground city spoken of in Hopi Indian legend. While the blacks and whites warred above ground the family would groove on each other in the Hole, living off food-trees and chocolate fountains until it was time to emerge and live in peace amidst the ruins of the apocalypse. It was a foolproof plan. Sad the rest of the people in the world were too ignorant to think of it themselves.

In order to keep a careful lookout for possible advance scouts sent by the Black Panthers, Charlie stole Doris Day's telescope from Melcher's house in Malibu and lugged it with him on his trip to an isolated area three miles up Devil's Canyon. The area was located deep in the woods off a fire road. Many of these fire roads led to the

Pacific. If worse came to worse, if the Hole remained undiscovered, Charlie planned to use these roads to escape any army, black or white, that might attack their desert paradise. One of Charlie's "special" friends, an old man involved in Los Angeles politics, had given him a master key to the fire roads in exchange for a simple blowjob. Some perverts would do just about anything for a suck.

Charlie and his family roared down one of these fire roads in four dune buggies covered in expensive ocelot furs (stolen from the mother of a family member) and spray painted swastika-like symbols used by the Process Church of the Final Judgment. In the back of the dune buggy lay machine guns mounted on pivots. They had covered the guns with large parachutes just in case the jeeps were being tracked by the authorities. Only the day before, a helicopter had hovered over the ranch for far too long. It had made Charlie uneasy, one of many reasons for this sudden exodus.

Around noon Charlie ordered his family to turn onto a short driveway that led to the campsite. They halted long enough to camouflage the entrance with brush, then continued on. Charlie imagined himself to be Moses leading the children of Israel out of Egypt. Unlike with the kikes, however, Charlie's family wouldn't wander around in the desert for forty years. The Promised Land was only a few feet away.

Though not as majestic as the underground city inside the Hole, this clearing would serve their purposes for now. It would be a perfect site for the ritual, the "favor" he'd promised his friends. Charlie had brought along his favorite kids in order to help with this most delicate operation: Bruce Davis, Bobby Beausoleil, Danny De Carlo, Tex Watson, Bill Vance, Mark Walts, Stephanie Rowe, Linda Kasabian, Gypsy, Ella, Sadie, Mary, Ouish and a host of others. About twenty in all.

They all squeaked with delight when they caught their first glimpse of the idyllic little field covered by a soft carpet of grass, almost enclosed by a barrier of trees. Their own private Garden of Eden.

In the center of the clearing was a birch tree that would work quite well as a tent pole. Charlie ordered some of his girls to begin setting up the tent, while others draped a parachute over the dune buggies in case yet more curious helicopters decided to fly overhead.

As he watched his family working diligently, Charlie wondered which of them he would honor with the privilege of becoming a sacrifice. He would need two volunteers: a male and a female to represent the androgynous *nagari* in the alchemical process. He knew the volunteers would make themselves known to him when the time was right. He trusted the universe, and in turn the universe trusted him.

All was.

Up.

Up through the misty interior of a tall and multilayered cumulonimbus cloud that appeared to ascend forever and ever.

Up.

Up through a violent storm located in the troposphere. Angry gusts of wind attempted to knock Aldrin off course more than once, yet he struggled on valiantly, even while bolts of lightning threatened to cleave him in two. The bolts shot past so closely he felt he could reach out and absorb the energy into his body, or perhaps wield the bolts like spears.

By degrees he managed to leave the storm behind him as he worked his way up through the stratosphere; up through delicate, puffy white patches of clouds and into a surprisingly pleasant, sunny area. It was almost like crossing a thin barrier separating the worst of the planet's winters—perhaps stored up here by a celestial intelligence once they were through wreaking havoc on the ground—from the best of its summers. But even this passed away after a time as Aldrin flew ever onward, gradually finding himself shivering in the coolness of the mesosphere, quite a dramatic change from what he'd experienced only seconds before. The coolness tapered off, then disappeared altogether to be replaced by a blazing heat in the exosphere. Fortunately, the heat was fairly tolerable, enabling him to continue soaring. He darted through it quick enough that it didn't do too much damage to his flesh.

Aldrin smiled, thinking of the empty rocket that would be leaving the launch pad at Cape Canaveral six months from now. On one hand he felt bad for deceiving the American people, but he knew full well they could not be made aware of the essential role that ritual magick played within the space program. Aldrin wished the public could be as mature as his fellow initiates, but the time wasn't right. El-Baz had explained the situation to his satisfaction, and El-Baz was never wrong.

Aldrin and Armstrong left the atmosphere side by side. To Aldrin, no one had ever really seen the stars until gazing upon them without the annoying barrier of an atmosphere blocking one's view. Aldrin was tempted to ignore the moon, simply allow himself to be carried off into the stars' waiting embrace. But one thought of El-Baz's stern, dark face caused him to reject such fantasies, and to continue toward the rocky moon....

For the first time in Aldrin's life illumination was coming beneath him (from Earth) rather than from above. It was a strange effect. When he faced forward his vision was obscured by darkness; when he glanced over his shoulder he found himself blinded by intense light. Earth appeared now to be a mere black dot, one side outlined by a silver arch, the other drifting off into misty obscurity. Aldrin couldn't believe he'd been standing on the surface of that dot only a short while ago.

Aldrin and Armstrong's journey actually took 169 days, though it seemed far, far less. Never once did they experience thirst or hunger. Their direction altered at such a slow pace that it was impossible to know the exact moment when they began soaring downward. The mysterious structures El-Baz had warned them about soon became visible. A 30-mile-high crystalline dome loomed up from the crater-scarred surface like a tattered fragment of a forgotten myth. The dome was a truncated icosahedron pocked by massive holes. Years past, the abandoned domes were no doubt ripped asunder by ferocious meteor showers. Aldrin and Armstrong now flew toward one of these holes. Once they'd flown within a distance that enabled them to study the ashy gray deadness of the lunar surface with some amount of clarity, Aldrin saw a series of castle-like structures located miles past the dome. They too seemed to be in badly need of repair. With the heightened curiosity of a school boy, Aldrin wished he and Armstrong could explore the millennia-old ruins. But their mission was a very specific one. El-Baz had advised them against straying from the script.

Of course, El-Baz had advised them on many matters before allowing them to make this journey. At one point Aldrin had asked him how he expected them to breathe in the airlessness of space. El-Baz had simply smiled (a rare occurrence) and told him to read "The Unparalleled Adventure of One Hans Pfall" by Edgar Allan Poe. From this story Aldrin soon learned a little-known scientific fact: "the expansion and compression of chest, commonly called breathing, is action purely muscular, and the *cause*, not the *effect*, of respiration." In a vacuum, therefore, the normal human body would "become habituated to the want of atmospheric pressure," and "the sensations of pain would gradually diminish."

"I find that hard to believe," Aldrin had said to the King.

El-Baz patted him on the back in that patronizing manner of his and told him to go home and wrap a plastic bag around his head if he didn't believe it.

Aldrin did so and was surprised to find himself in fine condition after three whole hours. Death by suffocation, it appeared, was merely a psychosomatic condition.

Yes, El-Baz had taught them quite a bit, which was why Aldrin was more than willing to listen to his advice not to disturb the ruins of the ancient civilization that had called this moon home before the destruction of the twelfth planet and the resultant pole shifts on the moon and Mars approximately sixty-five million years ago.

Aldrin and Armstrong alighted upon the eastern edge of Tranquility Base at twenty-three degrees west and zero degrees latitude on July 20th, 1969, a most special date for Farouk El-Baz and all those who worshipped the Egyptian god of resurrection: the day of Osiris' helical return over the pyramids at Giza, the day that Isis (represented by Sirius, the brightest star in the sky) was located at 19.5 degrees above the southeastern horizon. Over and over again El-Baz had drilled into Aldrin's head the following statement: the Egyptian hieroglyph for Isis was an equilateral triangle meaning "a doorway."

The touchdown was gentle. Aldrin sank to his knees and pressed his palms against the pebbles and rock fragments littering the desolate landscape. He glanced left and right, backwards and forwards, seeing only a horizon that dropped away on all sides. Then he turned his attention toward the sky. It was strangely fuzzy, as if he were looking back at the blue globe of Earth through dust-smeared glass—which, of course, he was.

Armstrong touched Aldrin on the shoulder and said, "We should get ready for the ceremony. We can't be late."

Aldrin nodded reluctantly, knowing full well that his companion was right. He wished he could just sit here and soak in the majestic desolation of the moon. But they had a mission to accomplish, a ceremony to consecrate.

It didn't take them long to find Surveyor III, the unmanned spacecraft that had landed on the moon in 1967 not long after El-Baz had been hired at NASA by a geologist named Ed Nixon, the brother of President Richard Nixon. Surveyor III alighted upon the moon on April 20th, a very special day: the birthday of Adolf Hitler. The moon was square with Saturn on April 20th, 1889. Sun trine Jupiter: the will to expand.

Yes, the will to expand, El-Baz, had said, *to the stars, if necessary.*

Armstrong discovered the secret cache within Surveyor III: the hidden chalice and vial. The chalice was made of pure silver, the vial of clear glass through which Aldrin and Armstrong could see no more than fifty milliliters of a swirling crimson liquid. The vial was no longer than one's little finger.

Once the chalice and vial were safely in hand, the two astronauts took to the air and flew back to Tranquility Base. At 3:50 P.M. Eastern Standard Time, Aldrin and Armstrong sat cross-legged amidst the "magnificent desolation" of the temple site to Isis. Aldrin whispered, "I am the wine and you are the branches," as he poured the blood of Christ into the chalice. Once the vial was empty he handed the chalice to Armstrong, who had been promised the first sip. They passed it back and forth, back and forth, until it was empty at last.

Aldrin's mouth became numb once again. He heard a voice whispering inside his head. *Rise.* The shaman? *Rise.* Armstrong uncrossed his legs and kneeled on the harsh terrain. *Rise.* Armstrong did the same. *Rise.* Aldrin felt a strange yearning in his gut, an alien passion building within his groin. *Rise. His penis became erect as he imagined yielding to the majestic man before him, melding with mythology in one extended second of pure ecstasy: Osiris and Apollo locked in a passionate embrace. Ah, yes....*

Silently, a fissure opened in the ground, a crack just large enough to accept Aldrin's penis. He fucked the moon mother, fucked her raw as Armstrong mounted his companion. Unconsciously, Aldrin had been preparing for this moment for years. Everything was so clear now. It was no coincidence that his mother's maiden name was

Marion Moon. This day had been planned since before his birth. The Winged White Warrior slipped his penis into Aldrin's rectum. The moon mother sighed and screamed at once, the *kalas* of a holy trinity ripping through her skin.

"But what will we do after we've completed the Communion service?" Aldrin asked El-Baz.

"Oh, you'll know," the King replied. "In a true magickal ritual, you must give yourself up to destiny."

Aldrin shook his head and laughed. "I don't want to be rude, sir, but do you know how crazy this sounds? I mean, we're involved in a historical moment here. Do you think we should really muck it up with all this... I don't know, mystical hoo-ha?"

El-Baz didn't shout or smile or respond in any way for quite some time... until at last he whispered sternly, "History is a magickal ritual. Where would we be without it? Stuck in the primordial goo, trying to figure out how to evolve limbs and lungs. Listen: we wouldn't be here without magickal ritual."

Aldrin sank his fingers into the rocks and closed his eyes and saw before him a tall bearded man with a hood drawn low over his face. He cast no shadow. A pair of ravens sat perched on either shoulder. The man knelt down beside Aldrin and whispered in his ear. Between his groans, Aldrin repeated what he heard.

"Bone to bone, blood to blood, flesh to flesh. Moved by the desire to create, from this hour our bodies are one."

Armstrong used his fingernails to scrape three trails of blood into his own bare chest. *Marks-of-Joy.* In a quaking voice he said, "With this blood, I devote, hollow, and sanctify my soul to the gods who live."

Simultaneously, Aldrin echoed the words of the Bringer-of-Ecstasy.

Awake, there is distance to conquer and space to shape.

Lebensraum... Sun trine Jupiter... the will to expand....

The Bringer-of-Ecstasy gouged out Aldrin's right eye with his fingers. Aldrin opened his mouth, slowly, slowly—*the camera lights and flashbulbs glared, but not one of them flinched... we'll probably never know how long the pharoahs' slaves took to build the pyramids... it was as if in making the selection the country had merely gone to a secret fraternity of self-assured superpilots who had made it through the mysterious door... the physical and psychological torture tests at Wright-Patterson... when the door appears, it is on the frontier between the visible and the invisible...*

　　　　　　　　　　　　　　　　　　　　ROBERT GUFFEY

for the door is never in the same place... it is constantly in motion... but all the candidates knew that everything we said was being scrutinized, even at parties... on one occasion it may appear on a mountain summit... a satellite going from north to south, probably in a polar orbit... Schirra played "Jingle Bells" on his harmonica... on another occasion it may appear in the depths of the sea... several hours later, Neil and Dave were aboard the destroyer Mason, *seasick but otherwise okay... to locate the door, look for The-Bridge-of-Opaque-Colors... I am the wine and you are the branches... the rainbow that is saturated with beauty... beautiful, beautiful, magnificent desolation*—and screamed with the borrowed voice of the Bringer-of-Ecstasy.

A few yards in front of him Aldrin could see the rim of a large crater. A white light shot up over the rim. The light coalesced into a portal, a doorway.

Armstrong dug his bloody fingers into Aldrin's thighs and shuddered with pleasure as he melted into his blood brother.

Something emerged from the door....

The family arranged themselves in a circle. As always Charlie sat in the center, singing a song. This time it was "Cease to Exist," which the Beach Boys had stolen from him and released as "Never Learn Not to Love" on the B-side of a 1968 single. Unfortunately, they changed the words "cease to exist" to "cease to resist," thus excising the vital Luciferian message of the song. If only they had left the words the same, the single would have been a chartbuster. Charlie was certain of it.

As he crooned the words, "I never had a lesson I ever learned/But I know we all get our turn/And I love you," Mark Walts suddenly released a cry of horror and leaped up from the circle, ruining the song. A large spider crawled up his arm. *Creepy-crawly*, Charlie thought. For the one second that Charlie saw the spider, he communed with it, became one with it, saw the world through its eyes. Then the decisive moment came: Mark slapped the spider off his arm. It fell to the grass and tried to scurry away, but Mark crushed it beneath his boot. This was the sign for which Charlie had been waiting.

Charlie threw his guitar aside and rushed the sixteen-year-old boy. He slapped him upside the head. "What the hell do you think you're doing?"

The boy cringed. "I-I'm sorry, I was scared."

"*Scared?*" Charlie pointed at the spider. "And you don't think she was scared?" He knelt down beside the insect, used his fingertip to caress its crushed body. He tried to will the spider back to life, but it was no use. It was beyond saving.

He glanced up at the boy, fire in his eyes. *Flame-Eyed-One.* "Better a human being," he whispered.

The boy glanced from side to side, as if looking for support from the rest of the family. He found none. They were all frowning at him. Charlie rose to his feet, pulled the .45 from his belt. He unlocked the safety and waved the revolver in front of the boy's face. "Has a spider ever polluted the earth? Has a spider ever killed?"

The boy's lower lip quivered. He wouldn't speak.

"Answer me!"

The boy whispered a single word: "No."

"But *you* just killed. You're a big man now. A killer of insects. Maybe you'd like to try your hand at bigger game." Charlie held the gun out to Mark.

The boy reached out tentatively, as if Charlie might pull the weapon away at any moment. Charlie urged him on with a nod. Mark grabbed the gun by the handle. He stared at it through confused eyes, as if he wasn't sure what to do with it.

"Go on," Charlie said, sinking to his knees. He pulled open his buckskin vest and tipped his head back, as if accepting a Communion wafer. "Christ said, 'My prophecy upon this wasted earth and upon the corrupt creation that squats upon its ruined surface is: THOU SHALT KILL.'" He giggled like a little child.

Mark shook his head back and forth. "No, Charlie, I can't hurt you."

"You're a big boy now. You must kill what you love."

"No!" Mark threw the gun onto the ground. He covered his head with his hands. "I can't," he whispered.

Charlie sighed. On his hands and knees, creepy-crawly style, he inched his way toward the fallen gun. He picked it up, checked to see if the safety was still off. "Too bad," he said. "I guess that means I have to kill *you* instead. Creepy-crawly."

"Creepy-crawly," the family echoed softly, rising to their feet. Some withdrew their hunting knives.

Mark had removed his hands from his eyes. He began to back away toward the woods. "No," he said, searching the eyes of his friends

ROBERT GUFFEY

for even one sympathetic soul. "I love you." It was clear from his tone that he didn't mean just Charlie. He was referring to all of them.

"We love you too," Charlie said. "The spider loved you. You did her a favor, we'll do you a favor. Never learn not to love, Mark. Cease to exist." He laughed self-consciously, then his lips curled into a snarl. "Cease to resist. The transition will be so much easier."

Tears filled Mark's eyes as the girls began reciting Charlie's poem "Never Say Never to Always" in an eerie sing-song that sounded somewhat like a nursery rhyme.

> *Always is always forever*
> *As one is one is one*
> *Inside yourself for your father*
> *All is none all is none all is none*
> *It's time to drop all from behind us*
> *The illusion has been just a dream*
> *The Valley of Death may not find us*
> *Now as then on a sunshine beam*
> *So bring only your perfection*
> *For then life will surely be*
> *No cold no fear no hunger*
> *You can see you can see you can see*

They advanced on the boy, the hot sunlight glinting off the steel blades in their hands. Mark bolted and ran.

This was his second mistake—for Mark, at least. For Charlie it was a blessing. His family needed the practice for the war that was surely coming.

Bruce Davis was the first to pursue the boy. Charlie stopped Bruce before he could get very far. He grabbed him by the shoulder, swung him around. "No." He turned toward the other family members, snapped his fingers and pointed at the fleeing boy. The family charged after him, some of them laughing, some of them screaming.

Charlie patted Bruce on the shoulders and stared into his dull, stoic eyes. With his shoulder-length hair and unkempt beard, he sort of looked like Charlie. Some people even called him Manson II.

Bruce was reliable and had done good work for him in the past. Hell, he'd proven himself long before he'd even met Charlie—perhaps beginning with Cheri Jo Bates on October 30th, 1966. He could very well have started his work even earlier. Charlie didn't know everything about Bruce, but he knew enough to be impressed by the Zodiac-killer-cover he had used to obscure the true motives of his crimes. Charlie was hoping to utilize a similar cover for the murders that were to come. Something to do with the damn Black Panthers, perhaps.

Charlie could feel the kill-lust surging just beneath Bruce's skin. His muscles were tense, more than ready for action. For *creepy-crawly.*

Charlie whispered in Bruce's ear, "You'll get your piece of the lamb, don't worry. Hop in one of the dune buggies and meet us on the fire road."

Bruce appeared as if he wanted to break away from Charlie's grasp and pursue the prey on foot. He restrained himself. He nodded once, his face never betraying any emotion whatsoever. In paradise, Bruce would make a perfect slave.

As Bruce headed toward one of the dune buggies, Charlie darted off into the woods. Despite his late start, he quickly overtook the other family members. His stubby legs could move faster than most people expected. He fancied himself a wolverine in human form—short, cunning, ferocious.

Charlie felt for the revolver in his holster, making sure it was there just in case he was forced to eliminate his prey from a distance. He preferred to meet Death head-on, up close and personal. Death, like sex, was an intimate experience. It should be handled slowly and unselfishly. One's friends should be invited to join in. This eliminates all forms of jealousy and helps to destroy the ego. All vital fluids should merge into one continuous stream, like a river in which a family can bathe as a sacrament to oneness.

Mark's problem was his inability to share with the others. He was an outsider in more ways than one. If he wanted to inflict pain, he should have asked someone's permission. Anyone in the family could have told him that killing an insect, or any non-human animal, was the ultimate sin.

Mark's first mistake was stepping on the spider. His second mistake, of course, was running from his fate. It would be much more painful this way.

But "mistake" was a subjective word. At the moment, from his constricted viewpoint, Mark probably thought it had been a mistake. From Charlie's enlightened perch he knew that Mark would thank him in the afterlife, for Mark's soul would sit at a table of heroes amidst all those who had died for a higher purpose.

At 12:05 P.M., on July 20th, 1969, Charlie and nineteen members of his family charged through the woods searching for their prey. Charlie was armed with the .45-caliber revolver, which sat in a holster on his hip, a twelve-inch Bowie knife strapped to his ankle, and a very special weapon that lay in a scabbard on his back: a two-foot ceremonial sword given to him by George Knowl, a member of the infamous biker gang The Straight Satans. (Knowl had assured him, "This is the same sword Wilfred Smith gave to Jack Parsons over fifteen years ago, man. Most people think this sword got destroyed when Parsons blew himself to bits back in '52, but they're fuckin' wrong. This is history I'm holdin' in my hands, Charlie, pure fuckin' *history*.") Charlie could feel the power of the sword surging through his blood.

He halted for a moment, crouched in the grass, sniffed the air. The prey wasn't far away. Mark thought if he reached the fire road he might be able to flag down a passing car. Charlie smiled. This was most unlikely, as the hunt was destined to succeed.

He heard Bobby calling his name—somewhere from the left. Charlie giggled. Yes, the left hand path. *Vama Marg*.

Charlie met up with Bobby near a birch tree on the side of the road. Bobby pointed at the empty road with his knife. "I saw him head out that way," he said, almost out of breath.

Charlie scanned the road and the surrounding woods with the intentness of a coyote, searching for the slightest sign of movement. Suddenly, he heard a scream. From the opposite side of the road, about ten yards away, a disheveled boy emerged from the trees pursued by a giggling Ouish. Though one of the youngest in the family, she could lose herself to death as well as any of them.

Mark ran into the middle of the road. At first it seemed as if he might dash back into the woods until he saw Gypsy and Ella emerge with knives raised. Since the woods were blocked to him on both sides, he continued running down the middle of the road.

Many yards behind Mark, Bruce appeared in Charlie's command dune buggy. Charlie ordered him out of the car. He slid behind the steering wheel, took off down the road, roared past Ouish, Gypsy and Ella. Charlie thought of the broken corpse of the beautiful spider. He thought of Fields, the supervisor at the Indiana School for Boys. He thought of Fields' favorite leather strap: three feet long, four inches wide, as thick as the first pencil-thin-dick Charlie was forced to suck at the age of thirteen in that most Christian of reform schools. The school had managed to do its job quite well. It had instilled in Charlie the cardinal tenet of Christianity: Thou shalt not kill... except for those who deserve it most. Fields' gravelly laugh, the sound of the wind whistling through the holes cut into the strap, the face of the sixteen-year-old boy who raped him in the feed bin while the guards stood and watched: all these images fed the fire in Charlie's mind as he rammed the dune buggy into Mark's back. Charlie heard a loud *crack* as the boy fell to the ground. He ran over him with both the front and back tires on the left side of the car. Charlie came to an abrupt halt about twenty feet away, then spun around so he could have another go at the boy.

Sweet Stephanie Rowe stumbled out of the woods and screamed when she saw Mark's body. She was only fourteen; she hadn't lived long enough to shed her fear of death as Charlie had inside a dozen penitentiaries. Fortunately, she was about to receive a crash course in such matters.

Ella and Gypsy tried to calm Stephanie. She thrashed wildly in their arms, broke away from them, ran to Mark. She knelt down beside him, caressed his head. He whispered something to her.

He was still alive.

Stephanie turned to the other family members and screamed, "What're you doing? I thought this was just a game. I thought we were all just playing a game."

Charlie pressed his moccasin-clad foot against the pedal and headed straight for Mark's crumpled body. For a moment Stephanie seemed as if she would remain in place no matter what, dune buggy bedamned. Charlie would have respected her for that. It would have meant she had risen above the fear that kept the piggies so enthralled.

But at the last second Stephanie scrambled to her feet and darted out of the way like a desert lizard. The dune buggy rolled over Mark at a terribly high speed. The resultant bump caused Charlie to leap into the air a few inches. He released a triumphant laugh, a sound like a whip slashing through air.

He slammed on the brakes, jumped out of the car. Bruce stood over the body, tipped his head to one side as if scrutinizing a dead bird. "Not dead yet," he said in his usual monotone, then pulled out his .22 caliber Iver Johnson and shot the boy three times in the chest.

Stephanie screamed.

Bruce turned to Charlie, nodded his head once. "He's dead now, I think."

Charlie performed an impromptu ritualistic dance around the body while singing a few lines from one of his songs: "I had a little monkey/And I sent him to the country/And I fed him on gingerbread/Along come a choo-choo/And knocked my monkey coo-coo/And now my monkey's dead."

Ella, Ouish and Gypsy laughed and clapped.

Stephanie released a howl of pain and leaped on Charlie, slashing at his face with her knife. She managed to cut him across his right temple before Bruce tackled her, pinned her to the ground.

Charlie tensed for a moment when he heard the sound of approaching vehicles. The vehicles rounded the nearby bend about a hundred feet behind them, and he saw they were only the dune buggies from his own battalion. Danny, Tex, and Sadie must have decided to retrieve them from the camp site.

Charlie bent down to pick up the fallen knife.

Sadie and the others leaped out of the vehicles. Sadie asked Charlie if he was all right.

Charlie just smiled. "Of course I'm all right. I can't die, nothing can die." He reached up to pull the long hair out of his face. When he lowered his hand, his palm was stained with blood. He frowned for a moment, then tossed the knife to Tex. "Show Stephanie. Show her how nothing can die."

Tex didn't hesitate. He knelt down beside her and poked her in the neck with the tip of the knife, drawing only a small amount of blood. This caused Stephanie to scream even louder than before. Bruce straddled her thighs, pinned her wrists to the ground.

Sadie asked her politely to quiet down as she stuffed a handkerchief in her mouth. "You don't want someone to hear us and ruin the fun, do you?"

Charlie turned to Ouish and said, "What's your time?"

Ouish withdrew a silver pocket watch she'd stolen from one of the many Bel Air piggies who liked to invite them up to their hillside pads for an orgy—and maybe even a beating or two if they were so inclined. "12:22," she said.

"Take it slow," he told Tex. "Drag it out as long as possible. I'll tell you when to finish it."

"Shouldn't we take her into the woods?" Sadie said, glancing overhead as if searching for invisible spies.

"There's no need for that shit," Charlie said. "We won't be disturbed. The only person who can see us right now is the man in the moon—and believe me, he won't tell. He's much, much too busy."

Charlie laughed. Everyone else laughed too, though they couldn't possibly understand the joke.

Charlie climbed into the back of the dune buggy. He popped open a warm can of Coca-Cola, dug into a brown paper bag for a peanut butter sandwich, and watched as the family took turns raping the girl. Bruce went first, slicing her in the neck as he fucked her. Charlie had to keep yelling his name to prevent him from losing himself to the ecstasy and ruining the entire operation. Bruce was forced to cut deep gouges in his own thigh to help himself climax without fatally knifing the girl.

Meanwhile Charlie sat on his four-wheeled throne, wielding his sword like a royal sceptre, and uttered the name of the next lucky participant.

Tex.

Then Bobby.

Then Sadie.

Then both Ouish and Ella.

Charlie watched the seconds fly by on the silver pocket watch. Sometime around 12:30, between Bobby and Tex, the girl stopped trying to scream. She closed her eyes and whispered incomprehensible words over and over again.

At 12:33 she stopped moving at all. She just stared up at the sky. She opened her mouth, but no sound came.

While Gypsy performed cunnilingus on the girl Bruce and Bobby sliced open Stephanie's stomach and abdomen. Bruce wanted to go further, but Charlie ordered him to back away. He told Linda to lap up the blood from the girl's stomach. She did so without hesitation. He tapped his sword against the side of the jeep and told Mary to rip out the girl's uterus once Linda was through consuming the *ojas* of her blood.

The rest of the family descended upon the blood. A mass of white flesh swept over the girl, desiring just a fraction of her *kala*. The family became one through the consumption of her essence. Charlie could feel their endless ecstasy rolling over him in tangible waves. Parsons' sword heated up slowly, burning the palm of his right hand.

At exactly 12:50 Charlie leaped down from the dune buggy, cut Stephanie's throat with his hunting knife, slicing from left to right.

Then plunged Parsons' sword into her heart.

Instead of blood, a white light shot up out of the wound. The light coalesced into a portal, a doorway about twelve feet tall and eight feet wide. It drifted away from the body and began to float down the road.

Charlie ordered everyone back into their vehicles. "Follow that light!" he said frantically.

The family climbed into the dune buggies, five to each vehicle. With Charlie in the lead, standing behind the machine gun mount and pointing at the light with Parsons' sword, the vehicles roared down the road toward the fleeing light.

"Faster!" Charlie urged. "Faster, *faster!*"

Charlie's Dune Buggy Attack Battalion sped into the white light and emerged on the eastern edge at Tranquility Base on the Earth's moon: twenty-three degrees west and zero latitude. Charlie couldn't quite believe his eyes, but knew exactly where he was when he saw a white man fucking another white man up the ass near the edge of an immense crater.

For a second the two men resembled all the "supervisors" at the Indiana School for Boys who had ever fucked Charlie up the ass. Just two more hypocritical, self-righteous Blue Meanies with too much power. All the piggies had to die, so why not these two as well?

Charlie's "friends" had asked for a rite of blood in order to balance the cosmic forces disrupted by the rape of the moon mother. The more blood the better. After all, the Aeon of Osiris was the Aeon of Death.

Charlie swiveled the machine gun mount toward the white men. He snapped his fingers and pointed at the targets with his sword. Sadie, Ouish, and Linda let fly a barrage of bullets into the astronaut's sky-clad torsos, blood and flesh spraying outward and coating the nearby crater. Charlie joined the massacre with his own shower of lead, blowing apart the skulls of the dumb piggies at the exact moment they turned around to see the terror that was approaching. The stupid expressions plastered on their faces just before their skulls blew apart into a thousand shards was worth all three years of Fields' whippings. Their expressions looked something like this: *Friggin' hippies on the moon?*

"Damn straight you fucking squares," Charlie uttered beneath his breath. "Grok this." He continued to propel bullets into their bodies long after they had already been mangled into formless piles of meat.

Charlie released his finger from the trigger, wiped the sweat from his brow with the back of his hand, exhaled noisily. "Whew! Looks like we're gonna have us a barbecue on the moon, what do you say?"

From the rest of the family came a string of: "Hey, that's cool, man," "Far out," "Like, trippy."

The family discovered that the moon possessed an atmosphere, for the blood-stained matches in Tex's pocket lit up fine when Charlie struck it across a lunar rock.

"Hey, my science teacher told me you couldn't light nothin' on the moon," Tex said.

"Your science teacher was wrong," Charlie said, holding the match up as if to prove the point. "I bet your science teacher didn't say shit about that glass dome up there neither. What the fuck did your science teacher know?"

Tex had no response.

Bruce and Danny kicked the bodies into the nearby crater, created a makeshift spit out of the telescope tripod in Charlie's dune buggy, then set it up over a fire that they lit in the bottom of the crater. As Bruce rotated Aldrin over the fire, the rest of the family formed a circle around him.

Charlie pulled out his guitar from the back of the dune buggy, sat Indian-style near the fire. "Now what was we talkin' about?" he said.

"'Cease to Exist,'" Sadie said.

"Oh, that's right." Charlie resumed the song right where he left off. Everyone else joined in: "Submission is a gift/Go on, give it to your brother/Love and understanding is for one another/I'm your kind, I'm your mind/I'm your brother/I never had a lesson I ever learned/But I know we all get our turn/And I love you." They had never sounded better. The acoustics on the moon were perfect.

ROBERT GUFFEY

By the time they had worked their way through "Sick City," "Garbage Dump," and "Eyes of a Dreamer," Aldrin was just about done. Bruce took the liberty to slice him up into fourteen different pieces. As Charlie nibbled on the penis, he reflected on the poetic irony of the situation: no doubt Aldrin had believed himself to be winning the favor of Osiris, not realizing that Asar (Osiris, the dead) "reflects the Fool, that is the Hidden Light that is 'A' between I and O (Isis and Osiris)," as the occultist Kenneth Grant once told Charlie at The Spiral Staircase, a hip hush-hush occult hangout in Topanga Canyon.

Of course, there's nothing more foolish than getting eaten by a bunch of "friggin' hippies on the moon," Charlie thought, pulling a strip of burnt flesh from between his teeth. He held his thumb up to Bruce Davis and winked.

After dinner the family wandered around on the lunar surface, just checking out the scene, seeing what was cooking (besides Aldrin and Armstrong). They were quite dumbfounded by the giant glass towers miles away.

"Dig those crazy castles," Gypsy said. "Can we look at them, Charlie? Huh, can we?"

Charlie permitted them to explore. With his guitar strapped over one shoulder, his magic sword lying in the scabbard on his back, the family rode toward the strange castle that seemed to be millennia-old, if not older still. The moon was silent, desolate, and as cold as Death Valley at night. In many ways it reminded Charlie of the first time he set eyes on the Spahn Ranch and knew he would call it home. Perhaps they didn't need to find the underground world of the Hopi Indians. Perhaps they'd found paradise right here.

Charlie was glad he'd agreed to help the Caput Mortuum and her Order in this way, otherwise he might never have witnessed this weird and wonderful landscape. Not only that, but he'd also gotten a good meal out of it and balanced the cosmic forces in the process. It was always best to save the universe when you could profit from it, he wasn't ashamed to admit it.

Charlie prided himself on his honesty. He couldn't stand hypocrites like Yul Brynner, Peter Sellers, Steve McQueen and all the other Hollywood big shots who'd paid his family to have sex with them on camera. Charlie was upfront about his "perversity." Why be ashamed of it? Charlie had managed to break down all the artificial barriers in his mind. He was *clear.*

All was.

They rode lazily across the sandy terrain for about twenty minutes, singing their favorite songs from "The Magical Mystery Tour." Abruptly Bruce stopped singing in the middle of "Strawberry Fields" and pointed up at a window in the highest tower of the castle.

"I thought I saw something moving up there."

"Then you must have damn good eyesight," Charlie said.

Bruce shrugged. "S'okay. Why don't you use Doris Day's telescope to see what's doin' up there?"

"I didn't bring it with me. It's still in the dune buggy."

"No, I think Sadie's playing with it. Sadie!"

Sadie popped her head out from between Linda and Gypsy in the back of the vehicle. She was twirling the telescope in the air as if it were a baton.

"Don't play with that, you bitch!" Charlie yelled and snatched it out of the air. "That's Doris Day's spyglass, fachrissakes!" Sadie began pouting. "And don't pout neither! We don't have time for that shit!"

Charlie lifted the telescope to his eye, peered at the high window, and saw someone waving back at him from the high crystalline tower.

Someone he'd seen before.

The man was thin and tall with a long gray beard that almost touched the middle of his chest. A hood was drawn low over his face, a dark robe covered his body. Charlie felt as if the telescope were peering into his own past.

He turned to Bruce and whispered, "Keep the others occupied. I'm going up there alone."

"But why—?"

"Just do it!" Charlie said. "I think I've got me some unfinished business up there."

Charlie left everything behind: his guitar, his spyglass, his dune buggy, his family. He walked across the desolate lunar landscape with nothing in his head except the vivid memory of a night that occurred twenty-two years ago, a night on which he discovered how to control pain through power, and power through fear. The night the fire in his stomach first erupted outward into his arms, down into his hands. Hands that could so easily... so easily....

It was much easier, however, when others killed for him. This was true control. True power.

ROBERT GUFFEY

It took Charlie a little over twenty minutes to reach the crystalline double doors that stood wide open at the base of the 1,000-foot tower. Charlie was reluctant to touch the walls, out of fear that they might crumble to fine dust. He passed through the doorway and entered a massive hall consisting of strange angles and mysterious protuberances that seemed to serve no useful purpose. He glanced up at the transparent ceiling and was fascinated by the fact that he could see up into the floors above. It looked as if the upper floors were paralyzed in free fall, trapped in time. The hall made Charlie feel disorientated, lost, alone. He didn't like these feelings. He'd spent his entire life trying to leave them far behind.

Fearing them.

This was not to be. He had to face his fears. Become one with them. One with paranoia. He had to become paranoia's mistress, love her, worship her, fuck her until she gave birth to metanoia. Total awareness.

Disorientated, lost, alone: Charlie approached a spiral glass staircase at the far end of the hall. Charlie's moccasins made no sound against the smooth, ice-cold floor. Tentatively, he pressed the tip of his foot against the first step; it did not break. He placed both feet on the step. He kept his eyes on the stairs as he ascended, watching the floor drop out beneath his feet. It was as if he were walking on the air itself. The son of man ascending.

He wound his way up the glass spiral, occasionally glancing to his right or left in order to take in the sights: all of it so similar, so predictable, so desert flat and limitless. It would be easy to gain complete control of such a kingdom. Perhaps Charlie himself could rule over it from this 1,000-foot crystalline tower.

With such thoughts slicing their way through his mind, Charlie approached the highest landing. From two stories down he was able to discern a dark mass moving about along the floor above. He felt like potential prey watching a shark through murky waters, apprehensive and fearful. This was good. The more fear he retained in his body, the more he had to use against others.

The dark mass became more distinctive as he neared the highest landing: a man in a dark robe pacing before a narrow window. At last Charlie reached the landing and placed his shaking hand on the knob. It turned before he even applied pressure to it, and the door swung inward.

The room beyond was rather large. It was completely empty except for its lone occupant, the Bringer-of-Ecstasy. The tall man turned and beckoned his guest forward.

Charlie took two steps, then paused. "Who—who are you?" he whispered, echoing words spoken twenty-two years before.

The man spread his arms out wide, as if to say that the answer was obvious. "Some call me the One-Who-Blinds-With-Death, others Father-of-The-Slain. I have many names. You may call me Bringer-of-Ecstasy."

At that moment Charlie knew he'd finally found the stranger who had guided him onto the Vama Marg using only a few well-chosen words in that darkened housing unit populated by young boys with vague, gray futures before them: maybe an unwanted child or two, a wife they'd smack around when it pleased them, a couple of impressive crimes (if they were lucky), accomplishments they could hold onto like faded photographs and show off to the other inmates in the federal reformatories that were their inevitable destiny. They would be assigned numbers. Become numbers. Unremarkable in every way. Unknown to the rest of the world.

Unlike Charlie.

Charlie had a far greater destiny laid out before him.

It had been shown to him in the power of a three pound, twelve inch iron bar pulled off a window sill in the Indiana School for Boys.

From beneath his dark cloak the Bringer-of-Ecstasy removed the iron bar and threw it onto the floor at Charlie's feet. It landed with a "clang": the sound of prison bars slamming shut over and over in Charlie's mind in the form of unending echoes, unending echoes.

"Take it," said the Bringer-of-Ecstasy. "It's yours."

Charlie stared at the iron bar, uncertain of what to do.

"Go ahead." The Bringer-of-Ecstasy spread his hand out casually, gestured toward the iron bar. "Kneel down, touch your fingers to it. You'll see. You'll see *everything*."

Charlie didn't like being told what to do, but he was curious nonetheless. Was this the *same* iron bar? Had the stranger kept it with him this entire time? For what purpose?

Cautiously, keeping one eye on the stranger, Charlie knelt down and touched the bar with the tip of his middle finger. Since nothing bad seemed to occur as a result, he wrapped his fingers around the bar and gripped it tightly, tightly.

Charlie

lifts the blanket over Krause's head… fire erupts outward into his arm, down into the iron bar itself

sees

again and again and again… motionless flesh

everything

again and again and again… ecstasy

the sun blazing over Golgotha… the air smells like death, the rot of motionless flesh… the son on the cross, his throat as dry as the sand covering the skull-shaped hill… he presses down on the rusty nails lodged in his feet… this helps him breathe, helps him ignore the awful pressure in his chest… whispers, *I need water, please…* wonders if his voice, the voice that once commanded whole crowds, is strong enough to even be heard… someone, he can't see the person clearly in the glare, at last proffers him a sponge soaked in vinegar… but it doesn't smell like vinegar… it won't be long now, he thinks…

(The-Bringer-of-Ecstasy: "After the effects of the soporific drug wore off, Christ awakened within a tomb. Joseph of Arimathea arrived and smuggled Christ into Egypt. His wife and son, Marie-Madeleine and Jesus Barabbas, fled to Marseilles while we pursued Christ all the way to Cairo. We kidnapped him, transported him to the Western hemisphere. There in a desert of the southwest we exacted our revenge on the son of the father, tortured him one final time before….")

the end… I wish it would come for me now, Christ thinks… now, before the Brotherhood receives the satisfaction of hearing me scream… oh, and scream I will… scream I will…

Christ lies naked in the burning sand, stretched out as far as possible, his hands and feet tied to wooden stakes pounded into the ground… a jury of thirteen surround the condemned man… the Brotherhood's executioner is tall and thin, has a long gray beard that almost touches the middle of his chest, a hood is drawn low over his face, a dark robe covers his body, and even in the scorching sun of the desert he casts no shadow.

("I knew well how Christ felt. I myself had once been condemned to a similar ordeal, hanging from the World-Tree-of-Knowledge for nine whole nights learning nine magical songs. But this didn't keep me from performing my duty.")

Christ squints, tries to peer inside the shadowy hood of his executioner... as the golden double-headed axe is lifted into the air, Christ sees the face of the stranger... though the features are quite dissimilar, he can't help but see himself reflected in that face...

("Fire erupted outward into my arm, down into the axe itself. I brought the axe down onto Christ's right leg just below the thigh.

"Christ screamed.

"The jury clutched each other in shared ecstasy. In the land of Eden Yahweh forbade Snake from sharing knowledge with early man. Snake had flown on feathery wings until that time, until Yahweh ripped them off and condemned Snake to crawling on its belly for eternity. Now the Brotherhood intended to do the same.

"The axe came down again and again and again as Christ continued to scream, crawling skewered and bleeding in the hot red sand, a crippled savior leaking life at the feet of the old gods... old gods with old vendettas.")

Charlie sees everything... sees Marie-Madeleine as she learns of her husband's death... sees the son of the Father... sees the widow's Jesus Barabbas fleeing to safer quarters... sees the widow herself... sees inside her... sees her very thoughts—she feels as if more than just her ambitions and ideals have been severed forever, amputated just as surely as her lover herself—sees the widow's sanity deteriorating as she renounces the Father, renounces the cross, renounces life itself... sees her flee Marseilles... sees her give herself to the Romans... sees her executed in secret... sees the wife of Christ transform resurrected with axe-blade swiftness into the widow of pain widow of blood

widow of the amputation

Charlie released the iron bar and staggered backwards. He heard the clang of metal against glass, raised his hand to his forehead. He felt dizzy once again, as if he were about to collapse face-down. He pressed his hand against the cool wall, steadied himself. He closed his eyes until the room ceased spinning.

The Bringer-of-Ecstasy said, "I have many names, as do you. The family tree of Jesus Barabbas is long and convoluted; obscure branches split off into dark areas best left forgotten by the royal lineage. But they can't be forgotten. Your father—not the man who gave you your name, but your real father, the one who wouldn't even stay around long enough to see your mother's belly rise—was no normal wanderer." The Bringer-of-Ecstasy walked slowly toward Charlie, placed his large hand on Charlie's shoulder. He leaned forward and whispered in his ear, "You have a purpose, you have a lineage. Don't let them use you like a puppet. If you try to assert your rights, they'll try to eliminate you. Perhaps imprison you, perhaps kill you."

The Bringer-of-Ecstasy removed his hand from Charlie's shoulder, strolled over to the window once again. "Either way, you'll have been manipulated. Manipulated and cast aside... as always." He turned his back on Charlie, stared down at the grayish landscape hundreds of feet below.

Manipulated.

Charlie's right hand tightened into a fist. He wanted to hit something, anything. This was always his reaction when he remembered the past, all the times his mother pawned him off on strangers, sometimes selling him for nothing more than a pitcher of beer. He remembered the time he asked her to buy him a guitar while he was stuck in McNeil Island Prison. Though she claimed she didn't have a dime to spare, she came back two months later with some pre-pubescent cunt under her arm that she and her latest husband had adopted for two grand. Charlie blew up at her at that point, told her he didn't want to see her or her fucking daughter again. This was the only request his mother ever granted him.

Cast aside.

He remembered the first chick he ever balled, the same woman who would later become his wife, the woman who left him while he was stuck in a prison cell serving a sentence for stealing money to send to her and the child they'd had together.

Manipulated.

He remembered the first girlfriend he'd convinced to turn tricks for him... or rather, he *thought* he'd convinced her. Turned out she'd already been balling half the guys in Los Angeles free of charge. When he'd asked her to hustle her ass for him, she jumped at the chance to pursue her favorite hobby and get paid for it at the same time. When she got busted for hustling in Texas, she wasted no time in telling the cops who her old man was. Even gave them the address. After a few sporadic visits in prison, Cynthia disappeared with all his money and possessions.

Cast aside.

Still staring out the window, the Bringer-of-Ecstasy said, "July 20th, 1969, the day of Osiris' helical return over the Pyramids at Giza; the day Osiris' sister and lover, Isis, is located at 19.5 degrees above the southeastern horizon at the Sea of Tranquility. Isis, represented by Sirius, is the brightest star in the sky, the most important star in the Egyptian calendar. Exactly 13,000 days from now, on February 21st, 2005, the geometry over the Sea of Tranquility repeats precisely as it did thirty-six years before."

The Bringer-of-Ecstasy turned slowly, faced Charlie. "Unclench your fists, Charles. You won't accomplish anything that way. Though you may not believe it, there are places on Earth where she can't harm you. Sacred places, like here, where I'm far stronger than she. You must take her to such a sacred place, and I'll do the rest. February 21st, 2005. Remember that date. They'll try their best to prevent you from claiming your proper position, your ordained birthright, before that date. That's the day the secret chambers beneath the Sphinx will be opened at last, revealing both the hidden path and the coming future… but only for the Chosen. The Elite. The holy, royal bloodline." The Bringer-of-Ecstasy laughed scornfully after uttering those words. "Or rather, the few members of the bloodline 'respectable' enough to be recognized officially by the Caput Mortuum. Even among the Elite, some are only outsiders looking in."

The Elite. Charlie thought of the list of "Beautiful People" the Caput Mortuum had suggested he eliminate in order to instigate the coming Apocalypse. But was this Apocalypse real, or was it simply a cover for the Caput Mortuum's true purpose: to set up Charlie and his family for a very big fall, a fall that would remove Charlie from the Big Picture for more than thirty-six years—13,000 days, at the very least?

If what the Bringer-of-Ecstasy had shown him was accurate, and Charlie didn't doubt than it was, then the Caput Mortuum was far more than just his informant and occasional employer… far more than just his traitorous enemy. That was nothing special. He'd had plenty of those in the past. No, the Caput Mortuum might be far more "intimately" related.

Charlie held out his balled fist and said, "If you don't want me to use this against them, what the hell else can I use?"

"Your mind would be an excellent start, Charlie. If you manage to survive the coming months, just remember: the Caput Mortuum and the Order will never be able to complete their grab for power 13,000 days from now if the proper ceremonial sacrifices are not completed on the preordained dates. November 30th, St. Andrew's Eve. February 2nd, Candlemas Day. April 24th, St. Mark's Eve. April 30th, Walpurgis Night. June 23rd, St. John's Eve. August 1st, Lammas Day. If any of the sacrifices on these dates are prevented, it will hopelessly upset their plans." The Bringer-of-Ecstasy ceased talking, simply gestured toward Charlie as if expecting him to complete the thought.

Charlie whispered, "I'll be able to take back what's mine. I'm tired of being everyone's fucking puppet." His fist untightened, his fingers splayed outward.

Somehow, even from across the room, Charlie could feel the man's touch on his hand; he could hear the man's voice whispering in his ear, though the Bringer-of-Ecstasy still stood beside the window: "Bone to bone, blood to blood, flesh to flesh...."

Charlie felt himself growing dizzy once more. The room began to twirl. He closed his eyes for a moment, but that failed to stop the queasiness in his gut. He opened his eyes, looked up at the unblinking stars that seemed quite distorted through the concave crystalline ceiling. The lunar sky looked unreal, like dark paint slapped upon a giant canvas. This was Charlie's last thought before his entire body shivered. He swooned and toppled onto the ground, the back of his skull slamming—*crack*—against the lunar glass.

When he opened his eyes once more, he lay in the middle of a dirt road beside a slaughtered body—the body of Stephanie Rowe. A few feet away lay the remains of Mark Walts.

Surrounding Charlie were Bruce and Tex and Ouish and Gypsy and the rest of his family. All of them were asleep. Content expressions lay on their faces, as if they had just eaten a large meal at a celebratory feast.

Charlie was about to yell at everyone to get the hell up and hide these damn bodies, but then he happened to glance up at the cloudless blue sky, at which point a strange calm swept over him. He lay his head back down on the dirt and just stared and stared. Somewhere up there the blood of the moon-rapists seeped into the magnificent desolation of the lunar terrain.

For some reason, this image focused Charlie thoughts. He knew what to do. He had to play a delicate game: pretend as if he were still following the Caput Mortuum's orders while distancing himself from the actual crimes. If the axe at last came down, as the Bringer-of-Ecstasy suggested it would, then only a few members of the family would receive the blows, not Charlie. Charlie would survive the Caput Mortuum's traps. He would use his mind.

Charlie felt confident for the first time in a long, long time.

On the evening of April 23rd, 2004, Charlie sat in a cell making scorpions out of twine.

It was a skill he'd developed in jail years before, just something to while away the hours, the minutes, the seconds. He had more then enough of all three of these.

When he didn't have twine he used the thread from his socks. Scorpions and spiders were his usual fare. They were more than just play toys, however. They were companions to whom he could talk and sing. Sometimes he sent them out in the world to do little jobs. He gave them names, he gave them personalities. He put little things in their pincers and sent them out in truth.

He was just now putting the finishing touches on a new trio of scorpions. He thought he might call them Wynken, Blynken and Nod.

A guard strolled by the cell. It was that new blond kid, Hoffman. The guard slammed his baton against the steel door and yelled, "Lights out in ten minutes!"

It was 11:20 already? Time always seemed to speed up when he was working on his little dolls.

Hoffman lingered by the door and whispered through a small rectangular window, "Hey, Charlie, I got your shit for you."

Charlie smiled, laid his scorpions aside, strolled over to the door. Hoffman slipped a scrap of torn newspaper beneath it.

"Here you go, Charlie my man. Peace."

As an after-thought, Charlie flashed him the sign for love with his left hand. Hoffman nodded and continued walking, the sound of his heels echoing down the hall.

Charlie reclaimed his seat, being careful not to crush his scorpions. He unfolded the scrap of paper. According to the date at the top of the page, it had been ripped out of the January 23rd, 2004 edition of the *Weekly World News*. Only four months behind this time, Charlie thought. Hoffman was getting better. Charlie spotted an article highlighted in yellow and scanned it briefly.

Police have interviewed witnesses who say they observed a group of four or five people at the grave site on the night of November 30, 2003. The witnesses reported they saw lots of activity around the grave for a period of two hours or so, after which the unidentified people left carrying a large object. Police believe that object was—

Charlie knew what this meant.

He folded the article into a paper airplane, tossed into the air. It soared gracefully about the cell. For a moment he imagined it flying through the thick pane of glass in the tiny window, toward freedom. But no. Instead it landed on its nose with a dull thud just inches away from the door.

This made Charlie giggle.

Idly, he turned to stare at the numerous photographs lining the featureless walls, all of them depicting the clear blue sky above Death Valley, otherwise known as Paradise, California. He sighed, knowing he would need more than a paper airplane to fly all the way there. Ah yes, he would need help from his little babies.

At that moment the lights went out in his cell. That was fine with Charlie. His babies worked better in the dark. So did he.

Within minutes, after a few flicks of his wrist, the scorpions were ready to travel.

What did that bumper sticker used to say? Keep On Truckin'….

Charlie placed a tiny note in each of the scorpion's pincers. He held them next to his mouth and whispered their various destinations. They seemed to nod their approval.

Charlie knelt on the cold stone floor and released his little babies. Wynken, Blynken and Nod scurried toward the impossibly thin space beneath the door. Their twinish legs made no sound whatsoever.

They were soon lost in darkness.

Charlie settled back onto his bed and listened to the music inside his skull, beautiful songs composed by Charlie himself.

Singer and songwriter, murderer and lover, father of scorpions, son of man, Charlie closed his eyes and watched the worlds spinning inside his head.

* * *

On the evening of April 24th, 2004, Sandra Good (known to her family as "Blue") returned to her small apartment in Hanford, California, not far from where her beloved Charlie was being held at the California State Prison at Corcoran. After putting her groceries away in the kitchen, she immediately sat down at a small wooden desk and began rereading *Delancie v. Superior Court*, 31 Cal 3d 868. There had to be something she was missing, some secret code embedded in the text that would remove the red tape from her path and allow her Charlie to stand before her in the flesh once again.

She longed to see Charlie, but The California Department of Corrections had been illegally preventing this since January of 1991. The Warden and the Director of the CDC both claimed that Sandra would be "too great a security risk." What did they think she was going to do, waltz into the prison with plastique strapped to her chest?

Though she'd been trying to sue the CDC for years, it didn't look like she'd ever get her rightful chance to see Charlie face-to-face and not through a television screen during one of those trashy tabloid shows. When she'd watched Charlie performing on the Geraldo Rivera show, she'd been struck by the fact that Geraldo looked more like a serial killer than Charlie did. She wondered how many boys Geraldo had buried in his backyard.

She wished she could walk into the prison and hug Charlie, just like she used to do back at the ranch, and talk about old times as if those prison bars had never closed shut between them. There was a concerted effort on the part of the government to keep this from happening. Perhaps they were afraid of the alchemical energies that would result from the mere touch of Charlie and Sandra, the joining of anima and animas, the serpentine nagari. If so the government would never allow Sandra to enter the Special Housing Unit, her legal rights bedamned, unless a miracle of Biblical proportions intervened.

Until then Sandra remained in her apartment pouring over obscure rulings in the legal code (except when she was forced to go out and earn a sustenance-level paycheck in order to pay for the research), trying her best to run rings around all the hurdles the devilish lawyers loved to drop in the average person's path. An attorney she had met with briefly some years ago had once denied the existence of a monolithic conspiracy ruling the legal system—which was rather laughable, considering Sandra's firsthand knowledge of such matters—when it was quite obvious that the legal code itself was a conspiracy against the people, as it was clearly written in esoteric language and obscure ciphers known only to the select few initiates into the Grand Eternal Sovereign Brotherhood of Ambulance Chasers or whatever stupid name it was known by in their smoke-filled back rooms at the American Bar Association.

The exact words of the attorney were: "Miss Good, you're being very naïve. If you can hire me I assure you I'll do my best to defend you. There's no more a conspiracy in the legal world as there is a—a man in the moon!"

This last statement had made Sandra laugh considerably. She'd left his office a few moments later, never to return. Ever since then she'd been defending her rights on her own as best she could. If she lost, at least it would be on her own terms.

Sandra continued to flip through the pages of the tedious document—wishing the entire time she could speed read, her eyes shriveling slowly into dry orbs of dust—until a quarter after seven, at which point she heard a strange scratching sound emanating from just outside her window.

She grew scared at first, for she thought someone might be trying to break in. Then she remembered what Charlie had always told her about fear. She rose from the desk, approached the closed window on the opposite side of the room just above her battered couch. She flicked off the living room light in order to make her fear even greater, making her that much more powerful.

She kneeled on the sofa and parted the dirty white curtains. She half-expected to see a human face wrapped in nylon peering back at her. Instead she saw three scorpions tapping claws against the glass. A wide smile broke out across Sandra's face. Ah, it had been so long since Charlie had sent his little friends for a visit. What a pleasant surprise.

She lifted the window, a cool breeze blowing in her face. The scorpions scuttled inside quickly, as if eager to save themselves from the cold. They crawled up her arm in single file. Wynken perched upon her shoulder and whispered in her ear.

It's time, he said eagerly, sounding quite like Charlie.

He hoped tonight was the night: April 30th, *Walpurgisnacht.*

Charlie sat naked in the darkness of his cell. It was ten minutes till midnight. Hoffman had just completed his first inspection, leaving Charlie alone with the shadows and his music and the sky over Death Valley.

Charlie concentrated on the photographs lining the walls, as he had done every night for the past twenty-five years—ever since Sandra had first begun providing him with the photos. Sandra had seemed genuinely puzzled by the request, which was all for the better. Charlie didn't want anyone knowing his plans. Surprise was everything.

Charlie had demanded that the photos be of the sky above Death Valley, particularly the area located in Eastern California. It didn't matter if it was morning or night, just as long as it was Death Valley. During one of the rare times he was allowed to talk on the phone, Sandra asked him how he could possibly tell the difference between one photograph of the sky and another. Charlie replied, "Don't worry, I can tell the difference. Don't try to pass off some phony shit on me, girl. If you want me to do my job good, you do yours."

Sandra had complied. With each message delivered by his little dolls, another photo went up on the wall. By and by, his entire cell became a panorama of azure skies punctured by an occasional patch of night, pieces of cottony clouds floating about here and there across the once-gray walls. Every night, from around 11:45 to 3:00, Charlie would perform the same ritual over and over and over again, waiting for the proper time to claim what was rightfully his....

Charlie meditated on the photos, trying to project himself onto the desert floor of Death Valley where he once lay with Sandra, Squeaky, and the rest of the family after jamming or making love or feasting in celebration of the Great God Pan. He remembered the feel of the warm desert wind on his face, the smell of the impossibly clean air, the taste of the particles of grainy sand that somehow managed to coat his tongue, the beautiful sound of silence (since few or no automobiles ever traversed the desolate tumbleweed-littered highways of the desert), and most of all the sight of an endless blue sky devoid of Los Angeles smog, which Charlie believed was the physical manifestation of the sinful acts so prevalent in the modern Gomorrah known as Hollywood. He remembered it all in great detail, so much so that the nondescript prison walls seemed to dissolve as the scenes captured in the photos grew larger and larger, engulfing Charlie with their unattainable majesty.

At this point the Death Valley skies would often snap back inside their glossy, rectangular prisons on the walls, leaving Charlie to stumble about his cell within a cloud of dazed confusion as he tried to recapture the ineffable image that had seemed only an arm's reach away. Every night the image grew ever more real, ever more tantalizing, ever more untouchable.

Until tonight, the night of the witches' sabbath.

For tonight everything changed. The image did not snap back at the last second. Instead Charlie plunged into the expanding skies and found himself falling a considerable distance through the freezing desert air of midnight. He fell ten feet and landed on his side, knocking the wind from his body. He lay gasping on the rough terrain for several minutes, sharp stones pressing into his bare flesh. At last he glanced upwards and saw an actual highway only a few yards away from him. He forced himself to rise to his feet, wrapped his arms about himself, rubbing his upper forearms in order to generate just a tiny amount of heat. Distantly, he saw a single yellow eye barreling down the highway. The sound of a motorcycle filled the immediate area.

Ignoring the cold and the pain, Charlie ran toward the highway. He stood in the path of the oncoming motorcycle and waved his arms far above his head.

"Help me!" he screamed. "Please, I need help!"

Charlie stared straight into that bright, impassive eye, trying to will it to stop with whispered incantations.

At 24030 Hawthorne Boulevard in Torrance, California stood the California Bank & Trust, a large structure that loomed over the much more modest buildings that surrounded it. It could be seen from many miles away, its dark slit-like windows staring down upon the citizens of this coastal suburb of Los Angeles like a sentient god trapped in concrete and plaster.

The California Bank & Trust (once called the Union Bank

Building) was constructed in 1973. The workers who had placed each brick in its proper niche, the pedestrians who drove by the building every morning on their way to work, even the men wearing pristine suits and ties who toiled in the building every day of their orderly lives, had no idea why the building was constructed in the first place.

It was built to contain the Caput Mortuum.

On the twelfth floor of the California Bank & Trust a horde of spiders made of thread, twine, dust and pieces of lint crawled beneath the double doors that led to Office 1200 and marched toward a defective Frigidaire that had once been bright white, but had since turned slightly yellow with age. The spiders attached tough strands of webbing to the refrigerator's silver handle, then pulled the door open. The little light flickered on to reveal a grayish metal reliquary in the shape of a human head. The intricate designs—the flowing hair, the full lips, the painted designs—that adorned the casket seemed to indicate the head of a woman, and a beautiful one at that.

The spiders connected their webbing to the stylized hair that flowed outward from the container in the shape of handles. With very little care, they jerked the line forward. The reliquary smashed onto the tiled floor; a gust of frosty air popped out of the container; jagged shards skittered about in all directions. Amidst the wreckage lay the severed head of a beautiful woman with long red hair and sparkling hazel eyes, eyes that snapped open in astonishment upon seeing the strange spiders. Her painted red lips (somewhat blue from the cold) curled into a snarl and released an angry, high-pitched scream.

Trying not to panic, the spiders dragged the head from the office and out into the nicely carpeted hallway. Now came the difficult part. They would have to drag the screaming head past the security guard without being detected.

First things first. In order to prevent the Caput Mortuum from screaming for help, they stuffed her mouth with silken webs. Though she continued to put up a struggle, trying to bite her way to freedom and such, the clamor was noticeably muffled.

The spiders skittered down the hall, past Bobi Hromas' En Agape office where the American Christian Trust coordinated their plan to program nuclear Armageddon in the Middle East. But that was an entirely different matter, one which did not concern the spiders at the present time.

The spiders paused in front of the elevator. One of them crawled up the wall and pressed the Down button with one of its many legs, then crawled back down the wall to join its brothers on the carpet. The spiders admired the carpet while awaiting the elevator. They were lovers of fine weaving.

At last they heard a distinctive "ding," the Down button became pink, and the gray elevator doors slid open. Fortunately, there was no one inside. The spiders dragged the head into the elevator.

As the elevator descended, the spiders went to work. They crawled up the golden-colored wall and pressed the Emergency button, stopping the elevator between the 6th and 7th floors. The spiders connected their webs to the square hatch in the ceiling and pulled. The hatch opened. After the spiders congratulated themselves on this maneuver, they crawled out onto the roof of the elevator. From here they lowered their webs onto the Caput Mortuum, then hoisted her up after them.

Carefully, they peered over the edge of the elevator. It was a long way down, but this did not scare the spiders. Nothing could dissuade them from completing their appointed task. Half the spiders descended to the bottom of the elevator shaft on their silken webs. Once they had reached the bottom and decided that everything was clear, they tugged on their web to indicate it was safe to send down the Caput Mortuum.

The spiders on the elevator made certain the webs connected to the head were strong enough, at which point they shoved her over the edge of the roof, lowering her to the ground at a slow rate. About five minutes later the spiders on the ground circled the head, cut the webs from Marie's beautiful hair, then signaled the others to come on down. The others did so with great excitement, for they were very close to their goal. Oh yes, quite close. They could *feel* it.

The spiders conferred on how to escape from the shaft. They decided brute force was in order. They sprayed one of the doors with a thin sheet of webbing and pulled it aside with a single, concerted effort. They glued the doors into place with more strategically-applied webbing, then pulled Marie into the shadowy basement. Out of the shadows emerged two security guards, their pistols drawn.

"All right, hold it right there!" one of them said. He seemed surprised when he realized that no one was inside the elevator, only spiders.

The spiders whipped strands of webbing around the guards' ankles and pulled, knocking their feet out from under them. The spiders swarmed over the guards, snatching their pistols away from them with the help of their webs. They bound and gagged the two men, hanging them from the ceiling. The guards swayed back and forth, their limbs dangling from the webs at awkward angles as if they were defective wooden puppets.

The spiders wound their way between towering, labyrinthine stacks of crates, eventually discovering the entrance to the stairwell. They climbed up the stairs, dragging the head behind them. Marie moaned in pain every time her head bumped against the edge of the steps. This process took a long time. Twenty-three minutes later, at 10:36 P.M., the spiders reached the door leading to the first floor. Three of the insects climbed up the door in order to peer through a tiny window near the top. They could see a lone security guard sitting behind a circular desk, nearly falling asleep. The spiders whispered their ideas to each other, then crawled back down the door to share them with their brothers.

Within minutes the trap was set. A dozen spiders hung the Caput Mortuum from the ceiling just beyond the doorway. They held her in place while the other spider turned the knob with a silken lasso. The door appeared to swing open on its own, as if an invisible man were traipsing through the doorway. This piqued the security guard's interest. He glanced up at the door, furrowed his brow, rubbed the sleep out of his eyes.

"Who's there?" he said, yawning. "Sean, Gerald? Did you find out what was wrong with the elevator?" A pause. "Hello?" He mumbled a series of invectives to himself, rose from the nicely padded vinyl chair with a groan. He patted the gun at his hip as if for reassurance. "Hello?" he said again as he placed his hand on the edge of the doorway and peeked inside. His last word echoed out into the stairwell.

At that moment the spiders on the ceiling released the Caput Mortuum. Moaning angrily the entire time, she swung forward on the web and slammed into the guard's forehead. A loud "thunk!" resulted from the collision. Before he even knew what had hit him, the guard collapsed facedown onto the ground.

The spiders released a few cheers, then cut Marie from the ceiling.

She landed on the guard's spine. It sounded like something cracked, but the spiders couldn't be sure. They dragged Marie across the shiny lobby floor, through the front entrance, and out into the quiet night.

They dragged the head two blocks to a waiting school bus: the black/white bus newly liberated from the Spahn Ranch by Blue herself.

Sandra slid out from behind the steering wheel and opened the double doors; the spiders crawled inside. She knelt down in order to pick up the Caput Mortuum.

"Good babies," Sandra said, patting a few of the spiders with her little finger. "You've done good work. Now go sit down and wait for your milk."

Since all the seats on the bus had been removed long ago, the spiders had to crash wherever they could find an empty space. They waited patiently as instructed.

Sandra removed the webbing from the mouth of the Caput Mortuum. The instant she did this the head began reeling off a litany of invectives far more creative than the ones that had spilled out of the security guard's mouth only minutes before.

"How dare you do this to me!" Marie said. "Do you realize who you're dealing with here? I'm Marie-Madeleine, the Caput Mortuum, the widow of—!"

Sandra held Marie out at arm's length and slapped her across the cheek. "Shut up, you bitch! I know full well who you are. I also know about the responsibilities that you've thrown aside and ignored, discarded like a piece of meaningless trash. You may have gotten away with it for a long time, but not anymore you cuntless old relic!"

Marie's mouth hung wide open. She was completely speechless, no doubt for the first time in her life.

"I-I can't believe this," she finally managed to whisper.

"Well, get used to it," Sandra said, lowering the Caput Mortuum into a makeshift box constructed of wooden planks Wynken, Blynken and Nod had found in a garbage can a few days before. The planks might give Marie splinters, but Sandra didn't really care. The woman deserved every moment of discomfort that was to come. Sandra shut the lid and locked it. Marie's screams were still discernible, though muffled to a great extent.

Sandra slid behind the steering wheel. From now on they would remain on the road, forever on the move, until it was time to head northeast, toward paradise.

Stealing the motorcycle wasn't difficult. Murdering the owner with his bare hands was difficult, but not the theft itself. Somehow, thievery had always come rather easily to Charlie. Of course, he was never able to hang onto the stolen property for very long, but no one was perfect.

After all, anyone could steal. It was actually stealing and getting away with it that took a unique skill, something Charlie knew he didn't possess. That's why he killed people instead. It was much simpler. At the moment, however, he wasn't interested in owning the bike forever, just long enough to get him to Ballarat.

Ballarat was a ghost town located on the edge of a twenty-five mile salt lake between Wingate and Ballarat Road. Charlie, having slipped into the motorcyclist's clothes, looked like any other over-the-hill desert rat trying to outdistance old memories—or perhaps even find lost miners' gold—amidst the ghosts that haunted the empty roads of these desert towns. Charlie rode southeast toward Trona, a village that lay only a few miles south of the Death Valley National Monument. Memories upon memories washed over Charlie. He remembered the day Cathy Meyers had first told the family about the Meyers Ranch snuggled high in the mountains bordering the National Monument. It was sometime during the beginning of October, 1968. The possibilities of such a remote location, so near to All Hallow's Eve, had set Charlie's mind on fire. It wasn't long before he packed his family into the bus (green at that time) and moved into the ranch, doing as best they could to make the Valley live up to its name. The first day they inhabited the ranch was October 12th, which just so happened to be Aleister Crowley's birthday as well.

Charlie retraced the path as if it were etched on yellowing parchment stored somewhere within his mind. After passing through Trona, he rode north on Highway 28, stopping long enough to pick up a tank of gasoline. About twenty minutes later he crossed the salt lake that led toward the ghost town of Ballarat. On the outskirts of town, hidden within the broken down ruins of what had once been a barn, Charlie discovered the command dune buggy he had hidden there almost twenty-seven years before, hidden for the express purpose of delivering him to the place of execution: Devil's Hole.

Charlie ran his hand along the dune buggy's metal frame, leaving a meandering path within the decades worth of dust that had collected upon it. He stroked the ratty remains of the expensive ocelot furs that still hung from the sissy bars, cleared away the dust from the swastika-like symbols of the Process Church painted on the sides, stroked the machine gun that sat mounted on a pivot. Yes, this might come in handy if the situation degenerated as fast as everything else in his life: his childhood, his marriage, his singing career. All he'd ever wished to do was defend what was rightfully his, whether that be his safety, his freedom, his heritage, and yet the universe itself didn't want him to win. It was about time the universe started answering for its crime… not in the half-assed way he'd gone about it before, but directly, through the Caput Mortuum herself. After filling the tank with gas Charlie slid behind the steering wheel and hot-wired the vehicle. Amazingly, it revved up with a roar as strong as it had possessed way back in 1969. He stormed out of the barn feeling somehow rejuvenated, as if a missing chunk of his soul had been stitched into its proper place. Skirting the east side of the salt lake, he rode south down Wingate Road for fourteen miles until he reached a white pole that had been pounded into the dirt to mark the hard-to-find access road to desolate Goler Wash, an almost surreal wasteland that had once been a bustling gold mining area but which now served as a resting place to abandoned Model T Fords, ancient ore-munching machines from the nineteenth century that had once been powered by nothing more high-tech than overworked burros, and a score of other relics from various eras thrown together in a confusing jumble by the vicissitudes of time. Charlie recognized many of the relics from his stay in the area almost three decades before. Because so many years had passed, he felt more sympathetic to their plight. He suspected he would be joining them in their graveyard sooner than later.

Charlie drove the dune buggy east toward the dry waterfalls that would mark the final stretch up to the Meyers Ranch. Very soon the terrain became too narrow and treacherous for even the command dune buggy. He backed up the vehicle and parked it near the mouth of Goler Wash. He began a seven and a half mile trek through the slit in the mountain, trying to remain fairly close to the steep cliff while also trying to avoid the needle-sharp barrel cacti that bloomed out of it.

Soon Charlie came upon the first dry waterfall of Goler Wash. The only route open to him was to climb the steep wall of rocks up to the top of the waterfall. He had done this long ago when he was much younger and in better shape. He looked carefully for footholds in the rocks, placing his leather biker boots on small protuberances that edged out of the cliff face just enough to allow him a slight boost upward. Inch by inch he pulled himself up to the top of the waterfall, where he immediately came upon a second waterfall. He headed right, rounding a sharp curve in the cliff that led to yet another waterfall. The moldering map in his brain told him to turn left. He rounded a wide, V-shaped curve, beyond which lay a series of four more dry waterfalls.

Seven waterfalls. He remembered the words of Kenneth Grant, head of the Nu-Isis Lodge, spoken during a celebration at The Spiral Staircase.

"In Hebrew the word for sword, *zain*, is attributed to the Twins, Set-Horus. *Zain* is the number seven, the number of sexual love. The letter *zain*, spelt in full, equals 67." Grant pointed out that 1967 was the year Charlie was released from Terminal Island after seven years of imprisonment. "*Binah*, the third cosmic power-zone or *sephiroth*, is also equal to 67. Thus, 67 signifies the womb of the Mother containing the twins, Set-Horus.

"*Zain* originally signified the womb through the symbolism of the Goddess of the Seven Stars, Ursa Major. In the Egyptian hieroglyphics the sign of 7 is of a god, symbolized by the axe, the axe being the weapon of Set, the opener of the Mother. In the language of the secret gnosis Set is identical with his mother, which is why his name means seven. Set and his mother, Typhon, were collectively the eighth power, the power that represented the height or summit.

"Charlie, I know you're Set reborn, I can feel it. But who is the Mother? Who is the woman who will complement you, help you reach the summit?"

At the time Charlie didn't have the answer to that question. Later, on the moon, he was shown part of the answer. The rest he would have to figure out on his own once he reached the place of execution.

After passing the seventh waterfall Charlie was forced to hug the cliff face for about a hundred feet while scooting along a precarious, thin ledge. This ledge brought him to a six-foot-wide passage leading downward to a dry creek bed. The creek bed consisted of a three-mile-long series of ragged dips and rises that tired Charlie quickly. He felt as if he were back on the sidewalks of San Francisco.

Beyond the creek bed lay a proper road. He followed the road for about five miles, passing several empty cabins, before coming to a crossroads. Crossroads were often the scene of paranormal phenomena; they were also preferred by occultists for use as the site of magical ceremonies. Charlie himself had used them for this purpose long ago. At the moment, however, he just wanted to go to sleep. For some reason he didn't remember this journey taking quite so long. The fork straight ahead would take him directly to the Meyers Ranch.

He reached his old home at 6:54 P.M. as the sun began to set, washing the sky with a hazy crimson-orange that looked so beautiful Charlie thought it was unreal at first. Laid out before him in a series of darkening silhouettes were the ranch house, a trailer, and a dozen or so outbuildings. Patches of barrel cacti grew amidst the tumbleweeds. The cacti were the only living things Charlie could see for miles around. The entire ranch had degenerated into a pitiful shadow of its former self. Where were the gardens filled with vegetables and the patches of wild strawberries? It had been so long since he'd tasted real fruit....

Off in the distance, somewhere behind the trailer, Charlie heard the echoes of Ouish and Mary and Squeaky and Sandra and Linda and Bruce and all the rest playing like children in the sand. He glanced at the cacti and wished they were strawberries. He wanted to taste one this very second. But nothing ever came easy to Charlie. He always had to work as hard as twelve men for the simplest pleasures. Unfortunately, he knew these simple pleasures were far behind him, lost in the traces of that distant wonderful hellish year: 1969.

Far away, hidden somewhere in the Panamint Mountains, a coyote howled for the first time of the night. He felt compelled to search out the singing voice, which soon drowned out the echoes of his long-lost family.

Early on the morning of May 5th, Charlie sat in the dry desert soil of Death Valley, pounding nails into wood, surrounded by nothing even remotely civilized, totally alone.

This was a new experience for Charlie. Even back in '68 he'd never had the Meyers Ranch all to himself. There had always been a hundred kids beneath his feet, all wanting guidance, all wanting food, all wanting love, all wanting *something*. The only other time in his life he had been alone was when he was sentenced to solitary confinement, but that wasn't quite the same thing: being alone in a little box as opposed to being alone in this desert vastness....

He was grateful to the current residents of Meyers Ranch for allowing him to stay. The scorpions, spiders, and bats were kind to extend such courtesy to a stranger in need of help. But this was just good policy. You never knew when a stranger might be a god in disguise. A wrathful god, at that.

Presently Charlie was not at the ranch itself. He had driven his dune buggy north into the triangular section of the Death Valley National Monument that overlapped with the north-western edge of Nevada. He sat building a small boat beside a deep pit of dark water known as the Devil's Hole.

The entire point of retreating to the desert thirty-seven years before had been to uncover the secret entrance into the underground caverns beneath Death Valley, the world the Hopi Indians referred to in their legends as the Third World, the world known to the Mayas of Yucatán as Mitlan. This world was ruled over by Ah Puch, the Lord of Death. In Mexico the Aztecs had known the Lord of Death as Mictlan, his Kingdom as Tlaxico. In Peru and Chile he was called Supai, whose subterranean home was simply "the Place of Death." Back in the late sixties Charlie had sent Bruce Davis to Central America in search of the entrances to these realms.

Charlie was certain this "Place of Death" existed beneath the desert. He himself had discovered the secret entrance in October of 1969; it was none other than the Devil's Hole itself. The Hole was fenced off by the Park Rangers, ostensibly because of its danger to casual visitors. Charlie knew the real reason: to prevent Charlie from discovering his underworld paradise. Indeed, the fence was hardly the sole barrier. After almost a year of visiting the Hole and watching the pale blind fish that sometimes bobbed to the surface, early in October of 1969 Charlie had—merely on a hunch—dipped his hand beneath the surface of the pool only to find that his flesh remained as dry as the desert air.

There was no water. It was an illusion, a simple trick of Maya,

ROBERT GUFFEY

Queen of Shades, cast over the Hole to obscure its true importance. Even in the world of the occult, the simplest tricks were the most effective—but not effective enough to fool Charlie.

Was it a mere coincidence that only a few hours after discovering the entrance, the Los Angeles Sheriff's Department arrested Manson for the final time? Of course not. This was the Caput Mortuum trying to prevent his underworld ascension. It was then that Charlie knew the Bringer-of-Ecstasy had been right.

Charlie stepped back a few feet to observe his work. Only a few more nails left to go. It was appropriate that he would finish the boat not long after Walpurgisnacht, one of the most important holidays of the year. He had been working on it ever since the day of his escape, carefully measuring each plank of wood so that they conformed to the intricacies of sacred geometry. It didn't pay to fudge on the details when building a hyperdimensional vessel to penetrate the land of the dead itself.

Charlie didn't doubt he would succeed. The universe itself was now conspiring in his favor. He *knew* this. After working against him for so long, the universe just *had* to change its tune. Today was May 5th, exactly 12,675 days after Aldrin and Armstrong had allowed themselves to be sacrificed to the moon goddess. (Charlie often wondered who those impostors were who sometimes wrote books or appeared on TV news shows to discuss their "alcoholism," a convenient excuse to explain why they didn't quite behave like the men who originally landed on the moon.) So much had happened since then. So many had died at Charlie's hands. He'd ruined so many lives, including his own, all for the benefit of a lying bitch of a goddess and her small, incestuous circle of acolytes—blind lap dogs, in truth. But he no longer needed them and their "special" knowledge.

He would circumvent the exclusive rituals of the "Illuminated" with his own homemade Ka vessel, penetrating the heart of the unknown with the Caput Mortuum herself tucked under his arm. All the invisible factors, the secret alignments and divinations that controlled the slightest details of people's lives, were in his favor. With the Bringer-of-Ecstasy on his side, the universe would have to give way and grant him passage to paradise.

Charlie kneeled down and ran his fingers over the surface of the boat as if he were stroking the thighs of a lover. With his other hand he reached down and dug his fingers into the dry soil. There was one other aspect of this site, this gated area around Devil's Hole, that infused the soil itself with sacred energy—energy that would help Charlie's passage to the Other Side. This area was the exact site where, almost two thousand years before, Christ was executed

the axe comes down again
and again and again
as Christ screams crawling skewered and bleeding in the hot red sand

by the Brotherhood of the Snake, a secret society formed to honor the old gods, particularly Quetzalcoatl, the feathered serpent who was so mistreated in the Garden of Eden. Charlie could feel the *ojas* of Christ's blood still lingering in the soil to this very day. The fact that this was the site of Christ's death had remained hidden to him until that moment on October 12th, 1969, when he had punctured the illusion cast over Devil's Hole with his bare hand. At that second he had recalled in minutest detail the information given to him by the Bringer-of-Ecstasy during Charlie's brief sojourn on the moon. And then came the sheriff and his pack of hounds....

Charlie pulled his fingers out of the soil and removed his hand from the boat. He withdrew a short black nail from a tool box, proceeded to hammer it into the juncture of two planks of wood near the stern. He wondered if this was the sound Christ had heard right before the smell of opium and belladonna wiped out all thoughts....

The last nail. Charlie stood, appraised his work once again. The boat appeared to be finished, but he could test it out over the course of the next few hours preceding the journey just to make sure.

Charlie draped a series of large blankets over the boat, then covered them with sand and rocks. From a distance, beyond the gated area, the boat would simply look like a slight rise in the earth. Perhaps it wasn't as complex an illusion as that cast over the Hole, but it would be enough to fool the stupid Park Rangers.

For a moment Charlie paused beside Devil's Hole to stare at the pale blind fish swimming just beneath the surface of the water. It was certainly an evil portent, enough to scare off even the least superstitious of visitors. A nice touch. Charlie had to give the Caput Mortuum credit; she was certainly a thorough illusionist, better even than her husband.

Peering within the Hole, he wondered if the bones of Christ had been tossed inside after the carrion eaters had had their way with the flesh. Perhaps Charlie would meet up with them soon.

Charlie hopped into his dune buggy and headed south toward the ranch, where he planned to sing to his boarders in order to repay them for their kindness and hospitality. And then later, after dinner, he would run with the coyotes and learn strange secrets through their songs.

The desert was filled with ghosts. Charlie could see them clearly, but only at twilight, only when he ran with the coyotes.

Tonight, as he'd done every night since his escape, Charlie had made dinner, played his newest songs for his boarders at the ranch (he'd never had a more appreciative audience), then rode his dune buggy into the desert to share tales—strange tales about magicians and golems and severed heads that ruled whole nations—with the coyote clan's wizened old storyteller and his twelve sons. Badwater was the lowest point in the desert—indeed, in the entire United States. Charlie found that ghosts were abundant here, particularly in the eyes of the dreamer, the eyes of the storyteller himself.

Tonight, as the sky deepened to twilight, he told the coyotes the tale of a black and white bus haunted by the spirits of children long dead, spirits who were later reborn into the new owners of the bus— beautiful teenage girls who once walked the pale, crater-pocked surface of the moon and longed to return.

"The moon is *not* crater-pocked," said young Coyote-Who-Hides-In-Daylight. "The moon is filled with lush green trees and whispering rivers that sing."

Charlie said, "Hey, listen, jack, I hate to disappoint you, but I *been* there." The circle of coyotes glanced at each other with blank stares, then snickered with amusement—all except for the elder coyote. "All right, all right, *don't* believe me, it doesn't matter. It's just a story, right? Why're you getting your fur all ruffled for?"

"I apologize for these young shitheads," said old Coyote-Who-Tells-Strange-Stories, throwing a hard glance their way. "Stupid people often can't tell the difference between religion and fiction."

The storytellers' sons giggled nervously, then hung their heads low when they realized their father was serious.

"I hear what you're saying, storyteller," Charlie said. "That's how we humans got this whole 'crucifiction' shit laid on us, but that's a whole nother story. Let's just stick to this story, okay?"

Coyote-Who-Tells-Strange-Stories simply nodded.

"All right," Charlie said, "what was we talkin' about?" He snapped his fingers. "Oh yeah, the black/white bus. You see, I was in the Spiral Staircase suckin' on a hookah when this fourteen year old witch named Snake came up to me and asked me if I wanted her to give me a blowjob. I asked her where her mother was. She said she was in one of the other rooms in the house getting fucked. I told her to go find someone else.

"Well, a couple minutes later this girl's father, a magic mountain man, comes stomping on over to me and wants to know what I done to his daughter. He was real angry. At first I thought he was challenging me to a fight. Then I realized he was challenging me to fuck. 'No one refuses my daughter and gets away with it!' he told me. Shit, I was never one to refuse a challenge.

"So we went out to the bus and I stuck my rod down the little Snake's throat. I fucked her ten or twelve times, even more. I fucked her so much I came right out her eyeballs and she cried my semen like tears. I went through her womb and out onto the other side. Her stomach became big with babies, and the dead children of the bus were reborn on Earth."

The coyotes were silent for a moment, then Coyote-Who-Tells-Strange-Stories said, "That's a nice story. Very romantic."

"Thank you," Charlie said.

"I can tell you have the touch of the storyteller within you. And yet you were never trained in the field?"

"Except in prison. You gotta be able to tell a good story to survive for two seconds behind bars."

"I understand. Since you're clearly a lover of fables, allow me to tell you a story."

Charlie gestured for him to continue. "Please. That's why I came out here."

"This is a story about the Sun and the Moon." The old coyote's eyes seemed to droop with exhaustion. He did not have long to live on this world, that much was clear. "The Sun and the Moon were in love with each other, but theirs was an unconsummated love. Oh, they *so* wanted to be together. But the Earth resented their love because He was all alone and would never love anyone except Himself. He wanted to punish them for their happiness. So He placed Himself between the Sun and the Moon. And the Sun forever chased after the Moon and the Moon forever chased after the Sun, but the Earth was always between them and they always seemed to be a day apart. They never gave up though. They never would. And the Earth would just laugh and laugh at their misery. Oh, how'd he'd laugh because he would never know their love and thus, he would never know their misery." The coyote's eyes drooped shut once again.

"Uh, is there a moral to the story?" Charlie said.

The coyote's eyelids fluttered open. He stared at Charlie with yellow, tired eyes. "The world doesn't want anyone to be happy," he whispered. The coyote turned to his sons and said, "Please, leave us alone. I have much to discuss with this man."

The sons wandered away, snickering to each other.

The old coyote watched them go, a tinge of sadness haunting his eyes. When his sons had at last disappeared into the reddish twilight, he turned back to Charlie and said, "Twelve sons, and none of them are storytellers. They're hunters and pranksters and thieves and some are even outright fools." He sighed. "I'm ashamed to admit this. I could blame it all on their mother, I suppose, but I know that's not entirely true. I went wrong somewhere. Perhaps I spent too much time telling stories, and not enough with my sons." He stared at the desert floor, as if trying to find an answer within its harsh simplicity. The next time he looked up at Charlie his eyes were stoic, his voice laced with a tone of inevitable finality. He had accepted what was coming.

"It's time for me to move on," the coyote said. "I long to embrace death, and yet the world doesn't seem to want to let me go. I think it's time I forced its hand. I want you to kill me, Charlie. Kill me and drink my blood. Every story I've ever told will drain out of me and into you. You deserve them far more than my sons."

For a time the two storytellers sat staring at each other as the sun sank behind them in the west. Charlie feared the wisdom in the coyote's eyes. He rose to his feet and approached him for that reason. He bent over and petted the tired coyote's snout. "All is love," Charlie whispered. He straddled the coyote's back, grabbed his neck, turned it to the left. *Crack* screamed the bones. Life left the body. Charlie bit into the back of its head, ripping off strips of fur and flesh. The blood felt hot and salty on his tongue and filled his brain with fire and cactus water and alkali flats and the seeds of a thousand stories.

A thousand stories.

Charlie stared up at the sky where large black birds circled menacingly. Strange red trails seemed to follow the birds as they flew. He wondered what kind of birds could release crimson streaks from their tails. These were very exotic birds indeed.

His entire attention became focused on those streaks. He seemed to merge with them, to follow the birds in their frenzied path through the air. He could feel the pressure of the arid wind on his face. He went twirling through the sky, not at all wondering how this was possible, just enjoying every second of the experience. As long as it lasted, that is.

For soon the illusion ended.

And worlds came rushing in.

Charlie saw the dead souls of the *Hindenburg* trapped in a beehive. He saw fifty-three World War II fighter planes descend into an ocean of fragile white glass. He saw the severed head of a kangaroo, garnished in sour cream, served on a silver platter to white men in tuxedoes. He saw a lemon slowly peeled open to reveal a compact, working replica of a human's insides complete with heart, liver, stomach, and intestines. He saw an egg cracked open on the edge of a sizzling pan, a gooey human eyeball with a blue pupil drop out onto the burning metal. He saw a giant human fetus with translucent skin moored like a zeppelin to the top of the Empire State Building. He saw a moon rocket sitting on a launch pad, encased in scaffolding of human bones. He saw a happy little girl blow out eight candles atop a dead preying mantis covered in white frosting. He saw a screaming hairless woman in a straight jacket, locked in a small room with soft walls from which hundreds of erect penises sprouted and spat at her until the floors were moist with pale fluids. He saw a team of surgeons staring in shock as thousands of live crabs swarmed out of a young soldier's chest wound. He saw two small boys slit open the stomach of a fat clown and pull out streams of brightly colored confetti in order to devour the sweet candies that lay deep within. He saw a laughing blue-eyed child riding a new bicycle through fields of mangled flesh scattered about Nagasaki moments after the blast. He saw two winos sitting on a trash-strewn sidewalk, passing their last drink back and forth as their city burned down around them. He saw a wounded tiger allow herself to be eaten by hyenas while her cubs ran for shelter. He saw the rays of the dawn sun shining on the red sands of Olympus Mons. He saw a teenage girl helping an old nude woman climb out of a bathtub filled with blood. He saw a pregnant woman reading a story to the daughter in her womb. He saw a spider dancing on a single thread directly above a young boy's face as he sat sleeping amongst old crates in a musty attic. He saw two men hugging on a busy city street while a light sprinkle of rain water kissed their shoulders. He saw the immense Coyote-Who-Devours-All running toward the corpse of the elder storyteller, traversing whole mountaintops with a single step. He saw Charlie pursued by a thousand ghosts from a thousand stories rising from the darkened desert floor.

A pair of ravens fly over the Panamint Range in Eastern California, across the endless landscape of arid desert, down 282 feet below sea level into the lowest point of North America. The entire area is filled with barrel cacti, salt lakes, alkali flats, alien rocks of grotesque colors.

Down.

Down, the ravens spiral in ever-tightening circles. Down toward the carcass of a coyote rotting amidst this remote vastness. The sky is a lush crimson, the color of blood, the color of sustenance. As the sun lowers ever westward, down into the land of the dead, the sky deepens to a royal purple. For some reason Kirlian auras are always most visible in this twilight darkness, at least this is what one of the ravens believes; Hugin is his name.

Far above Badwater, Hugin can clearly see where the target was standing only an hour before: Kirlian echoes of Charlie's recent past. There he stands, a formless black blob from which bluish flares shoot outward like a mini fireworks display. Hugin sees the aura bend over to pet the coyote on the snout. Charlie then grabs the coyote by the neck and wrestles it to the desert floor, biting into its head, snapping its neck, eating strips of its flesh raw as the bluish flares deepen to a purple that matches the sky itself.

Hugin can even detect brief snatches of Charlie's thoughts: fearing the coyote, approaching it for exactly this reason, becoming one with fear, drinking the blood of total awareness, paranoia, *coyotenoia*. Hugin knows he can track Charlie through his aura.

Lingering traces of his presence remain in the form of bluish-purple streaks staggering across the barren terrain, an area almost as isolated as the moon itself. He is certain the target is now within reach.

Hugin glances backwards and sees Munin performing loop-the-loops in the middle of the air. Hugin sighs, releases an ear-piercing shriek, bringing the raven to attention. He chastises Munin briefly, tells him there's work that needs to be done.

Stop clowning around, Hugin says. Go find the Bringer-of-Ecstasy. Bring him back to me. By the time he arrives here I should have tracked down Charlie.

And what if you haven't? Munin says.

Hugin just stares at him.

What? Munin says. I'm just asking a question. Aren't I allowed to ask a question?

Have I ever *not* found a target?

Yes. There was the time when—

That was *one* time. There was an unusual amount of sunspot activity that day. It wreaked havoc with the melonite in my brain.

Silence again. That evil stare.

All right, Munin says, I'm going, I'm going.

Be back by midnight.

Without a further word Munin darts off toward the southwest, down into the dark lands where the wolf of night devours the sun, and thinks, Who the fuck died and made Hugin king? Someone must've shoved a big, prickly stick up his ass this morning, no doubt about it.

Down into the western lands....

Hugin watched as Charlie's after image drank the blood of the coyote, savored its taste, rubbed the warm liquid on his face and neck, then ran toward a nearby dune buggy. Hugin followed Charlie's Kirlian trails out of Badwater about fifty miles southwest to a gash in the Panamint Mountains known as Goler Wash. Charlie left the dune buggy near the mouth of Goler Wash, then proceeded up the trail on foot. As Hugin flew deeper into the valley the Kirlian aura grew more distinct, which indicated that Charlie had passed through here only a short time ago.

Hugin soared between the steeply-cliffed walls over a series of seven dry waterfalls, and then down to a creek bed that led him to a manmade road. He watched Charlie staggering down this road as if in a hallucinatory daze. He continued walking straight until he came to a dilapidated ranch that consisted of a one-story house, a trailer, and a dozen or so outbuildings that were on the verge of disintegrating into dust. Charlie's aura disappeared into the house. He was still somewhere inside.

Hugin fluttered down onto a window sill near the front door. The window was just barely open. Hugin had to squeeze beneath it in order to get inside. He snagged a couple of feathers on the bottom of the window and ripped them off in the process of freeing himself. Thankfully, it only hurt for a few seconds.

Hugin hopped onto a nearby rafter that had fallen from the ceiling. A length of thick hemp rope lay on the floor like a dead snake. Much of the furniture was broken and had been pushed over onto their sides, becoming the home of spiders and scorpions.

Hugin noticed a trail of blood on the floor that led from the front door, deeper into the house. He lifted up from the rafter and flew into the kitchen adjoining the living room. All the cabinets were wide open. Packs of white rice, bags of potatoes, and dozens of canned goods lay scattered on the wooden floor. Amidst the pile of rotting food, flies and other dipterous insects had made themselves at home.

Hugin continued on, buzzing through the kitchen and into a small hallway that branched off into other rooms. The auras of bats could be detected in the rafters above him.

He heard a hellish, distorted cry erupt from the room at the far end of the hall. He fluttered toward the room with some apprehension, as he had never heard anything like this before. The door to the room was almost shut; nothing distinct could be seen through the crack. Hugin heard the scream degenerate into a whimpering gurgle. He squeezed through the door and found himself in a large bedroom. The remnants of a rusty king-sized bed frame stood beneath the broken windows, through which a storm of sand was blowing into the room. Charlie sat on the wooden floor, completely naked. Long strands of fine brownish-red hair grew from his back. His face elongated into a snout. Whiskers spouted like blades of grass on a high-speed film depicting the beginning of summer.

Hugin sat perched above the doorway, staring down at this scene in confusion. How was this happening? He knew he should fly out of there as soon as possible, but his morbid fascination stopped him. He had to see where Charlie's transformation would take him.

Charlie toppled onto his back and groaned with what sounded like a strange mixture of both pleasure and pain. As Charlie grew more and more feral, his screams became moans of ecstasy. He squirmed on the floor, his legs contracting, bones snapping. Here and there pockets of flesh bellied outward like tiny windblown sails, then just as suddenly deflated in upon themselves, growing as taut as hardened leather. His eyeteeth, encrusted with dried blood, lengthened into fangs.

Since Hugin had already seen what Charlie's normal teeth could do, he decided this would be a pretty good time to get the hell out of the room. He fluttered up from his perch, intent on buzzing out the door. Charlie's head jerked upward at the sound of his wings. He reared up onto his hind legs and leaped into the air, snatching Hugin's tail between his teeth. Hugin just barely escaped being bitten in two by the bloodthirsty coyote.

Hugin soared through the hall as fast as possible. The sound of talons scratching against the wooden floor grew louder and louder. Hugin almost slammed into a wall, so fast did he round the corner into the kitchen. He heard the coyote leaping into the air once again, the sound of jaws closing on air; he swore he'd felt the coyote's hot breath blowing onto his back. He rounded another corner, this time emerging into the living room. For a second Hugin was certain he would slip away. Only when he was standing in front of the window did he remember how difficult it had been trying to squeeze through that tiny space. Rather than search for another means of escape, Hugin tried to slip through once again. He almost made it. Halfway outside, he could feel the desert wind ruffling his feathers. He saw the full, pale moon high up in the starry night. The impact of the coyote against the glass sounded like the sudden slap of water against dry desert rock; it lingered beautifully in the air for a brief moment, then faded away to be replaced by the violent scuffling sound of talons tearing hopelessly against fangs, sharpened bone ripping into flesh amidst a patch of needle-sharp cacti.

Sandra Good parked the black/white bus near the mouth of Goler Wash, next to Charlie's old command dune buggy. So many years had passed since she'd last been here. She felt as if she were reentering a dream that had been cut off just before reaching the best part, the part where you lifted up from the earth and began to fly....

Sandra turned to her passengers and said, "Well, we're here, kids. It's been a hell of a wait, but we finally made it."

Many of the spiders had been sleeping. At the sound of Sandra's voice they became very excited, ready and willing to continue with the mission their father had provided them.

Just being around the spiders made Sandra happy. She thought of herself as their mother, even though she had had nothing to do with their creation. Charlie was wholly responsible for that. Only he could reach into the *Meon*, into the other side, and pull out the souls of all the children who had ever given their lives to the family within the black/white bus... pull them out and weave them expertly like thread into the twine used to create the spiders, the spiders who now danced on vinyl-wrapped chairs while awaiting their mother's next words. They had been awaiting these words since Walpurgisnacht. Unfortunately, the scorpions' message had been very clear: Sandra was not to enter the desert until the first quarter moon after Walpurgisnacht. The reason why was not given, but Sandra thought she had an idea.

After she tucked the makeshift reliquary under her arm, she asked the spiders to follow her outside. With only the sparse moonlight to guide them they maneuvered through the treacherous pass of Goler Wash, down to a creek bed that led to a barely passable road. For some reason she had the eerie feeling that dozens of eyes were staring down at her back. She looked up and scanned the dry waterfall above her. All she could see were a flock of black birds (crows, perhaps?) perched upon the rocks in a single, evenly spaced line. For a second she wondered if they were the ones spying on her, then just as quickly dismissed the thought as being too improbable even for her life.

It took her and the spiders almost two hours to walk the five miles toward the ranch, good old Meyers Ranch. Sandra was heartened to see the old place again, despite its degenerate state. It brought back so many fine memories. Fireside sing-alongs after dinner. Midnight swims in the pool. Playing hide-and-seek among the secret grottoes within the nearby hills. Dune buggy races in the desert. Sacrificing babies under the full moon. Ah yes, high old times.

Standing near a long defunct trailer, its dark eye-like windows staring inward into nothingness, Sandra watched the dimly lit main house where she and Squeaky used to help cook breakfast for the others. She watched as if waiting for something in particular, something she couldn't explain. She watched as one of the living room windows burst outward under the impact of a large, dark shape. The impact sounded like the sudden slap of water against dry desert rock; it lingered beautifully in the air for a brief moment. The falling shards of glass reflected moonlight as they sprayed outward like water from a hose. The sound of shattering glass was soon replaced by a new sound: talons tearing hopelessly against fangs, sharpened bone ripping into flesh. Within seconds this too faded away, to be replaced by a silence much deeper than that which had preceded the sounds of death.

Out of the silence, amidst cacti laced with moonlight and blood, came a dark figure padding across the rocky sand on four legs. Sandra stood perfectly still as she watched two yellow eyes grow larger and larger out of the midnight darkness. Though decidedly changed since the last time she had seen them, she had no problem recognizing the man within.

The coyote walked right up to Sandra, who kneeled down in order to be face-to-face with her old friend. Blood stained Charlie's mouth and paws. He raised one of his paws and laid it in Sandra's hands. Sandra stroked it lovingly.

"How you doing, Charlie?" Sandra said.

Charlie saw the spiders trailing off behind Sandra in even regiments. He nodded his head toward them as if acknowledging their presence, thanking them for everything they had done for him. Sandra could not hear the words that were exchanged between them, but the spiders seemed to respond in kind. Then Charlie turned back toward Sandra.

"I need the head," he said.

"She's right here." Sandra let go of Charlie's paw, then set the wooden box on the ground. She reached into her pocket and withdrew a tiny silver key. She had used a normal, everyday bike lock to keep the lid shut. Now she slipped the key into the lock, popped it open.

The Caput Mortuum sat at the bottom of the box, staring up at them with angry eyes. "—can't do this to me!" she screamed. "I'm the widow of the Savior himself! I—!"

"Oh, why don't you get a new act?" Sandra said.

Charlie dipped his head into the box, locked his teeth onto Marie's long red hair, then snatched her out while she uttered an endless string of venomous insults and hollow warnings.

Charlie walked past the house, the Caput Mortuum dangling from his fangs. Halfway across the ranch, he turned back to stare at Sandra. She could see his sad yellow eyes hovering there in the darkness. The eyes said, *I love you. I'll come back for you, Sandra. Goodbye for now.*

The eyes darted off toward the north, and soon disappeared into the endless midnight.

As the fifth of May edged into the sixth, Charlie approached Devil's Hole. With the Caput Mortuum dangling from his mouth, he leaped over the gate surrounding the Hole. The Caput Mortuum wouldn't stop screaming, but that didn't matter. No one could hear her all the way out here.

Charlie padded toward the hidden boat. He dropped the Caput Mortuum into the sand. She landed with a quiet *thunk* and rolled away a few feet, cursing Charlie the entire time. Charlie ignored her. He dug away the sand and rocks, then grabbed a corner of one of the blankets between his teeth and pulled it away, uncovering half of the boat. He circled the boat, then pulled aside the rest of the blankets.

"What do you think you're doing?" said Marie. "I'm not getting in that thing! Besides, there's nowhere to go. What are we going to do, float around in that pool? You're insane!"

Once again Charlie snatched her hair in his mouth, then plopped her in the middle of the boat. Charlie placed himself behind the stern and began to push the boat forward with his snout. The boat was now headed directly for the Hole.

"Are you the stupidest creature on Earth?" Marie shouted. "Can't you tell that's just a pool? There's nothing of interest there!" Marie's voice grew more high-pitched as her nervousness intensified. Charlie was pretty good at detecting the lie in someone's voice. Jail will do that to you. You can't lie around in bullshit for thirty-five years and not become intimately familiar with its scent.

Inch by inch the boat drew closer to the pool; the closer the boat became, the less venomous were Marie's demands. Rather than insulting Charlie, she offered him untold treasures for her release. She offered to kiss him, supposedly rendering him immortal. She offered him power, a throne beside her reliquary when the Order at last took over the world.

"I don't know what you've been told," she whispered, "but that's not an entrance into anywhere you want to go. It's not a hole. It leads *nowhere*."

Charlie simply continued pushing until a good portion of the bow hung over the edge of the pool. With one more shove, it would no doubt topple into the pool. Marie's eyes widened as she peeked over the bow. Pale blind fish stared back at her from below the dark water.

"In Christ's name, what do you want from me?" Marie yelled. "Who are you?"

"Please," Charlie said, "you must recognize your own blood. You've certainly spilled enough of it in your time to become familiar with it, you disembodied bitch."

For one moment Charlie saw the light of recognition in her eyes, at which point he gave the bow one final shove.

The boat toppled into the pool, but there was no sound of splashing water. It sank beneath the water and left no trace behind it, not even the faintest of ripples.

"*Not a hole*," Charlie echoed. He howled scornfully at the moon, then leaped into the baleful waters. Again, no sound. No trace.

Devil's Hole, empty once more, waited patiently for its next victim.

Charlie and the Caput Mortuum sat in a wooden rowboat sailing toward the center of the Earth.

They hadn't drifted far from Devil's Hole, the entrance to the underground Amargosa River. The river seemed to trail off deep, deep underground. On either side of them was a featureless, rocky bank from which he sometimes heard strange chittering sounds and the pattering of bare feet. Perhaps this was just his imagination, for he couldn't smell the presence of any living being besides Marie and himself.

Charlie sat on his haunches near the bow. Marie lay propped up against the stern, her eyes darting about from side to side as if expecting Death itself to emerge from the water and drag her down beneath the surface. She was at somewhat of a disadvantage. Her pitiful human eyes could see nothing but darkness within the subterranean cavern, while Charlie's feral eyes were made for penetrating the desert night. It was about time that Charlie had the advantage over the woman who had been trying to destroy him for the past thirty-five years.

"'Can't you tell that's just a pool?'" Charlie said, quoting Marie's own words. Marie remained silent. "Why've you been keeping this from me all this time?" Again, Marie said nothing.

Charlie recalled every journey he and the family had taken into Nevada just to visit Devil's Hole, where they would sit and stare at the strange water, longing for the inner earth. At one time he had even asked a pumping company how much it would cost to pump all the water out of the Hole. The company's immediate reply: $33,000. At the time he had wondered if that figure had been a code meant to clue him in on the occultic influence that was preventing him and his family from entering paradise. After all, there were thirty-three degrees in the Masonic hierarchy, near the top of which sat the Caput Mortuum herself.

Charlie had always thought it odd that such a strict patriarchy would allow a woman to reign over them. Perhaps her connection to the divine, as well as her sexless state, rendered her acceptable to the hierarchy. Why hadn't *They*—the men at the top—disposed of her a long time ago? Who could know? Who could fathom the minds of a secret society? Not even the members of the society itself, it if was truly effective.

"Why?" Charlie repeated. "If you'd let us come down here none of the bad shit would've gone down. We would've done your sleazo sacrifices for you—to keep the moon mother happy, or whatever crazy-ass reason you gave me back then—and then we could've hid out down here and the police never would've caught our asses. Me and Squeaky and Sandra and the others would've been happy down here. I didn't want to 'take over the world.' I didn't want to kick you off your throne. I didn't want anything to do with your fucking secret society. I had my family and that's all that mattered. I just wanted to be happy."

Charlie hung his head, thinking about all the perfect times in those early days right after being released from Terminal Island when it had only been him, Squeaky, Mary, Ouish, and Patricia driving the school bus (before it had become blackened with paint and goat's blood) from city to city, adventure to adventure. He remembered an incident in '67 when an old jailhouse friend gave him two pistols and a carbine, all of which Charlie ended up tossing into the bay. He could have sold them for quick cash, but couldn't bear the thought that they would inevitably be used to hurt human beings. He had been so idealistic then. Where had it all gone wrong?

"Why?" Charlie repeated. "Why have you been fucking with me this whole time? *Why?*"

Marie said nothing.

He knew where it all went wrong. He didn't need it spelled out for him. The high weirdness started when he hooked up with Robert and Mary Anne DeGrimston, the leaders of the Process Church of the Final Judgment, while Charlie and the family were staying at The Spiral Staircase in Topanga Canyon. When the DeGrimstons began offering him large amounts of cash, cash he needed to keep his family together, just to perform a small job here and there, Charlie couldn't refuse. "As long as it's nothin' illegal," Charlie had said, but he needn't have worried. After all, magic rituals weren't illegal if they didn't hurt others (directly, that is). These rituals didn't, not at first. The pain didn't come into it at all until much, much later—until Charlie was so far down the rabbit hole he didn't know what the real world looked like anymore. By the time DeGrimston had introduced him to the Caput Mortuum it had all seemed so natural, as if a talking severed head was an everyday phenomenon. He had even come to think of Marie as a friend, so much so that he refused to accept money from her or DeGrimston anymore. He would perform the rituals for free. And perform them he did, even on the surface of the moon.

"Why?" Charlie said, the word becoming an endless, angry mantra. "Why, why, *why?*"

Marie said nothing.

Charlie rose up on all four legs. The hair on his back bristled. He lowered his head, bared his fangs. A growl from deep in his gut erupted out of his throat. Saliva dripped from his fangs and onto the bottom of the boat.

At that moment Charlie smelled the presence of another being nearby. He glanced upward just in time to see Death descend upon him with black wings and razor-sharp claws....

Charlie and Marie found themselves standing in the middle of a dining car on a coal-black steam engine. Charlie was no longer a coyote; he was human once again. Marie, too, had regained her body. She looked stunning in a flowing scarlet gown, resembling nothing if not Crowley's vision of the Whore of Babalon. Charlie wanted to throw her down on the ground and beat the beauty out of her. But he held back. He felt embarrassed by all the high society snobbish types staring at him and his rumpled clothes with obvious disapproval. Various groups of people sat around the car drinking tea or coffee, reading the newspaper, having a quiet conversation. Charlie and Marie weaved their way through the lace-covered tables, trying to reach the door that led to the next car.

A waiter stepped in front of Charlie and shoved a tray full of teacups in his face. A silver teapot sat on the tray, wisps of steam floating out of the spout. "Hot apple cider tea," the waiter said through a wide, rictus-like smile.

The sweet-smelling aroma wafted into Charlie's nostrils. It was hard to resist. "No, man, not now. Uh, we'd rather explore the train, maybe find our room."

"You can explore the train any time," the waiter said. "But after this moment has long since dissolved into the past, will you ever be able to retrieve this particular cup of hot apple cider tea?"

Marie ran her soft fingertips along Charlie's forearm. She leaned near his ear and whispered, "I *am* thirsty."

Charlie could feel his penis hardening. He tried to get it under control. "All right... I suppose we can relax long enough to have one cup."

The waiter guided them to an empty table near a window. He seemed quite enthusiastic as he placed the cups of tea in front of them. "This will help smooth out a rather bumpy ride."

Marie pointed a red-painted fingernail toward a young couple sitting at the table next to them. "Can I have some of those little cheese biscuits they're eating?"

"Certainly, Madame," the waiter said and walked briskly away.

"It's been so long since I've eaten anything," Marie said, then took a sip of her tea.

"*Why?*" Charlie said through a scowl, continuing his interrogation as if it hadn't been interrupted by Death itself.

"Why haven't I eaten? Because I haven't had a body in two millennia, silly. Why do you think?" She smiled over the rim of her cup.

"You know that's not what I mean." Outside he could hear the tentative, chugging sounds of pistons beginning to turn. The station seemed to pull away from them rather than the other way around.

Marie sighed and rolled her eyes. "Isn't it obvious? I simply couldn't let you gain access to the land of the dead."

"Why *couldn't* you?"

Marie said nothing. Charlie slammed his fist against the table. Everyone turned to stare at them.

"Because," Marie whispered, "I thought you were going to use it as a base from which to attack me. I thought you wanted to dethrone me and prove that you were the descendant of the Savior."

"But that's cr—," Charlie started to say. With his peripheral vision he could see people still staring at them sideways. He wished they would just mind their own business. He lowered his voice to a whisper. "I didn't even *know* I was related to you people until I started doing these bullshit rituals for you. If you'd just left me alone, I never would've found out about it."

Marie took another sip of tea, her pinky protruding into the air. "Please, we simply *have* to keep track of all you people. We can't just let you bastards run around free. There's no telling what you might do. If there's one thing the Order doesn't like, it's surprises." She sighed. "No, we had to keep an eye on you, there's no question about it."

Marie said all of this in a very condescending tone. Charlie hated that. She reminded him of all the school teachers and prison guards and wardens and parole officers who'd ever "taught him a lesson" with the tip of a poisoned tongue or the end of a wooden baton.

"And how long have you been 'keeping track' of me?" Charlie said.

Marie rolled her eyes again. "Since you were born, of course. We thought if we put you in that 'school for boys' you'd be out of our hair for a good long while, but you just kept escaping over and over again. You were a persistent little shit, I'll give you that. But that's partly why I thought we might be able to use you. Unfortunately, I didn't give much thought to the possible blowback effects."

"Blowback effects? What the fuck are those?"

Marie smiled sadly. "I'm looking at them," she sighed.

There followed a moment of uncomfortable silence. Charlie didn't know what to do, what to say. He took his first sip of tea.

"Good tea?" Marie said. She didn't wait for him to answer. "Would you like to fuck me?"

Charlie was taken aback by the question. "What? I *hate* you. I want to *kill* you."

She grinned. "Is that a yes?"

Charlie placed his hands on his knees and glanced at the other passengers. They were all happy and laughing, telling each other jokes, gossip about mutual acquaintances, news of the day. How long had these people been on the train?

Charlie thought about all the people he'd killed. All those souls. Sacrificed for what? For her? Is *she* all he had left? Is *she* what he'd wanted all along?

Charlie grabbed Marie by her blue-veined wrist and pulled her toward him, leaned over the table and kissed her on her crimson lips. Their tongues intertwined. They kissed passionately for a very long time.

"Ahem, excuse me, Madame. Your cheese biscuits." Charlie heard the waiter's voice right next to his ear. He pulled away from Marie and glanced around, but there wasn't a trace of the waiter anywhere. Perhaps he had never been there. Charlie craned his neck over his shoulder, saw the waiter emerge from a doorway on the opposite side of the room, a doorway that seemed to be dripping pieces of itself onto the floor. An outline of liquid silver formed around the smiling waiter. He strolled toward their table in slow motion, crimson-trail-afterimages floating languorously behind him—visual echoes, infrared shadows of the position he had occupied only a second before. Sitting upon the metal platter in his hand was a wicker basket containing pale white biscuits—biscuits that squirmed over one another like worms.

"Ahem, excuse me, Madame. Your cheese biscuits."

Charlie snapped his head away from the strange sight and peered through the window. The train was barreling through a cavernous passage. Trapped within the diatomaceous earth, lodged up to their waists, were live human beings. They were naked and frail; it seemed as if an entire limb might snap off at the merest brush of a butterfly. Most disturbing of all were their tortured wails as their bony arms stretched outward, attempting to scrape the window with their long, cracked fingernails. They just barely missed the train, like Tantalus reaching for his fruit. The hellish sadness locked inside their sunken eyes radiated outwards in tangible waves and filled the entire dining car with pain.

Charlie doubled over, clawed at his gut. It felt as if the inside of his stomach were being eaten away by sulfuric acid. He remembered falling down a flight of stairs at his grandparents' house when he was five. He remembered one of his many "uncles" sitting beside him on the living room couch to lecture Charlie about the unreliability of women; the man's alcohol-laced breath smelled sour, felt uncomfortably warm against his cheek. He remembered his grandmother pulling him out of elementary school after he suffered a beating by a gang of stronger kids. He remembered learning about astrology from a book he'd found in a garbage can at the age of nine. He remembered his first orgasm at twelve when he allowed the boy down the block to touch him between the legs. He remembered the first time he cracked a multiplication problem at his grandfather's strident demand. He remembered the faceless state workers dragging him away from his mother. He remembered running away over and over and over again, trying to find her, regain her, always failing. *Why doesn't she pull me away from this nightmare just like Grandma did back in elementary school?* He remembered surviving on his own for many months, scrounging through garbage cans for food. He remembered being arrested for armed robbery, thrown into jail again and again. He remembered killing his first man with nothing more than his bare hands, felt the pain of the man's death in every cell of his body. He remembered entering a coal-black train. He remembered kissing Marie on the lips. He remembered doubling over, clawing at his gut, feeling as if the inside of his stomach were being eaten away by sulfuric acid. He remembered....

Just before the end, Charlie reached the center of the Earth. It was quite a beautiful place filled with chocolate fountains and food trees. Sandra and Squeaky were there; so was the rest of the family. They laughed and played creepy-crawly and sang songs, just like in the old days.

In the center of the Earth no one ever manipulated anyone else, you couldn't feel pain, and everyone always told the truth.

Beneath the central sun Charlie sat cross-legged in an endless field of wild strawberries and cranked out some old classics on his guitar while a chorus line of scorpions and spiders danced and performed back-up. The family linked hands and joined in.

All the songs have been sung

And all the saints have been hung
The wars and cries have been wailed
And all the people have been jailed
The world is yours, my friend
It's yours to begin or to end
In the eyes of the dreamer
In the eyes of the man
Take nothing from nothing
Brother, it's all just the same
For the loser is the winner
And there ain't no blame
It's just the end of the game
The moment is ever constant in the mind
Everywhere I look the blind leads the blind
Here's your chance to step out of time
There ain't no reason and there ain't no rhyme
For the trouble you bring is the trouble you bring
And a thing is a thing just a thing is a thing
In the eyes of a dreamer
It's in the eyes of a man

Then came the instrumental break. Charlie jammed on the guitar while Wynken, Blynken and Nod performed a complex soft shoe number. The music came down slowly. The central sun seemed to brighten and everything faded away into *ice-cream eaters so this faggot saw God screaming he let go of the body he was holding God, how he wanted something to say to the Captain spread a large umbrella over himself until I came to the point where the moor paths broke off Shock! Hexagram fifty-one! Oddsbodikins! but as he keeps on performing impossible acts clergyman paused in the street panic made them open at once set them to cleaning fish we sat on a bottle-glass boulder now there was little hope of escape the geometric design of the Machine was simple host-peoples and to replace it by the mass the comets have such a space to cross he looked doubtfully at the pristine white bed sheet round and round went the room there were two peepholes in the airlock from that height the approaching silver car was small indeed bravery is not enough it was a bitter winter there was the sound of marching boots outside now he could layer the goo i'm not sure believing in me is such a hot idea for he was not to remain a sailor, or a super-cargo these spheres enclose the Earth, which is at the center reason is dead (drying her eyes)*

*when comedians ask them if they're having a wonderful time i'm tired of pills
and needles bodies of both living and dead we're carried away so that the land
lay under a cloud for seven days it is it is all nothing is unseen food turned out to
be no problem the inquisitor shrugged i hate guys like that deep in his body, the
knotting heat began again there had been such a depth of ocean in his words you
fall down and they begin kicking you the rubber was on and he felt like a damn
fool while just a few hundred feet below I am yet six months before my time and
a pair of huge, square, black shoes and, well, it just* looks *niftier feeling nothing
and not tasting his snickers bars after what happened to the grandparents it was
a few months quiet if pressure were exerted upon this depression, the bed could
easily give way and buckle all public money shall be published from time to time
fragments of speeches came from his lips I have a few more words at my disposal
and I can't ignore that I told her that's how it is with guys in the TV world fake
bottles set in fake concrete and I had about made up my mind I would stay there
all night when I hear a* plunkety-plunk, plunkety-plunk

Marie floated down the Amargosa River not far from the capsized boat,
wondering how the hell she had gotten into this position. Today was
May 6th. Exactly 322 days from now would be February 21st, thirteen
thousand days after the raping of the moon mother, the day the secret
chamber within the Great Pyramid was to be opened. Of course, she had
no idea what lay within, but she assumed it would enable her to gain total
control over a world that had wronged her too many times to be forgiven.
She had gone far past the point of asking the Father why He had forsaken
her. Now she just wanted revenge.

Unfortunately, it didn't look like she was going to get it—at least
not today. Not on December 5th. Not ever.

Tch, she complained to herself while she stared up at the
stalactites that hung from the cavern ceiling far above her, you
go through nearly two thousand years of skullduggery and covert
machinations and all for what? For a stupid con—who's never even
read an entire book in his life—to mess it all up in the end? It doesn't
make any sense. There has to be more to it than that.

On the left side of the bank she suddenly saw a figure standing
there in the darkness. At first she thought it was nothing more
than her imagination. Then the figure bent over and reached out
for Marie's hair. He dragged her toward shore, lifted her up out of

the water. He was thin and tall with a long gray beard that nearly touched the middle of his chest. A hood was drawn low over his face and a dark robe covered his entire body. A raven was perched upon his shoulder, the very same raven that had attacked Charlie.

At last, Marie understood whose game she was in.

Strangely, knowing for certain didn't make her feel any better.

THE DIALOGUE

MUNIN: Did it work out like you wanted?

THE BRINGER-OF-ECSTASY: Of course. Did you ever doubt it?

MUNIN: No, but I still don't understand why Hugin had to die.

THE BRINGER-OF-ECSTASY: He's only dead for now. No doubt, we'll carry his body away with us when we return home over the Bridge-of-Opaque-Colors.

MUNIN: Was she worth all this chaos?

[The Bringer-of-Ecstasy stuffs the Caput Mortuum beneath his armpit and pats her on the top of the head.]

THE BRINGER-OF-ECSTASY: It doesn't matter. I only do what I'm told.

MUNIN: Are you kidding? No one can tell *you* what to do.

THE BRINGER-OF-ECSTASY: I'm afraid that's not quite true.

MUNIN: You're going to have to explain that one.

THE BRINGER-OF-ECSTASY: Mysteries shouldn't be explained—they should be experienced.

MUNIN: More secrets. It never ends with you, does it?

THE BRINGER-OF-ECSTASY: When the world is pregnant with lies, a secret long hidden will be revealed.

MUNIN: And what secret is that?

THE BRINGER-OF-ECSTASY: You're well aware of it. How many times do you need to be told?

[The Bringer-of-Ecstasy—also known as the One-Who-Blinds-With-Death, the Flame-Eyed One, Wand-Bearer, One-Whose-Eye-Deceives-Him, and Father-of-The-Slain—disappears slowly through the ambulating door that appears out of thin air. Munin fades away with him, melts into the ultraviolet end of the light spectrum, returning to the home of the old gods… old gods with old vendettas.]

[Exeunt]

Hail to the gods that are dead.

Decay in Amber

1

First the nightmare, then glass. Images of a giant rat gnawing at his testicles shocked him out of sleep. The light of high noon shone through amber glass, golden, the color of thick honey. The glass arced over the man's head for about three feet to either side of him, then curved downward and enclosed him. He could feel the cool smoothness of the glass beneath his naked back, see a V-shaped flock of birds soaring through the cloudless sky high above him, smell the intense odor of cheap beer suffusing every pore in his body. But he wasn't drunk. At least, he didn't *think* so.

He didn't know what he was... didn't know who he was... where he was.

He shot up to a sitting position, bumping his head on the glass, causing the bottle to tip downward in the water, nearly sinking him. Sinking him? He lay back down again, and the strange vessel ceased its rocking, and the waves receded once more.

Leaving the man to wonder how he had ended up naked, trapped inside a giant bottle, adrift in the middle of the ocean.

But wait, perhaps he wasn't in the *middle* of the ocean. Not quite. Though the water—tinted amber by the glass—stretched onward without end fore and aft of him, starboard and port offered the hazy view of land devoid of vegetation. The man concluded he was floating down a river as immense as the Nile at its broadest point, or perhaps even one of the Great Lakes. He wished he could somehow steer the bottle toward starboard; he seemed to be far closer to the land on that side. But how could he? The man could barely move for fear of sinking the bottle. Panic rose within him. How long could he last trapped within this… this *prison*? He didn't even know how long he'd been here up to this point. He felt thirsty, hungry, exhausted. What could he have done to deserve such punishment? What kind of a sadist would do this to him?

Something cool and wet tickled his spine. Yes, streams of water had seeped in when the bottle tipped backwards after his ill-fated attempt to sit up. A few tiny gashes perforated the bottle cap, allowing him to breathe but threatening to kill him if he tried to escape.

Escape? Was that possible? Could he fit through the neck of the bottle? Could he even swim? He didn't know. Certainly not all the way to shore, not in this condition.

He lay back, watched the sky, weighing the few possibilities open to him, wondering how the situation could get any worse.

The sky began to darken. The clouds seemed to gather out of nowhere. Within a matter of minutes he saw a thin smattering of rain drops pelting the glass above him. *God, no.* Even a slight sprinkle was enough to begin filling the bottle with water. *God, God, no—*

The wind whipped in from the port side, blowing him toward shore at a brisk pace. His heart rate quickened, quickened. Would the wind be brisk enough? Could he get within swimming distance of shore before the bottle sank beneath the waves?

As the featureless land formation drew ever closer,—almost as if it were bearing down upon him rather than the other way around— he began to realize that this was no ordinary shore, no sandy beachhead or fertile riverbank. No, this particular shore was made of concrete. And crouched upon its edge were a pair of gigantic beings with sharpened sticks in their hands, their eyes focused on *him*. The barest scintilla of hope that had risen within him during the past few minutes now dissipated as swiftly as fog in sunlight. What were these monsters planning on doing with him once they caught him?

He would find out soon enough, for as the wind drew him ever closer the two giants reached out as far as possible and tried to snatch the bottle with the ends of their sticks. Through the mist and rain he could not be certain at all of his first impressions, but the features of the giants seemed almost Mongoloid in nature, like the retarded adults he had taken care of that one summer in the special home.

The special home. A fleeting memory. He had been seventeen then. He'd considered the job an imposition, taking away time that might've been spent on more important matters. On what? He clenched his teeth and fists, trying, trying so hard to remember. If only he could concentrate....

Impossible. Not through the wind and the rain and the assault of the giants. At long last one of the beings managed to hook the bottleneck with the curved end of his stick and drew him slowly toward the concrete shore. The beings grew more and more immense as he approached them. They seemed to be at least forty feet high, the size of that other place, that strange fortress he'd lived in before... before....

Before what?

The giant had him now, the bottle clenched in his pale hand; he lifted it into the air, dangled it in front of his blue eye by two fingers. "Holy shit, Danny, look at this."

"Just a beer bottle," Danny said.

"No it ain't. There's a little man inside."

"Yeah. Yesterday it was the gremlin in your closet. I'm not fallin' for that shit again. My sister tells me there ain't no Santa Claus and I believe her."

"Fuck you. Look!" The unnamed giant thrust the bottle at Danny.

Danny peered at it. His eyes grew quite wide. "No fuckin' way," he whispered very slowly.

"Yes way." The giant pulled the bottle back and held it protectively against his chest. "And it's mine. *I* found it."

"Okay, okay. But let's show it to my sister. I bet she could tell you how to get some money for it."

Of course, by this point the situation had become quite clear to the man. These beings weren't mythical beasts. If anything, the only mythical beast in his vicinity was *him*.

He tumbled around in the bottle as the boys ran toward home.

2

"What d'ya think it is?" Danny asked.

Janice, Danny's older sister (she seemed no older than sixteen), kneeled down beside the bottle and with a look of absolute incredulity peered at the man trapped inside. She didn't say anything for awhile, just sat there on the beige carpet at the foot of the bed, twirling the ends of her long brown hair around her index finger, staring.

The man was glad his chaotic journey was over. He felt as if every inch of his already-fragile body had been battered and bruised on the way here. Now the bottle sat immobile on the pink comforter draped across Janice's fluffy bed. It was a far friendlier environment than those storm-wracked waves had been. Outside, hailstones pelted the closed window.

At last Janice managed to whisper, "It's amazing."

"Amazing?" Danny said. "Hey, that don't tell us how much it's *worth*."

"What do you care?" Billy said. (The man had heard Danny's sister refer to the other boy by this name.) "You didn't find it. You're not gonna get any of the money."

"I *know* that, dude. I'm tryin' to do you a favor here. Jeez!"

"I just don't want you to try an' say it's yours like you did with that hunting knife."

"That *was* mine! I picked it up first!"

"But I *saw* it first!"

Janice sighed and held up her hands. "Okay, just calm down." From her tone of voice, it seemed as if she'd said the same exact phrase a million times before. "This thing may not belong to either of you." Though disappointed, the two boys did not object to this statement. Apparently they respected the girl's opinion. She lowered her pretty face close to the glass and said softly, "What if... what if this thing came from, like, outer space?"

At which point the man rose to his feet and shook his fist at the girl. "I'm not a 'thing'!" Janice reared back, as if surprised that he could talk. "I'm a god damn human being and I want out of here! Let me out! *Now!*"

Janice, Danny, and Billy exchanged silent glances for a moment, unsure of what to do. Then Billy said, "Don't."

"Hey, how would you like to be trapped in a bottle?" Danny said.

"But what if it runs away?" Billy was obviously still worried about his money.

"You know what happens in movies when people open up things they're not supposed to," Janice said.

"I'm not a friggin' character in a god damn Disney cartoon," the man screamed. "I'm hungry!"

The kids seemed to understand "hungry." "What do you eat?" Janice asked.

"Anything. A slice of bread. I don't care."

Janice turned to Danny and Billy. "Well, I suppose we need to feed him."

"How're we gonna feed him if he's inside that thing?" Danny asked.

"Just drop crumbs into the bottle," Billy said.

Janice shook her head. "No. We have to get him out of there."

The man breathed a sigh of relief. Thank you God, he said silently.

While Danny and Billy left the room to fetch a slice of bread, Janice asked the man, "Who are you? How did you get in there?"

"I don't know. I can't remember."

"Do you have a name?"

He shook his head in frustration. "I can't *remember*."

"Are you sure you're not from outer space?"

The man waved his hand in the air as if to say, *Don't be ridiculous.* "I have fleeting memories, snapshots of my past, but I can't connect them to anything. They don't mean anything to me."

"Maybe you got bumped on the head or something. That's how it happens in the movies."

"This isn't a movie, this is my *life*!" He was practically jumping up and down now. "Where're those two brats with my food?"

Janice leaped to her feet. "That's not very grateful."

He realized he was blowing it. "Sorry. I'm just in an agitated state. It's not every day you find yourself trapped in a bottle without a stitch of clothes on." Janice turned her head away, as if she hadn't realized he was naked before that point. He could see that her cheeks were turning red.

"I-I'll try to find something for you to wear." She turned her back to him and opened the closet doors.

He got a real good look at her from this perspective. All in all, Janice was a nice little package. A bit too innocent for his tastes, but sometimes that had its advantages. Yes, back in the day he would've had a lot of fun with a girl like that—after plying her with a few drinks, of course. It was always a riot to watch the "innocent" façade break down after a few cold ones....

The man grew dizzy for a second. Slowly, he lowered himself to the wet surface of the glass. He waited for the room to stop spinning. Were these *his* thoughts? What kind of a life had he led... before...?

"Are you all right?" Now Janice was standing over him again. She held something in her hand.

"Yeah... yeah, I'm okay, kid. Just felt a bit light-headed, that's all."

"Well, I think I found something for you to wear." She held it up between her thumb and forefinger. A tiny pink nightgown. "I found it in my old Barbie doll house set."

"Forget it."

"It's all I have."

"What about Ken? Didn't he have any friggin' pajamas?"

"I lost all of Ken's clothing."

How the hell do you lose all of Ken's clothing but not Barbie's? He didn't even bother to ask. He just sat there in glum silence.

"It's all I have," she said, a touch of petulance in her voice. As if he would be disappointing her if he didn't do as she said. Yes, they develop that tone at an early age. Must be in the genes.

"Well, I can't put it on in here."

"How do we get you out?"

"Get a hammer and break the fucking glass!"

Janice seemed shocked by his language. She flung the nightgown on the bed and stomped out of the room. The man rolled his eyes. Somehow, he'd managed to find the one teenage girl on the planet who could be offended by the word "fucking." Where had he ended up, in some backwater Seventh Day Adventist colony?

A few seconds later the two boys returned with the slice of bread. They'd smeared grape jelly on it. Probably the only thing they knew how to make. He didn't care. He'd eat anything at this point.

They sat the plate down on the mattress, only inches away from the perforations in the bottle cap. He felt like Tantalus in that ancient Greek myth: tied to a tree with water up to his chin and fruit dangling above his head, both forever out of reach.

Danny and Billy just stood there staring at him as if expecting him to step through the glass like a ghost. The man sighed and said to Danny (who seemed to be the more reasonable of the two), "I think your sister left to go get a hammer. Maybe you should help her bring it back."

"Why does she need a hammer?" Danny asked.

The man closed his eyes. *To whack you upside the head, you stupid little shit.* He opened them again. "To get me out of here."

"Why don't we just pull off the cap?" Billy said.

"Does it *look* like I can fit through the neck?"

Billy hung his head, shrugged his shoulders. "I dunno."

It looked like the kid was gonna cry. Hell, you better say something. You need these little shits to get out of this mess. "Hey, kid, I'm sorry. I'm just feeling a little cross. I don't like being cramped up in here. I'm a bit claustrophobic, always have been." Was that true? He couldn't know, but it felt as if there was some kernel of truth to the statement. He *hated* closed-in spaces and would do anything in his power to break out of them. Break out...? Something niggling there in the back of his brain....

Janice returned with the hammer. She said to Danny, "Better turn on the TV, just to drown out the noise. We don't want Mom to hear and start snooping around." There was an edge of terror to her voice when she said this.

Danny switched on the small TV that sat atop Janice's dresser. It had a seven inch screen; the newscaster that appeared on it was black and white. The set seemed far too old, out of place in a teenage girl's bedroom. The newscaster was talking about a flood threatening to devastate valuable beachfront property in Malibu.

The man had two instinctual reactions to this information. First: Serves them right, the filthy rich bastards. Second: I'm in California. Of course. I've *always* been in California.

Janice said, "Maybe you better crouch down near the back of the bottle, just so you don't get hurt by the glass. Close your eyes too. You don't want slivers getting inside."

The doll was really looking out for him. It touched his heart. He did as she suggested, even turned his face to the bottle's circular bottom. For the first time he noticed the number 20 imprinted in the amber glass. Then he noticed his own reflection. It was shocking at first, and yet strangely familiar. Despite his haggard appearance,—sunken-in cheeks, unshaven face, dirty hair—he was handsome. In his late twenties. With a cleft chin, strong jaw, an aquiline nose that had been broken at some point in the past, piercing blue eyes, fair skin, almost feminine lips. He wanted to keep staring at his reflection. Instead he closed his eyes and braced himself for the coming explosion.

Janice gave the neck of the bottle a slight tap. Nothing happened.

"Look, don't pussyfoot around it," he said. "You want to be here all day? Just whack the son of a bitch!"

"I wish you wouldn't say things like that."

"Like what?"

"You know. That word."

Oh, Christ. He'd have to drop into the Little House on the Prairie, wouldn't he? "I apologize profusely, miss. I am much chastened and chagrined by my poor choice of invective. Now will you *please* demolish the motherfucker and get me out of here?"

Janice gasped in horror, then raised the hammer into the air. In the background, the newscaster said something about a place called Terminal Island in Long Beach. The name struck a chord in his memory. *Terminal Island.* The newscaster continued: something about a prison break. Yes, a dangerous criminal was loose in the area. Lock your windows and doors! Be on the lookout for this man....

The hammer came down on the glass with a tremendous CRASH! He could feel the vibrations jangling the nerves in his back teeth. Instinctively, he locked his hands behind his neck to prevent falling shards from damaging his spinal cord. Perhaps he'd been in dangerous situations like this before. Perhaps.

He turned slowly and opened his eyes. Most of the glass shards lay near the front of the bottle. The neck had been demolished. The opening was wide enough for him to walk out. He was free.

He glanced up at Janice, intending to thank her. But neither she nor the other two boys were paying any attention to him. No, they were all staring at the TV.

At him. His face. He looked different on the screen, but of course that was probably just the photograph. After all, it was hard to look handsome with those numbers hanging around your neck.

A caption at the bottom of the screen identified the escaped prisoner as Charles Henry Manning, convicted in 1998 on twenty-two counts of serial rape and murder. All the victims were young girls between fifteen and eighteen.

3

"Cool!" Billy said. "Can we keep him?"

"No!" said Janice. She raised the hammer again and came at Manning.

Manning backed up against the glass and raised his hands in the air. "No, please, wait!"

"Why should I?" Her lips, painted a subtle pink to match the light rouge on her high cheekbones, were twisted in a snarl. The girl had such pretty lips. "You're a murderer. A… a monster!"

"No! It's not true. I'm *innocent*."

Janice hesitated a moment. "How would you know? You said you can't remember anything."

"It's come back to me now." This, of course, was a lie. Seeing his mug shot had indeed jarred some brief memories: lying on a thin sheet draped over metallic grillwork, staring up at a filthy gray ceiling while sucking on a cigarette, trying his best to ignore the offensive stench rising from the shit-stained crapper in the corner of the 8 x 10' cell; sitting in the noisy dining hall, his only companion a puke-yellow tray containing soggy mashed potatoes covered in watery gravy with thin slices of artificial turkey and stale bread on the side, digging into this slop while feeling the hateful eyes of the other prisoners upon him; being attacked in the yard, the guards having to pull the hands of a large black man from his throat before…. That was all. He remembered nothing more.

But this didn't stop the words from pouring out of Manning's mouth: "That's why I had to get out of there. Because I was *innocent*. Somebody else did those crimes. If only they'd performed DNA testing like my lawyer wanted everybody would've known that. I would've been a free man. But the police didn't want DNA testing. No, they had their man and they couldn't be bothered with the truth. They framed me. I was just in the wrong place at the wrong time. Janice, can you imagine what that's like? Being accused of such a horrible crime, having all your friends and colleagues thinking you're... you're some kind of a *monster*? I lost my job, I lost my family, I lost my freedom. That was the worst of it. Losing my freedom. I'm claustrophobic by nature, can't stand closed-in spaces. Imagine being trapped in a little gray room, being told you can't leave for the rest of your life. Wouldn't *you* do everything you could to escape? Wouldn't you?"

Janice glanced around her bedroom. For the first time Charles realized how sparse the room was. Nothing hanging on the walls. No posters of rock musicians or soap opera stars. No gothic romances lining the book shelves. No half-completed diary lying open on a desktop cluttered with make-up and dolls. Just white walls. Very *clean* white walls. And the only books adorning her shelves were school textbooks, as lifeless as the blocks of stone that had surrounded him in prison.

She lowered the hammer. And said, "I don't know. I-I *hope* I would."

"Then you understand."

"I think so."

A moment of silence followed. Then Billy said, "So... so we *can* keep him?"

4

They decided he should remain their little secret. Charles was more than willing to stay, at least until he could regain a portion of his memory—the portion that could tell him where he had been headed when he broke out of that prison, and how he had ended up in this freakish condition.

The kids waited on him hand and foot. He was like a toy to them. Billy came over every day after school just to stare at him. Billy disturbed Charles the most. He kept asking him questions like, "So what was it like to kill those women, huh?"

"Listen, kid, I already told you. I'm innocent!" Of course, Charles couldn't be sure of that at all. Occasionally he perceived fleeting images from… his past? A past? A flash of young tanned skin covered in erratic swaths of blood. Scarred red wrists struggling to break free of the ropes that bound them. Smeared lipstick encircling the mean end of a billy club.

But were these his memories, or somebody else's? He didn't feel connected to them in any way, as if he were watching them on a television screen. Ambivalence was his only emotional response to the possibility that these images represented crimes he himself had committed with his own hands. He was bothered by the possibility; he wasn't bothered by the possibility. Hell, he didn't know what to feel. How on earth could he feel anything when he didn't even know who he was?

Despite his constant refutation of these crimes, Billy kept at him with the damn questions. "Did you ever slap the girls around when you did it to them? Did you ever stick your thing in her butt, like my Daddy does to Mommy?"

"You're one creepy son of a bitch, kid." Charles backed away from him and collapsed onto a pile of washrags that Janice had stuffed near the back of a makeshift house cut out of an old shoe box. It was pretty spacious, far larger than that cell on Terminal Island. He had a thimble full of food (bread crumbs) and an egg cup full of water. They gave him better stuff when he asked for it, but this was fine for now. He was just glad he didn't have to wait in that long line anymore.

Billy got down on his stomach and peered at him through the rectangular window cut into the box. "Did you use an axe like Jason or knives like Freddy?"

"You've been watching too many movies, kid."

"I don't watch as many as I used to, not since they started giving me the Luvox."

"I can't imagine why. Maybe you should chill out a bit. Get a hobby. Sports are good for you."

"I like boxing. I like how it feels when my fist slams into their face and the bones crunch and stuff. It's even better when they're not expecting it. Some of these sissies at school, they're like little girls. They cry when you break their fingers."

"Okay. Well… at least you're getting some exercise."

"I want to be like you someday."

"Five inches tall?"

"No, an escaped convict. I want to have a girlfriend who can drive the getaway car while I lean out the window and shoot at the police with a submachine gun."

"I can't say I've ever experienced that, Billy. Of course, I can't say I *haven't*, either."

"My daddy owns a lot of guns. He taught me how to use 'em in case the U.N. invades."

"The U.N.?"

"Yeah, he says the United Nations is gearing up to attack the United States with black helicopters and Russian tanks."

"It's good to have a strong role model, somebody who can teach you about the birds and the bees."

"I wish *you* were my daddy. My daddy's never been to jail."

"Give the old man a break. Maybe he's working his way up to it."

Billy seemed skeptical. "I *wish.*"

"In the meantime, did you have any luck finding that G.I. Joe doll? I'm getting sick of wearing this pink nightgown."

"Oh yeah, that's the whole reason I came over here, isn't it? Boy, I forget things real easily. The doctors say I have ADD."

"How could they sell your parents Luvox if they didn't say that?"

Billy stuffed the camo fatigues through the doorway. Charles stepped behind the curtain he'd rigged up around his bed and changed into the uniform. He suddenly had a brief recollection of his father (yes, a large bear of a man with premature white hair; this *must* be his father) standing in front of a mirror while telling Charles that he, too, would join the Army when he grew up to protect the United States from the Communists threatening to topple Latin America. "If the U.S. doesn't stop them," his father said, "you're gonna have to be strong. Stronger than everyone around you."

Charles remembered taking that advice to heart. He *did* grow strong. But he'd had no interest in joining the Army, not after hearing about his father being spat upon by veterans of World War II and longhairs alike upon his return from Southeast Asia. He had no interest in joining any organization, not even the boy scouts. He hated uniforms. Hated people. He would spend his life trying to run away from both of them. Inevitably, in the end, he would be forced to wear a uniform and cohabitate with other people twenty-four hours a day.

These sudden bursts of recall always caused him to grow quite dizzy. To steady himself, he grabbed hold of the plastic green lawn chair that had been liberated from the back yard of Janice's doll house. Once this moment of weakness had passed (don't worry, Father, it was only a moment), he stood up rail-straight, clicked his heels together, and began marching up and down the pitiful cardboard shack, laughing, laughing his head off.

"Are you okay?" Billy said. "D-do you like your uniform?"

"I'm fine!" he yelled. "Couldn't be better!" He was happy, happier than he'd been in the past week. He'd retrieved a huge chunk of his past in one sudden burst.

I remember you, Father, he said silently.

I remember why I hated you so much.

5

They tried to throw out the remains of the bottle, but he prevented them from doing so. He told them to hang onto it, hoping it would offer up some more clues as to how he had ended up inside it.

Janice left the remains inside the box, just in case her mother entered her room while she was gone and found the glass shards. ("Why would your mother come into your room while you're gone?" he asked. She shrugged. "You know, to see if I'm cleaning up after myself. I think they saw some show on PBS where this kid was hiding drugs under her bed. They want to make sure I'm not, you know, smoking weeds and stuff." Charles didn't say anything. He was too busy remembering the time he threatened to sock his mother in the jaw for trying the same routine on him. She didn't try it again. Another precious memory, restored.) He hadn't seen Janice's mother yet, thank God. Nor her father. To him they were just warbling voices that sometimes floated through the door like the disembodied parents on those old Charlie Brown cartoons. He hoped they stayed that way.

Charles felt so impotent. Minor annoyances that might have been stopped in the past with a simple threat were now, potentially, major obstacles worthy of his fear. He didn't like to be afraid. He'd never liked being afraid, not since... since what?

As he sat in the shoe box, his legs crossed Indian-style, meditating on the amber shards spread out before him like precious archaeological finds, he glanced up through the lopsided window; his idle gaze happened to alight upon the crucifix hanging above Janice's bed. And he remembered.

He remembered sitting between his mother and father every Sunday morning.

Listening to the hellfire and brimstone pouring out of the preacher's mouth like molten lava.

Watching the emaciated, tortured flesh of Christ squirming there on the cross as if He were actually alive, as if He were actually dying right there before his adolescent eyes.

Feeling the thorns clawing into His scalp, feeling the nails digging further into His gushing arteries, feeling the warm blood seeping down His bony arms and feet.

Tasting the body of the Savior on his tongue, the blood of the Son of God trickling down his parched throat.

And thinking: Pain. Pain is the key. Mother and Father love Christ because He's in more pain than they are. They love Him... they love Him more than they love me. But they don't really love *Him*. They love Pain. It's the only thing they respect, the only thing they'll ever respect. So if I want them to love me I'll have to give them Pain, I'll have to give it to them in spades.

He remembered, he remembered.

He opened his eyes and stared at the afternoon sunlight reflecting off the glass. Almost without thinking about it, he reached out and picked up a fist-sized shard. He drew it to his breast, then lowered the shard and began sawing the forearm between his elbow and wrist. Slowly. Back and forth. Slowly.

He smiled. With the pain came more memories.

6

At 3:11 P.M. Danny tip-toed into Janice's bedroom. Charles recognized him from his dirty sneakers, the laces of which were always on the verge of coming undone. Danny bent down in front of the shoe box while whispering, "Charlie? Charlie, are you awake?"

"If I had been I certainly wouldn't be anymore, not with you booming in my ear like that. Sounds like a PA system in my skull."

"Sorry. I tried to whisper."

"Well, whisper a little more softly next time."

"Do you mind if I bring you into my room for awhile?"

"Why?"

"Well, I don't think it's fair that Janice gets you all to herself. I'm the one who found you."

"Billy was the one who found me."

"Well... yeah. But it was *my* idea to go down to the river. If I hadn't've asked him he never would've—"

Charles waved his hand in the air. "Okay, whatever, get to the point."

"Well, I thought I could bring you into my room and invite some of my friends over and—"

"And show me off like a circus freak? Forget about it."

"It's not like I was gonna charge admission or anything—"

"Forget about it!"

"But what if—"

"If you don't haul your ass out of my room right this instant I swear I won't tell you any more stories about Terminal Island ever again."

Danny looked dejected, but he didn't argue. These kids seemed to respect *him* more than their own parents.

"Aw, all right," Danny said, dragging his feet behind him as he left. "Jeez, I didn't mean nothin' by it—" He shut the door behind him.

Charles relaxed again. Abandon *this* room to live with some snot-nosed brat? Why? The only bright spot in this whole absurd mess had been the girl. Janice Spindell. She'd told him her full name a couple of days before. She was quite a looker, and the fact that she wore her beauty with such unknowing innocence made her even more attractive. She was a firecracker waiting to explode. Her fanatic parents had kept her locked up in this little room for far too long. Girls like Janice didn't react well to confinement. When finally exposed to the joys of the real world, they displayed the behavior that a person without an immune system might exhibit when introduced to a small amount of bacteria. They go berserk, desperate to make up for all the pleasure that had been denied them in the past. Charles could sense a potential wildcat in the making, could actually *see* the waves of pent-up desire rippling just beneath her luscious pale skin.

He'd seen her naked more than once. Late at night, just before bedtime, she would dull the light beside her bed and begin taking off her clothes. Slowly. So slowly. First her blouse. Then her skirt. Her bra. Then she'd sit down on the edge of her bed, skinny out of her white stockings, her pink panties. She'd pull the braid out of her hair, shake her head in that seductive way only girls know, allowing the long chestnut-tinged hair to waterfall down her naked back. At no point did she look at him. At no point did she give the slightest indication of even knowing he was there. At no point did she seem to realize how sensual every movement of her body was to him. This made her even more enticing in Charles' mind.

He knew she had a boyfriend, some budding poet named Peter, but she wasn't allowed to talk to him on the phone. She wasn't allowed to do much of anything. Hell, she wasn't even allowed to stay out past nine o'clock. Peter the Poet must've been going out of his fucking mind. How many times had he been a mere finger's length away from her left tit or her cunt only to have it snatched away from him by the ticking of the clock? Pitiful, just pitiful. A living hell.

Charles didn't like waiting, never had. He didn't need to have any memories to know that.

Which made the situation even more torturous. He was worse off than Peter. Janice had clearly come to think of him as little more than a dog. Or a cat. Or a pet mouse. A lesser beast around which no modesty was required. Very few people ask Fluffy to avert its eyes while they change clothes.

That evening Charles lay on his blankets, hidden in shadow, stroking himself in time to the natural rhythm of Janice's unconscious striptease, trying to imagine the smoothness of her naked thigh, knowing he'd felt similar sensations before. Numerous times. But he could not recall them in detail, seeing only fleeting glimpses of faces. Young, pretty faces.

No names were connected to any of them.

As the diaphanous nightgown slid over her body he climaxed into his hand, whispering the name of the only woman he'd ever known.

7

The sound of shouting rose through the floor and into Charles' ear, ripping him out of a nightmare about mannequins. The dream was already starting to fade, like so many others he'd had in the past week. These days he didn't have much to do except sleep and dream and practice being a good pet.

For a moment Janice's high-pitched screams rose above those of her parents, but she was shouted down by her father. Charles glanced up at the red digital numbers glaring from atop Janice's night stand: 9:15 P.M. Ah, so that was the problem. Janice had stayed out fifteen minutes too late on a Friday night. Fifteen minutes. Poor kid.

Janice came bursting into the room, tears streaming down her cheeks. She flung the door closed—then at the last second thought better of it, snatched the doorknob, and gently pushed it shut. Without a sound.

Defeated, Janice plopped down on her mattress and stared at the ceiling. He could hear her crying in the dark, way up there on that fluffy mountaintop. He didn't know if he should ask her what was wrong, or just remain quiet as he'd done during her stripteases. He wasn't good at talking to women, never had been.

Wait a minute, was that true? How could he be sure? But his subconscious was telling him it was so, wasn't it? Perhaps he should trust it. He had nothing else to trust these days.

So fine, then. He wasn't good at talking to women. If he was truly guilty of the crimes the news channels had accused him of these past few days, that shouldn't be much of a surprise. And yet it *was* a surprise. He couldn't conceive of doing the things they said he'd done. He tried to imagine it, tried with all the hate he could muster up from his patchwork memory, but couldn't place the bloodiness of the deeds with these hands.

And why should he? Say he *was* guilty. So what? That was Back Then, in a world as far away from him now as Venus or Jupiter. Should he be held responsible for crimes he couldn't even remember? The second he awoke in that amber bottle he began a new life, with new rules, no matter what his subconscious tried to tell him. He was a new man, held back only by the limitations he created for himself.

He marched out of the box, crept over to the side of Janice's bed, and called up to her: "Are you all right, Janice?"

She gasped and jerked up to a sitting position, as if pulled by strings from above. Then he heard her sigh with relief as she peeked over the side of the bed. "Oh, it's only you. You gave me a scare." She laughed. "I've gotten so used to you, sometimes I forget you're there."

That made him feel good. Christ, maybe he should've stayed in the box. "Is there anything I can do?"

She wiped the tears from her face with the back of her hand. "Thank you. That's real kind of you. I-I don't know what you could do, though."

"I could listen."

She smiled. "Well, okay." She reached down and allowed him to step into the palm of her hand, then lifted him into her bed as if he were riding a freight elevator.

She sat on her side, propped up on her elbow, her face resting in her hand. Charles stood a respectful distance away, not too far from her chin.

"You can sit if you want to," she said.

But that would make him look even shorter! "I think I'd rather stand. So what's wrong?"

"Oh... it's my parents. It's *always* my parents."

"They do seem pretty strict."

"They're freaky. None of the other kids at school have parents like them."

"I know what you mean. My father was a captain in the Army.

ROBERT GUFFEY

He served two tours of duty in Vietnam. My mother was a religious fanatic. She'd sit around all day quoting passages from *Revelations* while trying to find new reasons to punish me. They were both born agains."

"Sounds like you're getting some of your memory back."

"I didn't remember anything until a couple of days ago, when I put on this uniform."

She giggled, as if noticing it for the first time. "It looks good on you."

"I hate it. It reminds me of my father."

"You hate him that much?"

"Yes. I can't tell you why exactly, I just *feel* it. I think he wanted to reshape me in his own image or... I don't know. It's still pretty fuzzy."

"That's what my parents want to do to me. They want to make me into an exact clone of *them*."

"Why were they yelling at you, because you were late?"

Janice rolled her eyes. "9:15 is late to them. What *planet* are they living on?"

"Where were you?"

"With Peter."

"You must like him, I guess."

"I hate him." Her lips curled into a sneer as she idly picked at a loose thread in the blanket. "I'm only going out with him because Mom and Dad hate him so much. He's just this pretentious, wanna-be poet. He writes me all these sonnets filled with dead swans. Dresses all in black. He thinks he's Allen Ginsberg or something. He's probably a faggot and doesn't even know it."

Charles had never heard her talk that way before. "Why do you think that?"

"'Cause he kisses like one." She rolled over onto her back, threw one arm over her forehead, and stared at the cottage cheese ceiling with a faraway look in her eyes. "I want a man who knows what to do with a woman. Someone who doesn't tip-toe around, asking my permission every time he wants to put his hand on my tit. Somebody who knows what he wants and just takes it."

After a moment of silence Charles said, "Sounds like you've given a lot of thought to this."

"I have. I want to get out of this place. I just need...." The hand on her forehead wilted into a fist. "I just need somebody to show me how."

Charles didn't know what to do at first. His subconscious was trying its best to reign him in. He ignored its nagging warnings as he scaled her rib cage. The black cotton blouse was slippery to the touch; he almost lost his grip a couple of times, but he didn't allow that to stop him. Within moments he was standing on her midriff, just above her bellybutton. He could feel her belly rise slightly with each intake of breath. She did not move, did not utter a word as he began the long walk up to her enticing white neck. He ran his hand along the smooth curve of her collarbone like a religious fanatic caressing a holy idol. He planted gentle kisses upon the massive wall of flesh, not even knowing if she could feel them. Still she said nothing.

Unclasping the first button on her blouse wasn't as difficult as he'd feared, only as difficult as removing a bedspread from a queen-sized mattress. He pulled the thin material aside, exposing her right breast. She said nothing. It looked so different up close. He could see all the imperfections in the mound of flesh, the pimples, the gaping pores, the thin silver hairs poking up intermittently around the pink aureole. And yet this unwelcome magnification did not serve in any way to lessen its erotic artistry, its monumental simplicity. He just stood there for a moment, admiring its beauty as it rose ever so slightly with each breath that Janice took, studying it as if it were a piece of kinetic sculpture under glass. Then he scaled the sculpture, kneeled down before the erect nipple, and began massaging it with both hands in slow circular motions.

He glanced up at her face when he heard the sound, that sweet little moan. Her eyes were now closed. Her fist remained on her forehead while the fingers of her left hand dug into the blanket. He quickened the pace in gradual increments. Her moans deepened. He twisted the nipple between both hands, hard, harder. He flicked his tongue back and forth across the nipple's crater-pocked surface. She raised both hands above her head and gripped the bedpost. He bit into the nipple, hard, still harder. Her hips began to shift back and forth with great violence. She whispered his name. Once. Twice.

He slid down her breast, crawled over her bare midriff on his hands and knees, planting kisses across the faintly silver hairs that covered her flesh like down. Her flesh: an erotic landscape waiting to be explored, a perfume-scented playground that stretched out before him promising further delights. In the quiet darkness of her girl-room scattered remnants of her adolescence hung all around him, as if accusing him of a crime with their silence. From her desktop a tiny regiment of stuffed animals stared at him disapprovingly with googly eyes made of cloth. He tried to ignore them.

She helped him explore her, reaching down to slip off her skirt, then her panties, being careful the entire time not to kick him off the bed by accident. She lay back down, naked except for her open blouse. She began playing with her nipples, smearing a small trickle of his saliva around her right aureole. She whispered two words to him. At first he wondered if he was imagining things. But then she said the words again, very precisely, as if she'd practiced the line more than once, perhaps having heard it in a movie.

He removed his clothes, though his nudity couldn't affect her pleasure in any way. She spread her legs for him, spread them as wide as possible. Such a simple gesture, this silent invitation, and yet it meant so much. He entered her, all five and a half inches of him. Remember, size doesn't matter, Charles told himself, not as long as you know what you're doing. But do I know?

It felt so strange to have her moist pink flesh surrounding him on all sides. A few pockets of air enclosed him, enabling him to breathe. Yes, now this was a claustrophobia he could deal with. He reached up for her clitoris and tickled it with all five fingers while he spread his legs out as far as they could go. This was no minor feat; it took great callisthenic skill. He must have been spending his time wisely in that exercise yard back on the Island. Even from where he was, he could hear her ecstatic moans. Janice raised her butt off the mattress and squealed, intoning the names of two-thirds of the Holy Trinity. As if *they* were the ones who were fucking her! For a moment Charles thought he was involved in a metaphysical gang bang, but no. A girl had to moan something while having an orgasm, didn't she? Why not something holy? Would her parents prefer that she invoke the name of some filthy pagan god or even Satan himself while she got fucked?

Something ripped inside her. Blood flowed over him in a sudden burst. This was such a surprise, he had no time to prepare himself. He almost drowned while being swept out of her vagina. Janice wouldn't let this setback stop her fun. She was lost in the initial throes of her first orgasm. She grabbed him by his legs and shoved him back inside her, deep inside the seeping redness. She used him like a dildo, stabbing herself savagely. He inhaled as much as possible every alternate thrust, holding the precious air in his lungs while immersed inside her. He suspected such dirty words had never been used in this household as many times and in such quick succession as in the past fifteen minutes. He hoped her parents were practicing their hymns downstairs, otherwise they might break in at any moment thinking their precious little princess had gone Linda Blair on them. Thankfully, this did not occur. Instead, the mad circling motions Janice was performing with her pelvis ceased ever so slowly, ever so slowly. The thrusts lessened in intensity. Charles had more time to breathe between each submersion. Then at last she released a quiet little sigh and remained still. She lay there for a moment, staring up at that same damn ceiling she'd been staring at her entire life (which no doubt looked quite different to her now than it had fifteen minutes ago) and contemplated the darkness in silence. Then drew Charles up to her chest and deposited him on her left breast. She didn't seem to care that he was covered in blood.

"You know what," she said, "I like you."

"I like you too," he said. "Does this mean we're going steady?"

"Of course."

"What about Peter?"

"Fuck Peter."

"I'd rather fuck you."

"You just did."

"Not quite." He gestured down at his erect penis.

A look of concern washed across her face. "I'm sorry. What should I…?"

"Just stay still, honey, and open those pretty lips of yours." He crawled up her throat and climbed onto her chin, leaving little bloody footprints behind him. He perched himself upon her lightly painted lips and began stroking himself. "Moan like you did a couple of minutes ago. Call out my name."

She did as he asked. It didn't sound like she was faking. She was good at this, real good.

A couple of seconds later he spurted a stream of milk-white come into her mouth. He was so excited, it streamed out of him like water from a fire hose; it overshot her tongue and went straight down the dark bottomless cavern of her mouth. For a moment he imagined being the first explorer to discover the Grand Canyon, seeing all that wide open virgin territory, and after an obligatory gasp of wonderment, after realizing "Hey, I'm all alone," dropping his pants and jerking off into that scenic panorama. A divinely-inspired tableau.

After the first two or three spurts, a few pearls dribbled onto Janice's lower lip. She licked them off with her tongue.

"Ever tasted that before?" he asked.

Her eyes widened. "Of course not!" For a second, her mother's voice crept into her tone. "It doesn't taste bad. But it doesn't taste good either."

"Probably an acquired taste."

"Smells like bleach."

"Really?" He'd never realized it had a smell.

She looked kind of funny at the moment. In order to stare directly at him, she had to cross her eyes. Like one of her stuffed animals. He laughed.

"What's so funny?"

"You."

"Do you love me?"

"Of course," he said.

"Say it."

"I love you."

She smiled. "Sorry about all the blood. My freshman Health teacher warned us it'd be like this, but I didn't think there'd be so much."

"S'okay. I'd like to clean up, though."

"I'm gonna have to throw away this blanket. How'm I gonna explain where the blanket went?" She set him down beside his box, so he could wash off inside the egg cup.

"Don't worry about it," he said. "We'll think of something."

He washed himself thoroughly (while Janice wiped the bloody footprints off her body with the now-ruined blanket), then she carried him back into bed with her. He lay on the pillow beside her ear. They spoke about a lot of things that night. Funny things, serious things, weird things. They got to know each other.

He fell asleep curled up on her chest.

8

Janice's parents grounded her indefinitely for her insolence the previous night. She pretended to be upset, pretended to cry. Inside, however, she was smiling. Wet with anticipation.

They made love all day Saturday.

All day Sunday.

During church services, right in front of everybody. It was Janice herself who came up with that idea. She smuggled Charles into church inside her skirt. Over the course of the entire service she reached orgasm eight times. She could hardly sit still. During the singing of the hymns she couldn't help but wiggle around in her seat, intoning the name of the Lord a bit louder than she'd intended. Afterwards Father McCollough called her aside and congratulated her on her enthusiasm. "It warms my heart to see a young person so enflamed by the Word of God. It's all too rare these days."

Janice blushed and stared at the ground.

"No need to be embarrassed, my child," the priest said. "If we had more teenagers like you attending church, the world would be free of sin within a few generations."

"Thank you, father," she said. "You don't... y-you don't... know how much that... that means to... me." She practically squealed this final word, as Charles was now doing something very clever with his tongue. She couldn't help but giggle.

McCollough laughed too. He said it was nice to see a teenager so jittery in his presence. After all, the Lord's representative *should* instill that kind of awe in the young. These days most kids reserved their respect for hedonistic rock singers and drug-addled movie stars. A few minutes later, while everybody was filing out the elaborate double doors, he congratulated Janice's parents on having such a devoted daughter.

This inspired such pride in their hearts that they lifted their indefinite punishment. At first Janice was upset, but later when they were alone again in her room Charles reminded her that if they could get away with fucking in front of God they could get away with fucking in front of anybody. They could fuck during Math class if she wanted. This so pleased her that she ran downstairs and told her parents she was going to willingly lock herself in her room and practice her hymns all day just so she could impress Father McCollough again next Sunday. Her parents smiled at one another and nodded. *You see, Frank? You see, Helen? The "experts" try to convince you that stern punishment only serves to make the child even more rebellious, but we've just proved the "experts" all wrong. Janice's future is bright. Maybe she'll grow up and attend seminary school. They accept female priests now, you know. Oh Frank, oh Helen, is it too impossible to dream that our very own Janice might become the first female Pope?*

Back in her room, Janice put an old .33 record on the phonograph her parents had given her long ago. ("CD players are creations of the Devil!") The album was a compilation of classic hymns performed by some famous London choir. Janice stripped to the hymns. She had all the moves down pat. She was a natural.

"You could be making a fortune with that routine downtown," Charles said.

"Really?" She was blushing again. "Maybe that's how I'll support us when we run away."

"Is that what we're doing?"

"Yes."

"When?"

She frowned. "I don't know. When I'm ready."

"When will that be?"

"I'll let you know." She unfastened the first button on her blouse. She was such a tease.

"Janice? Can I ask you a question?"

"Sure."

"Will you answer it?"

"Maybe."

"Did you know I was watching you all those nights when you were getting undressed for bed?"

She smiled. She unfastened the second button.

It went on like that for awhile. Everything else faded away from Janice's life. Friends, schoolwork, television, books. That was all just a blur, a half-formed papier-mâché background she swept past on a wave of multiple orgasms provided by a convenient, pocket-sized boyfriend invisible to almost everybody but herself. She didn't even allow Danny or Billy to *talk* about Charles anymore. She wanted him all to herself. Even the thought of him. Even the memory of him. Even his name.

As for Charles, he couldn't have been more content. He couldn't stand being away from her for even a minute. On those rare occasions when she had to leave him at home, he curled up in a pile of her unwashed panties and pretended he was riding inside her. Nice and safe and warm. So warm. He felt protected within her, as if nothing could hurt him while surrounded by her needful warmth.

They fell into a routine formed by their mutual obsession with one another. The routine seemed to benefit everyone involved. Janice's parents were pleased with her new, improved attitude. Janice's teachers were pleased with her high grades; they said she seemed to be *concentrating* better. (It was basic Pavlovian conditioning: recite complex trigonometry equations aloud for hours on end while receiving multiple orgasms and even the dullest of us will remember them.) Father McCollough was certainly pleased with her riotous performances in Church. A representative from A&M University in Texas happened to be attending services one day and offered Janice a music scholarship because he felt she would be "a most valuable addition to his own choir." Janice squealed with pleasure upon hearing the news, though the two events were not related in any way.

In this manner the routine continued for exactly six weeks and six days. On the seventh day, a Wednesday, the routine abruptly came to an end. The events surrounding this premature terminus were broadcast all over the network news and held most of Los Angeles enthralled for a better part of that afternoon and continued to do so well into the evening, after what remained of the body died in police custody. This is how it happened....

10

Janice had owned the black-and-white TV for years. Her uncle, who was far less fanatic about his faith than her parents, had given it to her on a whim. "I'm just gonna throw it out anyway," he'd said. Her mother and father had been dead set against it. They didn't think television was healthy for children. Many years before they'd read a Hal Lindsey book suggesting that both the television and the Xerox machine were inventions of the Devil. Somehow her Uncle had managed to persuade them that *black-and-white* televisions were devoid of Satanic influence. Thus, Janice had been allowed the keep the set.

Thus, Janice and Charles were watching it when the chase began.

Earlier in the morning Janice had convinced her parents, via clever method acting and the time-honored trick of pressing the thermometer beneath one's armpit, that she was far too sick to go to school. Unfortunately, she kept the thermometer in place too long, giving her a temperature of 102 degrees. Her mother was so concerned she decided to stay home from work that day and take care of her. No matter. She and Charles could fuck right in front of her nose and the haggard old bitch wouldn't notice. She was too stupid, lost in an imaginary world of angels and demons, sin and redemption.

Janice flung her pajamas onto the floor (if her mother walked in she'd simply say she was too hot to wear them, which wouldn't be far from the truth) and proceeded to whisper sweet nothings in Charles' ear. They fucked away the entire morning and the beginning of the afternoon, taking breaks to eat ice cream smuggled in from the kitchen. When two o'clock rolled around they were halfway through a bowl of Rocky Road, lounging at the foot of the bed watching old Foghorn Leghorn cartoons. Charles was just about to comment that a classic sequence involving cigarette smoking had clearly been edited out when a newscaster who looked rather like a Ken doll on speed interrupted the proceedings with a "special" news bulletin: a dramatic car chase was now underway on the 405 Freeway. A flotilla of police cars was in hot pursuit of a black 1967 Mustang. Both a police chopper and the network's oh-so-impressive "Eye in the Sky" helicopter were also involved in the chase. The scene cut to an aerial view of the pursuit.

"What's so 'special' about that?" Janice said. "Shit like this happens every day in L.A."

Charles shrugged. "Aw, it's good for ratings. People love chases, as long as they're not the ones being chased."

As if to prove that point, neither of them switched the channel. They hardly paused in their consumption of ice cream; perhaps there was very little difference between a fifty-year-old cartoon and a live police pursuit.

Along with thousands of other Angelinos, they remained glued to the set as the battered Mustang led the cops on a 120 mile-per-hour chase through Santa Monica, past Redondo Beach, Torrance, Carson, through Wilmington, and straight into Long Beach. They watched as the car drew closer and closer… to their neighborhood.

At first Janice thought it was funny. "Hey, they're gettin' closer to here!" She really got into the rhythm of the spectacle, applauding when the pursued car would deck it through a red light, just barely miss an old lady walking a dog, sideswipe a Volkswagen, wrench off the open passenger door of a parked car, blow a tire and keep going, the naked hubcap causing sparks to fly behind it like on a NASCAR racer. Which is what this was. A race. Entertainment for the masses. Charles was vaguely disgusted by it, but Janice seemed to be enjoying it so he didn't ask her to change the channel.

He didn't ask her to change the channel even as the sinking suspicion descended upon him that this chase was somehow connected to him.

Even as the Mustang crashed through a police barricade meant to stop it from entering a residential neighborhood.

Even as it wound its way through the labyrinth of suburban streets, somehow honing in on one particular block.

Honing in. On one particular street.

One particular house.

There it was on the TV screen: Janice's house shot from the intrepid "Eye in the Sky" news camera. Janice stared at Charles, open-mouthed. Charles just stared at the TV. He could've walked over to the window, but for some reason he chose to watch it on the screen. He couldn't hear the newscaster's commentary over the sound of the helicopters hovering above the house, but this was what he saw:

The Mustang screeched to a stop in Janice's driveway. The driver door swung open. Nobody got out. The police converged on the car, weapons drawn. The helicopter tilted slightly, enabling the cameraman to get a direct shot into the car. There sat a hysterical fat woman with long gray hair, thick glasses reflecting the smog-filtered sunlight, tears streaming down her sagging jowls. She already had her hands in the air, layers of fat settling down around her shoulders. The cops pulled her out of the car and shoved her face into the cement. One of the officers pressed his jackboot against her spine while another adjusted the handcuffs to fit around her massive wrists. She never stopped crying.

"Is that it?" Janice said, spreading her hands in the air. "I wanted to see a gunfight."

"There's always the next car chase."

"But the next one probably won't stop outside my house." She crossed her arms over her chest and pouted, looking more desirable than ever. She wore her petulance well. He decided to forget the sinking feeling in his gut. He reached out and caressed her inner thigh....

The door swung open. Janice slammed her legs together, crushing Charles between them. He heard Janice's mother say from the doorway, "What's all that commotion outside?"

Janice threw the blanket over her lap, then released Charles from the vice-like grip. "It's all over the news," Janice said, "you should've been watching it."

Her mother sighed. "I have better things to do than watch nonsense. What happened?"

"They chased a woman at 120 miles per hour all the way from Santa Monica, across the 405, through downtown Long Beach, and right up to our doorstep. Isn't it exciting, Mother?"

"I think it's horrible. The news just encourages such things by glorifying it. People want their... their 'fifteen minutes of fame,' so they hop into a car and lead the police on a wild goose chase. It shouldn't be allowed."

"It's not, Mother. The police are beating her up right now."

"Good. It's what she deserves."

"When are you going to let me drive, Mother?"

"Never, if things like this keep happening. Besides, it's very difficult to learn."

"I already *know* how to drive. They taught us at school and I've been watching Dad drive all my life."

Her mother sighed. "Oh, as if you can just pick it up like *that*." She snapped her fingers.

Janice lay back on the bed. "Forget it. You never let me do anything."

"I'm just saying it's not as easy as you think."

"All right. You know best." She kept her eyes locked on the TV screen. The fat woman was struggling, screaming something. A pack of cops encircled her, obscuring her from the view of the camera. The billy clubs came out.

"Are you going to keep watching that?" her mother said.

Exasperated, Janice smacked her tongue against the roof of her mouth. "Of *course*. I'm waiting to see if somebody gets *shot*."

"That's horrible! You must be running a fever!"

"That must be it."

"I'm going to talk to your father about getting rid of that TV set!"

"Yeah, you do that, Pretty Lady."

"We've got quite a tongue on us all of a sudden, don't we?"

"Same tongue *we've* always had. See?" She showed it to her.

Her mother was speechless for a second. "Just wait until your father hears!" she managed to sputter and slammed the door behind her.

Charles crawled out from underneath the stifling blanket. He wiped his brow of sweat and said, "Finally! Man, I thought she'd never leave."

"Shit, you can say that again." The unfamiliar voice came from below them. In tandem, Janice and Charles looked down at the carpet. There, peering up at them with an impish grin on his face, was a fifty-year-old bald black man dressed entirely in rags.

He was no more than six inches tall.

11

Sirens still screamed outside. Channel 11 had switched back to cartoons, the thrill of the chase having wound down to moribund scenes of a crazy fat woman being beaten to death. There was nothing titillating about that, nothing at all.

For a moment, before the switch, Janice's mother could be seen standing on her porch calling out congratulatory remarks to the police. Then Elmer Fudd appeared, blasting cartoon bullets at a smartass wabbit. If there was a subtext to this juxtaposition, Charles couldn't puzzle through it.

He was too busy gaping at the little black man standing on his carpet. ("His" carpet. For the very first time, he realized that he truly thought of it that way. "His" carpet… "his" home… "his" Janice.)

The stranger spread his arms and said, "Jesus Christ on a pogo stick, Hank, you ain't seen me in almost two months, can't you at least say hello?"

Charles opened his mouth; no words came. Who was this man? He seemed vaguely familiar, but….

"Charles?" Janice said. "Do you… do you know him?"

Charles closed his eyes, trying to place the face. "I… I don't know."

The stranger dropped his arms. "Is this a joke?"

Janice said, "He doesn't remember who he is. Can you help him?"

The stranger ran his hand over his smooth, hairless skull and blew out his cheeks. "Oh Lord, I didn't count on this."

"Who are you?" Janice said.

"Mr. Isaiah Jones, Esquire, at your service, miss." He bowed at the waist.

Janice wrinkled her brow. "What's 'Esquire' mean?"

"I have no idea, miss, it just sounds good."

Charles opened his eyes and studied the stranger: his kind, wide eyes; his distinguished salt-and-pepper beard; his lithe, swimmer's body. He had an ethereal aura about him, like that of a born dancer or a musical prodigy. But this gracefulness was offset by a deep sense of pain and loss that hovered over him like a dark halo. As with someone who had been forced to pack a hundred years of tragedy into only fifty.

A faint memory was niggling at the back of Charles' brain, but....

He shook his head. "I don't... I don't know you."

Isaiah turned to Janice. "How long has he been like this?"

"Since we found him."

"How long ago was that?"

"About two months."

"Have you been taking care of him?"

"Well, of course."

"I want to thank you for that, miss. I don't know what I'd do if...." Isaiah twisted the bottom of his patchwork shirt, wringing it nervously between both fists. "Well, I've found him now, that's the important thing." He turned back to Charles. "We can leave whenever you're ready."

"Leave?" Charles murmured.

"Yes, of course. We've still got a mission to fulfill. Don't you remember *that* at least?"

Charles willed the grogginess from his mind. He stood up straight on Janice's knee. "I'm not going anywhere. This is my... my home."

Isaiah's grin wavered for a second. The nervousness in his hands had infected his laughter, diluting it into a weak nasal whine. "Tell me this is one of your little jokes. You're pulling ol' Isaiah's leg again, right?"

"It's no joke, pal."

"We've been friends for over two years. We're *blood brothers*. We made a promise to each other, said we'd watch over each other to the very end. You don't remember any of that?"

Charles shook his head again.

Isaiah threw his arms in the air. "This is bullshit! We've got to get going! We've got a *mission*!"

"What mission?"

Isaiah let out an exasperated sigh. "I can't tell you in front of her!"

"There's nothing you can say that she can't hear."

"Listen, I know she saved your life, man, but that's no reason to go blowing the whole—"

"It's reason enough for me, stranger. Go ahead, spill it. What's the mission?"

Isaiah planted his hands on his hips and stared at the floor, as if running through the various possibilities flitting around in his brain. At last he said, "Do you know how you got into this… condition?" He waved his palm up and down, indicating Charles' diminutive size.

Charles' chest swelled with anger. "You think this is a fuckin' game? You think I know and I'm playing dumb? Why the fuck would I *do* that?"

Isaiah raised his hands in the air like a policeman directing traffic. However, his movements were far more graceful, far more fluid than any policeman's. Perhaps, instead, he resembled a mime pressing his hands against an imaginary wall. "Okay, okay," he said softly. "I'm just trying to figure out where to begin."

The words that followed, the words that poured out of Isaiah's mouth, were both strange and disturbing. He began not at the beginning, nor at the end, but close enough to both to satisfy everyone involved. He began with the grimoire.

ROBERT GUFFEY

12

Isaiah discovered the grimoire in the fourth year of a life-long sentence. The questions of why he had been given such a harsh sentence, or if he even deserved it, were both irrelevant. He was no less innocent than anybody else serving time within those gray, unforgiving walls.

The walls, like the prisoners within them, held strange secrets. Isaiah uncovered one of them while helping to renovate the library; he'd begun working there to earn money for cigarettes and candy bars and stamps to mail sad, rambling letters home to his older brother. While painting the east wall with a roller, he detected a slight bump. One of the bricks was loose. Ignoring the wet paint now dripping from its surface, he jerked it out with his bare fingers. Behind the brick lay a cool, shadowy niche that contained a small black tome bound in rough leather. The only identifying mark on the cover was an unreadable hieroglyph, or rune, that was silver in color and looked something like a crescent moon impaled on an upside-down broken cross. He opened the book. The pages inside were thin and brown, filled with wood pulp, as if the owner had made the book with his own hands. Each page, front and back, was covered in small crimped letters without indentations of any kind. The book was just one long paragraph.

The initial sentences were surrounded by quotation marks. They read as follows: "The sigil of Zamradiel is composed of a lunar crescent pierced by an arrow shot from a bow, both ends of which terminate in the letter G. The transfixed moon is the crucified flesh. The 'crucified' are those who have made the crossing of the Abyss. The letter G (*gimel*) signifies the 'camel', the ship of the desert, the vehicle by which the crossing is achieved. It is the letter of the High Priestess. This tunnel concentrates the influence of Set *via* the Black power-zone (Binah) that receives its light from the Stellar Sphere (Chokmah) and rays it downward through the abyss. The 17th *kala* is thus strongly charged with the atmosphere of Daath and of Death, both of which have close affinity with the *Lovers*."[1]

From that point on the book proceeded, over the course of nearly three hundred pages, to delineate the ancient alchemical secrets of transubstantiation. Lead into gold. Flesh into spirit. Death into life. Order into chaos.

At the moment Isaiah was more interested in the second function. For if he could somehow learn to transform flesh into spirit, then Terminal Island might be far less terminal than most believed, and the walls not so unforgiving after all.

He slipped the book into his prison uniform and smuggled it back into his cell. The incantations in the book were not totally unknown to him. He'd seen many of them while hanging out with his older brother. Since the late '60s Isaiah's brother had built up something of a reputation for himself in the occult underground of Southern California. He had changed his name to Lou Ishmael and made his living reading palms and Tarot cards for middle class white housewives, who were quite impressed by his "dark, mysterious" personality—so impressed, in fact, that his readings sometimes did not stop at just their palms.

This disgusted Isaiah. For years their relationship had been severed due to this and other disagreements between them. Isaiah had joined the Panthers when he was only eighteen. He'd read the teachings of Elijah Mohammed, *Soul on Ice*, and the autobiography of George Jackson before graduating high school. Louis, though ten years older, supported his brother's political affiliations but would never join such an organization himself. He believed in neither bullets nor ballots as valid methods of affecting change. Instead he performed what he called "private acts of chaos magick." For years

---

1 Grant, Kenneth. *Nightside of Eden*. Great Britain: Frederick Muller Ltd., 1977.

ROBERT GUFFEY

he'd been obsessed with the Kabbalah, the ancient teachings of the Rosicrucians, and the infamous writings on the self-styled "Great Beast" himself, Aleister Crowley. Isaiah wasn't impressed by such silly facades; he thought Crowley was nothing more than "another fat British faggot with too much time on his hands." So Louis tried to teach him the art of Voodoo instead, but Isaiah couldn't have cared less. He didn't go in for that mystical mumbo-jumbo. That was just Christianity wrapped in a different package. White skin, dark skin; it was still an empty box.

Isaiah put his faith in the concrete, in the here and now, in the transformative power of revolutionary politics. The more he learned about his Black heritage, the more he believed it was wrong to copulate with white women. Some of the brothers looked at it as a badge of honor, as if they were somehow getting back at the Man. Isaiah didn't see it that way. He was in no mood to be some white bitch's house nigger, exploited for an orgasm rather than for a bale of cotton. It was slavery with another name.

That his older brother would exploit himself in this way, to the exclusion of his own sisters, was nothing less than heinous. That he would turn his back on revolutionary politics for the ephemeral world of British occultism was nothing less than traitorous. Which is why he'd refused to speak to his older brother for ten years. Until 1982. When his string of luck ran out and he was nailed by the Man at last. Nailed for something he didn't even do. Isaiah Jones was innocent. Had been since he was born. It was impossible for a Black man to be guilty of *anything* in White America. Five hundred years of oppression absolved all ties to a corrupt justice system.

And yet despite this theoretical impossibility, he was nailed anyway. Nailed and stoned and spat upon and flung into Purgatory. Literally. After all, they didn't call it Terminal Island for nothing.

Strange things can happen to a man trapped in Purgatory. He starts rethinking the choices he's made in the past, and beliefs that seemed so deeply held only a few years before begin to drop away like dead skin. Isaiah began communicating with his brother again, through letters. At first his motive was somewhat selfish. He wanted to compile a prison memoir to beat all prison memoirs, even *Soledad Brother*, and Louis would be a trustworthy repository for his ongoing journal. But the letters abruptly switched from out-and-out political diatribes to a personal account of the dark emotions that had been dragging at his heart like a hook for over a decade, a sad eulogy on the death of his idealism, a final sighing gasp of the revolutionary optimism that had been so ingrained within him throughout his thirteen-year-long relationship with the Panthers. The transformation occurred when he received Louis' first response to his letters. It consisted of a single sentence:

Talk to me.

That's when the tears came, followed by the words.

The words were excellent therapy for him; they invoked emotions and memories he thought he'd forgotten. They led to a total restructuring of his worldview. They led him to a place of light where thoughts that had once been taboo in his world could now be acknowledged and openly discussed.

They led him to a place where the discovery of the Book was not only possible, but inevitable.

The letters delineating his spiritual evolution ceased, replaced with verbatim copies of the esoteric words in the Book. If anybody would know what they meant, it would be Louis Gates Jones.

And know them he did. Almost every day Louis mailed back Xeroxed copies of his letters complete with annotations in red ink describing the convoluted interrelationships tying each letter to every word, each word to every sentence, each sentence to every incantation. More importantly, he explained the function of each incantation and the exact process one must undergo in order to bring about the transformation of flesh into spirit.

He practiced year after year, sometimes alone, sometimes with a bunkmate who wanted him to "put a sock in it and go to sleep, why dontcha?" Isaiah used far less spiritual techniques to deal with such interruptions.

Within four years he had mastered the basic rudiments of the Art. One afternoon he caused a shank to disappear from the fist of an angry skinhead out on the exercise yard. Another day, in the cafeteria, he disassembled an apple into component atoms for exactly twenty-three minutes and reassembled it later on in his cell. It was nice and firm and juicy, not soft and dry like any other apple he'd ever been given in Purgatory. The process had not just preserved the original integrity of the fruit, it had *improved* it as well. He knew he was onto something big. He knew he was well on the path to breaking out of

Terminal Island.

Then came Charles Henry Manning. Charles Henry Manning *Junior*, to be exact. But he didn't like to be called Charles. That was his father's name. He despised his father. He wanted to be called Hank instead.

He took a liking to Hank at once. Hank didn't strut around with a chip on his shoulder like most white men. Despite his strapping frame, his hardened face, he was actually rather shy. Unlike every other inmate at Terminal Island, when Hank proclaimed his innocence Isaiah had no trouble believing him. He was too much of a fearful little boy at heart to ever have done the deeds for which he had been convicted. But the other inmates weren't aware of that. The other inmates hadn't spent almost twenty-four hours a day in his presence, seeing the hesitant way he moved across the cell, hearing the way his voice caught in his throat when he talked about his childhood, feeling the sadness and pain along with him as he described the perpetual Hell (a place that made Purgatory seem far less unbearable) his father had put him through for most of his young life. They knew none of this. All they knew was that a convicted child molester—worse, a child *killer*—had entered their precious sphere of influence. That the man maintained his innocence was irrelevant. They knew he was as innocent as every other man serving time within those walls.

They attacked him. Tried to, at any rate. But Isaiah protected him. Fought them off with the skinhead's shank which he could now materialize in his fist at will. The attackers were impressed by that trick, so impressed that Isaiah quickly gained a reputation as a "Mojo Man." Up to this point he'd tried to hide his budding talents from the other inmates, knowing full well that "Power told is power lost" (as the Zuni Indians liked to say), but in this situation it couldn't be helped. He would never have stood by and allowed Hank to undergo the indignities and torture they'd had in store for him. Later that night, in the cell, in the dark, Hank asked him how he'd made the shank appear out of thin air. That's when Isaiah showed him the Book. That's when he told him his plan. That's when he decided he couldn't leave without taking Hank with him.

While he continued to study, trying to determine how to apply the spell to two people rather than one, he also tried to keep an eye on Hank at all times. He was a lost little boy trapped in a world of animals; he required constant supervision, supervision that Isaiah could not give him twenty-four hours a day. There were times when he simply *could not be there* with him. Like that day he was working in the library. When Hank decided to take a shower. When the prison guards grew temporarily devoid of both eyesight and hearing, overlooked a gang of inmates marching into the isolated area, somehow became deaf to forty minutes worth of screaming.

Accidents happen. Sorry, child molester. Sorry, child killer. Accidents do happen.

Afterwards, Hank barely hung on to his sanity. Isaiah tried to comfort him as best he could. He hugged him to his chest while they rocked back and forth, back and forth. While Hank cried so, so hard. Whispering that he didn't think he could take it anymore. Couldn't go through that again. Wanted out. Out of this body. Out of life itself. Wanted out of this whole painful mess called Earth.

Isaiah said, Shh. Shh. It's going to be all right. We're getting out of here. Just a few more days. Just a few more days and I'll be ready.

I'm ready now. I want to *go*.

Isaiah grabbed his face with both hands and squeezed. Don't talk that way. I'm not going to let you. I'm not going to let you give up. We're both walking out of here together. I don't want you to die. I don't know what I'd do if…. Isaiah was crying now, the first time he'd cried in front of another human being since he was a child. Hank was crying too. They hugged that night, nothing more.

Later… days later… they went so much farther. And it felt so right. And Isaiah wasn't ashamed. And neither was Hank. He said so. Said it made him feel good. For the first time he felt good about himself. About the world. And it gave him a reason to deal with the pain. To persist.

While Isaiah continued his studies, practicing, practicing daily, preparing for that big day. December 22nd. The winter solstice. Louis assured him: that day would best hold the proper resonance required to open a channel to Zamradiel, Sentinel of the 17th Path.

Minutes after lights out, Isaiah began drawing the pentagram in the stone floor. He did it first with white chalk, then coated it with the blood of a live rat he'd hunted and trapped for just this purpose. On his chest as well as on Hank's he drew a sigil, the same sigil that appeared on the cover of the Book. He did it with a mauve-colored marker that Louis had sent him for exactly this purpose. Mauve was Zamradiel's favorite color.

Under the circumstances, of course, certain improvisations were required in the ritual. Ideally, human menstrual blood should be used to summon the demon. Zamradiel was associated with "the blood of the moon, the human female flux in its dark phase" according to the Book. Since no females were available, Isaiah had to demonstrate to the demon that he could tap into his own female side.

Stripped of their clothing, protected within the exact center of the pentagram, Isaiah and Hank performed the same act they had been engaged in night after night after night, unconsciously rehearsing for this very moment. Blood was let. It had to be that way. It was difficult not to utter a moan or a scream, there in the dark silence of the cell. Pleasure was so close to pain.

Blood pounded, pounded in Isaiah's head. He could hear the sound of tribal drums beating offbeat rhythms. They were so god damn loud. Couldn't anybody else in the prison hear them? No, don't think about anybody else. Lose yourself in the moment. Lose yourself.... Upon reaching the moment of orgasm, Isaiah intoned the demon's name in the key of "D."

It appeared in the form of a black pig covered in excrement, smelling of refuse and death. Then it was a magpie. Then a penguin. A piebald. A zebra. But not quite any of these, only distorted parodies possessing one wing too many, or too few eyes, or the wrong color, or the wrong size. At last it settled on its final form: the Spectral Hyena, known to certain African cults as the *Bultu*. It was so large its head almost touched the ceiling. Isaiah could see the prison wall behind it through its diaphanous skin.

The Hyena spoke to Isaiah. Silently. "You have summoned me from my sanctuary, Ville-aux-champs, in the heart of *Kabultiloa*. I pray you have done so for good reason."

Hank was trembling. Isaiah whispered to him, told him not to be afraid, it would all be over soon. He bent down and grabbed the long strand of silver hair he'd plucked from the dead rat for this very purpose. He held it above his head. "I've a gift for you, O Spirit Zamradiel."

The Hyena nodded. "Most excellent. Please lay it down at my feet."

Isaiah shook his head. The son of a bitch wasn't going to get him that easily. He dropped the strand of hair into an envelope, sealed it, folded it in half, then shoved the package outside the circle with the tip of his mauve-colored marker. *Priority mail to Hell*, Isaiah thought.

The Hyena hissed angrily, like a serpent. "I assure you the spell will work much more effectively if you lay the gift at my feet."

"Fuck you! Take it or leave it."

The Hyena hissed again. "Yessssss, O great and powerful 'master.'" This last word was uttered with obvious bitterness. "I obey." It lowered its mouth to the floor and lapped up the strand of hair with its long, black tongue.

"O Spirit Zamradiel, now that you have accepted my gift, I require of you a simple favor." He lapsed into silence, wondering if it was proper form to just launch into the request from here.

"Yessssss?" the Hyena said, a hint of boredom in its lilting voice.

"I require of you a simple transformative spell, a temporary metamorphosis of flesh into spirit for my companion and me."

The Hyena looked at Hank. "Is this your 'lover'?"

Hank buried his face in his hands and began to cry. Isaiah caressed the top of his head. "Yes," Isaiah answered.

The Hyena giggled. "Oh, said with such lofty pride! You've both condemned yourselves to Hell. God does not look kindly upon such illicit congress."

"You lie. I don't believe in a hateful God."

The Hyena responded with hysterical laughter. "Oh, is that so? How do you imagine I ended up in this position, serving scum like you? Because God is forgiving and beneficent?"

"I don't give a shit, you pitiful fuck! Just do what I asked of you."

"Very well, O great and powerful 'master.' I will fulfill your request to the very letter. That is my function, after all. To serve those who are far superior to me in spirit and intellect. Certainly that applies to you, does it not?"

"You're the one lappin' up rat hair, not me. Now will you just shut up and do your fuckin' job?"

"To the very letter."

The Hyena disappeared. That's when Isaiah realized his mistake. Too late.

Zamradiel had distracted him. He had not finished his demands, not entirely, not *precisely*. When dealing with the dark side, the devil was in the details. He had requested a "temporary" metamorphosis of flesh into spirit. Nothing more.

Zamradiel fulfilled his function. He turned Hank and Isaiah into living ghosts capable of walking through the thickest walls ever constructed on Earth. But only for a single second, immediately after which he restored them to flesh.

Zamradiel's definition of flesh was rather broad, for though he had indeed returned the pair to corporeal form... he had somehow neglected to return them *exactly* as they were before the transformation.

They were each only one inch tall.

Somewhere deep in the sunset halls of Ville-aux-champs, seat of the Order of the Shadow, a raven settled down upon an onyx pillar and uttered the hoarse mad cackle of a hyena. Isaiah saw the image and heard the laughter for a brief moment, then collapsed in the center of what now seemed a pentagram drawn by a giant. Consciousness faded away with the Ophidian current's ebbing hiss.

Zamradiel was no doubt amused by the misadventures that followed. Isaiah awoke in Hank's arms. He had dragged Isaiah's unconscious body through the bars and down the long green hall to the gate where the guards sat reading paperback books sent to the inmates as gifts. Gifts larger than a piece of paper rarely reached the inmates.

From there Hank dragged him into a dark hole at the base of the wall, outside the view of the cyclopean guards. Inside the wall Hank tried to wake Isaiah with kisses. Eventually it worked. Isaiah regained consciousness just in time to see the cockroach as it came at them from above, scuttling straight down the wall. Isaiah was equal to the creature in size; he was forced to wrestle it with his bare hands. Its chitinous hide was cold and hard to the touch, like steel. It was Hank who gave him the idea: "The shank! Remember the shank!"

Isaiah materialized the knife in his fist and sliced off the creature's antennae with two swift swipes. Then he plunged the blade through its eyes, and down and down into its face, its unprotected belly. It died quivering, uttering a high-pitched scream, its legs kicking in the air long after it had already expired.

Isaiah grabbed Hank by the hand and said, "Let's get the fuck out of here."

That wasn't possible. To them, the prison was the size of the Great Wall of China. They made it to the stairway that led down to the first floor as the pinkish rays of dawn began to illuminate the pastel corridor. They couldn't move about in the daytime. It was too risky. Too many inmates wandering about, eager to kill anything smaller than a prison guard. So they hid in the shadowy places, protecting themselves from the spiders and the rats when they had to, sleeping when they could. They traveled only at night, living off crumbs and slain insects. Once they made love in an air shaft, beneath a silken web billowing inches above them. The faint sunlight filtered through the silken canopy lent a sad, ethereal atmosphere to their slow, gentle thrusts. Their kisses were laced with a hint of desperation. They thought this might be their last time together. They were right, in a way.

The next evening they made their way into the kitchen. It was there, while standing beside a cardboard box of potatoes for perspective, that Isaiah realized Hank had grown an inch since the night of the transformation. Both of them had doubled in size.

"But that's great," Hank said. "That means we won't be like this forever!"

"Yeah, it also means we have to haul our butts out of here before we're too big to leave."

"How long do you think we have?"

"How the hell should I know?"

"You're the sorcerer!"

"I'm no fuckin' sorcerer. I'm an idiot."

Hank laughed. "You're not an idiot."

"I'll get us out of here. But we better do it tonight. Hell, Zamradiel might decide to turn us back the second we get past the gates. You know what happens then." He mimed firing a submachine gun.

"I don't care. Live or dead, I just want out of here."

So they made the decision. It would be tonight. Isaiah suggested the best way off the Island would be to stow away on the one truck they *knew* would leave in the morning, as it did every morning. The garbage truck.

Outside the kitchen, they tucked themselves in one of the numerous receptacles scheduled for pick-up and waited. The truck came just before dawn. Earthquake-sized jolts rocked them back and forth as the metal claw gripped the receptacles, lifted them in the air, dropped them into the truck's cavernous belly. They found themselves adrift in a sea of coffee grounds, black banana peels, hypodermic syringes, empty plastic bottles, soiled clothes, unidentifiable slime, and even used condoms. Everything would've been fine… if not for the rats.

They erupted out of the sea of refuse, a whole pack of them, each one as large as a cat, the thrill of imminent death causing their hair to bristle and their mouths to salivate. Isaiah told Hank to get behind him as he willed the shank into being. He stabbed the leader in the eye, eliciting a high-pitched wail that sounded like a woman being killed in a dark alley. Hank started to cry.

"You can't hold them off all by yourself!" Hank said.

"Not if I have to worry about you! Get yourself to safety!"

Hank was clearly reluctant at first. He didn't want to leave his lover alone. But he knew Isaiah was right. He had no experience with fighting, with violence of any kind. He would just get in the way. He climbed the mountain of trash behind him; the mountain sloped upward all the way to the lip of the truck. Isaiah was right behind him. The rats drove them all the way up the peak of the mountain where Hank lost it. The stress had become too much. He started blabbering, demanding to know where he was, how he had gotten here, who had done this to him? Was he dreaming? Was he dead? He scurried away from Isaiah, trying to seek refuge inside an empty beer bottle.

Isaiah screamed at him: "Calm the fuck down. What the hell're you—?" Then he realized that Hank had done a very smart thing. The rats couldn't get to him in there. During a moment of respite, while the surviving rats regrouped for a final assault, Isaiah glanced behind him and saw that Hank had fainted. He screwed the cap on the bottle to protect his body in case Isaiah didn't survive the next attack. He whispered his love to him while stroking the amber glass. He thought Hank looked beautiful when he was sleeping.

Perhaps only Zamradiel could have predicted that the truck would blow a tire at that exact moment, sending the vehicle into a tailspin on the bridge connecting Terminal Island to the mainland, flinging the bottle from its precarious position atop the mountain of refuse and down into the water below.

While the screams of Isaiah and the rats merged into a single wounded howl that sounded something like the cackle of a hyena.

The Order of the Shadow tries to be kind to its supplicants. Isaiah emerged from the crash with only minor wounds. His most serious wounds were emotional. He didn't know if he'd ever see Hank again. It was only after the truck had reached the City Dump that he realized it was within his power to track Hank down—*if* he was still alive. It should've been a simple matter to cast a location spell; such minor techniques were covered in the first chapter of the Book. But without the Book in his hands, he had to operate on memory. That wasn't easy. He cast the spell a total of eighteen times, leading him all over Los Angeles County. Fortunately, the Metro Rail will take you pretty much anywhere in no time flat and all for free—that is, if you happen to be only two inches tall. Or even three. Or four. Or five. For within a matter of days he found himself undergoing sudden growth spurts that left him at a height of six inches. Which was still short enough to ensure safe passage between the towering legs of the Metro Rail conductors. The conductors drove him from one dead end to the other as he tried to perfect the spell. But some locations were beyond the range of the Metro Rail. After the seventeenth try, when he found himself alone on the edge of the Santa Monica Pier with no Hank in sight, he decided to give up. He was about to leap into the swirling waters below when something told him to give it at least one last try. After all, seventeen was Zamradiel's number. He couldn't let the bastard have that satisfaction.

So he tried for #18. This time something inside him assured him it had worked. He just needed to get there. Of course, he'd hijacked plenty of cars before in his youth, but never at six inches high.

He slipped into the Mustang after the fat lady waddled inside the supermarket for a bag of groceries. Upon her return, as she shifted her considerable girth in the white vinyl seat and closed the door behind her, he popped up from behind the headrest and pressed the shank against her soft throat.

He knew what to say, played up his inner city accent. "All right, bitch, just be cool. Do what I say an' you won't get yo' self keel. Know what I'm sayin'?" She nodded while he smiled to himself. White people were so stupid, you could just spout out gibberish and they thought it was street talk. "'Twas brillig and the slithy toves, ho. Gone get some stank on my hang low if you gyre and gimble wit me bitch, you got that?" She nodded again. "Okay, good, now that we've established a sophisticated level of communication, please drive to the following residence."

He gave her the address. Everything would've been fine if she hadn't tried to ram that CHP officer off the freeway to get his attention. From that point on it was a pedal to the medal high speed chase. He didn't care. He wouldn't have to stick around for the consequences.

The second they reached their destination he ordered the fat woman to open the door, bounded out onto the sidewalk, scurried up the driveway, and squeezed underneath the front door at which point he heard two people screaming upstairs. He traversed the mountainous stairs, thanking the Lord he'd grown to six inches (such a trek would've been impossible just after his transformation), and darted between the nylon covered legs of a middle-aged woman screaming about people wanting their "fifteen minutes of fame." He hid inside a cardboard box filled with the remnants of a very familiar amber bottle and remained there until he heard the voice of his lost love say, "Finally! Man, I thought she'd never leave."

The very sound of his voice—

13

"—made my heart pound." Isaiah wiped the tears from his cheeks. "I-I'm sorry, I'm just so happy to be near you again."

Charles and Janice stared at him, speechless.

"What's the matter?" Isaiah said. "Why're you lookin' at me like that?"

"No reason," Charles said after awhile. "I'm just a bit... startled... is all."

Janice's red lacquered nails dug into the blanket. "I can't believe this."

"It's okay," Charles said. "We don't know that it's true."

"It's true," she said. Another uncomfortable moment of silence descended upon the room, then she said, "You haven't answered Charles' question. What's the mission?"

Isaiah sighed in frustration. He looked directly at Charles. "After all I've told you, you *still* can't remember?"

Charles shook no.

"Do you want to know why you were convicted?"

"I... I don't know...."

"Do you remember that your blood and semen were found at each of the twenty-two crime scenes, *on* the bodies, *inside* them?"

Charles closed his eyes. "No. No! You're lying!"

"I'm afraid not."

"What're you saying?" Janice whispered. "That he's guilty? That... that he raped and murdered all those... those girls?" Her face had turned sheet white.

"No." Isaiah said. "But his father did."

It hit him in the center of his brain like a spear. Charles tottered. The room began to spin. He fell off Janice's knee and crashed into the carpet.

Isaiah ran to him. "Hank!" He kneeled down beside him, rested Charles' head in his lap. "Are you okay, you okay?"

Charles tried to open his eyes but he couldn't—

—wriggle out of his father's vice-like grip. "You're gonna watch it, boy. You're gonna watch me do it to her. This is what she deserves. Her and all the rest of them. Filthy, stinking whores." He slapped her bleeding cheek. "Stop crying. Dressed like that, what'd you expect was gonna happen? What the fuck're you doing, boy? Don't you start bawling too! This is important. How do you expect to learn if you don't pay attention? Look, first you've got to check 'em real careful like. Just like this. Back in 'Nam some of 'em kept knives hidden in here. One of them even had a grenade. You think I'm lyin'? You'd be amazed at what you can fit in there. Just watch. Just watch, boy."

—couldn't open his eyes, no, no, please, don't make me open my eyes—

"Hank? *Hank?*"

Charles' eyelids fluttered open. Isaiah's face was close to his, far too close, almost as if he were going to—

"Get away from me!" Charles slammed his palms into Isaiah's broad chest, pushed him away.

"What's wrong?" Isaiah said. "Are you hurt?"

Charles rose to his feet. "I... remember."

"About the mission?"

He looked past Isaiah's shoulder and up. At Janice. "Everything."

Janice stood in the corner of the room, her arms crossed over her chest, facing the wall. "Janice?" he said. "We have to talk."

She turned around. Slowly. Refusing to look at him. "Yes. *We* do."

Charles moved close to Isaiah and said softly, "Listen, could you, uh, step into that cardboard box for a moment. Please?"

"Well, sure, I guess, but why should—?" For a moment his gaze shifted back and forth between Charles and Janice. His eyes lit up.

"Oh," he said.

Since there was nothing more to be said, he walked into the box. Charles watched him go. The man looked like a somnambulist.

Charles strode up to Janice's big toe. She remained still. "I can't talk to you from down here," he said. She sighed and got down on one knee, as if she were proposing. Perhaps she realized this, for she then lowered her other knee. She still wouldn't look at him.

"Let me tell you about my father," he said.

While outside, the helicopters continued to hover.

14

Perhaps it began with the helicopter crash. Perhaps it was even earlier. When Charles Manning Senior was a child. When his mother abandoned him on the doorstep of his alcoholic uncle. Who knows?

The Army was the only mother he'd ever known. They loved him, in their way. They stripped his mind and replaced it with nothing but cardboard memories. Silhouettes of relatives and friends and lovers. That is, if there had ever *been* any lovers. The Army taught him to hate the silhouettes. To shoot at them and kill them. To slice their testicles off with machetes and hang them from tree limbs upside down, fake teeth marks punctured in their throats to make the natives think vampires were roaming loose upon the land. Vampires working for the U.S. Army. Perhaps that wasn't too far from the truth.

All Charles knew of his father's past was what came pouring out of his mouth during the rage-induced tirades set off by his one-man crusades, his self-imposed tours of duty upon the "filth-infested" streets of Los Angeles. His crusade was a simple one: to divest the streets of sin and force it to live up to its angelic name. A scorched earth policy for dealing with urban decay. He often railed against Richard Nixon for not having the balls to go through with Operation Duck Hook, the plan to drop nuclear weapons on Vietnam. The plan that would have won the war. If only, if only....

If only Charles Manning had had his hands on that button, he would have....

But no. People like Manning were never given that kind of power. And so they lost the War.

Which meant that Manning had spent three years in a bamboo tiger cage, in the most hostile prisoner of war camp in Cambodia, for what? For a medal of honor? For nothing. Nothing at all.

His helicopter was shot down during Operation Watchtower. Sixty million dollars of heroin burnt up with the chopper. He and the pilot parachuted out and were taken prisoner the second they hit the ground. The soldiers stripped them naked and marched them through the center of the village while children threw stones at them. Manning enjoyed the pain, welcomed it. He laughed when one stone hit him in the face, a waterfall of blood rushing out of his nose. The pilot had already begun to cry.

They threw them in the same cage, began the interrogation. Manning gave them his name, rank, and serial number. The pilot... the son of a bitch little crybaby began blabbing immediately. The name of the operation, the heroin, everything. All within a few seconds. Manning didn't even think. He grabbed the man by the head and gave it a quick *twist*. There was a loud snap. The body fell to the floor. Just a pile of meat now. The thing didn't even have a name to him anymore, if it ever did in the first place.

The Vietnamese soldiers just stared at him with blank expressions on their faces. Acting shocked. As if they wouldn't have done the same!

They left him alone after that.

When he emerged from the cage three years later he felt cheated. Cheated out of the glory that should have been Uncle Sam's when the bombs dropped on Hanoi. But the Communists in the CIA had set up Richard Nixon, framed him to take the fall for Watergate, then pulled the rug right out from under the United States military. And gave Southeast Asia over to the Reds.

When they pinned the Purple Heart on his chest he stood up rail-straight and smiled for the cameras. But inside he was seething with rage. Inside he was already planning his revenge. While he'd slept in a cage the Communists had taken over the country. You could see that simply by switching on the television or watching a movie. Everywhere he turned sex was being worshipped like a false idol while the *real* Savior was spat upon. Just like *he'd* been spat upon by those fucking kids. The kids. The kids today were brainwashed, nothing more than media-controlled single-celled organisms crawling from one hedonistic sensation to the next with no idea of where they were going, no connections to the past or future. They were beyond saving. They needed to be destroyed. And to take their place would be the New Children, the children who would spring from his loins. His beliefs. His values.

But in order to do that, he had to marry.

He met Marie at a church social. She was young and pretty and devoted to God. He could overlook the fact that she was Hispanic. For the most part Hispanics were God-fearing people. They knew their place. Besides, Marie's knowledge of the Bible made up for any genetic deficiencies her heritage might pose for the children. She could recite any section of the Bible, chapter and verse, backwards and forwards, on command. That had to count for something. And besides, she was so innocent. So, so very innocent. Just look at her smile. Only an angel, a being devoid of all sin, could smile like that.

He discovered the truth on their wedding night. He had been so certain she wasn't like the others. But she was. Oh God, oh Lord, to hear the sounds she made underneath him. She didn't even try to hide the fact that she was *enjoying* it. So disgusting. He was forced to beat the sin out of her. It worked, as far as he knew. He never touched her again after that. Not for any reason at all.

Charles Jr. was born eight months later. Premature. Underweight. Weak. Well, that was just too bad. He'd have to work that much harder to overcome his deficiencies, wouldn't he? His deficiencies. Manning was beginning to regret his decision. If only he'd chosen a *normal* woman.

Manning took his son out on his first mission when he was only five years old. That's old enough. The same age Manning had been when his mother had... had... had left him on the....

They picked up the girl off Hollywood Boulevard. She was a sweet young thing, much younger than Marie. Barely sixteen. You could tell by the way she was stumbling around in those high heel shoes. Shifting from side to side, as if she were about to fall over, trying to keep that enticing smile plastered on her painted face, trying not to seem afraid. This was obviously her first time out.

And it would be her last.

Charles didn't see it. Not exactly. It was hard to see anything in the dark alleyway. Just brief glimpses in the rearview mirror. The girl thought it was odd to have a kid in the front seat, but she didn't complain. As long as she was gettin' the money, what the fuck did she care? Mostly he heard it. Heard him show her the Purple Heart. Heard her ooh and ah, as if she cared. Heard the rustle of her halter top being removed. Heard the short sharp zip of pants coming undone. Heard the back seat squeaking. Heard the girl moaning, saying bad words, real bad words. (Charles got smacked for saying such things at home.) Heard Daddy grunting like a pig, like a big fat pig. And in between the grunts he would quote words that Charles had heard thousands of times before. Passages from the New Testament. Revelations. Something about a scarlet whore. And then the sound of gagging, like when you get something caught in your throat. And the wild thrashing, like a fish flapping around on the bottom of a boat with a hook in its mouth. And the muffled screams. And the slashing. Like a fish being gutted. The soft, wet sounds as the innards are tossed in the trash. For the dogs.

Manning showed him his hands in the headlights. "This is what they look like inside. Smell it, boy." He held his hands up to Charles' face. "Take a good whiff. That's what they smell like. Just beneath the surface. Always keep that in mind. They might look good to you. On the outside. One day you might feel like *touching* one of them. If you do, keep this in mind." He smeared it all over the boy's lips; Charles winced and tried to turn away. Manning locked his head in place and coated his tongue with it. "This is what they taste like. This is what they *are*. Underneath. You see, you can't kill them, boy. They're dead already."

Charles remained in the headlights, watching as his Daddy dropped the slick wet body into the large blue dumpster beside the car. Charles wondered if that's what the dumpsters were put there for. For the bodies. Once you were done with them. Sort of like ashtrays.

Daddy lit up on the way home. Blue smoke rings rose up through the window, out into the night, into space. They seemed to turn into ghosts when they hit the air. Daddy didn't have to tell Charles not to say anything about tonight. Somehow, he already knew.

This is how it was almost every month. For years. Until Charles turned twenty-eight. He'd been living at home for most of those years, working minor jobs in restaurants and bookstores. He liked books. Particularly fairy tales. Sometimes he wrote little stories of his own. He liked to escape.

But there was no escape when they found him in the alley, closing the lid on the body. It was a stupid mistake. His father had told him to return and retrieve the Purple Heart he'd accidentally left behind. Charles had obeyed. What else could he do? He had no choice.

No choice when they interrogated him. No choice except to take the blame himself. After all, he'd heard the story a million times. When captured you gave up only your name, rank, and serial number. Anything more was grounds for…. A quick twist. A loud snap.

His father testified against him at the trial. Told them how odd he was. No ambition. Read books all day. Never went to the movies. Never had a girlfriend. Never went outside. Except at night. He should've figured something weird was going on when he started coming home at dawn, covered in sweat, his eyes so wild. Hell, he just figured he was on drugs or something. You know how kids are these days.

His mother testified too, just before her death. Told them about the blood-stained shirts in the laundry. She even gave them one. Of course, it wasn't his shirt but nobody knew that. His mother must have. Of course she did. But she, too, knew the penalty for treason. She wasn't a monster, though, not really. That's probably why she had the stroke the day after her testimony. She couldn't live with herself anymore, with the lies she'd learned to believe for the past quarter of a century.

They only found twenty-two of the girls. That was just one year's crop. The rest… had faded away from the history books, from memory, like one of those blue smoke rings he used to watch floating up from his father's lips after a particularly satisfying kill, floating up into the darkness where it would spread apart like taffy and transform into a frowning ghost just before it vanished. Forever.

Forever. That had been the sentence cast down upon him. And he'd accepted it willingly, like a good soldier will, intent on never giving up his secrets. Never. Not even if he had to take them to his grave. Until, that is, he met Isaiah. Who showed him that magic didn't exist only in fairy tales. Escape wasn't something you did in a dream. Love wasn't just a convenient plot device. Magic was real. You could use it to escape anything, even a dungeon. Or fight monsters, real ones. Or protect a loved one.

A loved one, like Isaiah. Like himself.

Charles Henry Manning, son of Charles Henry Manning. Same name. Same person. Same crime.

No. No, Isaiah showed him the foolishness of that kind of thinking. "You're not Charles Manning Junior," Isaiah said to him one night. "You're unique. You're *special*."

That night he changed his name from Charles to Henry. To Hank.

That night he proposed the mission.

"There's something I want to do after we get out of here," Hank said.

"That's it? Just *one* thing?" Isaiah grinned.

"Well, one special thing. It's kind of a… kind of a mission."

"That sounds like your father talking."

"It is. When I first told you about my childhood, what was the first thing you said to me?"

"I… said I was disgusted… I felt sorry for you… said I… I felt like killing your father."

Hank nodded silently.

"Oh, now wait a second—" Isaiah began.

"I want to do it. I *need* to do it. I need to feel there's actually some kind of justice in the world. All those women, all those *people*, dead because of a sick psychotic fuck like him. Sitting there in his couch critiquing the world through a television set, his belly hanging over his belt making him look like a giant disgusting toad, his Purple Heart inside its little glass case beside a half-empty can of beer. The king of the world. Judge, jury, and executioner." Tears began to stream down Hank's face. "Who made him God? Who the fuck made him God?"

Isaiah embraced him. Tightly. So tightly. And made him a promise. He'd stand by Hank's side no matter what. He'd support him no matter how dangerous "the mission." He'd give him the justice he needed.

With the shank they sliced each other's palms and gripped each other's hands. The promise was sealed with blood. Afterwards Hank stared at the blood on his hands and *knew*.

That red was not always the color of tragedy.

That blood could signify life just as easily as death.

15

Janice remained silent for a very, very long time.

"Please let me know what you're thinking," Charles said.

"No. Not until you tell me something."

"Anything."

"Do you still love me?"

"*Of course*."

Janice blinked away her tears. "Then this wasn't just some kind of a dream, some—" Her voice caught in her throat. "Some little fairy tale we've been living in for the past two months? This was *real*?"

"This was real. This is real."

She breathed a sigh of relief; a little laugh escaped along with it. She brushed the tears away with the back of her hand.

"I wish I could hold you," Charles said, "like a man. A real man."

"You *can*. You've been doing that all along."

"You haven't told me what you're thinking yet."

She took a deep breath. "I want to help you."

"Help me?" His brow furrowed. "With what?"

For a moment she just stared at him. "I know where we can get some guns."

16

They waited until long after midnight. By that time the helicopters and the police sirens and the news vans had melted into the darkness, in search of newer and better forms of violence to preserve on video. By that time Janice's father had come home and severely reprimanded her for her disrespectful behavior. She convinced him the fever was to blame. And besides, it was that time of the month. He said, "Oh, I see, I, uh—" and blushed and left the room.

In the quiet of the night her parents didn't hear Janice tiptoe out of her room. Didn't see her dressed in a heavy black coat, a black sweatshirt, black Levis, black boots, even black winter gloves. Didn't see her rifle through her father's desk drawer in the den. Didn't see her liberate the extra set of car keys. Didn't see her leave the house through the back door nor enter the adjoining alley through the gate in the backyard, nor climb the neighbor's fence and traverse their weed-infected backyard with the cat-like caution of a common thief. Which is what she was. Now.

She climbed the trellis, exactly as she'd done a million times before until such "nonsense" had become far too "undignified for a young lady like yourself" as her dad had often said. She climbed the trellis all the way to the second floor window. Tapped on the glass. First softly. Then not so softly.

At last Billy parted the curtains and looked outside. He opened the window, sleepy-eyed. "What're you doing here?"

"Playing a game. Would you like to help?"

"Sure. Where's Danny?"

"Asleep." She hooked her leg over the sill.

"What about the little man?"

"In my pocket."

"Wow. Can I see him?"

"If you're good, and help me out with the game."

"I will."

She planted both feet on the carpet, closed the window behind her. Quietly.

Then she kneeled down in front of Billy and said, "This is a game kind of like cops and robbers. Except you can't play cops and robbers without guns, right? So can you show me where your dad keeps his guns?"

Billy's eyes widened. "Are we gonna play with guns?"

"Sure. But we need to find them first. Kind of like Hide And Go Seek. But with guns."

"Oh, wow. Oh, boy." He was already starting toward the door.

"Wait." She grabbed him by the arm, raised her index finger to her lips. "We have to be very quiet. Like Elmer Fudd hunting wabbits. That's part of the game. You understand?"

He nodded. She released his arm and followed him out into the hall. Filtered moonlight illuminated the walls, which were decorated with a series of framed photographs depicting the maturation of Billy's father from infancy to adolescence to puberty to manhood. It was like an illustrated "This Is Your Life." In the earliest photo he seemed to be having a good time slamming two Hot Wheels cars together. At adolescence he was often depicted wearing a cowboy outfit, aiming his toy six-shooter at unseen enemies. At puberty, or just past it, his most common attire of choice seemed to be his school football uniform. At eighteen he was seen wearing an Army uniform. In the remaining photos his uniform remained the same except for the number of bars on his chest. Except for the earliest photos, in which he was wearing diapers, every single snapshot depicted him in a uniform of one type or another. At one time Janice had been impressed by this. Now she just thought it was odd. Unlike Charles Manning Senior, Billy's father had never been in a war but always wished he had. He loved war movies, particularly the ones starring John Wayne. Later war movies were unwatchable, he said. Like those

Oliver Stone movies. No action, just talk. If we wanted talk, would we be watching a movie? Hell no. There was no talk in war. Just blood. And sacrifice. And glory.

Billy's father (everybody called him "The Colonel" even though he'd never risen above the rank of lieutenant) had taken Billy, Danny, and Janice out on hunting trips for the past three summers. Billy and Danny were both seven years old during the first trip, and Janice had just turned thirteen. The Colonel taught all three of them how to shoot a deer at five hundred yards. Billy, having had prior experience almost since the moment he'd dropped from the womb, was a real whiz with the rifle. Not only would he shoot the deer, but he'd take out a couple of rare birds before the Colonel could stop him. Danny, on the other hand, couldn't quite handle the recoil and kept crying. The Colonel soon grew disgusted with him and focused his efforts on Janice. Janice bagged her first deer with the very first bullet out of her gun. She thought she'd feel guilty, having seen *Bambi* for the first time only recently, but in truth she didn't feel anything except a remarkable sense of accomplishment. By the end of the trip the Colonel assured her she was a natural. "You should think about joining the Army," he said. "The military needs a good marksman like you." She remembered feeling proud, as if there might be a chance for her somewhere beyond the walls of her little room.

Billy led her down the staircase and into the den at the back of the house. In the corner of the room stood a large rectangular safe the size of an average human being. Billy pointed at it and said, "They're in there."

Janice's heart fell. To be so *close*. "Damn. I suppose you don't know the combination, do you?"

Billy nodded and strode right up to the safe. He began spinning the tumbler. "James Bond," he said.

007. The door popped open with a slight *click*.

Janice peered inside. "Holy shit," she whispered, "James fucking Bond." Stored inside the massive metal box was at least one example of every single variation of the concept of a gun that had ever passed through the minds of men. Rifles, automatic rifles, repeating rifles, repeaters, recoilless rifles, air rifles, shotguns, sawed-off shotguns, muskets, hand guns, automatics, semiautomatic pistols, semiautomatic rifles, squirrel guns, carbines, long rifles, revolvers, pistols, sub automatic machine guns, even flare guns and a toy six-shooter (perhaps included for sentimental reasons); they were all there, complete with ammo, ripe for the picking.

She pulled Charles out of her left pocket and showed him the contents of the safe.

"Damn," he said, "you weren't kidding when you said you knew where to find some guns."

Janice smiled. She could see he was impressed. She wanted so very much to impress him, to show him she could handle dangerous situations as well as anybody who'd ever been in jail. Hadn't the Colonel said it himself? She was a natural.

"Hello, little man," Billy said.

"Yeah. Hey, kid."

"Janice said two bad words."

"Oh, I'm sorry," Janice said.

"Doesn't matter to me," Billy said. "I just hope Daddy doesn't—"

She heard the sound behind her and spun around. He loomed large in the doorway like a giant bear, a black silhouette surrounded by a halo of faint moonlight streaming in from the living room skylight. An incomprehensible groan emerged from the silhouette.

He shambled towards her. She froze. How could she ever defend herself against *that*? It didn't even occur to her that there was a safe full of guns behind her. Charles was yelling something, telling her to do something, but she couldn't hear any of it. Her entire mind was focused on the object in the Colonel's beefy hand.

An amber bottle. Swinging from his fist. Golden liquid dribbling down the side of his hand.

He was wearing a bathrobe and had three days worth of hair growing on his face. She'd never noticed how *gray* his hair was until this moment. Or how sallow his cheeks were. Or how dark the rings under his eyes had become. At one time, many years before, she'd had an innocent crush on the distinguished Army man, but now….

But now he was singing the theme song to *The Green Berets* and doing a very poor job of it. He was swaying back and forth. He barely made it across the room. It took him a very long time to focus on Janice's face. "Who's there?" he mumbled. "Jan? Is that you?" His breath smelled like Scotch.

Janice shoved Charles back into her pocket. She zipped the

pocket closed for safe keeping. "Yeah. Uh, hi." She smiled and waved.

"What're you doing here?"

"Just dropped in... to say hi."

He wavered for a moment more, then managed to say, "That's nice of you. I don't get to see too much of you anymore." He slurred the words.

"Well, you know how it is. I'm a little too old to be playing with Danny and Billy now."

"Yeah, well." He burped, then grinned. Proud of himself. "You've done a lot of growing up lately."

She laughed nervously. "You can say that again." He didn't appear to be at all aware of Billy's presence in the shadows beside her. Or the safe gaping open right behind her.

He couldn't take his eyes off *her*. "You've grown into an attractive young woman. Have I ever told you that, Jan?" He moved in close to her.

"No. No, I don't think you have." She could hear Charles' muffled shouts rising up out of her jacket. He was trying to punch his way out of her pocket.

The Colonel stroked her thigh. "When you were born you fell out of the pretty tree and hit every branch on the way down."

"Um... okay." Was that a compliment? "I'm really flattered, *sir*,"—she emphasized the word "sir" as she tried to wriggle free of his roving hand—"but you see, I'm not really interested—"

He didn't seem to be listening. His hand traced the curve of her butt as he leaned in to kiss her on the neck. She hooked one foot around his ankle, then slammed both palms into his barrel-sized chest. He toppled backwards over her foot like a redwood felled by a chainsaw. The bottle went flying through the air, spilling alcohol all over the carpet. His head hit the floor with a dull thud. His skull bounced once slightly, then lay still. His eyelids fluttered closed.

"Oh God," Janice said, covering her mouth with her hand, "I hope I didn't kill him or anything."

Billy waved his hand. "Aw, I find him on the floor like that almost every morning. No big deal."

Weird. She'd known the Colonel all those years and had never realized he had such a serious drinking problem. She wondered if her parents knew. Probably. Just another of the many "dark" secrets they'd kept from her over the years.

Then she felt the wrenching at her side again. She unzipped the pocket and Charles popped out like a jack in the box. "Why'd you lock me inside?" he said angrily.

"I was trying to protect you."

"We're supposed to be working *together*."

She gestured toward the Colonel's body. "Problem solved."

Charles just stared at the body.

Isaiah popped out of her right pocket. He applauded. "Pretty handy, little lady. Do you know Judo?"

"You don't need to know Judo to deal with someone as blitzed as him."

"Hello new little man," Billy said to Isaiah.

Isaiah held his clenched fist in the air. The old Panther symbol. "What's up?"

Billy peered at him closely, squinting his eyes. "You're a little nigger."

Isaiah lurched back. "What the fuck you say?"

Janice gasped. "Billy, please!"

Isaiah said, "You're lucky I'm only six inches tall, boy, otherwise your butt would be spread out from Tijuana all the way up to San Francisco by now."

"He doesn't know what he's saying," Charles said. "It's his father speaking."

The tension dissipated. They all glanced down at the pathetic drunk sprawled out on the alcohol-soaked carpet and knew that Charles spoke the truth. From experience.

Janice turned her back on the Colonel and stared at the safe. "Let's get this over with."

"Janice," Charles said, "I have to ask you this one last time." She started to protest, but he cut her off. "For *my* sake, if not yours. Are you sure you want to go through with this? It's not too late to go back. All you have to do is turn around and walk back into that house next door and go on with your life, just like you've always done."

"But you wouldn't be coming with me if I did."

"No. You know I have to go through with this. With or without your help, I *have* to go through with this."

"Then so do I."

"No. No, you don't."

Yes she did. What was in store for her without Charles? Men like the Colonel, pawing at her with meaty hands? Boys like Peter, writing her poems about dead swans? Fanatics like her father, ranting about the Will of God? What about her Will? Only a fool would turn her back on the only genuine *experience* she'd managed to salvage from a lifetime composed solely of vicarious TV thrills, second hand wisdom gleaned from sanitized textbooks, and empty platitudes no doubt translated inaccurately from some two thousand year old scroll. She was tired of lies. Tired of the world as it was described to her by "wise men" long dead or "wise men" living today who might as well be dead. She didn't want to hide from death. She didn't want to run from death. She wanted to grab it by the throat and control it. Make it work for her. Make it dance for her. Make it bow before her and kiss her feet with its cold tongue. She knew such power was possible. She felt it when Charles was inside her. When his body, his mind, his blood, melded with her own. When his life, his semen, shot inside her. When she felt his heart cease beating for a fraction of a second. In that moment she felt him die, felt herself die. Both dead together, alive together. In that single moment she knew she had the power to kill him, just as he had the power to kill her, if they ever pushed their love far enough. Past that one instant. Past that plateau. If they just kept it going. One orgasm after another. One heartbeat less and less. Each moment of ecstasy bringing them closer and closer to exhaustion, to death. Sometimes, at the height of it, she felt she could fuck him all day. Endlessly. Without food or water or surcease. Until, at last, death overcame them. With love.

That's why she couldn't do it. Why she couldn't go back to that room, that terrible suffocating womb. Why she couldn't abandon him for nothing more than the promise of a life without risks. She knew what that kind of an existence was like, had known it for sixteen years. Sixteen years was too long. Sixteen years wasted. Sixteen years without Charles inside of her. She wouldn't live that kind of life, not for one second longer.

Which is why she didn't respond to Charles' comment, except to reach out and grab the rifle she recognized from the hunting trips. She loaded it with ammo. It felt so natural, like riding a bicycle.

Charles let out a quiet sigh. Relief mixed with sadness. "Better grab a .38 as well."

"Which one's that?"

"That one over there."

She grabbed two of them. Along with a .45.

"Snag a .22," Isaiah said, popping out of her jacket. "Doesn't weigh much and you can strap it to your ankle."

Charles told her that was more than enough, but she refused to listen. She snatched up a Luger. Though she didn't even know its name, she was absolutely certain she had to possess it. (For no other reason than she thought it looked sexy, having seen one strapped to the hip of a Nazi in a WWII film. John Wayne didn't appear in that one.)

"Which one do I get?" Billy said.

Janice had almost forgotten about him. She glanced at the contents of the safe once more, then pulled out the toy six-shooter. She kneeled down in front of Billy and placed the toy in his little hands. "We're done with the first half of the game. Now I want you to take your six-shooter up to bed with you and go to sleep. When you wake up tomorrow morning, you can start hunting for us. We'll all be hunting each other, all four of us. You know, like Tag."

"What about Danny?"

"He'll be playing too. When you see one or all of us, you shoot. If you get all three of us you win."

"All four of you. Danny makes four."

She laughed. "Right. All four of us."

"What do I get if I win?"

"What do you mean what do you get? You win!"

"So? I don't get a prize or anything?"

Janice sighed. "Okay, okay, you win ten dollars. Is that good enough?"

"How about I get it now?" He held out his palm.

"What? You haven't won it yet!"

"Maybe I should go next door and tell your parents you're stealing my dad's guns."

Janice clenched her teeth. "You little—!"

"Just give him the ten dollars," Charles said.

"He deserves it," Isaiah said. "That's one bright kid."

Grumbling, Janice pulled out the roll of bills in her pocket. It was all the money she had in the world,—the savings from her brief job at the Catholic preschool last summer—mixed in with a healthy wad of cash that had accidentally fallen out of her mother's purse and into Janice's Levis. She took a ten off the top and slapped it into Billy's palm.

"I want a twenty," Billy said.

Janice grabbed him by the shirt collar and began shaking him. "If you so much as utter a *word* to my parents about what happened here tonight I'm going to—!"

"It doesn't matter," Charles said.

"What?" Janice said.

"It doesn't matter. We'll be long gone by tomorrow morning." Charles said to Billy, "Listen, kid, we're about to go off on a secret mission. It's kind of like James Bond stuff, you know? If you go around blabbing about what you've seen tonight, you'll be giving the bad guys a better chance to track us down. So we'd all appreciate it if you could just chill out for awhile and maybe think of this as our little secret, okay?"

Billy nodded. "Okay."

"Now give him an extra ten."

Janice reluctantly slapped another bill into the boy's palm.

Charles said, "Now take that on up to your room, hide it under your pillow, and catch some shut-eye. We'll let ourselves out. Okay?"

Billy nodded, waved goodbye to Janice and Isaiah, then left the room.

"That was amazing," Isaiah said. "You've got a real way with kids."

"He certainly does," Janice said, smiling to herself as she wondered what theirs would look like. Would the first one be a boy or a girl?

Then she realized who she was talking to. The smile vanished and she flushed slightly. For a moment she was afraid that Isaiah could read her thoughts. After all, he *was* some kind of sorcerer wasn't he? She still wasn't used to the idea of Charles and... and him. Together. She felt genuine gratitude toward Isaiah for having done so much to protect her Charles in prison. If not for him, she and Charles never would have met. She realized that, of course... nevertheless, she didn't want them to be together again. They couldn't possibly have what she and Charles had together. Charles could go *inside* her. All the way inside her. How many other men could lose themselves within their lover's body, sleep and dream within her, allow his thoughts to wander in quiet meditation without fear of harm knowing he was protected always by a fortress of flesh made for him and him alone? Dedicated only to him. Occupied only by him.

As far as she knew, her relationship with Charles was totally unique in the history of the entire world. Could Isaiah give him that? Could anybody?

The dreamy smile returned to Janice's face. She hoped Isaiah *was* reading her mind. Let him know now what he was up against: a love that transcended all of history. What was Isaiah compared to that? What was he?

After dropping some more ammo into her backpack, she came up with an idea. She removed an automatic pistol from the back shelf. "Oh no, not *more* guns," Charles said. She slipped the pistol into the Colonel's right hand (unloaded, of course), then sauntered out of the room, leaving the safe open behind her.

"That'll confuse him," she said. "He's so wasted, when he wakes up he'll think *he* did something with the missing guns."

Isaiah chuckled. "He'll probably think he killed somebody."

Janice flashed back once more to that Sunday afternoon in the woods when she shot her first deer. How proud she'd felt when the Colonel patted the small of her back and said those stirring words, "You're a natural." But now that she thought about it more closely, she realized the Colonel's hand had remained on her back far longer (and far lower) than necessary. This realization stripped a bit of the patina from that memory. An ineffable feeling of sadness fell over her. Memories like that are hard to come by. You can't afford to lose even one.

17

Isaiah said, "Pull over here. Keep the motor running."

For the past twenty minutes Janice had been driving northeast, keeping her father's shiny black Lexus well within the speed limit. Isaiah, who stood on the dashboard peering out into the cool clear night, pointed at a Lexus parked in front of a two-story house. The car looked exactly like her father's.

"If you follow my directions, this'll only take a second," Isaiah said. He'd talked her through the procedure twice before they'd even left her room, but he wanted to accompany her just in case. He didn't know how much she could handle in one night. For a Catholic white kid trapped in the suburbs of Long Beach most of her life, she had balls. Bigger balls than a lot of the asswipes he'd met in prison. He could see why Hank had... fallen in love with her.

When Hank had pulled him aside for a private conversation in his cardboard box, he'd expected the worse. But the worse had already occurred. To find out that he and the girl had somehow... somehow... become lovers. After everything he and Hank had been through together. After having trafficked with demons, clashed with monsters, nearly died in each other's arms. After having searched from one end of the South Bay to the other for him. To be betrayed. In the end.

And yet... and yet... he knew he hadn't been betrayed. Not out of malice. Not on purpose. Hank had had no memory of who he was. The fact that he had even survived his ordeal, that someone as capable as Janice had been kind enough to take him into her home, was a miracle for which he would be eternally grateful. He shouldn't be surprised that Hank might…. Well, he'd heard of the Florence Nightingale syndrome: wounded soldiers who fell in love with their nurses. This was a common enough occurrence, and not isolated to the battlefield. Perhaps that's what this was. A temporary infatuation, nothing more. He'd come to his senses after a couple of days. So would Janice. This was no life for her. She'd realize that… wouldn't she?

A hole had been blown in his chest the size of the wounds in Jesus' wrists. Why deny it? He felt like tearing his eyes out, he felt like crawling into a dark forest and dying, he felt like strangling Janice with his bare hands.

He felt as if a pair of ragged claws were tearing away at the inside of his stomach, a pitchfork raking a furrowed path through his lungs, a knife slicing away at the back of his temples. That bitch. That fucking white bitch, how dare she touch him. He was mine. Meant for me. Only the hand of God could have brought us together like that and then you come sashaying into our life with your skinny little body and innocent violet eyes and lacquered fingernails. Innocent my ass. Probably fucked half the football team before she was fifteen. You know how those Catholic girls are. They can't control themselves. They see a piece of meat, it's theirs. The more exotic the better. That's all Hank is to her. A precious little doll to carry around in her pocket. A good luck charm, like a cheap trinket you buy in Tijuana as a souvenir for the "girlfriend" you're never going to see again once you cross back over the border. A warm dildo with limbs. No batteries required.

A bitch like her would've been little more than roadkill for him back in his Panther days. Shit, she wouldn't last more than a second against him. If he wanted to get rid of her, he could do it without Hank ever knowing. Make it look like an accident. If he….

If he.

If he was a monster. Like Hank's father.

He wasn't. He wasn't.

He didn't want to bring pain into the world. Not anymore. He'd outgrown those days. Ever since prison. Ever since his brother began talking to him again. Ever since Hank….

It was just temporary. Just a phase Hank was going through. He'd work his way through it and come back to him. Janice wasn't a whore. She was a nice girl. She wasn't out to get him. She probably loved Hank for the same reasons *he* loved him. Which meant they had more in common than anyone else in the world. Work with her, Isaiah. Throw all the paranoia and the hatred away and work with her. Besides, he and Hank *needed* her. Needed her to fulfill the mission….

The mission was built on baby steps, had been all along. They were taking one of those steps right now, as Janice darted out of the car with Isaiah clinging to her shoulder.

"Get down low, behind the trunk," Isaiah whispered. "Whip out the screwdriver."

Janice already had it in her hand. She had the first screw out within seconds. Then the second. The third. The fourth. Damn, Isaiah thought, this bitch... girl... is pretty fuckin' quick with her fingers. He glanced up at the house. All the lights were out. Nobody was walking the streets. Good, good.

Janice removed the stranger's license plate and replaced it with her father's. Her hands shook slightly as the four screws turned slowly, slowly into place.

"Do we have to go through this all over again?" she said. "Can't we just drive off and I'll put the new one on later?"

"No. A cop will stop us for sure if he sees you drivin' around without a plate. It's better to do both at the same time."

After she'd finished with the last screw, she scurried over to the trunk of her dad's Lexus and began the same process all over again. Her hands shook a bit more this time.

"Calm down," he whispered, "there's no hurry. The criminal who acts like he's doing nothing wrong is the one who never gets caught."

This seemed to relax Janice. She took a deep breath and continued the task as if she was doing nothing more out of the ordinary than changing a tire. They finished in silence; once the plate was attached she stood up and strode back toward the front of the car. Poised. Nonchalant. Like a model walking a runway.

She slid behind the wheel, shut the door, and glided away into the night. Just a normal teenage kid taking an innocent late night drive. Nothing odd about that. Nothing odd at all.

"Everything go okay?" Hank asked from the headrest. He held

onto Janice's hair to keep himself from falling.

"This is one cool kid," Isaiah said. "Where'd you get such fast fingers?"

"Must be all those piano lessons my mother shoved down my throat," Janice said.

"Nah." Isaiah dismissed the comment with a wave of his hand. "You're a natural."

She smiled when he said it, but he didn't know why.

18

After crossing over into Torrance they made another switch with a black Lexus parked outside a bar called The Crystal Lounge. Janice barely needed Isaiah's help this time.

From there they drove to the apartment building where Charles' father had moved after the publicity surrounding his son's capture had brought down upon his quiet suburban home an endless flock of news reporters hungry for a brief quote or an impromptu tirade or even a fist thrown at a camera lens. Charles' mother had mentioned the new address in a letter sent to him just before her death. She wanted him to keep writing her. It might be good therapy for you, son. To work out your emotional problems.

She probably felt it was safe giving him the address in jail. After all, even if he was emotionally unstable, how could he hurt them from behind bars?

They pulled up to the curb outside the two-story building on Carson and Cabrillo. It was pretty sleazy. His father was living above a liquor store across from a fleabag hotel called The Hotel Pride. A speed freak was huddled inside a glass phone booth screaming into a receiver. They couldn't hear what he was saying.

Leading into the building stood a gate colored a puke-brown. It just rattled when Janice tried to open it. "Damn," Janice muttered, "what do I do?"

Charles sat inside her left pocket again. He could feel the bulge of the loaded .45 cocooned within the lining of her inside pocket. "Go around the building," Charles said. "Maybe there's another way in."

To their surprise, upon rounding the corner of a seedy "beauty salon," they discovered that the puke-colored gate offered security only against the easily discouraged. On the opposite side of the building was nothing but open air leading into a packed driveway. The first floor of the building consisted of storage garages. The apartments were on the second floor, numbered 1 to 6. They wanted #4.

Janice was strangely calm. She didn't appear to be nervous at all as she climbed the stone steps one by one. The door to #4 was painted the same color as the gate outside. Janice slipped her right hand into the jacket, got a firm grip on the handle of the gun, then knocked on the door with her left fist. Hard. Three times.

A throaty grumble emerged from behind the door. "What the fu—" Silence. "It's two-thirty in the fuckin' morning!" More silence. Then the rattle of a door knob. Janice's right index finger slid over the trigger. The door opened only a crack; a gold colored chain stretched out over the shadowy divide from which an acne-scarred face and a bloodshot brown eye could be seen staring at her with suspicion. The face belonged to a woman. A very old black woman.

Janice's finger slid away from the trigger. "Uh... is Charles Manning here?"

"*Manning*?" She shook her head over and over again. "No, no, he's gone. Gone." She started to close the door.

"Wait!" Janice slammed her hand against the door. "Where'd he go?"

The old woman looked tired. Very, very tired. "He moved when his wife died. I used to live in the one-bedroom next door. I needed a bigger place. For the grandkids. They're asleep." She was silent for a moment. "I'm not sayin' I'm glad she died. She was a nice woman. Loved God. Talked about God all the time. But I needed the extra bedroom."

"Wh-where'd he go?"

The old woman's eyes narrowed. Her suspicion had returned. "Why do you want to know?"

Janice removed her hand from the door. "I'm his daughter."

"No. No, his wife never mentioned no daughter to me."

"I'm not her daughter. I'm *his* daughter. She didn't like to talk about me much."

The old woman's eyes widened. "Oh. I see. Well." She glanced over her bony shoulder. "He did leave a forwarding address for his mail. Let me go get it." She closed the door. Janice breathed a sigh of relief.

Charles wondered how far away he'd moved. Was he close by? Would they still be able to get to him tonight? He wanted this to be over with. Now.

The door opened again. The old woman thrust a skinny arm beneath the chain. Held within an arthritic, claw-like hand was a yellow post-it note. "Thank you very much," Janice said as she accepted the note. She glanced at it, then stuffed the paper into her pocket. Right beside Charles. Who groaned in disappointment as his eye caught the most prominent word on the page. *Florida*.

Just when Janice was about to walk away the old woman said, "Hey. You know the son? The one they arrested for killing all those girls? You know him?"

Janice turned around long enough to say, "They arrested the wrong man," then continued walking.

19

The image burned within Charles. The image of that evil, murdering son of a bitch lounging on a sun-drenched beach in Miami, ogling the girls in bikinis, waiting for the prime opportunity to relaunch his killing spree. While Charles rotted in prison. Getting beat up. Raped. Attacked by monsters of all kinds, human and otherwise. Nearly losing his sanity. His life. While his father sipped his beer like a teetotaler, spending the money from mother's life insurance policy on... what? A stash of new knives, perhaps? The spree had probably already begun. The monster wouldn't be able to contain himself for long. It was a compulsion for him. He was addicted to blood, pain, the smell of death. And most of all... fear. Charles Henry Manning Senior was a vampire who lived off the fear he generated in others. In his son, for example. Who had no doubt provided a steady stream of nutrition for his father from the minute he was old enough to understand the concept of pain.

The image. The image of a vampire basking in sunlight.

Drove him. Drove him and Isaiah and Janice. Out beyond Los Angeles. Across state lines. Into Arizona. Through a desert that stretched on into New Mexico. Through Texas. Down. Through the rolling hills of Mississippi. Down. Through the Appalachians in the southwest of Alabama. Down. While the image unreeled in his brain.

The image. The image of an innocent young girl, only one of

hundreds, dying because he was too afraid. Too afraid to speak. Too afraid to stand up to his father long after the inherent weakness of adolescence had ceased being a convenient excuse. Too afraid to kill a monster that should have died long ago. Before it was even born. The image.

Drove them down.

Into Florida.

Into the sunny paradise known as Dade County where thousands of old men went to die.

Where one old man had gone to kill.

20

The level of tension among them fluctuated depending on the circumstances. Sometimes it was the weather. Sometimes it was the lack of food. Sometimes it was the *vato loco* trying to bust through the window with a crowbar. (Charles found it shocking how much violence was evoked from otherwise normal people when they came within arm's reach of what they thought was a young girl traveling alone in a car. When they discovered that she was not alone, when she introduced them to her good friends Commandant Luger and Monsieur .22 Automatic, they seemed to regain their manners very quickly and bend over backwards to remove themselves from Janice's proximity so as not to offend her delicate sensibilities.) Sometimes it was the frustration of knowing that a young girl might be dying at the hands of a monster while they sat stuck in traffic behind an accident on a Texas freeway.

And sometimes, more often than not, it was outright jealousy.

Charles tried to assuage their feelings, but this was a Sisyphean effort at best. No matter what he did, he was going to hurt somebody he loved very much. During their second night on the road, after having driven for almost fifteen hours straight, they pulled into a rest stop along the highway. Janice needed sleep the most. He could tell she also needed his attention, his comfort. He explained to Isaiah that he would be sleeping with her tonight.

"Just tonight?" Isaiah said.

"Tonight. Tomorrow night. The night after that. As long as she'll let me."

"So that's how it is." Isaiah tried to hide his pain with a casual shrug. "It's cool. I understand. You have to do what you have to do."

"Please don't be that way."

"Be what way? Fuck you, don't tell me what way to be! Go on, go be with your woman. She can dress you up like Barbie. You can have a lot of fun together."

"We already did that."

Isaiah just stared at him for a moment. "What, had fun?"

"No, no. I had nothing else to wear that first night, so she gave me a Barbie nightgown. It was pink."

Despite his best effort to maintain his stone-faced facade, Isaiah's lips quivered unsteadily and his anger dissolved into erratic laughter. "You son of a bitch," he said between giggles, "how can you fuckin' make me laugh during a time like this?"

"I'm sorry. I didn't mean to."

"Like hell you didn't." After the laughter had run its course Isaiah said, "I'll always be your friend, you know."

"I know. I *have* to do this. You understand why, don't you?"

Isaiah nodded. "I think so."

"I've never had a girlfriend. I need to know what that's like."

Isaiah nodded again. There was nothing left to say.

"Maybe," Charles said, "in the future—"

"Don't even say it. Just leave it hanging, okay? Just leave it hanging."

"Okay," Charles said softly. "Okay."

Isaiah slept in the glove compartment.

21

That night, while curled in the soft folds of her sweater just above her left breast, he told her of his decision. He was surprised, and a little pleased, to see tears welling up in her eyes. She didn't even need to say it.

"I love you too," he whispered.

They both closed their eyes. He could feel the beat of her heart against his whole body. Its rhythmic sound was as soothing as a lullaby.

Sleep came easily for both of them.

When they awoke the next morning, both he and Isaiah had grown an extra inch.

22

A stasis had been reached among the trio. Now that the guidelines had been set, they all agreed to operate within them. For the most part they stuck to that agreement. Besides, the journey was fraught with so many dangers, they didn't have enough time to let personal animosities get in their way. They had to work as a team. And they did this. They did this very well.

They dealt with the bad weather.

They dealt with the lack of food.

They dealt with the occasional carjacker trying to bust through the window with a crowbar.

They dealt with the frustration of knowing that only distance prevented them from ridding the world of a tremendous evil.

They dealt with all of this and more, but nevertheless tempers would occasionally flare and the wrong word would be uttered and uncomfortable silence would descend upon the car for a very long time. Until something threatened to impede their progress. Then the tension would dissipate, as if by magic, and they would band together to overcome this new obstacle before them.

In this way they traversed the breadth of the United States of America in a little over three weeks. (The trip might have been shorter if not for that incident with the psychotic policeman in the Appalachians; but that's another story, for another time.)

In this way they reached their destination.

In this way they penetrated to the heart of Heaven.

And tracked down the Devil himself.

23

From California to Florida, from Torrance to Miami, Charles rehearsed the scene in his mind. Over and over and over again.

He saw it in a number of different ways, from a number of different angles, under a number of different forms of lighting. Like a scene in a movie reshot fifty, sixty, a hundred, five hundred times with the same actors, the same lines, the same camera equipment. But a different interpretation each run-through. One subtle, one violent, one fifteen minutes, one fifteen seconds, one dramatic, one comedic, one artful, one exploitive, one solarized, one pixilated, one in freeze-frame, one in split-screen, one in extreme close-up, one in slow motion, one in black and white, one in color.

This last run-through was definitely in color.

He could see the brightness of the blood trickling down the girl's face as Father began to slice into her with a razor blade,—just as he'd done with that redhead behind the Safeway when Charles was eight; he'd removed her face in one piece and forced him to wear it as a mask to his school's Halloween party; Father had been so proud of him that night when he came home with the first prize ribbon for best costume pinned to his chest—while Father did something disgusting to her with his wooden strap-on, a favorite toy of his, the one he'd carved in the exact shape and likeness of a thermonuclear missile, while he sang nursery rhymes to her and told her to hush, hush my child, if you keep screaming I'll have to send you home, and then the pain will stop, and you wouldn't want that now, would you, we're just getting star—

This is the point in the scene where Father suddenly glances up at the sound of the door being kicked open and sees Janice standing there in the doorway with a gun in each hand and Charles perched upon her right shoulder. The combination of expressions on Father's face is classic: shock, confusion, fear. Charles points his finger at him and says, "You're going to pay for your crimes now, old man!"

"Maybe so," Father says, "but I'll take this one with me!" The blade plunges toward the girl's throat.

"NOW!" Charles screams.

Janice pumps two bullets into his father's skull; his head explodes, showering wet redness across the naked girl; the headless corpse topples backwards, the strap-on coming loose with pieces of blood and flesh still clinging to it. But at least the girl is saved. She's wounded, yes, but she's alive and she'll heal. Just like Charles. Just like Janice. Everybody is saved. Close in on Janice and Charles kissing. Fade to black and fade out.

From California to Florida, from Torrance to Miami, rehearsing the scene in his mind. Over and over and over again.

Not one of these scenes matched the reality of it.

ROBERT GUFFEY

24

He was an old man sitting in a rocking chair.

He looked far, far older than Charles had described to her.

He was short too, and shrunken, with skin like that of a fetus preserved in formaldehyde.

He rocked back and forth in darkness, watching an old black and white movie on a television set that was larger than anything else in the room. W.C. Fields was doing something funny with a potted plant. But the old man was not laughing.

He might have been sleeping. He looked up at them groggily when they walked into the room. Nothing had to be kicked in. The door to the tiny apartment had been unlocked.

"Is… this him?" Janice said.

Charles stood on her right shoulder. Isaiah stood on her left. "Yes," Charles whispered.

The old man's eyes widened upon seeing Janice. "You? Who're you?"

Janice shut the door behind her and locked it. She removed the .45 from her jacket. "My name's Janice Spindell. I'm gonna kill you."

The old man was silent for a moment, then he broke out into a phlegmatic coughing fit.

Janice felt confused. Part of her wanted to offer him a cup of water. She kept her finger on the trigger. She shifted from side to side.

"Why?" he finally managed to squeeze out between coughs.

"Because. You're evil." She shook the hair out of her face, held her head up with pride. "I'm your son's lover."

"Charlie?" The old man laughed, almost provoking another coughing fit. "Charlie's never had a *lover*. He never will. Doesn't have it in him. He's too god damn stupid."

"He's brilliant!"

"What the hell is this? You one of those serial killer groupies? You been writin' him letters in pri—" Then he stopped, and his face went white. "Charlie escaped. He's not in prison anymore. They called me and told me. Yesterday. Or was it... a few weeks ago?" He shook his head. Looked off into space for a few seconds. Then glanced back at Janice. "Did you help Charlie escape? Is he here, in Miami?"

"I'm right in front of your face!" Charlie yelled.

The old man's gaze darted about the room. "Charlie? Is that you? Wh-where're you hiding?"

Charles sighed in frustration. He leaped up and down on Janice's shoulder and waved his arms. "I'm right here!"

The old man leaned forward and squinted, squinted in the general direction of Janice's shoulder. "Wh-what is that?" He reached out for the eyeglasses sitting on the end table beside him.

Janice aimed the gun at his face, ready to fire.

"NO!" Charles said. "Wait. I want him to see me."

Shaking, pale hands covered in liver spots and varicose veins lifted the thick glasses to the old man's nose. He leaned forward again. "My God."

"Hello, Father. You don't look very happy to see me."

"How did... what've you done?"

"Escaped your little trap. Unlike all your other victims, all those girls you butchered."

"That... *I* butchered? *Me?*" He opened his mouth wide, as if wanting to laugh and scream at once. But he did neither. "You... son of a bitch. You killed me. You broke my heart. Gave your mother a stroke. Drove me out of my home, the one you lived in for most of your god damn life. I took care of you, thought you were telling me the truth when you said you wanted to write, that you needed 'time to practice.' Meanwhile what were you doing? Beating, raping, *murdering* children? Where did you come from? Not from me. Not from Marie. You came from Hell! You're some kind of god damn devil. I know it now. Just *look* at you. At least I can die knowing *I'm* not the one to blame. Too bad Marie didn't have that chance."

"Shut up," Charles whispered, "shut up."

The old man looked at Janice. "Has he got you believing this, these lies?"

The gun wavered in her hand. "I—"

"He's crazy. Can't you see that? Can't you see he's the devil?"

"Shut up," Charles whispered, "shut up."

"Shoot him," Isaiah said.

The old man saw Isaiah for the first time. "My God, my God, what is it?"

"Before he tries something," Isaiah said.

Janice was sweating. The metal was growing slick in her hand. "Charles?"

"Shut him up," Charles whispered, "shut him up."

"*Kill him!*" Isaiah screamed.

"I'd do it myself," Charles said, "if I was only big enough to hold the gun."

The old man made a move for something on the end table. Janice squeezed off a shot. The bullet blew a huge chunk out of the old man's chest. He lurched back against the sofa, his head bouncing up and down like a demented jack in the box. He gargled half-formed words, red froth bubbling out of his mouth. He tried to lift his right hand. She pulled the trigger again. This one got him in the stomach. Serpentine intestines spilled out onto the floor along with a spray of blood. But still he wouldn't die. The half-formed words kept trying to claw their way out of his shattered face. Ghostly words. Shadow words.

Janice fell to her knees, almost dislodging Charles and Isaiah from her shoulders. She sank her fingers into the carpet as if she were going to dig her way through the floor. Her stomach heaved. The drive-through breakfast from earlier that morning came waterfalling out of her mouth, some of it smacking the floor with such force that dew-sized particles sprayed back into her face. The stench of the old man's guts hung in the air, in her lungs, in her mouth, in her nostrils. It'll never leave, she thought, it'll always be stuck there.

"My God," she whispered, "what did you make me do?" She could feel them there on her shoulders. Clinging to her.

"I… I didn't make you do anything," Charles said. "You did it all by yourself. You *saved* us."

The old man's bare feet were only inches away from her. Clustered around them were a variety of objects that had fallen from the end table. A steak knife. A racing form. A ballpoint pen. A porcelain plate. A greasy fork. A half-eaten pork chop. A tiny crucifix dangling from a silver necklace.

"Where's the gun?" Isaiah said.

She glanced around, saw it lying behind her near a basket of unfolded laundry. She rose to her feet and picked it up. She wiped the vomit from her lips with the forearm of her jacket.

"We've got to get out of here," Charles said.

"Are we sure he's dead?" Isaiah said.

Janice forced herself to look at what was left of him. He'd stopped gargling. Stopped reaching... reaching out... for what?

Off in the distance, she could hear the sound of sirens.

"It's time," Charles said.

Janice nodded. She slipped the gun back into her pocket and opened the door. This was a large apartment building, filled with tenants. Mostly old people. The hallway outside was empty, but she could feel them all there just behind their locked doors, listening, listening for her... or perhaps not... she could hear the sound of TVs blaring at various points along the hall... perhaps they were trying to drown out the sounds, her sounds, the sounds she'd made in the little room behind her. She shut the door.

She didn't have to force herself to stroll, to take her time. Instinct had taken over.

The criminal who acts like he's doing nothing wrong is the one who never gets caught.

She was a natural.

25

They ditched the Lexus that night. Stole a Cressida, switched the plates twenty miles down the road, hauled their asses north. Hugging the coast up through Georgia. South Carolina. North Carolina. Virginia. D.C. O sweet land of liberty, of thee I sing.

They tarried awhile in the capital. Janice had never seen the White House before. Or the Washington Monument. She thought it looked like a big dick, a big white dick with flags for pubic hairs. Charles and Isaiah couldn't stop laughing at the analogy. She felt like a comedian for a while. It felt nice.

She knew then. She knew she'd been right. The old man had gone for that steak knife, hadn't he? He'd tried to kill them, just like he'd killed the others. She'd been acting out of self-preservation. And for Charles, of course. And Isaiah. At least she'd given the old man a chance to have his say before the end. That was far more than he'd ever done for his victims. God, all those victims… all those helpless little girls….

She hoped they could get some rest now. The whole ordeal, the blood on her hands, the stench still lingering in her nostrils, would have been worth it if only those girls could get some rest.

Some rest. That's what she needed right now. She was tired of running; she just wanted to settle down somewhere. Alone with Charles. Start working on having those kids.

A boy. She decided the first one would be a boy.

By the time they reached Maryland both Charles and Isaiah had grown to eight inches.

26

They settled down in Baltimore. Charles told them that this had been the home of Edgar Allan Poe back in the 1800's. They'd called it Pig Town back then, because of the massive slaughterhouse that had been located in the center of town. Poe was one of Charles' favorite writers. He particularly liked "The Telltale Heart" and "The Black Cat" and "Hop-Frog" and "The Cask of Amontillado."

Charles read Janice these stories one night from a tiny Penguin paperback no more than sixty pages long. They were the only books he could manipulate with his own hands. He propped the book up against the slope of her naked breast and recited the words to her in an appropriately somber manner. Afterwards, she asked him if Poe had had a father like his. "Maybe," Charles said, "but I hope not." They went to sleep after that, Charles curled up in the crook of her neck and shoulder.

They were living in a one-bedroom apartment on the edge of downtown Baltimore. Despite Janice's wishes to live alone with Charles, Isaiah continued to sleep in the living room. Where else could he go? They couldn't turn their backs on him.

The apartment was within walking distance of Janice's new job. She'd landed a gig in a strip joint called Angel's. Charles wasn't sure it was safe, but Janice insisted this was what she really wanted to do. In order to get the job she'd had to lie to the owner and tell him she was eighteen. Charles had shown her how to get a fake ID with a fake name. She'd chosen her new name herself. Amber.

She didn't know if the man believed her, but he gave her a job anyway. Maybe he was desperate for a new face. Or pitied her. Or saw that gleam in her eye and just *knew*. Amber was a natural.

Indeed she was. For months the three of them lived off her tips alone. While Charles and Isaiah grew larger in slow, slow increments.

By spring Charles was no longer small enough to fit inside her. She'd cried that first night, when she realized what was happening. Their relationship was changing. It was never going to be like it had been. Never.

Charles told her not to worry. One phase of their relationship might be coming to an end, but a new phase was beginning. As long as they loved each other, what did it matter? Besides, just think, in a few months they would be able to make love like normal people. He would be able to hold her like a real man. She nodded, then he made the tears go away by kissing them one by one.

By summer he had reached the height of four feet. The size that Danny had been right before she ran away. For some reason, Danny was the only person she could think of when Charles fucked her for the first time like a real man. She hadn't thought about her brother in months. Charles came within a couple of seconds. "I'm sorry," he said, "I'm not used to...." "It's all right," she whispered, patting his hair like a child. She didn't come that night.

Nor on the succeeding nights. The larger Charles became, the further they drew apart. They still shared the same bed. They still fucked. They still ate breakfast together. They still went out to see movies with one another. Sometimes he went to watch her dance at work, once he'd grown large enough not to be mistaken for an adolescent. But something was missing.

Ever since regaining his height, Isaiah had fallen into his old ways. He'd been picking up extra money by selling marijuana. Charles, on the other hand, still hadn't gotten a job. He hadn't decided what he wanted to do yet; he claimed he was still adjusting to his return to "normalcy," if indeed that was the proper word to describe his tumultuous life prior to the transformation.

Janice had never tried marijuana before. She had never tried any drug before. One night during her first week on the job, just before she was scheduled to go out on stage, one of the girls offered her a line of cocaine. Janice had refused violently. Perhaps this was the final remnant of her Catholic upbringing taking hold.

She was somewhat less reluctant when Isaiah offered her a toke off his pipe. They were sitting around watching TV, some old Jimmy Cagney movie about gangsters. Charles was gone, out roaming through the local bookstores no doubt. Janice and Isaiah didn't get along very well. They were rarely alone together in the apartment, and when they were they had to suffer through long uncomfortable silences. It wasn't pleasant for either of them. She knew he still hated her for stealing Charles away from him; and she hated him for being the only other person on the planet who had known Charles' love. She often wondered what it was that Charles had seen in this coarse black man. She wouldn't be surprised if Isaiah also wondered what Charles saw in *her*.

The first few hits didn't make her feel anything. I knew it'd be no big deal, she thought, it's just a bunch of hype. Then she started giggling. She'd never realized how funny Jimmy Cagney could be. Pretty soon Isaiah was giggling right along with her. She didn't quite remember how it happened. Didn't quite know who suggested it. She got up and showed him her best moves, the ones that really seemed to enthrall them, that drew in the biggest tips. She remembered Isaiah laughing and applauding. Remembered the feel of his hand caressing her stomach beneath her t-shirt. Remembered him unbuttoning her Levis; the feel of his beard bristling against her thighs as he went down on her there in the living room, on the couch, Jimmy Cagney still ranting in the background. Remembered taking his hand and leading him into the bedroom at one point. Remembered toppling against the mattress, the one she shared with Charles, and drawing Isaiah down upon her, caressing his broad shoulders, his muscular back, his spine, clutching at his firm butt and pushing him deep inside her; he felt so large inside her, filled her up, satisfied her, not like... not like... neither of them uttered a word, nothing but incomprehensible grunts and moans, not even during that final moment when they spasmed against one another and she closed her eyes and buried her face into the crook of his neck and shoulder and lightly bit his flesh to muffle the extended cry of pleasure that burst from her lips... neither of them said each other's names....

ROBERT GUFFEY

Afterwards, the silence returned. The uncomfortable silence. It hung between them as they lay side by side on the sweaty sheets, staring up at the ceiling. She could hear him breathing hard in the darkness. Faintly, the sound of the TV could still be heard drifting in from the living room. She waited for him to say something. Anything. She could still feel the aftereffects of the orgasm rolling through her body like ocean waves. It had felt good, so very good. They both knew it. There was nothing to say. Nevertheless, she thought the silence might drive her insane.

Finally she broke it: "We have to get dressed." She didn't need to say why.

She followed the haphazard trail of clothes into the living room, throwing his shirt and pants and underwear back at him like footballs. She could barely button her Levis, her hands were shaking so much. She took a deep breath, then offered to make them dinner. He said: That would be nice, Janice. Thanks. She made them chicken salad with garlic bread.

27

When Charles came home Isaiah and Janice were sitting on the couch eating dinner, watching a Cagney movie. *White Heat.* Janice leaped up and kissed him on the cheek. She offered to make him a chicken salad. She was over brimming with enthusiasm. He said okay. It was odd to see her so happy. They hadn't been doing too well lately. He didn't know why, but he'd been meaning to talk to her about it. He followed her into the kitchen. He couldn't get a word in edgewise. She just kept babbling about a wide variety of topics, everything from the customers at work to the weather. She was acting like some teenager. Then he remembered that she *was* a teenager.

When she'd finished making the salad they all sat down together. With Charles in the middle. Janice and Isaiah didn't have to tell him anything. He sensed it. A subtle tonal change in the silence between them. This wasn't the silence of hostility. This was something else. Then he knew. Somehow, he knew. He started crying. He lowered the bowl of salad into his lap and wept into his hands. "How could you," he whispered, "how could you?"

Janice tried to hug him, but he pushed her away. He threw the bowl of salad at the television set. Isaiah decided to leave. Charles didn't stop him.

They argued for seven hours straight, from 9:00 P.M. to 4:00

A.M. Janice kept saying, "It just happened, it just happened" over and over again. She came up with theories as to why she did it. She'd wanted to experience everything that he had experienced, wanted to know exactly what he had seen in him—

Charles had his own theories. He wasn't good enough for her. Couldn't fuck right. Couldn't last long enough in bed.

That's bullshit, she said. You think I'm that shallow?

I don't know what to think. All I know is that when I couldn't be your little toy doll anymore you tossed me aside.

And there it was. Out in the open at last. What they had been dancing around for so long.

He wasn't small anymore.

That was the only "problem," the only thing that had changed in their relationship. This relationship that had been so perfect only six months before.

Janice denied it. That wasn't the problem. She didn't care about things like that. She loved him.

They why'd you fuck Isaiah behind my back?

God, I don't know. I don't *know*, all right?

No, it's not all right! Do you want to end it, is that it?

The question was thrown right back at him: Do *you*?

Silence. Uncomfortable silence.

They stood there, separated by a distance greater than the five feet between them, not looking at each other. The carpet suddenly held a great fascination for both of them.

The question hung in the air, unanswered, for a very long time.

At last Charles whispered, No, I don't.

I don't either, Janice said.

That didn't end the argument, though. Nothing could. Finally it was pure exhaustion that did it. Janice was crying, and so was Charles. They hugged one another in the bed. As the sun rose, a deep crimson seeping in through the shades, they made love. At the moment of climax he found himself wondering if the two of them had done it here, in their bed. Janice whispered his name and said she loved him. He told her the same thing. Wondering if it were true.

28

Somehow, incredibly, they fell back into the same routine. Isaiah returned after three days. One morning Charles woke up and saw him lying on the couch. He didn't say anything to him except, "Good morning." Neither mentioned Janice. They acted as if nothing had happened. From them on Charles made certain the two of them were never alone together.

Despite this facade, the image of them having sex with each other tore away at his insides. He couldn't expunge it, couldn't sleep, could barely eat because of it. Then one day, out of nowhere, the solution presented itself to him.

He made the pass at Isaiah while he was fixing dinner in the kitchen. At first Isaiah didn't respond, perhaps thinking he was imagining it. Then it became too obvious to ignore. Isaiah went for it. They did it in the bedroom. It was so soft and slow, like that first time in their cell. But it was so much better here, without those bars pressing in on you, and the sounds of the prisoners next door delivering a running commentary on your love making. The walls were surprisingly thin in prison.

He made him promise not to tell Janice. He also made him promise not to touch her ever again. "If you do, it'll all end," Charles said. "You'll never see me again."

Isaiah said, "I understand." They lay there in the dark, beneath the blankets, listening to the silence.

29

The promise was unnecessary.

Charles wasn't really surprised when it happened. He met her in the alley behind the club every night after work. To accompany her home, like a gentleman. After all, the streets of Pig Town were unsafe after midnight, particularly for an innocent young lady like Janice.

He brought along a rose plucked surreptitiously earlier in the day from a merchant on the street corner. He would present it to her, bowing like a Victorian suitor, and she would smile and lift it to her nostrils. He would offer her his elbow, she would accept it, and on the way back home he would ask her to marry him. She would accept. They would kiss, right there on the street corner.

He arrived in the alley at the exact same time he always did. It was almost as if she wanted him to catch her.

To see her in the arms of the woman, kissing passionately, there under the naked yellow bulb by the trash bin. The woman was named Tory, or Tanya, or Tammy. Something like that. She was over thirty, though she said she was twenty-five. Blonde, big fake boobs. A real looker. He'd seen her dancing on stage with Janice any number of times. The thought had never even occurred to him.

He dropped the rose to the ground and ran away.

He was sitting on the couch when she came home at one. He'd told Isaiah to go.

"Where were you?" she said, a touch of petulance in her voice. "I had to walk all the way home by myself."

He punched her in the stomach. She crumpled to her knees, gasping for breath. He told her what he'd seen.

The first words she was able to squeeze out were, "You think I don't know about you and Isaiah?"

He unclenched his fist, lowered himself to the couch.

There was no argument. She packed her bag and left. He didn't try to stop her. In fact, he didn't say a single word. Neither of them did.

Isaiah came home about three hours later and found him sitting in the same exact position, staring at the blank TV screen.

They made love in the bedroom, in the darkness, in the silence.

30

Janice moved in with Tanya. They got along well together. There were no jealousies between them. Tanya really listened to her.

She listened to it all. The whole story. She had no trouble believing it, not the way that Janice told it. Not the way she handled that .45 she kept in her purse. She kept it there partly for protection. Partly for sentimental reasons. To remind herself it had all happened.

One afternoon, around two o'clock, the doorbell to her apartment rang. She'd just woken up, having worked all night at the club. She threw on a bathrobe and opened the door.

And found herself staring at her father.

His lower lip quivered as he began to cry. "Honey...."

He opened his arms. She was surprised at how easy it was to fall into them. Her tears moistened the shoulder of his tweed coat.

"Honey," he said three or four times in a row, stroking her long hair. "I thought I'd never see you again."

"How did you...?"

"A private detective. It took so long. Two years, God, two years."

Had it really been that long? She hadn't realized that so much time had... my God, my God, what did I do to them?

"You don't really hate me, do you?" her father said.

"No, of course not."

"Your mother thinks... because of that argument...."

"What argument?" She didn't know what he was talking about. "I love you, Daddy. I'm so sorry I haven't called. I didn't think... I just didn't think...." What else was there to say?

Tanya walked into the room, tying the belt around her fluffy white bathrobe.

Her father pulled away, embarrassed. "Oh," he said, "who...?"

Janice turned toward Tanya and said, "This is my father." Tanya's eyes widened with a mixture of apprehension and curiosity; she smiled and said hi. Janice turned back toward her father. "This is Tanya, my... roommate."

"Nice to meet you," her father said. "I feel like a fool barging in here, but I had to know...."

"It's all right," Janice said, "sit down." She gestured toward the sofa, then asked Tanya to get them both a cup of coffee.

When Tanya had left the room her father said, "I don't want to drive you away again, or offend you. Everyone warned me about not being too pushy. I just need to know. Are you happy? Are you happy here?"

Janice thought about it for a second, then smiled. "Yes. I'm happy here."

"What do you do? For a living, I mean."

Janice took a deep breath. "I'm a dancer."

An expression of relief passed across his face. "Ballet?" She could see him thinking about all those lessons she'd begged him to pay for. All those hours of practice.

"Kind of. More like performance art."

"Okay." The expression of relief wavered slightly; she could almost see the ominous images of NEA-funded hedonism flitting through his brain. That, at least, was better than the truth. "As long as you're happy, honey, that's all that's important." He patted the back of her hand.

The realization fell upon her so suddenly: he wasn't quite the ogre she'd always thought he was. He was just trying to do the best he could. It was kind of charming, seeing him so nervous, so eager to please her. She felt awful for having put him and Mom and Danny through so much pain. Danny. He was twelve years old now. Almost in high school. She felt her eyes misting over again when she thought about it.

"Honey... can I please ask you one more thing?"

She smiled. "Anything."

"Do you… still pray to God? Do you still believe in Him?" His brow was furrowed so, his eyes filled with concern, his lips pursed with worry.

Janice thought of seven things at once. A steak knife. A racing form. A ballpoint pen. A porcelain plate. A greasy fork. A half-eaten pork chop. A tiny crucifix dangling from a silver necklace.

"I don't know," she whispered at last. She wasn't looking at him. She wasn't looking at anything. "Ask me again later."

31

Isaiah picked up the slack, paying the bills now abandoned by Janice. Which meant selling more than just marijuana, but hell, that was okay. He'd made connections in town. Money was easy to get a hold of when you had connections.

Not only was Isaiah content with the situation, he was happy. Happy to serve Charles night and day. As long as he had Charles all to himself, everything would be fine….

Charles withdrew deeper and deeper inside himself. He never left the apartment. He barely ate, except when Isaiah forced him. Sleep was a necessity that had long ago abandoned him.

He watched TV now and then. Sometimes he even read a book. He never got all the way through it, though.

He was too busy thinking. Thinking about the past. Thinking about that one brief period in his life when the curse of memory had posed no problem for him. When the blood-gorged images of his childhood did not intrude upon his daily thoughts as regularly as a train pulling into a station, as often as the clicking of the little hand on the clock beside his bed. He had taken to staring at the clock for hours on end, wishing he could turn back the hours and the minutes and the seconds of his life and prevent the unfolding of the chaos-woven course that had led him to this space, this moment, prevent the deeds his quivering hand would perform if left unchecked, if allowed to undo the consequences of a past that had already begun to decay.

Acknowledgements

I'd like to thank the following people for their crucial assistance: Eric Blair, Chris Doyle, Wendy Sappo Dunn, Will E. Ford, Joe & Karen Guffey, Melissa Guffey, Randy Koppang, William V. Lee, Catherine Bottolfson McCallum, Henry Morrison, Wally Munk, Rose O'Keefe, and Elisabeth Perkins.

Also, the following titles were particularly helpful while writing the novella "Widow of the Amputation": *Men from Earth* by Buzz Aldrin and Malcolm McConnell, *Manson in his Own Words* by Nuel Emmons, *Nightside of Eden* by Kenneth Grant, *Lie* by Charles Manson, *The Odin Brotherhood* by Dr. Mark L. Mirabello, *Complete Stories and Poems* by Edgar Allan Poe, *The Family* by Ed Sanders, and *The Manson File* by Nikolas Schreck.

About the Author

Robert Guffey is a lecturer in the Department of English at California State University–Long Beach. His most recent book is *Bela Lugosi and the Monogram Nine*, coauthored with Gary D. Rhodes (BearManor Media, 2019). 2017 marked the publication of *Until the Last Dog Dies* (Night Shade/Skyhorse), a darkly satirical novel about a young stand-up comedian who must adapt as best he can to an apocalyptic virus that destroys only the humor centers of the brain. Guffey's previous books include the journalistic memoir *Chameleo: A Strange but True Story of Invisible Spies, Heroin Addiction, and Homeland Security* (OR Books, 2015), which *Flavorwire* called, "By many miles, the weirdest and funniest book of 2015." A graduate of the famed Clarion Writers Workshop in Seattle, he has also written a collection of novellas entitled *Spies & Saucers* (PS Publishing, 2014). His first book of nonfiction, *Cryptoscatology: Conspiracy Theory as Art Form*, was published in 2012. He's written stories and articles for numerous magazines and anthologies, among them *The Believer, Black Cat Mystery Magazine, Black Dandy, Catastrophia, The Chiron Review, Hypnos, The Los Angeles Review of Books, The Mailer Review, New Reader Magazine, Pearl, The Pedestal, Phantom Drift, Postscripts, Rosebud, Selene Quarterly Magazine, The Temz Review, The Third Alternative,* and *TOR.com*

www.ingramcontent.com/pod-product-compliance
Lightning Source LLC
Chambersburg PA
CBHW031100030726
47496CB00002BA/302